Join the army of fans who LOVE Scott Mariani's Ben Hope series . . .

'...eadly conspiracies, bone-crunching action and a tormented ...o with a heart . . . Scott Mariani packs a real punch'
...dy McDermott, bestselling author of *The Revelation Code*

'...ick, serpentine, sharp, and very very entertaining. If you've ...t a pulse, you'll love Scott Mariani; if you haven't, then ...aybe you crossed Ben Hope'
Simon Toyne, bestselling author of the *Sanctus* series

'...ott Mariani's latest page-turning rollercoaster of a thriller ...es the sort of conspiracy theory that made Dan Brown's ... *Da Vinci Code* an international hit, and gives it an ...ection of steroids . . . [Mariani] is a master of edge-of-...-seat suspense. A genuinely gripping thriller that holds ... attention of its readers from the first page to the last'
Shots Magazine

'...u know you are rooting for the guy when he does some-...ng so cool you do a mental fist punch in the air and have ...bite the inside of your mouth not to shout out "YES!" in ...e you get arrested on the train. Awesome thrilling stuff'
My Favourite Books

'...f you like Dan Brown you will like all of Scott Mariani's ...k – but you will like it better. This guy knows exactly ... to bait his hook, cast his line and reel you in, nice and ...ow. The heart-stopping pace and clever, cunning, joyfully serpentine tale will have you frantic to reach the end, but reluctant to finish such a blindingly good read'
The Bookbag

THE BACH MANUSCRIPT

Scott Mariani is the author of the worldwide-acclaimed action-adventure thriller series featuring ex-SAS hero Ben Hope, which has sold millions of copies in Scott's native UK alone and is also translated into over 20 languages. His books have been described as 'James Bond meets Jason Bourne, with a historical twist'. The first Ben Hope book, *The Alchemist's Secret*, spent six straight weeks at #1 on Amazon's Kindle chart, and all the others have been *Sunday Times* bestsellers.

Scott was born in Scotland, studied in Oxford and now lives and writes in a remote setting in rural west Wales. When not writing, he can be found bouncing about the country lanes in an ancient Land Rover, wild camping in the Brecon Beacons or engrossed in his hobbies of astronomy, photography and target shooting (no dead animals involved!).

You can find out more about Scott and his work, and sign up to his exclusive newsletter, on his official website:

www.scottmariani.com

By the same author:

Ben Hope series
The Alchemist's Secret
The Mozart Conspiracy
The Doomsday Prophecy
The Heretic's Treasure
The Shadow Project
The Lost Relic
The Sacred Sword
The Armada Legacy
The Nemesis Program
The Forgotten Holocaust
The Martyr's Curse
The Cassandra Sanction
Star of Africa
The Devil's Kingdom
The Babylon Idol

To find out more visit **www.scottmariani.com**

SCOTT MARIANI

The Bach Manuscript

avon.

Published by AVON
A Division of HarperCollins*Publishers* Ltd
1 London Bridge Street
London SE1 9GF

www.harpercollins.co.uk

First published in Great Britain by HarperCollins*Publishers* 2017
3

Copyright © Scott Mariani 2017

Scott Mariani asserts the moral right to
be identified as the author of this work

A catalogue record for this book is
available from the British Library

ISBN 978-0-00-748623-6

Set in Minion by Palimpsest Book Production Ltd, Falkirk, Stirlingshire

Printed and bound by
CPI Group (UK) Ltd, Croydon, CR0 4YY

MIX
Paper from
responsible sources
FSC™ C007454

This book is produced from independently certified FSC™ paper
to ensure responsible forest management.

For more information visit: www.harpercollins.co.uk/green

THE BACH MANUSCRIPT

PROLOGUE

Nazi-occupied France
July 16th, 1942

All four family members were at home when they came.

Monsieur and Madame Silbermann, or Abel and Vidette, were in the salon, relaxing in a pair of matching Louis XV armchairs after a modest but excellent lunch prepared by Eliane, the family housekeeper. Vidette was immersed in one of the romantic novels into which she liked to escape. Abel, meanwhile, was frowning at an article in the collaborationist newspaper *Le Temps*, in which he was reading of much more serious matters. Things in France were growing worse. Just a little over two years since the crushing might of the German Wehrmacht had rolled virtually unopposed into the country, each day seemed to bring a fresh round of new horrors.

Seated at the piano, framed by the bright, warm afternoon light that flooded in through the French windows, their seventeen-year-old daughter Miriam was working through the most difficult arpeggiated right-hand passage of the musical manuscript in front of her, pausing now and then to peer at the handwritten notes, some of which were hard to read on the faded paper.

Though she played the piano with a fine touch, Miriam's particular talent lay with the violin, at which she excelled. The real pianist of the family was her little brother. At age twelve, Gabriel Silbermann's ability on the keys was already outstripping that of his teachers, even that of his father. Abel had been a respected professor of music at the Paris Conservatoire for over twenty years until the venerable institution's director, Henri Rabaud, had helped the Nazi regime to 'cleanse' it of all Jewish employees under the *Premier Statut des Juifs* law, which had come into effect the previous year, 1941.

Since losing his post, Abel Silbermann had managed to get by teaching privately. Things were not what they had been, but he had always convinced himself that the family money, dwindling as it was, would get them through these difficult times. Abel was also the proud owner of a fine collection of historically important musical instruments, some of which he'd inherited from his father, others that he had picked up over the years at specialist auctions in France, Switzerland, and Germany – all before the war, of course. It had nearly broken Abel's heart when, six months earlier, he'd been forced to sell the 1698 Stradivarius cello, one of the most prized items from his collection, to help make ends meet. He often worried that he might have to sell others.

But Abel Silbermann had far worse things to fear. He didn't know it yet, but they were literally just around the corner.

'*Merde, c'est dur,*' Miriam muttered to herself. Complaining how tough the music was to get her fingers around. Gabriel could rattle through the piece with ease. But then, Gabriel was Gabriel.

'Miriam, language!' her mother said sharply, jolted from

her reading. Her father permitted himself a smile behind his newspaper.

Miriam asked, 'Father, may I get a pencil and add some fingering notes? I promise I'd do it very lightly, so they could easily be rubbed out afterwards.'

Abel's smile fell away. 'Are you mad, girl? That's an original manuscript, signed by the composer himself. Have you any idea what it's worth?'

Miriam reddened, realising the foolishness of her idea. 'Sorry, Father. I wasn't thinking.'

'It shouldn't even be out of its box, let alone being defaced with pencil marks. Please tell your brother to put it back where he found it, in future. These things are precious. This one most of all.'

'I'm sure Gabriel knows that, Father. He calls it our family treasure.'

'Indeed it is,' Abel said, softening. 'Where is Gabriel, anyway?'

'In his cubbyhole, I think.'

Things had been hard for Gabriel at school since the Nazis invaded. He hated having to wear the yellow star when he was out of the house. Some of the non-Jewish kids pushed him around and called him names. As a result, he had become a rather solitary child who, when he wasn't practising his pieces and scales, liked to spend time alone doing his own things. His cubbyhole was the labyrinth of nooks and crawl-spaces that existed behind the panelled walls of the large house, connecting its many rooms in ways that only Gabriel knew. You could sometimes catch him spying from behind a partition through one of his various peepholes, and you'd call out, 'Oh, Gabriel, stop that nonsense!' and he'd appear moments later, as if by magic, and disarm everyone with his laughter. Other times he could stay hidden

3

for hours and you'd have no idea where he was. Like a tunnel rat, his father used to say jokingly. Then they'd started hearing the terrible stories coming from Ukraine and Poland, from everywhere, of Jews hiding under floorboards and in sewers while their people were transported away for forced labour, or worse. Abel had stopped talking about tunnel rats.

'I do wish he'd come out of there,' Vidette Silbermann said. 'He spends too much time hiding away like that.'

'If he's happy,' Miriam said with a shrug, 'what harm can it do? We all need a little bit of happiness in this terrible, cruel world.'

Vidette lowered her book and started going into one of her 'In my day, children would never have been allowed to do this or that' diatribes, which they'd all heard a thousand times before. Miriam's standard response was to humour her mother by ignoring her. She moved away from the piano and picked her violin up from its stand nearby. Her bow flowed like water over the strings and the notes of the Bach piece sang out melodiously.

That was when they heard the growl of approaching vehicles coming up to the house. Brakes grinding, tyres crunching to a halt on the gravel outside, doors slamming. Voices and the trudge of heavy boots.

Miriam stopped playing and looked with wide eyes at her father, who threw down *Le Temps* and got to his feet just as the loud thumping knocks on the front door resonated all through the house. Vidette sat as though paralysed in her chair. Miriam was the first to voice what they all knew already. '*Les Boches.* They're here.'

In that moment, whatever shreds of optimism Abel Silbermann had tried to hang onto, his prayers that this day would never come, that everything would be all right, were shattered.

From the window, the dusty column of vehicles seemed to fill the whole courtyard in front of the house. The open-top black Mercedes staff car was flanked by motorcycle outriders, behind them three more heavily armed Wehrmacht sidecar outfits, a pair of Kübelwagens and a transporter truck. Infantry soldiers were pouring from the sides of the truck, clutching rifles, as Abel hurried to the front door. He took a deep breath, then opened it.

You can still talk your way out of this.

The officer in charge stepped from the Mercedes. He was tall and thin, with a chiselled, severe face like a hawk's. He wore an Iron Cross at his throat, another on his breast. The dreaded double lightning flash insignia was on his right lapel, the sinister *Totenkopf* death's head skull badge above the peak of his cap. Just the sight of those was enough to instil terror.

'Herr Silbermann? I am SS Obersturmbannführer Horst Krebs. You know why I'm here, don't you?'

Abel tried to speak, but all that came out was a dry croak. When Krebs produced a document from his pocket, a high-pitched ringing began in Abel's ears. The paper was a long list of many names. It was the nightmare come true. Some Jewish families had fled ahead of the rumoured purges. Abel, choosing to disbelieve that anything quite so abominable could happen in his dear France, had made what he was now realising with a chill was the worst mistake of his life by staying put.

'You reside here with your wife, Vidette Silbermann, and your children, Gabriel and Miriam Silbermann, correct? I have here an order for your immediate deportation to the Drancy camp. Any resistance, my men are ordered to shoot without hesitation. Understood?'

Drancy was the transit camp six miles north of Paris that

the Germans used as a temporary detention centre for Jews awaiting transportation to the death camps. Abel had heard those rumours, too, and refused to believe. Now it was too late. What good would escape have done them, anyway? All fugitives would be picked up long before they reached the Swiss border.

'Take me. I care little for my own life. But please spare my family.'

'Please. Do you think I haven't heard that before?' Krebs pushed past Abel and strode into the house. His soldiers clustered around the entrance. Abel found himself looking down the muzzles of several rifles. The hallway of his genteel family home was suddenly filling with troops, their boots crashing on the parquet, the smell of their coarse tunics mixed with leather polish and gun oil a harsh and alien presence. The Obersturmbannführer turned to his second-in-command and said sharply, 'Captain Jundt, seize everyone whose name appears on the list and have them assembled here in the hall. Make it quick.'

The captain snapped his heels. '*Jawohl, mein Obersturmbannführer!*'

Jundt relayed the command and soldiers surged into the salon to seize both Miriam and her mother, who was mute with horror and virtually fainting as they half carried, half dragged her into the hallway. While his men carried out his orders, Horst Krebs strolled around the downstairs of the house and gazed around him with appreciation for the Silbermanns' good taste. Krebs did not consider himself a barbarian, like some of his peers. He came from Prussian aristocratic stock, spoke several languages and, before the war, had published three volumes of poetry in his name. By chance, he had studied music at the same Halle Conservatory founded by the father of Reinhard Heydrich, the SS chief

6

whom the Czech resistance had assassinated only the previous month. Reprisals there had been harsh and were ongoing. Krebs intended to pursue his own duties here in France with equal zest.

Noticing the piano at the far end of the salon by the French windows, Krebs strolled over to inspect it. It was a very fine instrument indeed, a Pleyel. His keen musician's eye passed over it, taking in the beauty of such a magnificent object. Maybe he would take it home to Germany as a trophy of war.

Then Krebs' eye settled on the manuscript that sat on the piano's music rest. He raised an eyebrow. He picked it up with a black-gloved hand, and peered at it.

Behind him, the hallway echoed with the cries of Madame Silbermann and her husband's pleas as the soldiers forced them to line up at gunpoint. Captain Jundt was yelling, '*Wo is das Gör? Où est the gamin?*' Demanding to know the whereabouts of young Gabriel, whose name was on the list. Jackboots thumped on the stairs and shook the floorboards above as more troops were dispatched to search the rest of the house.

Krebs heard none of it. His attention was completely on the manuscript in his hands as he studied it with rapt fascination. The age-yellowed paper. The signature on the front. Could it be the genuine thing? It was amazing.

Handling it as delicately as though it were some ancient scroll that could crumble at the slightest touch, Krebs replaced the precious manuscript on the music rest, then swept back his long coat and took a seat at the piano. The six flats in the manuscript's key signature showed that the piece was in the difficult key of G flat major. He removed his gloves, laid his fingers on the keys and sight-read the first couple of bars.

Astonishing. If this was the genuine item, he wanted it for himself.

In fact, on consideration, he could think of an even better use for it. He and the now-deceased Heydrich were not the only high-ranking Nazis with a passion for classical music. What an opportunity for Krebs to ingratiate himself at the very highest level.

'*Entschuldigung, mein Obersturmbannführer*—' Jundt's voice at his ear, breaking in on his thoughts.

'What is it, Jundt?'

'We cannot find the boy. Every room has been searched but he is missing.'

'What do you mean, you can't find him? How is that possible?' Krebs was more irritated by the interruption than the news of a missing brat. 'He must be hiding somewhere.'

'The parents and sister refuse to say where, *mein Obersturmbannführer.*'

'They do, do they? We will see about that.' Krebs rose from the piano stool and marched towards the hallway. Moments like these called for a little greater authority than the likes of Jundt could summon up. Krebs drew his service automatic from its flap holster.

As Krebs reached the crowded hallway, he heard a sudden sound behind him and turned in surprise to see the young boy who seemed to have appeared from nowhere and was now racing across the salon, heading for the piano.

Jundt shouted, 'There he is!' as though his commanding officer were blind.

Miriam Silbermann screamed, 'Gabriel!'

Krebs realised that the boy must have been hiding behind the wood panels, watching him as he sat at the piano. Running to the instrument, the twelve-year-old snatched the manuscript off its rest, and clutched it tightly. He yelled, 'Filthy Boches, you won't take our family treasure!'

His elder sister screamed, 'Run, Gabriel!' One of the soldiers silenced her with a harsh blow from his rifle butt.

And Gabriel ran, still grasping the precious manuscript to his chest as though nothing could persuade him to let it go. He made for the French window and slipped through, dashing towards the lawned garden and the fence at the bottom.

Krebs watched him go. Then calmly, unhurriedly, he walked towards the French window. Stepped through it, feeling the sun's warmth on his face.

The boy was running fast. If Krebs let him run very much further, he would reach the fence and disappear into the trees, and it might take an entire Waffen SS unit all day to scour the surrounding countryside in search of the brat.

Krebs raised his pistol and took careful aim at the running child's back. It was a long shot, but Krebs was an accomplished marksman.

The gun's short, sharp report cracked out across the garden. Inside the house, Vidette Silbermann howled in anguish.

The boy stumbled, ran on two more staggering paces, then fell on his face and lay still.

More screams from the house, once again cut short by the soldiers. The Obersturmbannführer walked over to where Gabriel Silbermann lay dead, hooked the toe of his shiny jackboot under his body and rolled him over. A trickle of blood dribbled from the child's lips. He was still clutching the music manuscript as if he wouldn't give it up, even in death.

Krebs bent down and removed it from the boy's fingers. It sickened him to see that there was blood on it, but not because it was the blood of an innocent child he had just killed. Rather, it was like seeing a rip in an old master painting. The manuscript had survived all these years, just to be indelibly stained by the blood of a filthy Jew. Disgusting. Krebs carefully slipped the precious object inside his coat before more harm could come to it. Then walked back towards the house to resume his duties. A pretty much routine day had turned out to be a lucky one for him.

Soon, the rest of the Silbermann family would be taken to their temporary new home at the Drancy internment facility, along with more than thirteen thousand other Jews rounded up by Nazi troops and French police in what was known as '*Opération Vent Printanier*', or 'Operation Spring Breeze'. From Drancy, not long afterwards, Abel, Vidette and Miriam would find themselves on the train that would deliver them to their terrible fate.

Only one of them would ever return.

Chapter 1

Oxfordshire
Many years later

The country estate covered a spread of some thirty acres, a fraction of the grounds it had commanded in former, grander days, but still large enough to keep the big house well secluded from neighbouring farm cottages and the nearby village of Wychstone. The estate was entirely surrounded by a ten-foot-high stone wall, built long ago by an army of local labourers. Its main entrance gates were tall and imposing, all gothic wrought-iron and gilt spikes, set into massive ivied pillars crowned with carved stone heraldic beasts of Olde England that had guarded the gateway since 1759 and bore just the right amount of weathering and moss to convey an impression of grandiosity without looking scabby and decayed.

Neatly hidden among the ivy of the pillars were the electronic black box and mechanism for opening and shutting the gates, as well as the small intercom on which visitors had to announce themselves in order to be let in; the rest of the time, the gates were kept firmly shut. Nor could you see it from the ground, but the walls themselves were topped all the way around with broken glass cemented into the stonework, to deter unwanted callers. Technically illegal without a warning sign, but the property's owner was little concerned with their duty of care to protect the safety and wellbeing of potential burglars, vandals or other intruders.

Entering the gates and following the long, winding driveway that led through a corridor of fine old oak trees and eventually opened up to reveal the clipped lawns and formal gardens and then the house itself, few people could have failed to be impressed by the scale and majesty of one of the nobler country piles in the region. The manor stood on five floors, comprising over thirty bedrooms and many more reception rooms than were ever in use at any given time. Its multiple gabled roofs sloped this way and that. The red and green ivy that clung thickly about its frontage was kept neatly trimmed away from its dozens upon dozens of leaded windows. Clusters of chimney stacks poked like missiles into the blue Oxfordshire sky, providing a lofty perch for the crows that circled and cawed in the tranquil silence. Down below, parked on the ocean of ornamental gravel surrounding the big house were rows of Aston Martins and Bentleys and classic Porsches, nothing as vulgar as a Ferrari.

The place might have been the personal residence of someone extremely wealthy, a marquis or a viscount, or the ancestor of some Victorian merchant dynasty still reaping the fruits of the family empire. Old money. Or new money, like a dot-com multimillionaire or whizzkid software developer who'd struck lucky with some new gimmick that had set the world on fire. Whatever the case, they would have required a live-in service staff to keep it on an even keel. At least one butler, maybe two, plus the requisite contingent of housekeepers and kitchen staff and gardeners. Or else the fine house might have been open to the public, as a gallery or a museum or a National Trust heritage venue ushering crowds of visitors through its many grandiose rooms during the months of the tourist season.

It was none of those things. Instead, it was a place of business. A going concern, providing a variety of services to its clients. A polished brass plaque above the doorway read, in bold gothic font, THE ATREUS CLUB. Named after a king of ancient Greece, the father of Agamemnon and Menelaus, not that the name bore any connection to the nature and purpose of the establishment. A nature and purpose to which, in turn, few people were ever privy.

The Atreus Club was strictly private, hence the locked gates, and hence the broken glass on the walls. Members only. Expensive to join, and only certain individuals need apply to enjoy the secluded and discreet haven it provided for its exclusive, distinguished membership.

And for good reason, considering some of the activities those pillars of society enjoyed there.

Behind a tall balcony window, up on the fourth floor, one of those activities was currently taking place. The room was large but quite sparsely decorated. It had been a bedroom, and sometimes still was used as such, depending on need. Today, though, it was something else. At its centre stood an antiquated wooden school desk, the kind with the flip-up top and a recess for an inkwell. In front of it was a larger teacher's desk, behind which stood an equally old-fashioned classroom blackboard, complete with chalk and duster. Scrawled in slanting chalk script across the board were the words, *I must not be a naughty boy; I must not be a naughty boy.* Over and over.

At the far side of the room, in the light from the tall window, stood a metal frame, seven feet high with a steel bar supported between sturdy mounts either side. Attached to the overhead bar, arms raised above his head by the rubber manacles and rubber chains that bound him firmly in place, stood one of the room's two occupants. He was naked apart from his socks. A man in his early sixties, grey-haired, tall, slightly stooped, and not in the best of shape physically. His bare buttocks were pinched and somewhat shrivelled and very white, except for where they were striped red from the whipmarks that the room's other occupant had spent the last few minutes inflicting on him.

She was blonde-haired and attractive in a stern, Slavic kind of way, and at least forty years younger than her client. But not naked, not yet, as specified by the instructions that had to be followed to the exact letter. All part of the expensive services provided by the Atreus Club. And this particular client had specified, as he always specified on his frequent visits here, that the girl be wearing a mortarboard and one of the abbreviated black academic gowns that Oxford University tradition dubbed a Commoners' gown. Both items duly obtained from the official university outfitters, Shepherd and Woodward's of the High. No expense spared. Aside from the academic garb and the matching black fishnet stockings, garters and suspender belt, she was wearing nothing else. Again, as per instructions. The instrument of torture was a whippy rattan cane, the type that schoolmasters had once used to inflict corporal punishment on disobedient pupils, back in the day. The client had never been caned at school, however. He had always been a model pupil, set for academic glory.

'Have you had enough, you bad, *bad* professor, you?' the blonde asked with a wicked smile on her red lips. 'Professor' was what she was instructed to call him in their fantasy role-play. She spoke with an Eastern European accent that drove him even more crazy.

'No! Hit me again! Ah!'

The client's cry of pain and pleasure was drowned out by the whoosh and sharp crack of the cane as she whipped it through the air and added another fresh, livid stripe to his pale rear end. The velvety tassel on her mortarboard swung with the movement.

'Again! More!'

Whoosh. *Crack.*

This could go on for quite some time. As the blonde knew very well, because it usually did and she was his regular pick. She had the technique down better than any of the other girls. Something in the wrist action. For some reason, she was a natural at it. He knew her as Angelique, which, needless to say, wasn't her real name.

Another piece of information the client lacked was that the private session he was currently enjoying was, in fact, anything but.

The tall, mature oak tree on the front lawn was about as close to the house as it was possible for a hidden observer to get without being spotted from the windows, and you could reach it easily enough by darting from hedge to bush. Plenty close enough, for the man who was perched high up in its branches. The only challenging part of his job had been getting over the wall unscathed. The rest was easy. Almost fun. He had an excellent view through the window in question, and at this range the telephoto lens on his camera was capable of producing crystal-clear close-ups of both the client and the girl whipping him.

The watcher wasn't so interested in the girl. The client was another matter. Just a few more snaps, and the watcher would descend unseen from his perch and make his way back out of the grounds and over the wall to his vehicle.

The watcher permitted himself a smile as he watched the

blonde step back to give herself space, then swing the cane and whack the old perv again. He could almost hear the snap of the thin rattan against soft, loose, white flesh. Framed in the viewfinder the client's eyes were rolled upwards and his mouth was open with a sigh of ecstasy.

The shutter clicked one more time.

A perfect shot.

Someone was going to be happy.

Chapter 2

Ben Hope sat on the edge of the single bed with his old green canvas bag wedged between his feet and gazed around him at his strange, yet so familiar, surroundings.

And wondered, *What the hell am I doing back here?*

In some ways he felt like much the same person who had once lived in this very room, slept in this very bed, done all the things that a restless nineteen-year-old with the devil inside him and too many troubles for his young mind to bear is wont to do. In other ways, he was a very different person now. Twenty-something years of the kind of existence Ben had led since leaving this place couldn't but profoundly change a man, if it didn't kill him altogether.

But one thing was for sure. The place itself had barely changed at all during his long, long absence. Old Library 7 still had the same fusty smell of a building overdue for renovation by a century or longer. The yellowed and chipped woodwork of the ancient bow window was maybe a little more in need of repair. The carpet was still worn in all the same places he remembered. The thinly upholstered armchairs were the same ones he'd sprawled in evening after evening, meant to be reading but usually ending up asleep with the book upturned and dog-eared on his lap. Even the battered desk was original equipment, still bearing the black marks of cigarette burns and the scar from the time he'd smashed a bottle against it in some drunken fit of anger.

He'd been angry a lot of the time back in those days. Drunk even more of the time. Not the best of memories.

The only thing missing from the room was the old piano that had once stood over by the window, its place now taken by a saggy couch. Which seemed to make more sense. Quite why the college authorities had ever seen fit to put a piano in an undergraduate's room had always been a mystery to him. He'd never even opened the lid, having never attempted to play a musical instrument of any variety in his life before or since.

Ben stood up and walked by where the piano had been. He undid the Victorian sash window latch, painted over so many times that it needed force to open it, and worked the stubborn window frame upwards until it was far open enough to lean out.

The view of the quadrangle below was exactly the same as it had been twenty-something years ago, with the rear façade of Meadow Buildings facing him. The wide open space of Christ Church Meadow lay beyond. Here in the middle of a hundred and sixty thousand people, the college's nearly forty acres of unspoilt fields and woodland were a tranquil haven for wildlife, and for Ben. He could smell the river and hear the traffic rumble in the distance. It was a crisp and sunny Easter-time morning, in the break between Hilary and Trinity terms, and the usual troop of camera-toting tourists was bustling about the quad. Spanish, judging by the barking narrative of the guide who was busily ushering them around the hallowed college grounds.

It seemed an ironic coincidence that he should have been given his old room. Or was it? Maybe he had Seraphina to thank for it, looking up old records and being over-efficient.

Perhaps she thought he'd go all mushy and nostalgic and be forever grateful to her for the gesture. In which case, she obviously didn't know enough of Ben's history with the place, or the circumstances under which he'd left it.

Which in turn brought him once again to asking himself the same question that had been in his mind ever since he'd arrived in Oxford early that morning.

What the hell am I doing back here?

Ben knew what.

It had been a spur of the moment thing. A snap decision. Perhaps not, in retrospect, the wisest idea he'd ever had. Perhaps he was getting sentimental, after all. Which wasn't like him, or so he would have preferred to think. But he was here now. One night, and tomorrow he'd be sixty miles away having his business meeting; then soon after that he'd be home again at Le Val, getting on with life and work.

It was no big deal. He'd survived worse things in his time.

He looked at his watch. They'd still be serving breakfast in Hall, and he needed a coffee. But he felt grubby after the long drive up from Normandy and decided to take a quick shower first. Old Library was, as its name suggested, the oldest block of undergraduate accommodation within the college buildings, and convenience of facilities hadn't been uppermost in the minds of the architects back then. Each floor had just one communal bathroom, which in Ben's case was down the musty-smelling corridor from his room, past a series of deep-set oval windows and down a short flight of creaky steps.

The bathroom was still pretty much as scabby and mouldy as Ben remembered, and the plumbing still howled like a werewolf at full moon. He showered in tepid water, dressed quickly, then locked up his room. The oversized door key he'd been issued at the Porter's Lodge on arrival was the same Victorian affair he'd used back in the day. He slipped it in his pocket and hurried downstairs and out of the iron-studded door of Old Library. The way to the Great Hall was through a small cloistered quad, which until about 1520 had been the site of an eighth-century priory. Lots of history in this place. But right now Ben was more concerned about missing his morning coffee, and he quickened his step up the grand staircase to the Great Hall.

That hadn't changed either, with its grand vaulted ceiling and richly wood-panelled walls hung with scores of old gilt-framed portraits of Oxford luminaries through the ages whose names Ben had never cared to remember, and the three immensely long tables on which those students brave enough to consume college food took their meals. Ben vaguely remembered hearing a while back that some big movie production had used the hall as a location. Something about a boy wizard, he remembered, but that was all. He didn't watch a lot of movies.

Breakfast time was winding to a close. A few people were filing along the self-service aisle on the left of the hall, picking up pastries and croissants and being poured coffees by the college staff. Ben got himself a mug of black coffee, nothing to eat, and took it over to sit on his own at the bottom end of one of the long trestle dining tables, not too far from the door, intending to gulp down his coffee and slip away without having to get into conversation with anyone.

He glanced at the faces of the others in the hall. They were mostly about his age, and he supposed they were old members from his year, here like him to attend the college reunion. Some of them knew each other and had bundled together into little groups, their laughter and excited chatter echoing in the huge room. He didn't remember them.

But he quickly remembered the college coffee at the first swallow. It was just as bad as ever. Something on a par with British army coffee, a comparison Ben hadn't been able to make back in those days. It was too vile to gulp down in a hurry, so he sat sipping it, alone with his thoughts.

That was when a voice from behind him said, in a tone of astonishment, '*Ben Hope?*'

Ben turned, coffee in hand, and looked at the guy standing there, carrying a tray laden with a pot of tea, cup, saucer, jug of milk, bowl of cereal, glass of orange juice. For a second or two they stared at one another. The guy was a little older than him. Neither short nor tall, thin nor plump. Light brown hair beginning to show a dusting of grey around the temples. The face was very familiar. Even more than the face, the eyes. Sharply green, filled with a mischievous kind of sparkle as they peered closely into Ben's.

'Ben Hope, it *is* you, isn't it? Of course it is. My God, how long has it been?'

'Nicholas? Nicholas Hawthorne?'

'Thank God, you remember. I was beginning to think I must have aged beyond recognition. Not you, though. You haven't changed a bit.'

'I know that's not true,' Ben said. 'But thanks anyway.' He motioned at the empty space next to him at the table. 'Will you join me, Nicholas?'

'Why, gladly.' Nicholas Hawthorne settled himself on the bench seat beside Ben. There was that strange, hesitant uncertainty between them that you got when old friends who had gone their separate ways were reunited after many years, and the ice needed to be rebroken. 'It's just Nick these days,' he said with a smile. 'I only use Nicholas as a performance name. The agent's idea. He says the formality of it is more appropriate to the classical market. But never mind

21

boring old me. What about you? You're the last person I ever expected to see here.'

'Me too.'

'What have you been doing with yourself all this time?'

'Oh, this and that.' The fact was, very little of what Ben had done in the last couple of decades could be discussed in anything more than the vaguest terms. Even if he could have talked about it, and hadn't been the kind of person who preferred to keep things to himself, the details would only upset most normal, gentle folks for whom his life of risk, trouble and danger would seem alien, even frightening. He'd come prepared for that. His strategy was to provide the briefest and sketchiest account of himself possible, keep it vague and dodge direct questions. He said, 'I live in France now.'

'Business or pleasure?'

'Bit of both.'

'Are you married? Children?'

Ben shook his head. The easiest answer. The truth was complicated. Like most things in his life.

'I wouldn't have thought so, somehow. Not the children part, anyway. Nor me. Too busy with work.' Nick paused. 'Actually, what I heard is, you ran off and joined the army. Did very well there, or so the rumour went.'

'You shouldn't listen to rumour,' Ben said.

'Very true,' Nick said, laughing. 'Not that I was the least bit surprised to hear it.'

'No?'

'Absolutely not. I mean, the wild man of Christ Church, the legends of whose exploits still echo around the college walls?'

'I don't know about that,' Ben said. He hoped he wasn't about to be treated to one of the stories. They weren't ones he wanted to hear.

22

He didn't have to. Nick seemed to pick up on his unwillingness to discuss the legend that had been young Ben Hope, and quickly changed the subject.

'It's so good to see you again. What on earth brings you back to Oxford?'

Ben replied, 'As a matter of fact, you do.'

Chapter 3

Which was true, in a sense. Though only a few days earlier, the name Nick Hawthorne was just the vaguest scrap of a distant memory, a faint echo from another life. But some echoes have a way of coming back to you just when you least expect them.

Ben had been sitting in the prefabricated office building across the yard from the old stone farmhouse, tucked away at the heart of a fenced-off compound deep in the sleepy backwaters of rural Normandy. A place called Le Val, a place he had strayed away from too many times. A place he now felt happy to call home. Spring was springing, the sun was shining, and all was pretty much okay with the world, apart from the fact that he was working on a Sunday, and the stack of paperwork piled on his desk that he had to finish ploughing through by lunchtime.

The joys of running a business. But he couldn't complain. The enterprise he co-directed from this secluded base along with his partners, Jeff Dekker and Tuesday Fletcher, was growing steadily every quarter. Ben and Jeff had founded it a few years back and it would soon get to the point where they might have to expand to a second location, somewhere suitably remote and isolated, maybe further south where the climate was softer and they could spread out a little more.

For the moment, though, they were rattling on just fine and had established a comfortable, if by necessity slightly detached due to the nature of the business, rapport with the majority of the locals. In an area where most folks were farmers, or cheese makers, or small-scale cider and calvados producers, the idea of a bunch of British ex-servicemen setting up a tactical training centre to instruct military, police, hostage rescue and elite close-protection teams in some of the finer points of their trade must have seemed a little odd. The tall perimeter fences, KEEP OUT signs and roving German shepherd guard dogs might equally have unsettled one or two folks, not to mention the crack of high-velocity gunfire that was often to be heard rolling over the countryside from the safe confines of Le Val's five-hundred-metre range. They certainly unsettled Jeff's new fiancée, Chantal Mercier, who taught at a local primary school and frowned upon such gung-ho activities. Ben could see trouble ahead there, but he kept his mouth shut and didn't interfere with his friend's affairs.

Right now, Ben had his own affairs to deal with. And he heartily wished someone would come and interfere with those by relieving him of all this damned bureaucratic red tape. *Paperasse*, they called it in France. Ben had other words to describe it. Jeff often joked that you needed a licence to fart in this country, and he wasn't far off the mark.

The latest irritation they had to deal with was the need for a special import licence to obtain firearm components, even though the contents of the Le Val armoury were already itemised and catalogued down to the last screw and spring. There was a guy called Lenny Hobart in Surrey making what he claimed were the world's best, lightest and most stable tactical sniper bipods out of titanium and carbon fibre. Ben and Jeff were interested in trying them out and maybe buying in a few to use on the rifle range, where Tuesday had taken over as head sniper instructor to the SWAT teams who came to Le Val to train.

And so, Ben was due to travel up to Surrey in a few days, meet Hobart at the Stickledown shooting range in Bisley and put one of his prototypes through its paces at twelve hundred yards. At that kind of distance, where the wind was fickle, the very curvature of the earth came into play and even a microscopic amount of rifle cant could knock a bullet's point of impact way off course, anything you could do to improve the chances of hitting your mark was a definite boon. If the new bipod lived up to the claims of its inventor, Ben planned on coming home with half a dozen, with a view to ordering more.

Enter the French government, who in their wisdom now insisted on making him trawl through an additional raft of forms just to obtain a few inert bits of machined titanium, carbon fibre, spring steel and rubber. Making the world a safer place.

Ridiculous. You could do more hurt to a person with a candlestick.

Ben spent a few more minutes soldiering on through reams of officialese that might as well have been written in Yupik or Pawnee, then decided to give it a break. He was leaning back in his chair and enjoying his fourth untipped Gauloise cigarette of the morning when it occurred to him that he would be more usefully employed working on clearing the backlog of emails in his spam folder.

The Le Val email server had been getting bombarded with a lot of unsolicited mail recently. Offers of cut-price Viagra, phishing scams of one kind or another, and so many messages from prospective Russian brides called Tatiyana or Olga or Mayya, invariably 28 years old and offering to send images of themselves that Ben had been starting to wonder what Tuesday was getting up to online. He was getting almost as fast with the delete button as he was with a pistol.

Working his way through the pile, Ben came across an undeleted message from somebody called Seraphina Lewis. He glanced at the name for a fraction of a second before his finger gave its reflex twitch and got rid of it. Nice try, he thought. An unusual name. Intended to draw attention, maybe, as the scammers and phishers became more sophisticated in their techniques. The part of Ben's mind that still recalled anything from his theology studies from two decades earlier, before he'd dropped that future life to join the army and then the SAS, flashed up the name Seraphina as being the feminine derivative of the biblical Seraphim from the Book of Isaiah. Why he still retained such information inside his head, he had no idea. The Seraphim were the fiery-winged beings, high-placed in angelic hierarchy, who fluttered around the throne of God in heaven. Maybe the oblique reference to 'the fiery ones' was supposed to convey a subconscious image of hot, burning passion. Or maybe it was meant to project a sense of purity and innocence to catch the unwary recipient and lure them to read more.

Either way, by the time those thoughts had flickered through his mind at the speed of light, the email was already in the trash and he was turning his attention back to his paperwork.

But then Ben hesitated. Something else was unusual about the message. More than the name, it was the email address itself. He could see it still imprinted like a ghost image on his retinas: the suffix *@chch.ox.ac.uk*. The official domain name for Christ Church, Oxford.

Ben's old college. Which, as strange as that seemed, meant that the email was genuine, and meant for him. Ben hesitated a moment longer, then clicked open the trash folder and saw the unread message there at the top, above the collection of Viagra ads and Tatiyanas and Mayyas waiting to be permanently binned.

'Okay, Seraphina,' he muttered to himself, 'let's see what it is you wanted.' Donations to help restore some crumbling part of the college's architecture, no doubt, or to pay for de-moling the Dean's private garden or restore the paintings in the art gallery that nobody ever looked at anyway. He clicked again, and the message opened.

Strange indeed, but stranger things had happened in his life.

Chapter 4

The message wasn't the begging letter he'd expected. Rather, it was a month-old invitation to all former members of the 'House', that being the rather grand name by which his old college Christ Church colloquially referred to itself, studiously avoiding the word 'college' as a way to elevate itself above its smaller, less prestigious siblings. None of which could boast having a city cathedral as their college chapel, for instance, or thirteen British prime ministers and at least one English monarch among their illustrious alumni.

Somewhere close to the bottom of that list, way down there beneath the King Edward the Seconds and the William Gladstones and the Anthony Edens and the Lewis Carrolls – lower still than the likes of the infamous archbishop-turned-pirate Lancelot Blackburne and the German cokehead aristocrat Gottfried Von Bismarck – was the very little-known name of a certain Benedict Hope, Major, British Armed Forces, Ret. Though apparently not so little known as to be excluded from the invitation that had now unexpectedly, and slightly belatedly, landed in Ben's lap. The hard copy of the letter that the college had presumably sent out ahead of the email must have ended up in the Le Val shredder weeks ago, unopened, along with a ton of junk.

With mixed feelings, he read on.

29

Seraphina Lewis, as it turned out, was the new college administrator tasked with tracking down and reaching out to old House members. Christ Church was a bit like the SAS: once you were in, you were in for life. Even if you left there under the darkest of clouds. Even if you had almost set fire to the place on at least one occasion, and in a separate incident hurled down three flights of stairs a fridge containing a roast pheasant and a bottle of expensive champagne belonging to the son of the Italian president, almost causing an international flap in the process. Such trifling matters seemingly were omitted from House records, in a spirit of forgive and forget.

The invitation read:

Dear Old Member,

This is to remind you that you are cordially invited to attend a special Easter reunion for all Christ Church Alumni, to be held on Wednesday, 12 April. The event will include refreshments in the Deanery Garden and a celebration dinner in the Great Hall (gowns to be worn). In addition, this year we are delighted to invite you to a private recital in the college chapel by Old Member and former Christ Church Organ Scholar Nicholas Hawthorne, who since leaving the House has gone on to become an internationally acclaimed classical recording artist. Nicholas will be performing works by William Byrd, Olivier Messiaen and Johann Sebastian Bach on the cathedral's magnificent Rieger organ. I hope you will be able to attend, and warmly look forward to welcoming you back in person to Christ Church for this very special event. Accommodation will be available within college at no extra cost for Old Members and spouses.

Warmly, Seraphina Lewis, Christ Church (1993)

Ben stubbed out his cigarette, lit a fresh one, and leaned back from the desk to think. The date of the event was only three days from now, the email having sat ignored in the spam folder all these weeks. His automatic inclination was to dismiss the matter without a second thought and not even bother replying. He hadn't been back to Oxford since the brief time he and his then-fiancée Brooke Marcel had rented a house in Jericho, in the west of the city. Much had happened since then. Too much.

But then Ben thought about it some more, and felt himself slowly softening to the idea of attending the reunion. Not all his memories were bad ones. He remembered a moonlit summer's night many years ago, sitting under the ancient cloister arches near Old Library with Michaela, the two of them listening to the strains of one of Nick Hawthorne's late-night organ practice sessions emanating from where the cathedral nave adjoined the far corner of the cloister.

Though Nick had been the eldest by some margin, he'd been a key member of the 'gang of four': him, Ben, Michaela and Simeon. They'd all met during Ben's second year at Christ Church, which would turn out to be his last, and become good friends. When you could drag Nick away from his music, he was fun company, knew the wickedest jokes and could drink real ale like it was going out of style.

Simeon Arundel had been a very different personality. Like Ben, he'd studied theology. Unlike Ben, he'd been heavily committed long-term to the subject and would go on to see it through to the end by being ordained as a vicar. Michaela Ward had been a first-year student of PPE, Oxford's abbreviation for Philosophy, Politics and Economics. And she'd been Ben's first serious girlfriend, though the relationship hadn't lasted long. Following their break-up, Ben's life had reached an unhappy point where he terminated his studies and left university. Then, in the wake of Ben's dramatic departure, the friendship that had always existed between Michaela and Simeon suddenly deepened and they'd got together, married and settled in a village not too far from Oxford. As it turned out, those two had been meant for each other.

Ben would never forget either of them. Or the way they'd died, many years later.

With Simeon and Michaela gone, the original gang of four had been halved. Which might have impelled the survivors to keep in touch – but Ben and Nick never had. Ben was aware that it was his fault, since keeping in touch had never been his forte. Now after all these years, the thought of seeing Nick again filled him with a bittersweet feeling. Maybe it was time to rebuild the contact between them. The date of the reunion fitted right in with his planned trip to Surrey. Bisley was only an hour's drive away from Oxford, and it would save him having to find a hotel in nearby Guildford.

It was a spur of the moment thing. A snap decision. Ben thought *fuck it*, leaned forward, hit reply and started typing his response to Seraphina Lewis.

Two days later, he was slinging his old green bag on the front seat of his shiny silver BMW D3 Alpina Bi-Turbo, a replacement for the blue one he'd ditched at the bottom of the River Arno in Florence before Christmas, speeding off up Le Val's bumpy track, past the gatehouse and away.

If he'd known how things were about to turn out, Ben would have stayed at home. Or maybe not. Because trouble seemed to draw him like a magnet. And trouble was coming, just as it always seemed to. Especially when your name was Ben Hope.

Chapter 5

'I still can't believe it's you,' Nick Hawthorne said. 'Feels like such a blast from the past.'

'Feels strange for me too,' Ben replied. 'Being back here after all these years. Time seems to have stood still.'

They'd finished breakfast and were walking down the stone staircase from the Great Hall. Sunlight shone from the archway that led to the south-east corner of Tom Quad.

'Speaking of time,' Nick said, 'do you have any plans for the rest of the morning, or lunch?'

'None in particular.'

'Only, I'm having a few people over at my place for drinks and a bit of a buffet this lunchtime. Nothing formal, you know. It's a way for me to loosen up with a few laughs and a couple of glasses of wine before tonight's performance. Why don't you come?'

'I'd like that very much,' Ben said.

Nick looked pleased. He glanced up at the clock that adorned the massive Tom Tower, which straddled the college's entrance and loomed over St Aldate's. 'There are still a couple of hours before the first guests will start to turn up,' Nick said. 'If you like, we could head over there now. Give us a chance to catch up a bit on old times. And if you don't mind, you can help me set up the buffet while we're chatting.'

'On one condition,' Ben said.

'What's that?'

'You make me a cup of real coffee.'

'Done. You ready? Let's go and grab a bus. I live up in north Oxford, going towards Summertown.'

'No car?'

'I bought one last year, an Aston Martin,' Nick said with a casual wave. 'Total white elephant. I never even use the damn thing.'

'Business must be good if you can afford a car like that,' Ben said. He was still hurting from the cost of his new BMW.

'I get by,' Nick replied with a grin. 'You must tell me all about yours.'

Ben had so far avoided divulging much about what he was doing these days, except that he co-ran a business in Normandy. He shrugged. 'It's nothing that exciting.'

'I'm sure that's not true at all,' Nick replied.

They strolled up the hill to Carfax, which was the bustling hub of the city centre and more choked than ever with buses and milling shoppers. At Carfax Tower they jumped on a double-decker going north up Banbury Road, and climbed to the empty top deck to sit at the front. To Ben, it felt like being a student again. Except back in his day, you were allowed to smoke upstairs. Do it now, and they would probably cart you away to serve ten years in a max-security prison.

They took their seats, Nick by the window, Ben by the centre aisle. Small tremors rocked the bus as more passengers boarded downstairs. Nick was about to resume their conversation when heavy footsteps came up the double-decker's stairwell. The footsteps paused at the top of the stairs, then approached. Nick glanced back, Ben felt him go as tense as a spheksophobe near a wasp's nest.

'Oh Christ, it's one of them,' Nick muttered *sotto voce*.

'One of who?' Ben asked him.

'Crusties. Beggars. Whatever you call them. They cause a lot of trouble on the buses. Don't make eye contact with him. Maybe he'll leave us alone.'

The guy was on his own, walking up to the front of the top deck with a shoulder-rolling swagger to his step and a cocky grin on his face. He was large, over six feet tall and thick-chested, somewhere north of thirty. Which meant he probably hadn't taken a shower since his twenties. It was hard to tell which were dirtier, his jeans, hoodie or his straggly hair and beard. From under heavy brows he eyed Ben, then Nick. He raised a grubby finger as if it was a gun and pointed it at them.

'You're in my seat.' The guy's voice was harsh and crackly. Ben got a whiff of body odour and unwashed clothes coming off him like rotten cabbages, mixed with the sour smell of stale booze.

'We'll move,' Nick said quickly, starting to get up. Ben touched his arm to still him.

The guy's eyes flickered back to Nick and lingered there. 'I know you.'

Nick seemed to hesitate and looked uncomfortable for a moment. He replied anxiously, 'I . . . I don't have any money for you today.'

'You're in my seat,' the guy repeated. Heaping on the menace. Trying to.

Ben turned to gaze up at the guy from where he sat. He motioned at the empty deck and said, 'Plenty of seats free for you back there. How about you make yourself comfortable a few rows behind us, where I can't smell you?'

'*Ben, no,*' Nick warned in a low whisper.

'You mean, don't provoke him?' Ben said. 'This moron was born provoked. But that's okay. He doesn't worry me.'

35

The big guy fixed Ben with a glare. His pupils shrank down to the size of pinheads. Eyes rimmed red. 'I don't think you heard me, arsehole. This is my seat.'

'I heard you fine,' Ben said. 'Except I don't see any reservation signs. And I like the view from up front here. I think we'll stay.'

The hand pointing the finger disappeared into one of the pockets of the guy's hoodie. It came out again clutching a small paring knife.

'Oh, God,' Nick quavered in Ben's ear. 'I *told* you—' Like it was Ben's fault that one of the passengers was waving a blade at them.

'You got a mouth on you,' the guy said. 'Maybe I need to teach you a lesson.'

Ben looked at the paring knife. 'Thanks, but I already know how to peel potatoes.'

'Give me your fuckin' wallet, prick. Now.'

The bus was starting to move. The driver obviously hadn't bothered to check the fish-eye mirror above him that gave a view of the upstairs. Or maybe these things happened so often on board that he'd given up caring. Welcome to the city of the dreaming spires. Ben had almost forgotten how colourful the streets of Oxford could get at times.

The big guy reached out with his free hand to steady himself against the sudden lurch of the transmission as the bus lumbered forwards. Then the driver braked sharply as a couple of kids darted across the road in his path. The big guy rocked on his feet. The knife stayed pointed at Ben.

Ben used the momentum of the braking bus to come forwards out of his seat, faster than the big guy could register. In the next instant, the knife was out of his hand and in Ben's. Boggle-eyed with surprise, the guy swung a clumsy roundhouse punch Ben's way. Ben could have run down to the nearest coffee shop to order a takeaway espresso in the time it took coming. He trapped the arm, twisted it up and under the guy's ribs and behind his back, and used the leverage to dump the guy into a seat a row back on the opposite side of the aisle. Up close, the guy smelled even more strongly of stale sweat and booze. He tried to struggle and kick. Ben jammed him up against the window and pinched off the carotid artery at the base of his neck to shut down the blood flow to what little brain he had.

It normally took between five to eight seconds before the subject lost consciousness. This guy's system had been running on bad fuel for so long that his bloodstream was already starved of oxygen, and he held out for much less time. Ben kept the stranglehold clamped down tight until he felt him go limp.

The bus rumbled on up the street.

Nick was staring.

Ben checked the big guy's hoodie pockets. He found nearly fifty pounds in rumpled and grimy notes, along with a small bottle of ecstasy pills and a paper bag containing some dried-out magic mushrooms. 'That's your lesson for the day,' he said to the unconscious hulk as he counted the money and shoved all the stuff in his own jacket pocket. 'Cost of doing business with the wrong people.'

'What did you do to him?' Nick gasped.

'He's just grabbing forty winks,' Ben said. They were approaching another stop, crowded with people waiting to board. 'Smells in here. I vote we change buses.'

Chapter 6

'I can't believe what you just did,' Nick said for at least the dozenth time as they hopped on another bus going the same way. 'Oh, my God!' He was as high and starry-eyed as a young boy after his first ever pint of beer. 'I mean, how did you *do* that?'

'It's just a simple gimmick. A granny could do it. I'll show you sometime.'

'It's incredible.'

'It's nothing.'

This time they took a seat downstairs, in the back. Not a knife-wielding mugger in sight. 'What did you call them?' Ben asked.

'Crusties. Didn't used to be a problem, but now there seem to be more of them all the time. When they're not selling dope or drinking in the streets, they're intimidating people for cash.'

'Well, there's one who might think twice next time,' Ben said.

'I'll bet. I suppose you've done a public service.'

'He said he knew you. What's that about?'

Nick paused a second before replying. 'I've given him money now and then.'

'Voluntarily? Or on demand?'

'They can be pretty forceful. It's hard to refuse. I'm not like you, Ben.'

'It doesn't take much just to say no. Extortion and bullying don't deserve a reward.'

'Giving in is just exacerbating the situation, I know. But I suppose part of me feels sorry for them.'

'You'd be feeling sorrier all sliced and diced with a knife hanging out of your guts,' Ben said.

Nick couldn't argue with that. 'What are you doing to do with the, erm, items you took from him?'

'You want them?'

'I don't think so. Not my style.'

'I'll dump them in the first toilet I pass. Except the money. I'll find a better use for that.'

'Spoils of war?'

'I wouldn't call it that.'

Nick sat smiling and shaking his head in amazement for a few moments. Then he said, 'Actually, I don't know why I'm surprised by what you did back there. I shouldn't be at all. Considering.'

Ben looked at him. 'Considering what?'

'I don't just mean, you know, the wild things you got up to when you were a student. It seems you had a pretty amazing military career. Which would suggest to me that that idiot back there got off pretty damn lucky.'

'And how would you know that?'

Nick shrugged. 'Well, I have a confession to make. I looked you up.'

'You did?'

'A few months ago. Now that we have all this wonderful technology at our disposal, I was getting all mid-life-crisis-ish one evening and googled the names of a few of our old friends. I was horrified to learn of the deaths of Simeon and Michaela. I was doing a concert tour in Japan when they had their car accident, and I'd no idea. Came as a complete shock. I still can't get over it.' Nick shook his head mournfully. 'That makes you and me the last of the old gang, doesn't it?'

Ben said nothing. For two reasons. First, because he knew full well that the fatal crash had been no accident: he'd been there and witnessed it. And gone on to avenge the lives of his dead friends. Second, because of the private history that existed between him, Simeon and Michaela. Things that Nick didn't know, some of which not even Ben himself had known for many years, and which would remain a secret forever. Ben stayed silent, waited for Nick to go on.

'Anyway, there aren't a lot of Benedict Hopes in the world. I found your business website, with your photo on it, which was how I knew it was you. I forget the name of it now. Le something.'

Ben had never liked his picture being on the website. Jeff's idea. 'Le Val,' he said.

'That's it. Your bio doesn't offer a great deal of information. Which I presume is intentional, because you can't reveal much about your history. But I can guess.'

'Can you?'

Nick shrugged. 'Tactical training centre. What is that?'

'What it sounds like,' Ben said. 'We train people.'

'People? Anyone? People like me?'

'I don't think it would be your thing, Nick. Military and specialised police units, mainly. Some private outfits, too.'

'What a strange world you live in. I had no idea such things existed.'

'It's just a job,' Ben said.

'Sounds like a little more than that.'

'Keeps me out of trouble,' Ben lied. More truthfully he

40

added, 'It's been going a few years now. We might be expanding before long. Maybe southern France, or maybe further afield in Europe. Don't know yet.'

'I don't suppose there's much call for that kind of thing in Britain.'

'Too many legal restrictions,' Ben said. 'Unless you're the Ministry of Defence. That lot can do whatever the hell they please.'

Nick pursed his lips and nodded. 'What did you do before that? It seemed from your bio as though there was a few years' gap after you quit the army.'

'Oh, this and that,' Ben said.

'So secretive?'

Ben shrugged. More than ever, he wished he wasn't so easy to look up online. Damn that Jeff Dekker.

'Let me guess,' Nick said, smiling. 'You were a professional assassin. Taking out corrupt dictators, or polishing off enemies for the mob.'

'You've been watching too many movies.'

'A secret agent, then.'

'I helped people,' Ben said, just to steer the conversation away. The bus was rumbling slowly northwards through Oxford. He was thinking about flouting the regulations and lighting up a Gauloise.

Nick raised his eyebrows. 'Helped people?'

Ben shrugged again. Why couldn't they just have discussed the weather, like everyone else? He said, 'Sometimes people need help.'

'The kind of help that they can't otherwise get?'

'That kind of thing,' Ben said.

Nick was a shrewd guy, and he was looking at him with thoughtful eyes. Ben decided to say no more about himself. 'So who's coming to lunch?' he asked.

'Just a few pals. Music people, mostly. They're an all right bunch. You'll like them. One of them is my old professor, Adrian Graves, whom I haven't seen for – crumbs, must be a couple of years. Where does the time go?'

Ben was wondering the same thing, as well as when he'd last heard anyone say 'crumbs'.

Nick went on, 'He's an interesting character. Probably the most knowledgeable authority on baroque and classical that I know.'

'I'm looking forward to meeting everyone,' Ben said. It wasn't strictly true. He would have preferred to spend the time alone with Nick, the two of them catching up in private as reunited friends should. But you couldn't have everything.

They got off the bus on Banbury Road and walked the rest of the way. Nick lived in a quiet leafy street where imposing old three- and four-storey Victorian townhouses stood behind fancy black and gilt wrought-iron terrace railings. The Aston Martin, covered in pigeon droppings, was parked on the street outside a house with a black door with a lion's head brass knocker. The buzzer panel discreetly mounted to the side with three name labels on it aside from Nick's. 'I'm on the top floor,' he explained to Ben as he opened the door and led the way inside the hall.

In fact, as Ben soon understood as they reached the top of the house, Nick's apartment comprised the entire upper floor. From the tall window outside his door there was a view of the University Parks woodland, cricket pavilion and the River Cherwell beyond.

'I bid you welcome to my humble abode,' Nick said, showing Ben into the apartment. The inside was modern compared to the exterior, airy and surprisingly large. The walls of the main living space were adorned with expensive-looking artwork and even more expensive-looking oriental rugs covered sections of the gleaming hardwood floors. But what instantly drew the eye more than anything else was the sunlit bay near the window, dominated by a shining ebony-black grand piano and a contrastingly ancient-looking, highly decorated keyboard instrument that Ben guessed was either a harpsichord or a clavichord. He was a little hazy on the difference. Whatever it was, it and the grand piano nestled together facing in opposite directions, the new and the old like two halves of a yin-yang symbol. They were the focal point of the room.

'You have a very nice place,' Ben said.

Nick grinned. 'How about a coffee for the hero of the buses?'

'Please, don't start that again.'

'Okay. I'm sorry. Then how about a coffee for a very old friend that I'm extremely happy to have met up with again?'

'Sounds better,' Ben said. 'Me too.'

'A deal's a deal,' Nick said. 'And I don't think my coffee will disappoint.'

Nick disappeared down a hallway that led to the kitchen, whistling some bright little tune as he got busy. Ben heard cupboard doors banging, cups and saucers clinking. In his host's absence, Ben walked over to admire the piano. The gothic-script lettering above the keyboard and on its side said BOSENDÖRFER. It was quite a beast.

Ben liked music a lot, some kinds more than others, and often wished he'd taken up an instrument in his life. If he had, it would most likely have been the tenor sax, inspired by his favourite jazz players. Like Bird, of course, and Coltrane, and Sonny Rollins and Dexter Gordon and a host of others. He enjoyed listening to a good pianist, too, even though he wasn't as much of a fan.

Nick's piano was a beautiful object, no doubt about it.

Neither it nor its antique counterpart showed a speck of dust and they both screamed *loving maintenance* in sharp contrast to the neglected state of the car in the street outside. It was pretty clear where Nick's priorities lay.

Moving away from the instruments, Ben gazed at a couple of the portraits on the walls, both very obviously dating back to bygone centuries. One was of a man with a lean, gently thoughtful face, silky frills at his neck and cuff, a powdered wig like a judge's on his head. The name plaque on the gilt frame said JOSEPH HAYDN. The other picture showed a heavier, more austere-looking jowly fellow with thick lips, a wedge of double chin, a frock coat and a slightly different kind of white wig, proffering in his one visible hand a small sheet of musical notation as if to say, 'Here's a little ditty I just wrote, especially for you. And you'd better like it.'

Ben peered closer and saw that this was the famous Johann Sebastian Bach, whose organ music he would be hearing Nick play that evening.

He found a different likeness of J.S. Bach elsewhere in the room, in the shape of a small alabaster bust resting on the glass shelf of a corner display cabinet. This Bach didn't look very pleased at all, wearing an intense, challenging scowl that followed you wherever you went. He was just one of a number of collectables on display in the cabinet, mostly music related: other composer busts of all the usual suspects, Mozart, Beethoven, Schubert, and some that Ben knew less well such as Berlioz and Messiaen; then there was a metronome inlaid with mother of pearl, a violin bow, an ivory piano key, a framed lock of hair purporting to have belonged to Frederick Chopin.

On the middle shelf, propped up on a little stand, was an old handwritten music manuscript that resembled the one in the Bach wall portrait, though it was proportionally a shade larger and consisted of several sheets bound together with wax, instead of just one.

Ben moved close to the cabinet to peer at the manuscript. The paper was splotched, faded and yellowed with age but the handwritten musical notation was almost entirely legible, apart from a curiously shaped, russety-coloured stain that covered part of the right bottom corner and obscured some of the last stave and a few notes. Written music notation was double-Dutch to Ben at the best of times, and this looked like a scrawl. The only part of it he could make out was the composer's signature at the top of the front page, which made his eyebrows rise.

J.S. Bach

'Like a moth to the flame,' Nick's voice said behind him. Ben turned. Nick was returning with the coffee. The rich scent of some serious dark roast was already filling the room.

'Everyone goes straight to that manuscript,' Nick said, carrying the tray to a coffee table. 'And they all ask me the same thing. What must it be worth, and aren't I taking a massive risk not keeping such an obviously priceless relic locked up in a vault?'

'So what's it worth?' Ben asked.

Nick chuckled. After a dramatic pause he replied, 'It's worth precisely zero. Zilch. Don't be taken in. It's a fake.'

Chapter 7

'You could have fooled me,' Ben said. 'It looks real enough. But then, I'm hardly an expert.'

Nick laughed as he set the things down on the coffee table and took a seat in a nearby armchair. 'Join the club. I'm just a humble instrumentalist, not exactly one of your hardcore scholars or collectors who scour the earth ready to part with eye-wateringly vast sums for original manuscripts. I picked that up as a novelty for a few pennies in a crumbly old backstreet music shop in Prague when I was there for a concert last October. Believe me, if it was the genuine item, it'd probably be worth as much as this apartment and everything in it, plus that daft car outside. But it looks the part and is a great conversation piece among my musician pals. We're a dull lot, I'm afraid.'

Ben peered back through the glass at the manuscript. 'I suppose that stain on it would lower its value, though. If it was the real thing, I mean.'

'I amuse myself by telling gullible souls that Bach spilled coffee on the paper while he was composing. You should see their faces at the idea that the great man would actually do such a thing as sit at the keyboard with a steaming mug next to him, like any other human being.'

'Is that what the stain is, coffee?' Ben asked, peering at it. Through the glass, it was hard to tell.

'That's what it looks like to me,' Nick said. 'One thing I do know, old Johann Sebastian was nutty about the stuff. Of course, coffee was very much the craze across Europe at that time. He loved it so much that he even wrote a piece of music as a homage to it, a mini comic opera called the "Coffee Cantata".'

Ben glanced back at the stern face on the portrait. 'He doesn't strike me as the comic type.'

'Oh, don't let that austere front fool you,' Nick said with a wave. 'Bach loved nothing more than to have a good time, in all kinds of ways. He was the father of twenty-two children and he was extremely fond of his grub, not to mention wine and beer. He was sixty-three when he sat for that portrait, but he could still enjoy himself. I'm trying to remember how the "Coffee Cantata" goes. Oh, yes—'

Nick recited:

'Oh, how sweet coffee tastes,
More delicious than a thousand kisses,
Milder than muscatel wine.
Coffee, I have to have coffee,
And, if someone wants to pamper me,
Ah, then bring me coffee as a gift!'

'Sounds like he had it bad,' Ben said. 'Even I'm not that addicted to it, yet.'

Nick smiled and pointed at the cups on the table. 'I'm willing to bet you soon will be, once you try this. Come and drink it while it's hot.'

The coffee tasted as good as it smelled. Ben took it black, no sugar, the way coffee ought to be. He nodded his appreciation. 'Now I *am* an expert in this department,' he said. 'And that's no fake. It's the real McCoy. Colombian?'

'Brazilian Sierra Negra,' Nick said, looking happy. 'Something special, isn't it? Better than the bilge water they serve in Hall, at any rate.'

Ben drank some more, then shook his head, thinking back to the manuscript. 'It's a strange world where someone would go to the trouble of counterfeiting something like that.'

'Welcome to the music world. You'd be amazed at the fakery that's out there. Do you seriously imagine, for instance, that I could afford a real lock of Chopin's hair? There's only one validated example in existence, and that's in a museum in Warsaw.' Nick motioned towards the cabinet. 'That one there was most likely put together from the sweepings off the floor of a pet-grooming parlour.'

'That's one way to make use of dog hair,' Ben said, thinking of the state of the floor of the Le Val office after four German shepherds had been lying around in there. 'I was thinking of stuffing pillows with it.'

Nick smiled. 'I should point out, however, that not everything I possess is phony. That harpsichord there, for example. Made by Jacob and Abraham Kirckman, London's finest craftsmen of their day, circa 1775. Double manual, six hand stops, cabinet of oak, mahogany and tulipwood, all hand-inlaid. I had it professionally rebuilt six or seven years ago. Cost me an absolute bomb.'

'You can see where the money went,' Ben said.

'And hear it. Listen.' Nick jumped to his feet, went over to the harpsichord and dashed off a few fast, tinkling bars. 'Scarlatti. Hear the quality of the sound?'

'I have to say the piano appeals to me more. That's an impressive Bosendörfer you have.'

'And we had some fun dragging it up the stairs, I can tell you,' Nick said. 'You want to hear something?'

'You don't have to play for me.'

'My pleasure.'

Nick switched seats to the piano stool. With his back to

the window, framed in the sunlight, he laid his hands on the keyboard and the room filled with the rich resonance of the grand piano. He played for a minute or so, while Ben watched and listened. The piece was slow and melancholic, yet majestic and powerful. The deep tones of the Bösendörfer projected a weight of emotion that throbbed through the soundspace around them and transported Nick off to another world as he sat there, swaying and rocking soulfully to the music he was playing.

Ben said nothing until Nick stopped and sat back, smiling at him. 'What was that?' Ben asked.

'"*Ich ruf' zu dir, Herr Jesus Christ*",' Nick said in faultless German. '"I call to you, Lord Jesus Christ". It's a chorale prelude. Originally an organ piece, of course. They didn't have pianos like this back when it was composed.'

'Didn't sound that old to me.'

'Amazingly timeless, isn't it? That's what you get from the grand master. He was way ahead of his time.' Nick nodded up at the portrait Ben had been looking at before.

'Bach?' Ben was surprised.

'Johann Sebastian himself. Some of the real purists would say it was heresy even to play Bach on a modern-day piano, let alone commit sacrileges like use the sustain pedal with these old pieces.' Nick shrugged. 'I say, if it sounds good, why not?'

'It did,' Ben said. 'Thank you for letting me hear it.'

Nick came away from the piano and returned to his armchair to pour them some more coffee. It was only now that Ben noticed that he was wearing copper bracelets on both wrists. Nick sipped his coffee and then leaned back in the armchair, rubbing his hands as if they were hurting him. He caught Ben looking. 'Spot of the old arthritis,' Nick admitted. 'Sign of the years creeping up on me, I suppose.

Last thing a keyboard player needs is the curse of stiff fingers. Not so bad, now that spring is here.'

'Does the copper help?'

'A bit. But not as much as the special medication I use. The best in the world.' Nick winked. Ben didn't press him for details.

They chatted for a while longer, mostly about classical music and current affairs, of both of which Ben had little more than a passing knowledge. As midday approached, Nick frowned at his watch and said he ought to start getting things ready for the lunchtime buffet. Ben was ready to help out. A deal was a deal.

While Nick busied himself gathering up the coffee dishes, he motioned in the vague direction of the kitchen and asked if Ben could start getting the food out of the fridge and laying it out on the side. Ben obligingly headed up the passage to find himself faced with four identical white doors, any of which could have been the kitchen. He tried one, but it was locked.

'That's the spare bedroom,' Nick said, coming up behind him with the coffee tray. 'Kitchen's at the end.'

'You keep your spare bedroom locked?' Ben mused.

'That's where I keep my terrorist cache of explosives and weaponry,' Nick said casually. 'You'd never guess I was plotting the overthrow of western civilisation, would you?'

'Your secret's safe with me,' Ben replied with a smile.

The kitchen was spacious, airy and well organised, with faux-marble worktops, a solid oak dining table and matching bespoke wall units. The two friends worked quietly and efficiently, to the strains of soft choral music playing from Nick's hi-fi system. Male bonding had never been so gently domesticated as this. For Ben, it beat erecting an improvised jungle camp or circling the wagons in readiness for an enemy assault any day.

As Nick washed up the coffee cups, Ben took the platters of food from the tall American-style fridge and set it on the side to peel off the cling film wrap. The sandwiches were exactly cut into little triangles, crusts trimmed away, colour-segregated into white bread and wholemeal; one third tuna and mayonnaise, one third ham and pickle, and one third some sort of anaemic-looking paste. For the vegetarians, Nick explained. Ben pulled a face.

Next they had to transfer tubs of stuffed olives, hummus and other dainty finger food from the delicatessen into bowls, which Ben found neatly stacked in a cupboard. Then came the drinks: wine glasses and a selection of reds and whites, some nice barrel tumblers and carafes of pressed fruit juice and lemoned mineral water for the non-drinkers. Ben didn't think Nick had got in enough bottles of wine, but he made no comment. The whole thing was a little too precious for his tastes: he said nothing about that either.

After that, the oak dining table had to be moved from the kitchen into the main room, and everything laid out nicely. Napkins, knives, forks, paper plates, and some straw coasters judiciously provided in case anyone did anything as horrible as set a glass down on top of one of the fine keyboard instruments. Most members of his social circle were far too cultivated to commit such a ghastly act, Nick explained, but you never knew. He told a horror story about some clumsy oaf who once elbowed a whole pitcher of Coke into the works of someone's Steinway baby grand. Needless to say, that person was *not* invited today.

'Dear me,' Ben said, tutting. He had himself once broken into a music museum in Milan and there personally, deliberately, smashed the leg off a priceless historic pianoforte.

A painful tale that he chose not to share with his friend at this moment, or any other. Ben had had his reasons for what he'd done, but something told him Nick might not understand.

Soon afterwards the first of the guests began to arrive, and not long after that, the place was filling with the buzz of polite chatter and laughter. Nick had selected a different CD from the collection that filled an entire bookcase, and the choral music had given way to some kind of lively baroque stuff with booming cellos and crisp harpsichords.

For Nick, completely in his element, the proceedings were just getting underway. For Ben, though, his visit to his friend's apartment felt as though it was coming to an end. Even as the first introductions were being made, he was getting itchy feet to make his excuses and leave. But he didn't want to appear rude. He'd stay just long enough to drink no more than two glasses of wine, munch a couple of sandwiches, pay his social dues, before telling Nick he had to make tracks.

Everyone he spoke to was part of the Oxford classical music scene, in one way or another. Ben was introduced to an organ restorer, to the manager of the Holywell Music Room where Ben had once attended a Bartók string quartet recital, and to a bunch of others whose names and occupations escaped his mind seconds after he'd met them. One of the guests was a tall, slightly stooped, grey-haired university academic in a beige suit with a yellow bow tie, whom Nick greeted like a long-lost friend. 'Ben, I'd like you to meet Adrian Graves. Adrian, this is Benedict Hope, an old chum from the House. He's here for the reunion.'

An old chum. The Nick Ben had known back then would never have used expressions like that.

Handshakes, blether blether, yakkety yak, delighted to

meet you, how fascinating, will you be at the concert, all the expected chit-chat. Ben smiled and nodded his way through the intros and gleaned that Graves was Nick's former professor and a renowned musicologist and expert in ancient something-or-other, now semi-retired. Graves had brought along his wife, whose name was Cressida, or maybe Cynthia, or Camilla – three passes of small talk and boom, it was gone from Ben's memory. He studiously avoided saying anything at all about himself, and trusted Nick to keep what little he knew under his hat. Which limited Ben's options for interactivity even more than his painfully obvious lack of involvement with the local music scene.

As more people turned up and the buzz of chatter stepped up a notch, Ben retreated to the edge of the crowd on the pretext of grabbing a second glass of red wine and another tuna sandwich. He resolved to drink his drink and be on his way.

Being on the sidelines was more interesting to him. Ben was no psychologist, but he'd been engaged to one long enough to pick up a few pointers. Brooke believed that you could learn a huge amount about a person's inner state of mind just by observing them, listening to their talk, noting the dynamics of their behaviour with others. Ben agreed with that idea. All his life he'd had an eye for noticing the small things that most people didn't. And he'd noticed something about Professor Adrian Graves the instant they'd been introduced.

Now Ben filled his last moments before leaving by watching him at a distance. What he saw confirmed his first impressions.

Something seemed to be gnawing at Graves. He was restless, clearly preoccupied, his face busy, eyes darting here and there as he took frequent sips of wine and stood around looking edgy. As Nick went off to greet the latest arrivals Graves was left talking with his wife. Whatever she was saying to him, he didn't seem to like it. His anxious face now flushed with irritation, he said something snappy to her that Ben didn't catch over the ambient noise, banged his empty wine glass down on a sideboard and stalked pointedly away from her. The way stressed-out people do in uncomfortable social situations, he hovered about the periphery of the room alone, pretending to be engrossed in the paintings, peering at the instruments. In psychology terms, Brooke would have described Graves' behaviour as a kind of displacement activity. Like yawning or fidgeting or developing a sudden fascination for a blank space on the wall when you'd much rather be somewhere else.

As Ben watched, Graves wandered over to the display cabinet, where he spent a long time staring at Nick's fake Bach manuscript as though completely captivated by the sight of it, coffee stain and all.

Ben wondered what was up with the guy. It was mildly interesting to watch him. But not interesting enough to warrant sticking around to see more. If Ben and Brooke had still been together, she could happily have spent the rest of the afternoon speculating about what sort of Freudian malaise was at the root of Graves' behaviour. Left to his own devices, Ben personally didn't care all that much. He drained the last of his wine and then threaded his way through the crowd to where Nick was deep in animated conversation with a tall woman who looked like a skeleton in a black dress, a single olive on the plate in her hand.

'Listen, Nick, I have to make a move,' Ben said, gently interrupting.

'So soon?'

'Hope to catch you later, at the concert,' Ben said. 'But

just in case we don't get a chance to talk, here's my card. I wrote my mobile number on the back.'

Nick took the card, looking disappointed that Ben was going. They said their goodbyes. Ben wished him good luck for tonight. 'Not that you need it.' Then smiled at the skeleton lady, said a few nice-to-have-met-yous on his way out, and left the apartment.

Out in the quiet, empty street, Ben breathed a sigh of relief as the claustrophobia of the noisy party quickly wore off. 'Freedom at last,' he muttered to himself. He stood for a moment, savouring the stillness and space around him.

Maybe he'd been living in the countryside too long, he thought. 'What do you think?' he said to a pigeon that was perched on Nick's Aston Martin.

The pigeon stared at him, crapped on the car and then flew off.

Chapter 8

Long ago

Sometimes it seemed to them as though the whole world was made up of nothing but words. Words, words, every day a storm of words, coming at you so hard and fast from all directions that you could barely digest the information in time for the next torrent. Lecture after lecture, until the voices appeared to merge into a babble of confusion that echoed around your head, enough to drive you crazy. Book after book, until the dots on the pages became meaningless and floated in front of your eyes and remained hovering there even in your dreams.

Which was what made these moments all the sweeter and more magical. Moments of pure stillness, where you could just drift awhile, and share a silence with someone so close to you, and simply be.

The wine they'd drunk earlier was cheap and rough, but neither of them cared. The night was warm, just the merest kiss of a gentle breeze through the dark cloister. She rested against his body with her arms wrapped around him, saying nothing, gazing into the deep black shadows, imagining that the glow of his cigarette was an orange star billions of light years away in a galaxy nobody knew about. Nobody but them.

She could feel the tightness of his muscles, and knew that such moments were the closest he could come to being relaxed, like a compressed spring that was never fully unwound. Ben never spoke about the bad things in his life, but Michaela sometimes saw the pain that seared his blue eyes like lightning in a summer sky. Things she was too young to understand, even though she was only eleven months younger than he was. Hers had been a sheltered life, up until now. His had not. That was all she knew, but she wanted to make him happy because she loved him with every molecule of her being, more than she could ever have imagined it was possible to love anyone.

Some days, it seemed he could never be happy. Tonight, she thought he could.

No words. Just being. Listening. Enjoying. The voice of the organ drifted down from the cathedral tower and echoed through the darkness of the cloister, mingling with the night air. In those hours when the college slept, nobody minded. Nick could play until dawn if he wanted to, because as organ scholar he had the keys to the ancient studded oak door in the far corner of the cloister, which led up the narrow staircase to the hidden chamber where the heart of the instrument lay.

He'd started his practice after midnight. Just messing around at first: the opening Hammond organ riff from the rock classic 'Smoke on the Water' by Deep Purple had made Michaela chuckle. Jon Lord was one of Nick's organ heroes he often raved about. Johann Sebastian Bach was the other; and now the organ was filling the sweet night air with the haunting, cascading music of a minor-key fugue, its lines intertwining and swooping and soaring like the flight of birds – or so she pictured it. The music seemed to pulse with its own life, making her think about the new life that pulsed inside her, so fragile, so tiny, yet growing imperceptibly each day.

Michaela hadn't told him yet. She hadn't told anyone. She was still waiting for the right moment, afraid of what Ben's reaction might be. Terrified, too, of what her parents would say when she broke the news to them. She was only eighteen. So many plans had been made for her future. Now, she suddenly no longer had any idea what lay ahead. Doubts often gripped her. Would she and Ben have a life together? What would it be like? He could be so wild, even reckless. Michaela worried that her family would never accept him.

She reached up and ran her fingers through Ben's hair. Ever so gently, he grasped her hand and kissed it.

'I love you,' she whispered.

'I love you too,' he murmured in reply, and the sound of it, and her total and complete faith in his sincerity, rocked her heart and made her want to cry with happiness.

If the baby was a boy, she'd already decided she wanted to call him Jude.

Chapter 9

Ben returned to the college on foot rather than taking a bus. The April sunshine was warm, and he took off his leather jacket and slung it over his shoulder as he walked. He liked walking, because it forced him to slow down. And because he could smoke without getting arrested, even though he was almost out of Gauloises.

On Ben's way back towards the city centre he walked by a beggar who was slumped in a doorway opposite St John's College. He was a man in his forties with sunken cheeks and matted hair and a cardboard sign made from a torn-up box that said HUNGRY + HOMLESS PLESE HELP. No knife. That counted for something. No dog, either. Some of these guys used their pets to extract sympathy from folks, when in fact it wasn't the animal's best interests they were most concerned about. Ben had once triggered one of them into a rage by giving him canned dog meat instead of money. But this guy looked as genuine as he did pitiful. Ben stopped and dug out from his pocket the fifty pounds he'd taken from the crusty. 'Here you go, buddy,' he said, and walked on as the guy sat there clutching his money and staring after him.

Ben spent the next couple of hours wandering through the grounds of Christ Church Meadow and down to the river beyond. The air was full of spring and the scent of

59

daffodils as he followed the footpath along the bank of the Isis to the college boathouses, where he stopped a while and watched the shimmer of the sunlight on the water, letting thoughts and memories play freely through his mind.

For all the bittersweet emotions it kindled for Ben to be back here, Oxford was an undeniably beautiful place to live and he was happy that Nick had found his niche here, enjoying a normal and safe and happily closeted existence doing what he loved. Just like Simeon and Michaela, in the cosy comfortable warmth of the country vicarage not far from Oxford. Normal people, living out their blissfully sheltered lives. Until one day, the real world reached out and snapped them up and it was over.

Ben wondered what it must be like to be a normal person like the members of the old gang. He envied them in a lot of ways, but at the same time he knew that if he had his own life to live all over again, most of the choices he'd made in his time, however crazy or reckless they might have seemed on the outside, would remain unchanged. Maybe he was simply preordained, deep down in his DNA, not to be like normal folks.

Afterwards he slowly made his way back up the path and past the moored narrowboats and river cruisers to Folly Bridge, where he rejoined the busy streets and headed up past Tom Tower and the front of Christ Church to the city centre. Remembering that he was short on cigarettes he strolled down the High Street in search of the venerable pipe shop and tobacconist's he used to frequent long ago, only to find to his chagrin that it had closed down and become a blasted travel agent.

But some things hadn't changed. He crossed the street and walked inside the old covered market, which was exactly as he remembered it from years ago. He spent a while exploring, and bought a bottle of good wine to drink in his room later that evening after the concert. Thinking of the concert made him think of the dinner in Hall that would precede it, which in turn brought to mind that Seraphina's email had stipulated that gowns had to be worn for the event. With mixed feelings Ben recrossed the street and walked down to the university outfitters to buy one. There were different types of academic gowns, depending on status. Ben's lowly status required a Commoners' gown, which was a truncated waist-length affair made of flimsy black material that made you look like some kind of half-arsed Batman. His very first action on dropping out of university all those years ago had been to douse his gown with lighter fluid and torch it. The new one was identical. Ben hated the thing, but rules were rules.

Dinner was dinner, too. Feeling stupid in his gown, Ben found himself seated among strangers and said little to anyone. It was his second depressing social experience of the day, and he left before the main course. He ditched the gown, jogged up the hill to the centre, bought fish and chips at Carfax Chippy, and took the satisfyingly greasy package back to Old Library 7 where he washed it down with some of his wine. In France, drinking claret this good straight from the bottle would probably have been regarded as a crime of sorts, but what the hell. Then it was time for the concert, to which he was looking forward in the hopes of seeing Nick again.

It was a leisurely thirty-second walk around the corner from Old Library to the arched doorway of the cathedral. The famous Seraphina Lewis was there on duty, as diligent as an army sentry but a lot noisier, to meet and greet the arrivals, tick off names on a register and usher them through the grand entrance. Ben liked cathedrals, not because he was particularly pious, but for their serenity. As a student, he'd often attended evensong and other choral services, just to drink in the atmosphere.

Christ Church Cathedral was exactly as he remembered it. If things had gone the way they should have between him and Brooke, they'd have been married here. Privilege of being an old member. Needless to say, things had not gone as they should have.

But Ben wasn't here to dwell on unhappy memories. He'd come to hear Nick.

The concert began promptly at eight-thirty. For the next hour and a half, the cathedral was filled with the celestial voice of the great organ. From the thunderous put-the-fear-of-God-into-you tones of Johann Sebastian Bach toccatas and fugues to the intriguing dissonances of Olivier Messiaen, Ben enjoyed every note of it. It wiped his mind clear and transported him to another place. He was proud of his friend. Nick was up there doing what he loved, and doing a damn fine job of it. When the final notes of the last piece died away, Ben would have stayed another ninety minutes.

He hung around afterwards and was the last to leave, but didn't see Nick and supposed he must have been waylaid or had things to attend to. Ben gave up waiting for him, sorry that he was missing this last chance to see his friend. As much as he'd have liked to stay in Oxford another day so they could go out for a few drinks together, he had to leave first thing in the morning for the meeting with Hobart at Bisley ranges, an hour's drive away. Shame.

On his way back to Old Library, Ben turned his phone on and found there was a text message there from someone who'd tried calling him during the concert.

It was Pam Hobart, Lenny's wife, informing Ben very apologetically on her husband's behalf that tomorrow's rendezvous would have to be cancelled as Lenny had been taken ill with a bout of gastric flu.

And just like that, Ben's plans were suddenly all in pieces. He texted back to say he was sorry to hear the news, wishing Lenny a speedy recovery and promising to set up another meeting when he was better.

Great. Now he'd have to go home empty-handed; the rifle shooting activities at Le Val would just have to make do without the world's greatest bipod for the moment. Ben was mildly irritated, but he couldn't call his trip a complete waste of time. He was pleased to have hooked up with Nick again. Now they'd re-established contact, Ben was determined not to let it lapse.

Maybe he would stick around Oxford, after all. There was no pressing need to dash straight back to France, as Jeff and Tuesday could manage fine without him for just a little longer. He'd pay a visit to the college admin office in the morning to check that he was clear to hold onto the room another day.

His mind made up, Ben ambled back through the cloister and up the groaning bare wooden staircase to his room. The remainder of the wine he'd bought earlier was there waiting for him, seductively calling, 'Drink me'. He was about to flop in the armchair when he changed his mind, and for old times' sake grabbed the bottle and went back down to the cloister. He sat on the same cold stone ledge he used to sit on, and in the peace of the night he smoked his last three Gauloises, listened to the bats flapping about the cathedral tower and savoured the rest of the wine.

He thought about lost friends and wished they were there, but he wasn't lonely. He'd been alone for most of his life, and he relished solitude as much as he liked the darkness.

Sometime in the early hours, he carried the empty bottle upstairs and went to bed.

Chapter 10

Nick Hawthorne treated himself to a taxi home after the concert. He was happy with the evening, and thought he hadn't performed too badly. The organ had sounded great as it ever had, in all the years he'd known it. The truth was, the only remaining original part of it was the case, dating back to about 1680. The actual guts of the instrument were a modern replacement from the late seventies. He often wondered what the old one would have been like to play.

All in all, a successful night. The only downside was that his hands hurt after the performance. He couldn't flex his fingers without wincing. Of all the rotten luck, for someone in his line of work to get arthritis of the hands at such an early age. Nick had two consolations. One was that the jazz pianist Oscar Peterson had suffered from the same condition for much of his life. If it didn't stop Oscar, it wouldn't stop him.

The second consolation was waiting for Nick back home. On arrival he hurried straight to the spare bedroom, unlocked the door, slipped inside and turned on an infrared side lamp that filled the room with a crimson glow. Out of habit, he locked the door behind him.

The reason Nick Hawthorne kept the spare bedroom locked at all times was because it contained his large collection of plants. When it came to horticulture, he was highly specialised: *cannabis sativa* was the only species he'd ever attempted to grow. He was pretty adept at it, too – so much so that it had become something of a hobby with him. Only the females produced smokable marijuana; the males were there for pollination purposes only. He'd learned how to nurture his crop with all the right light conditions and nutrients, maintaining the soil pH in perfect balance for optimum growth. The resulting overproduction was far more than he could actually use himself, even if he'd planned on spending all day every day stoned out of his wits, which was far from the case. So many plants filled the room that it looked like a set from a jungle movie. He'd taken out the bed long ago to make room for them all. Aside from the sideboard and tables all covered in pots, the only remaining furniture was the large recliner chair in which he often spent his evenings, bathed in the submarine glow of the infrared lamp and drifting through an extremely pleasant haze as he partook of the evil weed.

Nick's cannabis use was the only illegality he had ever committed in his life. He felt absolutely no guilt about it whatsoever, as he justified it on purely medical grounds after having tried every noxious pill and potion the doctors could offer him, and all they'd done was cause a whole raft of side-effects without relieving the symptoms of his condition. Deciding the medical profession were essentially no more than quack salesmen for pharmaceutical corporate giants set on poisoning everyone, he'd gone natural and never regretted it. The stuff worked. It was the only medicine that eased the pain in his hands after playing. Plus, it relaxed him, and that was just what he needed after a gig.

The room was kept much warmer than the rest of the apartment. Nick bolted the door shut behind him, then slipped off his coat and dumped it carelessly on the floor in his haste to attend to his needs. He opened the sideboard cupboard where he kept his stash of the crumbled dried leaves, along with his extra-large-size Rizla papers. He spent a few moments carefully rolling up a joint, which made little lances of pain jolt through his fingers, but the discomfort would soon be relieved. Then he went over to the recliner, settled deep into it, relished lighting up the joint with his Dupont Mozart lighter, and began to puff away contentedly.

It wasn't long before he felt the herb working its magic. The delicious familiar sensations began to wash over him, his muscles drooping, heart rate slackening until he could have sworn it was beating once a minute. A smile curled his lips and he closed his eyes, letting the recliner support him like a big, soft hand gently cupping him in its palm. The echoing remnants of the evening's performance played in his head. Then they, too, relaxed and softened, gradually slowly faded away to transcendent silence . . . and Nick Hawthorne was one with the Cosmos.

Some eons later, Nick's eyes snapped open. At first, disorientated, he thought it was the vividness of his dream that had startled him awake. But the bubble of the dream was popped, and the thumping sound that had woken him was still there.

Thud.

Crash.

Nick stopped breathing and he went rigid with sudden tension. He peered at his watch by the dim light of the infrared lamp and saw that it was ten to four in the morning. He'd been asleep for five hours.

He sat bolt upright in the chair as he heard another muffled thump from somewhere beyond the bolted bedroom door, not far away.

There could be no question. Someone was inside the apartment! But who? His mind was still clouded from sleep and the lingering after-effects of the cannabis, and for a couple of moments he thought maybe some of his music pals had turned up in search of a late-night party. Or maybe one of the lunchtime guests had left something behind and come back to get it. But no, that couldn't be. Nick was certain he'd locked the front door on his way in.

That was when he clearly heard the heavy, aggressive footsteps thumping about the apartment, and the strange voices of at least two men, and his guts twisted up with the realisation that whoever was inside his place, it wasn't his friends. They were intruders.

Nick struggled to contain his panic and think straight. From some part of his brain bubbled up the memory of something he'd read: that what the Americans called home invasions, or what the British police called 'creeper burglaries', were reportedly on the rise in the UK. Creeper burglars were the kind who were content to enter their victims' properties even when someone was at home, because in the case of a confrontation they had no qualms about beating your brains out with a hammer or stabbing you to death.

All sliced and diced with a knife hanging out of your guts.

Except these guys weren't doing a lot of creeping. It sounded like a herd of elephants in there.

Nick slowly rose from his chair and advanced through the red-lit jungle towards the bedroom door. He placed the palms of his shaking hands flat against it and pressed his ear to the wood, listening, barely daring to breathe in case they detected his presence in here. The thought suddenly hit him that they might see the streak of infrared light under the door, and he reached out and turned off the lamp, plunging the jungle into pitch black. He froze in the darkness,

67

listening to the intruders crashing about. As terrified as he was of what they might do to him if they found him, the thought of the mindless damage they could be causing to his precious possessions, just for the hell of it, frightened him even more. Any moment now they might start smashing his instruments to pieces, or urinating on them and God knew what else. His beautiful Bosendörfer. Worse still, the irreplaceable Kirckman.

But what could he do? He was completely helpless to prevent the worst from happening. This wasn't America, where you could come bursting out brandishing a home-defence shotgun and send the bad guys packing, or even give them the blasting they deserved and still be on the right side of the law.

Call the police, quick. Nick fumbled in the darkness for his coat, thrown down on the floor earlier. Finding it, he fished his mobile phone from the pocket. He was poised to start dialling 999 when he stopped.

What are you thinking, you bloody fool?

Here he was standing among enough home-grown cannabis plants to stock a garden centre, and he was about to invite the police into his home. Madness. Not in a thousand years would they believe all this was for his personal use only. He could see the headline in the *Oxford Mail*: CLASSICAL PERFORMER CHARGED WITH DEALING DRUGS. Reputation in shreds. Career gone. He'd have to sell the apartment. His mother would be scandalised. It was all too awful to contemplate.

Get a grip on yourself, Nick. Do something!

But what?

He could still hear the burglars banging about, and the sound of their voices through the door. One of them was making a joke about something. The other one laughed.

They weren't speaking English. Was it Polish? Romanian?

That was when it suddenly occurred to Nick that the solution to his problem was staring him in the face. He couldn't call the cops, but he could call someone. Someone who wouldn't be afraid, like him. Someone who could wade in and handle this situation like swatting a couple of flies. The human equivalent of that home-defence shotgun Nick was so badly lacking right now.

Ben Hope.

Nick fell to his knees on the floor and groped in his coat pockets for the business card Ben had given him earlier that day. He shone the glow of his phone over the back of the card and saw the mobile number handwritten there. He punched in the digits with a trembling finger and clamped the phone to his ear, crouched on the floor of the dark room as though he was saying a prayer of penitence.

Nick almost wanted to sob with relief when he heard Ben's voice in his ear before the second ring. Four in the morning, but he sounded wide awake and alert. Like a kick-ass justice-dealing machine ready to spring into action.

Nick cupped his hand over the phone and spoke in a raspy, urgent whisper. 'Ben, it's me, Nick. Listen—'

'Why are you whispering? What's up?'

'I need your help, right now,' Nick croaked. 'There are *intruders* in my apartment.'

Ben Hope wasn't one to waste time on idle chat. 'Call 999. Stay safe. On my way.'

'I can't call the pol—' Nick began to explain, but then the line went dead. He stood up, still clutching the phone, listening through the door and realising that something was different. He could no longer hear the intruders. He stalked closer to the door and pressed his ear against it.

Dead silence.

Had they gone? They must have.

A moment earlier, that would have been the most wonderful relief in the world. Now, Nick was almost disappointed that he wouldn't get to see Ben Hope kicking their sorry arses after all.

He slowly, tentatively, unbolted the door and eased it open a crack. Still not a breath of sound or movement from out there. The worst of the danger seemed to have passed, but all the same his heart was fluttering with mixed dread and fury at the thought of what evidence of horrible damage he was about to find in his home.

Nick stepped nervously out into the pitch-dark hallway and turned towards the living room at the top of the passage, where he could see a faint rectangular outline of light around the edges of the door. His legs felt shaky under him. He reached out a hand to find the light switch.

Then a powerful grip clamped hold of his arm and he cried out in terror as he felt himself being jerked forward off his feet. As he fell, something hard and solid hit him a brutal blow to the face and he felt his nose break.

The light came on. Nick was on the floor, groaning, blood bubbling from his broken nose. He peered through a veil of pain, craned his neck upwards to look at the trio of men standing over him and looking down at him as if he was a dog turd they'd stepped in. The one who had kneed him in the face reached down and grabbed a fistful of Nick's hair, making him cry out again as he forced him to stagger upright. The man pressed the web of his hand against Nick's throat and pinned him against the wall.

Helpless and unable to speak or move, Nick stared at his trio of attackers. Big, hard-looking men, all wearing dark clothes. They had broad shoulders and angular, ruddy faces, and eyes that gazed back at him without any trace of compassion. As though he was just an object to them, not even human. To Nick, that was the most terrifying thing of all.

One of them shouldered past, yanked open the spare bedroom door and peered through, flashing a small torch around the inside. He grinned.

'Like I said, boys. It's a fuckin' greenhouse in here.' Speaking English now, thick with the accent of the language Nick had heard them talking in before. Eastern European, but he still couldn't place it.

Such things were the least of Nick Hawthorne's worries now. The man pinning him by the throat drew back his other hand in a clenched fist.

Nick saw little after that. The punches kept coming, hard and violent. He felt his teeth break, with a horrible crack that filled his head. Then he was back down on the floor, heavy kicks striking at his stomach and sides and groin and legs, with nothing he could do except curl up and try to protect himself and hope it would be over soon.

One of the thugs said something that Nick couldn't have understood, even in English. Then he felt the pincer grips seize him by the arms, and his body being lifted off the floor. They half-carried him into the living room, dragging his limp feet along the floor. He was groaning and half blind with pain, and only caught a fleeting glimpse of the wreckage of the room. Why were they doing this to him? He didn't understand. He didn't deserve this.

'No,' he tried to plead. But all that came out from his shattered lips was a bubbling moan.

They dragged him towards the window.

Chapter 11

Ben had wanted to ask why Nick couldn't call the police, but there was no time to lose over questions. He hurriedly pulled on his jeans and boots, put his leather jacket on over the dark T-shirt he'd been sleeping in, and left Old Library at a sprint.

The BMW was in the college car park to the rear of Meadow Buildings, across the quad and through a gated arch. Ben threw himself behind the wheel, and moments later the snarl of his exhausts broke the serenity of the silent meadow.

He skidded out of the college grounds and sped up St Aldate's. One-way systems and pedestrianised zones weren't a priority for him, and nor were speed limits as he hustled northwards through the night. Oxford never quite sleeps, but at four in the morning its centre comes closer to being deserted than most modern cities. He hit seventy miles an hour on Cornmarket, and eighty on Banbury Road, before he had to brake to avoid running down a bunch of drunks clowning around in the middle of the street. Moments later, he was roaring into the tranquil part of north Oxford where Nick lived.

Only to find that it was no longer so tranquil. And that he wasn't the first emergency responder to arrive on the scene.

The houses and trees of Nick's street were lit by the swirl of blue from the squad of vehicles that half blocked the road. Ben kerbed the BMW opposite and got out. The other side of the street he could see the door to Nick's place hanging open, police hovering outside like guards. The top-floor windows were lit, and more lights were coming on in neighbouring houses all around as residents woke up to the goings-on. An old man stood framed in his doorway on Ben's side of the street, wrapped in a dressing gown and squinting across at the police cars and the glare of blue lights. He looked confused and distressed. 'What's going on?'

Ben made no reply. A short distance away, a female uniformed officer was taking what looked like a witness statement from a young man and woman in their early twenties who stood huddled and pale at the side of the pavement. They were dressed as though they'd been to a party. Passers-by, rather than neighbours. The guy was clutching a phone at his side. Ben thought he must have been the one who called 999, if Nick hadn't.

Closer to the apartment entrance, Nick's Aston Martin was boxed in by a chequered Thames Valley Police Vauxhall Vectra and two unmarked detective cars. One was a Plain Jane Mondeo and the other was some kind of seventies' American muscle car as wide as a river cruiser, blue lights twinkling from behind its grille. As incongruous as it was, Ben gave it only a glance. A chill gripped his insides as he saw the paramedic unit clustered near the entrance to Nick's building.

They'd backed their ambulance up close, but they hadn't gone inside, because their focus was down here at street level. Emergency medical equipment was spread out over the pavement, which was strewn with shards of broken glass. Glancing up at the shattered pane of the top-floor window of Nick's apartment, Ben understood where the glass had come from. But the paramedics had their backs to him, blocking out what they were doing. He needed to see, even if he didn't want to.

He hovered impatiently as a second police Vectra came screeching onto the scene and then ran across the street for a better look, his heart thumping. The WPC spotted him and left her witnesses for a moment to step towards him with her arms spread to ward him away, but he pushed by her. A cold, sour wave of fear washed through him.

He knew. Even before he got a clear view of what the paramedics were working on, he knew.

Then he saw it. The chill gripped his guts and his vision seemed to telescope into a tunnel, while the sounds of radios and frantic activity were muted in his ears and nothing existed except Ben and the grim sight in front of him.

The body had fallen from the top-floor window above. It hadn't hit the pavement, because its drop had been arrested by the spiked iron railing below. A man's body, fully dressed in beige chinos and a bright blue shirt. Hanging over the railing with his arms and legs dangling limp. A spike protruding either side of his spine. In the amber of the streetlights and swirling blue of the emergency vehicles, the blood that was dripping from the railing and pooling on the ground, running along the cracks between the paving stones and coursing in little rivulets off the edge of the kerb into the gutter, looked oily and colourless.

It was Nick Hawthorne. His head was hanging at an angle that made his face visible, or what was left of it. From his busted nose and teeth, it looked like the fall wasn't the first injury he received at the hands of the intruders. He looked as though he'd been in a bare-knuckle prize fight, and lost badly in the first round. One eye was swollen completely shut, the other wide open in a frozen stare of terror.

When you hit rock bottom, your deepest dread realised, the nightmare come starkly true, that leaves nowhere else to go. Now there was nothing left to be afraid of. Ben closed his eyes for a moment, stilling himself, gathering his strength. Then he reopened them and felt the fear gone, replaced with icy calmness.

He looked back up at the smashed window above. He could see shapes and shadows moving around up there, which he knew were police officers examining the scene. He couldn't believe how fast they'd got here.

He stood behind the paramedics as they struggled to get his body off the railing. If they were in a hurry, it was only to get the mess cleared up, not because their patient was in need of urgent medical assistance. He wasn't going anywhere but the John Radcliffe mortuary, across the city in Headington.

'Sir?'

Ben turned. The WPC, her face half blue in the lights, wisps of mousey hair sticking out from under her hat. Jabs of static and voices blurping from her radio. She looked drawn and tight-lipped, as if she wanted to throw up and was fighting to hold it in. Ben wondered if this was her first impaling. Cops had a dirty job and saw some pretty bad things. But they couldn't begin to imagine some of the things he'd seen.

'Sir, I need you to step back, please.'

'What happened here?' Ben asked, already building the scenario in his mind. Nick had said there were *intruders*, plural, in the apartment. It would have taken at least two men to throw him through the window with enough force to shatter it like that. Perhaps three.

Ben glanced across at the witnesses. The young woman

75

was crying, her male companion awkwardly holding her and patting her back as if to console her, though he looked as shocked as she did. Ben saw two possible options there: either they'd happened on the body after it had already hit the railing, or else maybe they'd seen Nick come out of the window and drop to his death, which would have been twice as horrifying and accounted for the shell-shocked looks on their faces. In that case, they might also have seen the perpetrators running off, which could have happened before, during, or after calling the police.

If the couple had observed Nick's killers flee the scene, Ben expected that any moment now the cops would hustle them into a police car and whisk them off to the station to help the cops with their enquiries, on what was going to turn out a long and sleepless night for all concerned.

'I have to ask you to step away, please,' the female officer repeated more firmly. 'This is a crime scene.'

Crime scene. If the cops had thought it was a deliberate suicide or simply a case of some stupid drunk falling out of a window, either way they'd be calling it an accident scene. The fact that they were calling it a crime scene confirmed for Ben that the witness couple must have seen Nick fall and the bad guys make their escape moments later. If the police hadn't turned up so uncharacteristically damn fast, he might have been able to talk to them himself, and get a description of the attackers. That chance was blown now. Ben was upset about it.

'Okay, officer. I didn't mean to get in the way.' Ben stepped back. The female officer gave him a look that said, 'Don't go anywhere, we might want to talk to you' and hurried back to the witnesses.

Moments later, as Ben had expected, the WPC was joined by another officer who led the witness couple to one of the marked Vectras and took off with the flashing blues lighting up the trees along the street. Ben seemed to have been forgotten about for the moment, which suited him fine. He needed to learn more, which wasn't going to happen standing out here with the uniforms. If the plainclothes guys were upstairs in Nick's apartment, that was where Ben needed to be too.

Chapter 12

Nobody saw Ben as he entered the building and hurried upstairs. He met a couple of Nick's downstairs neighbours on the first-floor landing, who looked pale and bemused and asked him if he knew what was going on, but he brushed by them without a word.

When he reached Nick's floor he saw the apartment door lying open and slipped inside, silent as a shadow. Ben's ability to blend into his environment and move about without being seen or heard had been noted as off-the-scale exceptional by his first instructors in the SAS. Time and practice had made him much better at it since.

The apartment looked as though a small bomb had gone off inside it. Furniture was overturned, paintings torn off the wall, the glass display cabinet broken and knocked on its side with Nick's music collectables all spilled over the floor. The precious harpsichord had been shunted so roughly to one side, leaving scuff marks on the polished hardwood floor, that one of its three legs had folded under it and the instrument was listing at an angle like a beached ship.

From where Ben stood hovering near the entrance he could see through the open doorway that led to Nick's kitchen. Halfway down the passage, the spare bedroom door that had been locked earlier was hanging ajar. There was a glow of red light coming from inside the bedroom. Ben wondered what that was about. A strange yet familiar smell hung inside the apartment, and it seemed to come from that open room. He wondered for a moment what that was about, too, until he realised what it was, and put it together with the red light.

In the middle of the devastation of the living room, two plainclothes detectives and another uniformed officer were clustered together deep in conversation. The older detective was doing most of the talking, which told Ben that he was the superior officer. He was a short, reedy individual with dyed black hair oiled over a balding crown and a moustache that twitched as though it was going to fall off when he talked. From the moment Ben saw him, he had the strangest impression that he'd seen him somewhere before. For the moment he couldn't pin it down, but it would come to him.

The younger plainclothes guy looked to be maybe a couple of years older than Ben, and a couple of inches taller at around six-one. He was dressed more casually than his superior in jeans and desert boots. He had a craggy, weathered face that looked as if it had been beaten out of Kevlar, and watchful eyes that were locked on the older detective with all the expression of a rough plaster wall, but Ben could tell that he wasn't impressed with the guy.

None of them noticed Ben's presence, until he stepped towards them and interrupted their conversation with, 'So what's with the incredible response time, guys?'

They all turned around. The one with the craggy face showed no change of expression, but the older detective flushed the colour of liver. 'Who the hell are you?' he demanded.

'I might ask you the same question,' Ben said.

Which might not have been the best way to win the guy's

favour. Ben was still trying to place him. The moustache bristled like a startled cat as the older detective broke away from the group and stepped aggressively towards Ben, puffing himself up to look bigger. 'I'm Detective Superintendent Forbes, Thames Valley Police, and this is a closed crime scene. Who the hell let you in here?'

'You'd have to ask them.'

'What's your name?'

'I'm Ben Hope.'

'Occupation? Address?'

'Businessman. I live out of the country. I'm in the UK on a work-related visit.'

'And you have a reason for being here at four in the morning?'

Ben was getting tired of the rapid-fire interrogation. 'That's my friend stuck on the railings down there. All the reason I need, wouldn't you say?'

'How do you know the victim?'

'We were at college together, here in Oxford. Long time ago.'

'Were you close?' Forbes asked the question without a trace of sympathy. Ben was definitely not liking him very much.

'I wouldn't say that exactly. Yesterday morning was the first time I'd seen him in more than twenty years.'

'So, in fact, you hardly know him at all,' Forbes said, arching one eyebrow as if Ben had just admitted to a criminal offence. 'Therefore I repeat, why are you here?'

'I'm sentimental,' Ben said. 'And I don't like it when people throw innocent folks out of windows. Especially when I was just getting to know them again. That's why I'm here. What about you?'

Perhaps sensing the rising tension between Ben and his

superior, the younger plainclothes guy stepped forward and introduced himself. 'I'm DI Tom McAllister.' He spoke with a Northern Irish accent that was only slightly attenuated from however many years he'd been on the Thames Valley force. 'I was first on the scene, less than five minutes after it happened. By the time I got here it was already too late to do anything for your friend. I'm sorry.'

'You must live nearby,' Ben said. 'It took me less than fifteen to get here from the centre, from when he phoned me.'

McAllister shrugged. He had an open, ruggedly sincere face that Ben liked. Which wasn't a usual reaction for Ben when dealing with cops.

McAllister replied, 'I don't, but I happened to be driving through the area when the radio call came through.' Ben noticed he was holding a ring of car keys, the old-fashioned one-piece metal kind you could puncture someone's throat with. The leather key fob medallion featured a fierce-looking fish and bore the emblem BARRACUDA. The American muscle car parked down in the street. Ben thought that maybe if he lived in Oxfordshire and had a big V8 rumbler like that and nothing better to do on a balmy April night, he'd be driving about at four in the morning too.

'You say he phoned you?' Forbes asked.

'Check his phone and you'll see my number was the last call he made,' Ben said.

'And where were you at the time?'

'At our old college. I'm staying there. You want my room number too?'

'Just making sure we have our facts straight,' Forbes said. 'So you're in Oxford on business. What kind of business might that be?'

Ben gave one of his standard vague replies. 'I'm a security

81

consultant.' It would take ten seconds to look him up and find out about Le Val and his military background. If they poked a little deeper they'd soon hit the brick wall of MoD secrecy concerning the true nature of Ben's past, and the fun would begin.

'Security consultant. That covers a lot of ground, doesn't it?'

Ben looked at Forbes. 'Am I a suspect?'

'Not at this time.'

'Just as well, because that won't sit well with me. If you want proof of where I was at the time of the incident, the next thing you'll want to check is the registration number of the silver Alpina down there in the street, and the footage from the speed cameras I just tripped on my way here. All of which gives me a pretty good alibi, so you needn't think about giving me any crap.'

'Nobody's giving you any crap,' McAllister put in.

'No?' Ben said. 'I'm only trying to help here. So far I haven't heard anyone saying much about catching the people who killed my friend.'

McAllister nodded and pulled a grim face, as if he could barely wait to get his hands on them, either. Judging by the guy's rough, scarred knuckles, Ben would have said McAllister had got into a few scrapes in his time.

'And what exactly did the victim say to you on the phone?' Forbes asked.

'What do you think he said? He was scared, same way you would be if you woke up at four in the morning to find a bunch of intruders smashing up your home. He needed my help to deal with it. I got here too late. End of story.'

Now Forbes was staring at Ben with a look of extreme suspicion. 'Deal with it?'

'I didn't say I was going to shoot them,' Ben said. 'Though it wouldn't be a bad idea.'

McAllister was looking at Ben as if to say, *take it easy.*

The moustache twitched. 'Then what were you going to do?'

'Ask them politely to leave,' Ben said. 'With the gentlest touch of persuasion.'

'Dealing with violent attackers is the responsibility of the police, not the public,' Forbes said in a hectoring tone. Ben noticed the way McAllister gave an exasperated eye roll behind his superior's back. Ben was thinking that if he had to work with this guy Forbes, Forbes might end up getting thrown out of a window too.

'Then it looks like we all failed him,' Ben said.

Forbes asked, 'Why would he call you and not us?'

'I think we both know the answer to that one.' Ben pointed through the open passage towards the doorway of the spare bedroom. 'It's obvious he didn't want the police here. You can almost smell the marijuana from outside. And judging by the infrared lamp, he was probably growing the stuff.'

'He was virtually farming it,' Forbes said. 'Tell me, Mr Hope. How long has your friend been dealing drugs?' He folded his arms smugly, as if he could already see the headline. *Thames Valley police unmasks kingpin drug lord.* 'It's obvious this was a deal gone bad. Happens all the time.'

'You're dead wrong, Forbes. He used the cannabis for arthritis pain. You can verify that with his doctor in about three seconds. He'd already tried every type of conventional medication going. But I can't blame you for wanting to wrap this up nice and easy. That's what a hack like you does best, isn't it?'

Forbes turned a shade of purple. He took a step closer to Ben, which forced him to look up as he scrutinised Ben's face. 'Do I know you from somewhere?'

The fact was, while they'd been talking, Ben had

remembered where he'd seen Forbes before. Take away the moustache, give him some more hair on top and knock off twenty-odd years, and the memory was as sharp in Ben's mind as though it had happened yesterday. Ben allowed himself a cold smile as he played it back. He was pretty sure that Forbes' colleague McAllister would enjoy the story. For the moment, he decided to spare Forbes the humiliation.

'Something amusing you?' Forbes said.

'My friend just died. I'm not in a laughing mood.'

'Then why are you looking at me like that?'

Ben leaned closer to him and sniffed. 'Thought I could smell something. Must be my imagination.'

'I've had enough of this nonsense,' Forbes said. 'Let me remind you, Mr Hope, that you're trespassing on a crime scene. So I suggest you bugger off before I do pull you in for questioning.'

Ben melted Forbes with a long, hard glare that lingered so long that McAllister was starting to get edgy. There was nothing more to be said. Ben turned and walked away.

Outside, the police SOCO unit had erected a forensic tent over the railings. The ambulance had gone, and the broken glass on the pavement was all cleaned up. All that was left of Nick was the blood congealing in the gutter.

Ben walked slowly across the street to his car and drove back through the city of dreaming spires. By the time he stepped out of the Alpina in the college car park the first light of dawn was breaking, washing the trees of the meadow and the old limestone buildings of Christ Church with red and gold. The air was fresh and sweet, and Ben filled his lungs with it to try to flush out the sour taste of death and violence that wouldn't go away. Maybe it never would.

As he made his way towards Old Library he paused in the cathedral cloister. Listening to the silence of the organ that Nick Hawthorne would never play again. It was too late to go to bed, and even if it hadn't been, Ben knew he couldn't have slept. He wondered if the killers were sleeping.

First Simeon and Michaela. Now Nick too. All gone. Ben was the last of the gang left.

Someone was going to wish he wasn't.

Chapter 13

Long ago

The independent cinema off Cowley Road in east Oxford was called the Penultimate Picture Palace, and it was famous for several reasons: for belonging to a guy who was equally notorious for having a life-size replica shark sticking out of the roof of his house, and for screening the kinds of movies the corporate cinema chains didn't show, like Bertolucci's Last Tango in Paris.

Young Ben Hope didn't care about sharks any more than he did about watching the middle-aged Marlon Brando dressed like a hobo act out sordid rape fantasies with a teenage Maria Schneider. What appealed to Ben about the PPP was that it was famous for being the kind of rough and ready joint where you could smoke and drink to your heart's content and nobody would hassle you. And if you could survive the late-night walk back to college through the jungle of east Oxford without getting mugged or poisoned by the temptations of the kebab vans, it all made for a fine evening out.

At nineteen, he could already see that the world was changing. One day these places would be sanitised out of existence. Until then, he intended to experience them fully.

It was after pub closing time when Ben and Michaela left

the cinema, along with the small crowd who'd just sat through the epic double bill screening of Fellini's Roma and Satyricon back to back. Michaela's choice of movies, because she was into all that arthouse stuff. Ben hadn't objected. He had a pack of Woodbines and a quarter bottle of Teacher's blended scotch, because his student allowance didn't extend to the single malt stuff, and that had been plenty enough to keep him contented through the four-hour marathon even if he hadn't been able to understand a damn thing that was going on. The night was warm and the stars were out, they were young and in love and they set off towards home at a slow walk, hand in hand, talking and laughing about stupid things.

He felt good in her company. It was a perfect moment for him and he wanted it to go on forever.

The bikers had gathered outside a fish and chip place on Cowley Road that was closing up for the night, munching greasy food out of paper wrapping and knocking back cans of lager as they stood around ogling their row of Harleys and Jap cruisers parked on the kerbside. Eight or nine of them, hanging tough. Studded leather and cut-off denims and long hair and tats, the whole works, designed to demonstrate what badass outlaws they were.

As Ben and Michaela ambled closer, she tugged his arm and looked at him with worried eyes that glistened in the streetlights.

'Maybe we should cross to the other side.'

He chuckled. 'What are you worried about?'

'They look nasty.'

'Don't be silly. They're all for show. The tattoos probably aren't even real.' He squeezed her hand reassuringly. They walked on. A couple of the bikers stared at Michaela. Ben looked at the motorcycles and wondered what it would be like to ride one.

Then a biker with a bushy beard and an overhanging gut

called out raucously, 'Show us yer tits, love.' It must have been the best witticism his mates had heard all night, because the rest of them all fell about racked with mirth.

Michaela tugged at Ben's arm again and she shrank close to him, wanting to quicken her step to get past them. But Ben slowed his. He gazed at the fat biker. 'Why don't I show you something else instead?'

What came next was more than Ben had intended to happen. But it couldn't have worked better if he'd planned it that way. Still holding Michaela's hand he stepped off the kerb, planted one foot against the side of the nearest motorcycle, and gave it a push. The machine toppled off its sidestand and fell over, bumping into the one next to it. Which fell also, and hit the one next to it in turn.

The bikers watched in dumbfounded horror as the entire row came crashing down in a perfect domino effect. Mirrors crunched. Handlebars twisted. Lovingly polished chrome exhausts scratched and dented. The worst disaster imaginable.

Michaela was boggling at Ben, almost as aghast as the bikers were. Scarcely able to believe what effect one little push could have, he burst out laughing. Which perhaps, in retrospect, was adding a touch too much insult to injury.

The fat biker let out a shrill scream. He dropped his beer can and went waddling over to rescue his Harley as if it were an infant trapped under the rubble of a collapsed house. The rest of his mates joined him, yanking at crumpled handlebars and cissy bars in a desperate attempt to disentangle and right their beloved machines. But everything was so badly locked together that they'd need a crane, and maybe an angle grinder too.

The fat biker turned on Ben with froth bubbling at the corners of his mouth and murder flashing in his eyes. 'I'll fucking have you for that.' He reached inside his jacket. His fist came out clenched around the handle of some kind of small, tatty-looking pistol and he pointed it at Ben, teeth bared in hatred.

Michaela let out a frightened cry. Ben just stared at the gun, because he'd never seen one before and part of him was genuinely curious about it. He had no idea what kind it was, whether it was even real or a blank-firing starter pistol. There was something he'd heard of called a Saturday Night Special, a favourite concealment weapon among gangs and hoodlums. Maybe it was one of those.

Whatever it was, he didn't want it pointing anywhere near Michaela. He pulled her behind him, so that he was shielding her with his body. Then stepped towards the fat biker, reached out and, before the guy had a chance to react, whipped the gun out of his hand. The move took about a third of a second. Ben didn't have any way of knowing it then, but before too long, military experts in unarmed combat would tell him he had a natural talent. In the years to follow, he would learn to do it even faster, against far more dangerous opponents.

In the blink of an eye, Ben went from having never seen a real gun to pointing one at a living human being for the first time in his life. He would have expected his heart to be thudding like a steam hammer and his hands to be shaking, but he felt strangely calm and felt no fear as he aimed the pistol at the fat biker's face.

The rest of the bikers scattered, sprinting off in all directions. The fat one stood his ground, but only because he was paralysed with terror. His eyes were so wide, Ben thought his eyeballs were going to drop out like two hard-boiled eggs.

At that moment, the most awful smell filled the air. The biker had shit his pants. He stood there knock-kneed for a moment, mouth opening and closing; then his eyes rolled back in his head and he collapsed in a dead faint.

'Oh, my God!' Michaela covered her face with both hands.

Ben tossed the gun into the litter bin outside the chip shop. He looked down at the unconscious biker. The smell was bad enough to make your eyes water. The whole spectacle was so insane, Ben started laughing even more loudly than before. 'Did you see that?'

For some reason, Michaela didn't find it even faintly amusing. Recovering from the initial shock, she rounded on him angrily. 'Ben, we have to get out of here, NOW!'

He was about to reply when there was the whoop of a siren and the street was suddenly swirling with blue light. The police car slid to a halt at the kerbside. A male and a female patrol officer got out. She was tall and sandy-haired, he was dark and reedy. The WPC ran over to the body on the ground while the male cop glared at Ben as though they'd stumbled across a murder scene.

'I never touched him,' Ben said, pointing. 'He's just fainted.'

As if to prove him right, the fat biker's eyes suddenly snapped open. Like a man awakening from a nightmare only to find it really happening, he let out a yell and started trying to scramble to his feet. He took one look at the cops and broke into a lurching run, the best he could manage with his leather jeans full of warm shit. The WPC went to restrain him, but the biker shoved her out of the way and ran a couple more paces before he stumbled in his desperate haste to escape, and fell on his face. Before he could get up again, the male officer pinned him bodily to the deck and started cuffing his hands behind his back. 'You're under arrest!'

Then suddenly the male cop was recoiling off the fallen biker, staggering upright and looking down in alarm and disgust at the front of his nice, neat uniform, which Ben now saw was covered in the biker's excrement. It was everywhere on him. His hands were dripping with it.

Ben started laughing so hard, he thought he was going to throw up all the whisky he'd drunk. Michaela became even angrier with him. 'For Christ's sake, Ben!'

She wasn't the only one. The male cop came storming up to him, his face turning aubergine purple with rage. 'What the hell are you laughing at, sonny?'

'Like a pig in shit,' Ben cackled. It was a whole new meaning to the expression, and he thought it was the funniest thing he'd ever come up with.

'Right! I'm taking you in too, for insulting a police officer!'

And so began Ben's first ever arrest, though it wouldn't be his last, followed by a night in the cells at St Aldate's police station down the street from Christ Church. An incident that, later, would almost cost Ben his military career before it had even begun.

You never forget your first serious love. Just the same way you never forget your first serious brush with the law, and the face and name of the cop who booked you. In Ben's case, the arresting officer that night was Constable Forbes, Thames Valley Police.

You live and learn. Ben never did anything quite like that again.

But it would be only a matter of a few weeks before he did something even worse.

Chapter 14

It was ten in the morning when Ben saw the crusty appear from among the crowds and buses on busy Queen Street near Carfax Tower. The guy was doing the circuit, just as Ben expected from what Nick had told him. For an aggressive, intimidatory beggar like this one, the whole central area of Queen Street, Cornmarket, and all the little surrounding lanes and side streets, was a target-rich environment bound to yield decent takings for a dishonest morning's work. Swaggering cockily about his hunting grounds, the crusty didn't seem the least bit cowed from his experience just the previous morning.

Some people never learn.

Ben was skilled in the art of one-on-one surveillance, but it didn't take much skill to follow a target like this one, who lived in his own world and cared about nothing much except where his next free handout was coming from. Nor was there much artistry in the way the crusty went about his business. Ben watched him collar three unsuspecting victims for money, two in Queen Street and a solitary woman he accosted in Shoe Lane. Both of his male targets were smaller than him, which generally applied to most men, and both were younger, underconfident guys who were easy to push around. Ben could have intervened on their behalf, but his strategy was to hold back for now. The time for intervention would come later, once Ben had him in a less public place.

When the crusty finally got on a bright green Oxford Bus Company double-decker heading for Cowley and the Blackbird Leys estate further east, Ben hung back and was one of the last passengers to board. He took a seat at the rear of the lower deck, where he could watch all movements onto and off the bus. Then all he had to do was sit back and wait for the right moment to test his theory.

Cowley Road had changed a lot over the years. Various dives Ben had once frequented and had great affection for, like the iconic Bullingdon Arms pub where Irish ceilidh musicians once gathered for impromptu jam sessions over pints of the best Guinness to be had anywhere outside of Dublin, were gone, now replaced by slick, plastic wine bars. The old Penultimate Picture Palace was no longer, either, which saddened him. But he had things other than reminiscences on his mind.

As he gazed out of the window Ben ran back through the clues once more. At the time he'd noticed certain small things yesterday, he'd dismissed them as unimportant. The fact that the crusty had apparently been so quick to recognise Nick on the bus, and that Nick had seemed uncomfortable about being recognised, and then his slight hesitation when Ben had asked him about it later on, had seemed like nothing. Ben hadn't been surprised to find illegal pills and magic mushrooms in the crusty's pockets, either. Nor had he made anything much of Nick's reference to his 'medication'.

But since last night, all those apparently disconnected elements were coming together in a way that made Ben see the whole picture very differently. If Nick was growing weed, he'd have to have got the seeds from somewhere. Nowadays it was possible to obtain cannabis seeds online with virtually total freedom, but maybe a man like Nick Hawthorne wasn't worldly enough to know that. Or maybe he was worried about dodgy internet purchases being traced back to him. For the sake of privacy, a cautious fellow with too much to lose might have preferred a face-to-face cash transaction. Which would by necessity have brought him into contact with members of the city's soft-crime elements. Ben was now almost convinced that Nick had been buying dope from the crusty. That was how they knew each other. That was what Nick was trying to hide, in his cautious way.

The problem was when soft crime unexpectedly hardened. You never really knew who you were dealing with, or what they might be capable of. A guy with a pocket full of harmless-enough seeds could turn into a guy waggling a knife in your face. Or, under certain circumstances, a guy who might get together with a bunch of like-minded cronies and decide to throw you out of a window.

The question was, what circumstances? Ben didn't know. He was working on an incomplete theory. But he would soon find out if it was right or wrong.

When the crusty disembarked a few minutes later, Ben got off and tailed him down the street. A hundred yards further on, the crusty paused at the entrance to a shabby alleyway between an Asian grocer's shop and a takeout pizza place, glanced furtively around without noticing Ben following him, and darted out of sight.

Ben quickened his step to catch up and saw his target entering the doorway of a flat down the alley. The door wasn't locked, and the crusty walked in without a key. It was either his place, or he was visiting. Either way was fine by Ben. He counted down thirty seconds to let the crusty get well inside the place, then slipped silently after him. The doorway the crusty had gone through was all peeling and scabby. Someone had stencilled graffiti on it, with a picture of a petrol bomb and a slogan that said KEEP WARM – BURN OUT THE RICH. A little way beyond the doorway, the alley opened up into a patch of wasteland used as a dumping ground for local traders. An old shed stood derelict among knee-high weeds, next to a skip overflowing with garbage and a row of council wheelie bins.

Ben retraced his steps back to the door, eased it open a crack and then entered the flat, as quiet as a breath of air. The interior was even dingier than the exterior, and smelled strongly of damp carpets, cheap cooking, body odour and the smoke from illicit substances. The crusty had gone clumping up a flight of stairs to what Ben presumed was a bedroom. Pausing at the foot of the stairs, Ben listened and heard voices. Five minutes passed, then he heard the creak of the bedroom door opening and withdrew out of sight as the crusty re-emerged and came clumping back downstairs, counting out a rumpled sheaf of cash and shoving it in his pocket.

That's what a drug deal looks like, Forbes, Ben thought.

The crusty stepped back out into the empty alleyway. He lingered a moment near the doorway to take out a baccy tin and light a roll-up kept inside it, then turned to start heading back towards the street. Ten to eleven in the morning. Another busy day ahead.

But his schedule was about to be disrupted.

Chapter 15

Ben was on him in three fast strides and knocked him unconscious with a hard blow to the side of the neck. The crusty went as limp as a scarecrow cut loose from its post. Ben caught him under the arms as he fell, and dragged him back down the alley towards the patch of wasteground.

It wasn't a killer blow, by any means. Ben hadn't intended it to be. You could never judge these things perfectly, but he expected the guy to wake up in about five minutes. It took seven, by which time Ben had already started on the fresh pack of Gauloises he'd bought from Havana House that morning. He was using the illegal flick knife he'd found in the crusty's pockets to clean under his fingernails.

Lying on his back against the inside of the derelict old shed, the crusty stirred, then his eyes fluttered half open one after the other and he croaked, 'Where am I?'

'Somewhere none of your pals are going to come and help you,' Ben told him. 'It's just the two of us. Your lucky day.'

The crusty's eyes focused, and sudden recognition forced them open wide. 'Oh, fuck. It's you.'

'Scared? You should be.'

The crusty started to struggle in his panic, trying to get up. Ben pushed him back down with his foot. 'I see you got yourself a new blade. You really shouldn't go about armed like that. Someone might get hurt.' He folded the blade shut and slipped the weapon into his own pocket.

'What do you want from me, man?'

'I think you know exactly what I want from you,' Ben said.

The crusty gave up trying to struggle. He lay on the filthy, rotted shed floor, breathing hard. 'Look. Okay. Take my money. Tell Gluebrush I'll have the rest by Saturday. That's a fuckin' promise. Tell'm!'

Ben shook his head. 'Do I look like I'm collecting for some loan shark?'

The crusty's eyes filled with confusion. 'You a cop?'

'Wrong again,' Ben said. 'You're going to wish I was a cop. If I'm right about you, you're cat meat.'

'What the fuck, man?'

'Here's what we're going to do,' Ben said. 'I'm going to ask you questions. Each time, I'll start counting, one, two, three. If I haven't had an answer when I get to three, I'll break something. Fingers, wrists, ankles, nose, teeth, you get the picture. You're a big guy. Plenty to break. And I'm a very violent person. Once I get started, I can't stop. We could be here all day. Do you understand what I'm telling you?'

The crusty nodded up and down as far as his head could move.

'Here we go, then. First question. What's your name? One. Two—'

'P-Paul. Paul M-Midworth.'

'Where d'you live, Paul?'

'Rose Hill.'

Ben took out the grubby, much-thumbed document he'd removed from the crusty's pocket, the Job Seeker's Allowance booklet that he used to sign on for his dole money, with his full name and address and social security number written

97

at the top. Paul Midworth, aged thirty-one, did indeed reside in Rose Hill. 'You passed the first test, Paul. Let's keep the truth coming. Ready?'

'Yes! What the fuck, man—'

'The guy who was with me on the bus yesterday. Know him?' Ben started counting. 'One . . . Two . . .'

'What guy?'

Ben sighed. Then reached down, grabbed Midworth's wrist and twisted it almost to the point of breaking. Midworth let out a shriek.

Ben didn't let go. 'It's going to hurt a lot worse when the bones come ripping right through the flesh. Did you sell him gear?'

'Yeah!'

'How often? When's the last time?'

The crusty rolled his eyes in agony up at Ben. 'I don't know! Now and then. Not for months. It was just a few fuckin' seeds, man.'

'Why'd you go after him? Did he owe you money? Flash a little too much cash under your nose, enough to tempt you to go and look for more?'

'I never done anything!'

'And all I have to do is believe you. Who are your friends that you took along? Did you pay them, or did they do it just for kicks?'

'I swear, whatever you think I done, man, you're getting it wrong.'

'Think carefully, Paul. I'm going to rip this arm right out of its joint.'

'Aagh! What's your problem? I said I didn't *do anything*! I SWEAR!'

'Where were you last night, between three-thirty and four in the morning?'

'Home!'

'Alone? Got a girlfriend who can vouch for you?'

'I was alone, man. But I fuckin' promise you . . .' Midworth was crying now. His words trailed off into a pitiful mutter.

Ben let go of him. 'Get up. I said get up.'

Midworth got shakily to his feet. The shed was small and cramped, and there wasn't much room for two people, especially when one of them was built like an ox. The rotted floor sagged under his weight.

'Here's your knife,' Ben said, taking it out. He thumbed the release catch on the handle to pop the blade out with a sharp click, then handed it to Midworth.

Midworth took the knife, peered at it in his hand and then peered uncertainly back at Ben with pink teary eyes.

'That's twice I've humiliated you,' Ben said to him. 'First yesterday on the bus, and again just now. Made you look like the pathetic, snivelling, weak coward that you are. I'll bet you'd love to get even with me. Teach me that lesson you said I needed. Carve me up good and proper. So here's your chance. Stick that switchblade in me.' He touched his chest. 'Right here.'

'Don't fuck with me.'

'Seriously,' Ben said. 'Stick it right in there and give it a good twist. Make me bleed. Cut my heart out. What are you waiting for?'

'You'll break my arm.'

'No,' Ben said. 'I'll take you apart slowly, piece by piece. But only if you fail. Come on. I know you can do it. A tough guy like you, who carries a knife to show how big he is, likes to shove people around? If you can beat a defenceless guy to a pulp and throw him out of a window, you won't have a problem.'

'I didn't hurt anyone.'

'I'll make it easy for you. Hands behind my back. Eyes closed.'

Shaking his head, Midworth backed away as far as the confines of the shed would let him. He dropped the knife. 'This is a fuckin' terrible mistake, man.'

'You made it.'

'Let me go. Please.'

Ben had spent most of his adult life around dangerous men. He'd worked with them, and against them, all over the world, for a lot of years. He'd met few who were as dangerous as he was himself, but many who had come close, and he'd learned to understand exactly what qualities and mindset were needed in that kind of individual. Whether they used their skills for bad, or whether they used them for good as Ben had, what they shared was the ability to cross a line that ordinary people could not cross. It is a hard, hard thing to actively, wilfully, hurt or maim or kill another living human being. That was why murdering psychopaths were mercifully rare, and why brave men who could do whatever it took to serve and protect the innocent were in such short supply and great demand.

Ben Hope was one of those men. And he could see that Paul Midworth was not one of them. He just didn't have the makings of a killer.

Which was good news for the world. But bad news for Ben. Because it meant his theory had been totally, completely wrong, and that now he was going to go right back to the beginning and work this thing out.

'I didn't do nothing,' Midworth sobbed. 'I didn't hurt nobody. Please, man. You've got to believe me.'

'I do believe you.'

Midworth fell to his knees on the dingy shed floor, bent over with his head in his hands, and wept like a little boy.

'No more carrying knives,' Ben said. 'No more taking money from people. No more dealing drugs. That life is over for you now, Paul. Clean yourself up and get a job. I know where you live and I'll be watching you.'

Ben picked up the switchblade, folded it shut and slipped it into his pocket, then left Midworth cringing there in a heap and walked away.

He walked all the way back to the college, thinking hard. By the time he arrived there, he knew where he had to go next.

Chapter 16

On his way into north Oxford, Ben phoned Jeff on the Alpina's hands-free system to tell him the Hobart meeting had fallen through and that he might be held up in the UK for a couple of days due to a separate matter. Jeff knew Ben too well to ask for details, and Ben knew Jeff too well to offer any, fully aware that both he and Tuesday would drop everything and be there like a shot to help him if they suspected the least hint of trouble.

Ben wanted to deal with this alone, his way.

The big black Plymouth Barracuda was parked outside Nick's place, dwarfing every other vehicle in the street and looking more like a gangster's ride than a detective inspector's. No other police cars were in sight, nothing left to mark the crime scene except the police tape cordoning off a section of the iron railings. Ben parked the Alpina across the street and crossed over. As he passed the American car, a ferocious barking erupted inside without warning and he turned to see a large German shepherd dog launching itself at the window to get to him, making the whole car rock on its suspension. Ben paused to admire the dog. It reminded him of his own shepherd, Storm, and for a moment he yearned to be home at Le Val.

Ben let himself inside the house using his Yale bump key,

climbed the stairs to the top floor and limboed between the strands of police tape blocking Nick's apartment door. Ben walked into the wrecked living room and called out, 'Hey, McAllister.'

Tom McAllister appeared from the kitchen, blinking in surprise to see Ben. 'How did you know I was here?'

'Does anybody else in Thames Valley Police drive a Yank tank like that?' Ben said.

'What powers of observation you have, Mr Hope.'

'They say it's the ones who blend in that you have to watch out for.'

'That's just what I want them to think,' McAllister replied with a crooked smile. 'Tell you the truth, I won the car in a poker game. I've no idea why I keep the damn thing. One day someone'll do me a favour and pinch it.'

'I don't think your German shepherd will let that happen.'

'His name's Radar.'

'Police dog?'

'Was,' McAllister said. 'He was too aggressive for the job. Couldn't tell the good guys from the bad guys half the time.'

'I know the feeling,' Ben said, eyeing him.

'You don't trust the police much, do you?'

'What were you doing in Nick's kitchen, hunting for leftover tuna sandwiches?'

'No, I was just admiring the nice copper pots the man had. There's a Mauviel skillet worth half a week's pay. Had a lot of great recipe books, too.'

'What are you, a frustrated chef or something?'

'In my dreams.'

'Anything would beat working with your idiot of a boss.'

'Forbsie?' McAllister shrugged. 'So is that what you came back here for, to tell me what I already know?'

'No, I came back here to figure out what I'm missing,'

Ben said. 'Something about this situation isn't making sense to me.'

'Me neither. But you shouldn't be here. You may have noticed the tape on your way in. That's intended to indicate that members of the public – that would be you – are meant to keep out.'

'Must have missed it,' Ben said. 'Then again, keeping me out is hard to do.'

'So I noticed. You're not the kind of fella who's easily stopped, are you?'

'Is that your intuitive impression?'

'Partly. I also looked you up.'

'Everybody does these days. I must be more interesting than I thought.'

'What was it, SAS?'

'You wouldn't find that information on my record.'

'Not the records the MoD would allow the likes of me to access, that's for sure. The ministry got in a right flap when I tried to poke my nose in. Not that I'd have found anything I didn't already know.'

Ben raised an eyebrow. 'And how would that be?'

'I knew one or two of those fellas in Belfast,' McAllister said, 'back at the tail end of the Troubles, before I got out of the place. You've got the look. You could grow your hair and beard a yard long and walk around looking like John frigging Lennon and you'd still have it.'

'Didn't know I was that obvious.'

'Not to Forbsie. But like you said, the man's an eedjit.'

Ben sighed. 'Well, now you know who I am, just don't call me "Major", okay? I don't like it.'

'Oh, I'd never do that,' McAllister said. 'I demonstrate a lack of respect for authority. Or so my superiors are always telling me.'

Ben looked at him. 'I think you're the most unusual cop I've ever met.'

McAllister pulled another crooked smile. 'You have no idea.'

'Then you and I just might get along,' Ben said. 'Mind if I take a look around?'

'Would it stop you if I said yes?'

'No, but it might spoil this nice entente we're having.'

Ben walked over to the door of the spare bedroom and peered inside. The large recliner chair in the middle of the room was surrounded by tables and stands on which dozens of plants had stood, before the thieves had raided it. You could see the water marks and rings where the pots had been, and little piles of spilled earth. The room reeked of stale cannabis smoke and compost. The infrared lamp was still burning. Ben noticed the deadbolt that had been fitted to the inside of the door.

'It's as we found it,' McAllister said. 'Cosy little setup yer man had in there, with his comfy chair and more greenery than the botanical gardens. I wouldn't mind a room like that myself.'

Ben said nothing and returned to gaze at the wreck of the living room. After that morning's process of elimination, he was looking at a blank sheet, sucking in every detail to try to make sense of what he was seeing. 'Looks just the same as it did last night. Nothing's been touched?'

'Not yet. Forensic examiner got held up. He'll be here in twenty minutes.'

'I'll be gone by then,' Ben said. 'So what's your take?'

McAllister frowned and pursed his lips as he gravely surveyed the scene. 'Forget drug deal gone bad. And I don't think they came here to do murder. Looks to me like an aggravated robbery, pure and simple.'

Ben nodded. 'Maybe.'

'You don't look convinced.'

'I don't think it's quite that straightforward,' Ben said. 'Your average burglars wouldn't be interested in artwork, and there's no way they'd even try to cart a piano down the stairs even if it was worth a fortune. But that leaves plenty of stuff here they'd have gone for. Like that stereo, for a start. They wouldn't have trashed it.' He pointed at the expensive Pioneer sound system that had been hurled to the floor along with the rest of the contents of the bookcase it had been resting on. Nearby, a home cinema unit had been kicked over, along with the super-size flat screen and Blu-ray player that were now lying in a mess of wires.

'I'm with you there,' McAllister agreed. 'That's a grand and a half's worth of TV they've left behind. But I'm thinking, the kind of guy who can afford to live in a place like this and lets the birds crap all over his Aston Martin has money to burn. He could have had piles of cash lying around, for all we know. Or a bunch of jewels and gold watches. Maybe they just filled their pockets and ignored the rest of it.'

'I was here just a few hours before it happened. I didn't see money lying around. Nick wasn't that ostentatious. He only let the birds crap on the car because he wasn't into the wealthy lifestyle thing. In any case, he was a classical organist, not a rock star. He was doing okay, but I don't think he was a millionaire.'

'Then they came for the weed,' McAllister said. 'Your friend had a bit of a habit, to say the least. Maybe someone else got wind of the wee forest he'd grown for himself in there. That would explain why they hit this place and not any of the neighbours.'

'I already thought of that,' Ben said. 'But if they came for the weed, then why smash the whole place up?'

McAllister shrugged. 'Just being bad bastards. I've seen it all before, believe me. Got called out to a robbery at a stately home last month. You should've seen the mess. What they couldn't load into their van, they pissed and shat on just for kicks. Takes all sorts.'

Ben shook his head. 'I don't buy your theory, Inspector. And I'll tell you why.'

Chapter 17

McAllister was looking at him, frowning and waiting for more. Ben said, 'Nick played an organ recital at the cathedral last night.'

'We know that. So what?'

'So, his hands were probably hurting afterwards,' Ben said. 'It was a worsening problem for him. I think he was more worried about it than he let on. My guess is, he came home and went straight into his smoking room for a joint, because he was in pain. He'd have bolted himself in, because he was obviously cautious that way. Then he relaxed in his chair and must have smoked himself asleep. That's why he was still dressed when it happened, because he hadn't gone to bed.'

'Go on.'

'Then around four in the morning, the noise of the intruders woke him up and he called me. Still bolted into his smoking room. See the point I'm making?'

'Why does it matter where he called you from?'

'It matters, because it means that they were already smashing the place up before they knew about the drugs, because otherwise they'd have kicked the door down and gone straight after them. If they didn't, it's because they were looking for something else. Something other than the usual kinds of loot a burglar looks to steal, stuff that's quick and easy to sell on through their usual channels.'

McAllister considered it. 'Okay. Makes sense, so far. Then what were they looking for?'

Ben shook his head. 'That's what I'm missing. Whatever it was, they didn't touch any of his other stuff. Like a targeted robbery with a specific intention. Which is generally the domain of professional thieves. And that's where the mystery is here. A contradiction. Pros wouldn't have turned the place over like a bomb crater. They'd have taken what they came for, in and out. Instead, this bunch must have smelled the dope through the bedroom door and seen an opportunity to score something extra for themselves.'

McAllister thought about it, and nodded slowly. 'You're saying they were working for someone else.'

'That's the only way this makes any sense,' Ben said. 'They were paid to come and take something very specific. The drugs had nothing to do with it. But this was strictly amateur night. Whoever hired these rent-a-thugs didn't pay a top-dollar price, that's for sure.'

'So they sniff the dope and they figure out it's coming from the bedroom,' McAllister said, walking through the motions. 'At this point maybe they don't know anyone's in there, but they'd soon find out when they discovered the door was bolted shut from inside.' He stopped at the door and turned to look at Ben. 'Why didn't they just kick the door in? There's not a mark on it.'

Ben said, 'Maybe Nick came out before they had a chance to break it down. They grabbed him and started beating him, which is how his face got all battered. Then they dragged him over here to the window, knocking that harpsichord sideways on their way. And flung him through the glass.'

'Bastards. But why kill him?'

'No masks,' Ben said. 'Like I said, amateur night. Maybe he saw their faces.'

'In which case they thought they had to rub out the witness.'

'That's one possible alternative. The other is they killed him just for the hell of it. Like you said, McAllister, bad bastards.'

'All right,' McAllister said, putting up his hands. 'It's a credible enough theory as far as it goes. But until you know exactly what they took, and therefore what someone else instructed them to take, it's just supposition.'

Ben paced slowly around the room, scanning every inch. His eye landed on the shattered remains of the toppled glass display cabinet. He sank into a crouch next to it.

'Don't touch anything,' McAllister warned him.

'As if,' Ben said. He took the switchblade from his pocket, flicked it open and used the long stiletto blade to sift around in the mess of broken glass.

'I'd pull you in for carrying that,' McAllister said.

'Except you're not exactly a run-of-the-mill cop.'

'Any other hardware I should know about?'

'No gun,' Ben said. 'I told you, I'm a businessman.'

'Right.'

Ben went on sifting carefully through the broken glass, at the same time recalling the things he'd seen inside the display cabinet the day before. Nick's collection of small alabaster composer busts were lying about among the wreckage. So was the phony lock of Chopin's hair, the metronome, now smashed with its mechanical innards hanging out, and the various other musical knick-knacks Ben remembered seeing on display.

All except one.

'Something's missing here,' Ben said. 'His Bach manu-script.'

'His what?'

Ben rose to his feet, clicked the knife shut and put it away. He turned and pointed at the Bach portrait on the wall. 'See the sheet of musical notation he's holding in the picture? It looked like that, except it was several sheets. It was definitely here. And now it's gone.'

'Would you recognise it? Any identifying marks?'

'Apart from the fact it's allegedly hundreds of years old and not exactly something you'd see every day, just two. Namely the signature of Johann Sebastian Bach on the front, and a brown stain that covers about quarter of the bottom right-hand corner of the same page.'

'What kind of a brown stain?'

'Nick said it was coffee. Could be mildew. Or something else. It was hard to tell.'

'So where is this thing?'

'You're the detective. You tell me.'

McAllister pulled a face. 'Maybe your friend took it out of there.'

'Or maybe someone else did.'

'Is it valuable?'

'Nick said it was a fake,' Ben replied. 'But what if he was just saying that? Or what if he only thought it was? Doesn't matter. If someone wanted it badly enough to kill for it, they must've believed it was genuine.'

McAllister puffed his cheeks. 'A music manuscript. Jesus, that's way out of my area of knowledge.'

'And mine,' Ben said.

'We'd be talking about a very specialised robbery.'

'But a substantially narrowed list of potential suspects,' Ben said. He stared at the floor and started chewing his lip.

McAllister was frowning as if he was highly uncertain

about this new theory. 'What else can you tell me about this manuscript?'

Ben said nothing.

'Hey. I asked you a question.'

Ben was silent.

McAllister stared at him. 'Hello? Anyone at home?'

Ben made no reply.

McAllister's frown turned to a look of annoyance. 'Are you going to stand there all day like Mum's chance?'

'I'm thinking.'

'If you're onto something that can help me catch these bastards, I need to know.'

Ben already knew enough about this Tom McAllister to have worked out he was a pretty shrewd and capable officer. That was why Ben was saying nothing more. Because a smart cop like McAllister had a better chance of catching Nick Hawthorne's killers than most policemen Ben had known.

And Ben didn't want them caught. Not by the police. If that happened, the worst fate that could befall them would be to end up in a nice warm cell with three meals a day, at the expense of law-abiding taxpayers. That was a little more comfort than these men deserved.

Now it was McAllister's turn to be silent as he stood watching Ben, as though reading his thoughts. 'I hope you're not thinking what I'm thinking you're thinking.'

'That's a lot of thinking,' Ben said. 'Watch you don't blow a fuse.'

'You know what I mean. And I know who you are.'

'No,' Ben replied. 'You don't know the first thing about me.'

'I don't have my head up my arse like Forbsie. I've a pretty good idea what a man like you is capable of. And I don't

112

want trouble. I hate these shites as much as you do. But if we start finding more dead bodies lying around—'

'That's not what I do,' Ben said.

'Don't kid me. I can see it in your eyes. Think I haven't seen that look before?'

Ben said, 'I mean, I wouldn't leave them lying around. No mess, no trace. They'd disappear, like they never existed. And when I catch them, they'll wish they never *had* existed.'

'You're warned.'

Ben looked evenly at the cop. 'So are you, Inspector. Because believe it or not, I like you. You seem like a good guy. So don't get in the way.'

McAllister was returning Ben's steady eye contact as the two of them squared off like opponents before a fight. 'Get in the way of what?' he asked.

'Of what happens next,' Ben said.

Chapter 18

Long ago

'Slow down! You're going to get us killed!'

The race was lost. The Porsche 928 had run out of acceleration, or the driver out of bottle, and it began to fall back as the nose of the cherry-red Lotus edged past. The overtaking manoeuvre had been just a little hairier than Ben had anticipated, what with the articulated lorry bearing down on him from the opposite direction. Foot hard against the floor, he ducked back into his lane just in time as the lorry blasted past with its driver's fist jammed angrily on the horn.

The lorry driver wasn't the only one annoyed with Ben's road antics. 'Ben! That was insane!' Michaela had to shout to be heard over the yowl of the engine. Maybe she'd have been shouting anyway.

The classic 1972 Lotus Elan was Simeon Arundel's. In those days few students had the luxury of possessing their own cars and the spiffy red two-seater had earned Simeon a dashing reputation at college, although in truth he was a very prudent driver and kept to strict limits. By contrast, in the two years since he'd passed his driving test the Lotus was the quickest car Ben had been able to have a go of – it could only do about

120 but handled with verve – and he was enjoying extracting every ounce of its performance. Enjoying it a little too much, from the look on Michaela's face.

'Did you have to get into a race with that bloody Porsche?'

'The guy was asking for it,' Ben laughed, glancing at his vanquished enemy shrinking to a dot in the rear-view mirror. 'We taught him a lesson.'

'Fabulous. Now you've got that out of your system, can we try and get there in one piece, please?'

He glanced at her. She really was fuming. 'Come on. Where's your sense of adventure?'

'I really don't know. It must have run off with your sense of self-preservation.'

Ben reached across and squeezed her hand. 'Forgive me?'

'I forgive you, but just be more careful in future.' She rolled her eyes. 'What am I saying? You're Ben Hope.'

It was a glorious, sunny early October day in Noughth Week before the start of term, and he and Michaela were travelling the sixty miles from Oxford to her parents' place near Caterham for a party. It would be the first time Ben had met her family. Things were getting serious. Simeon had been only too happy to lend them the car for the occasion.

Michaela's father, Magnus Ward, was something in the stock market and her mother Lydia was the senior manager of a private clinic. The wealthy couple lived in a large mock-Tudor home on three acres of landscaped gardens. The semicircular driveway was shaded under a giant willow tree and, by the time Ben and Michaela rolled up, already filling up with cars as other guests began to arrive for the party. The Wards' social events were legendary, according to Michaela.

'See. I got us here, didn't I?' Ben said as he swung into the driveway and slithered to a halt just inches from someone's Jaguar.

Michaela had softened a little since his road-racing escapade

115

earlier, but now turned to him with a frown. 'Promise me you'll be on your best behaviour, all right?'

'I always am.'

'That's what worries me.'

They got out of the car and walked up towards the big house. Lydia Ward was a prim, neat lady with pearls and Margaret Thatcher hair. She greeted her only daughter with a flurry of kisses, then held Michaela's shoulders and stepped back to scrutinise her as though she hadn't seen her in months. 'Are you feeling all right, dear? You look a little off colour.'

'I'm fine, Mother,' Michaela said, wriggling out of her grip with embarrassment. 'And this is—'

'Of course. Hello, Benedict, how lovely to meet you at last. We've been hearing so much about you.'

'Good to meet you too, Mrs Ward,' said Ben, giving her his nicest smile. If being on his best behaviour included allowing people to call him Benedict, so be it. He looked down at the small Pekingese dog that had appeared at Mrs Ward's feet. He was sandy-coloured with a black face and bulging eyes that were fixed upwards, checking Ben out.

'Meet Hamlet,' Michaela said. Ben crouched down to pet him. Hamlet licked his hand. Mrs Ward looked amazed. 'He's normally quite diffident towards strangers.'

It had been prearranged days earlier that Michaela and Ben would be staying the night. Mrs Ward snatched a moment away from greeting the guests to lead the young couple upstairs and show them their – pointedly plural – rooms. 'You'll be sleeping here, Benedict.' Indicating up a long passage to a door as far away as possible from Michaela's. 'Cousin Eddie will be in the room next to yours, dear,' she said to her daughter. Michaela looked pleased to hear that Cousin Eddie was coming. 'He's a golf pro, you know,' Lydia Ward told Ben, as though Ben was supposed to be impressed. He smiled politely. Best behaviour.

Back downstairs, Michaela's father had appeared, smelling of cigars and acting a little vague and distracted as he was expecting some business guests to arrive at any moment. He and Ben shook hands. 'Good to meet you, Benedict. Heard a lot about you. Care for a drink?'

'Whisky,' Ben said, and caught Michaela's warning look. Might have slipped a little there.

Magnus Ward was thrown for a second. 'I – uh – I think there might be a bottle of scotch in the study. I'll fetch it.'

Soon the event was getting into full swing. The day was so fine that the party spilled out into the gardens behind the house, whose striped lawns stretched for acres to the woodlands in the distance. Thirty or more guests gathered on the poolside terrace, where the caterers had set up a lavish buffet and barbecue. Magnus Ward kept a pretty good wine cellar, too, but Ben was content with his whisky. He carried the bottle with him, in the likelihood of his wanting a refill. After being introduced to about a thousand people whose names he forgot the moment he heard them, he drifted over to the barbecue and helped himself to a chicken drumstick. Michaela homed in on him through the crowd, touched his arm and kissed his cheek and cautioned, 'Don't drink too much.'

'Have I misbehaved?'

'No, you're being perfectly sweet. Mother likes you.'

Ben was relieved he'd managed to earn the Ward stamp of approval, thus far. But Hamlet was the family member who seemed to have taken the biggest shine to him. The Peke was trotting around everywhere behind him, gazing up adoringly. 'You haven't been feeding him chicken, have you?' Michaela said with a frown. 'It upsets him.'

'No, he just follows me. He and I are getting along great.' Ben waggled his half-eaten chicken drumstick at Michaela. 'You tried any of this?'

'Ugh, no.' She pulled a face and her hands went to her stomach.

'It's good.'

'I'm feeling a bit queasy. Think I must have a tummy bug or something.'

Ben was sorry to hear she wasn't feeling well. The real significance of her queasiness, however, would not be revealed to him for more than twenty years.

Soon afterwards Michaela got accosted in conversation by some family friends, while her father singled Ben out to regale him with tales of the stock market and political affairs chat. 'What do you think about this Saddam Hussein fellow, Benedict?' The Iraqi Army had recently invaded Kuwait, causing chaos to oil prices. Magnus Ward was concerned about the effect it was having on his investments, but expressed certainty that Hussein would soon back down in the face of US military threats and market stability would return. He blustered on about it until Ben offered his view that, 'No, Saddam won't back down. That's not his way. Then the Americans will launch everything they've got at him, and there'll be full-scale war in the Gulf. It's going to get ugly. I wouldn't bet on oil prices recovering any time soon.'

Suddenly Magnus Ward didn't want to talk politics any more, leaving Ben alone and wondering if he'd said the wrong thing. He sat at a garden table to one side of the patio, drank some more of his scotch (thinking the bottle must have a leak because it was going down strangely fast) and ate more chicken, content to be on his own with Hamlet who, it had to be said, was the most interesting new acquaintance Ben had met so far.

Ben's moment of solitude didn't last long. He was happy to see Michaela coming back, but not so happy to see the red-faced loudmouth who came swaggering through the party calling 'Ciao' left and right and plonked himself down beside them soon afterwards. 'This is Eddie Carver,' Michaela said. Ben was in the middle of introducing himself when Eddie rudely cut him off by braying, 'So how's my favourite little cousin, then?' and insisted on giving her a big expansive hug that almost knocked the drinks off the table.

Ben sensed he wasn't the only one to have taken a dislike to Eddie. Hamlet must have been feeling that way for a long time, and was eyeing him with hostility from where he sat between Ben's feet. Ben reached down and stroked the dog's little head. *You and me, pal.*

As Eddie began prattling on about the celebrities he'd been teaching to play golf, none of whom Ben had ever heard of, Michaela's mother wafted across from the house and asked Michaela if she'd be a dear and come and help prepare the strawberries.

'Take the dog with you,' Eddie said. He added under his breath, 'The horrible little mutt,' but only Ben heard it over the buzz of the party.

'I think he'd rather stay here with his new best friend,' Michaela said with a smile. Then she was gone, and Ben was stuck with Eddie.

'So Michaela tells me you're one of the god squad,' Eddie said to Ben.

'I'm sure she didn't put it that way.'

Eddie shrugged. 'Whatever. Said you're set on getting ordained, and all that crap.'

'All that crap,' Ben repeated. Funnily, he'd been thinking the same way about it himself, the last few months. The more he'd become focused on a future in the church, the more he'd begun to realise that it was not the right one for him. The trouble was that he'd wanted it so long, with no room in his heart for any other dream or goal, that the future he now envisaged seemed blank and empty.

'They ought to scrap all that religion nonsense,' Eddie declared on behalf of all Mankind. 'Do you play golf, Benjamin?'

'No, I don't play golf, Eddie. And the name's Ben.'

Hamlet growled at Eddie from under the table.

'You watch it,' Eddie warned him, pointing.

'You shouldn't point at him,' Ben said. 'He senses it as a threat.'

'That's exactly what it is. I swear, if he bites me—'

'You don't like dogs?'

'That's a rat monkey, not a dog. He stinks, and I don't like the way he's looking at me.'

'Dogs understand everything you're thinking,' Ben said. 'If he doesn't like you, it's because he knows you don't like him.'

'Is that a fact?'

Ben decided he wanted another chicken drumstick. Maybe he would give a bit to Hamlet, after all. 'Stay,' he said softly to the dog, then got up and made his way over to the barbecue where they were just taking a fresh load of chicken off the grill. As Ben was helping himself, he glanced back and noticed Eddie aim a sly kick at Hamlet's head under the table. The little dog yelped and slunk away with his tail coiled tightly up between his hind legs.

Ben laid down his plate. He stalked back towards the table. Eddie saw him approaching, saw the look on his face, and his eyes opened wide with sudden panic as he realised that Ben was coming right for him. Eddie started getting up, but it was too late.

Ben grabbed him by the neck, pulled him close and said, 'How about you try kicking someone your own size?'

Eddie struggled, but Ben wouldn't let him go. The table toppled on its side, sending Eddie's wine glass splashing over the back of a woman's dress nearby. A less refined crowd might have started chanting, 'FIGHT! FIGHT!', but not this one.

Some people started crying out in alarm, including Eddie himself who was squealing like a piglet as Ben gripped him by the collar and the belt and dragged him towards the swimming pool. A few of the male party guests stepped up to stop the fight, but saw the expression on Ben's face and halted in their tracks.

The next moment, Eddie was airborne. He hit the water with a tremendous splash that soaked the guests who failed to get out of the way in time. Floundering wildly in the water, Eddie just had time to gurgle, 'You bastard!' before he began to sink.

That was when Ben realised Eddie might be able to golf, but he sure as heck couldn't swim.

The party dissolved into total mayhem. Hamlet stood at the edge of the pool, barking. Almost everyone else was screaming and yelling, dozens of accusing fingers and horrified looks directed Ben's way. Magnus Ward pushed through the panicked throng crowding the poolside, roaring, 'What the devil is going on here?' Eddie was now just a thrashing blur at the bottom of the pool, and not about to come up for air any time soon. Ben would have jumped in to rescue him, but Magnus beat him to it, stripping off his jacket and diving into the pool with a splash. Two more brave souls followed his example, and moments later the bedraggled, spluttering Eddie was being hauled out of the water like a big fat trout.

Someone shouted at Ben, 'You bloody psychopathic maniac!' Next Michaela was running over from the house, with Lydia Ward in her wake. Hearing the yells of, 'He tried to drown Eddie!', she stared at Ben with so much disappointment and hurt in her eyes that he almost regretted what he'd done.

Almost.

The party never recovered from the drama. Magnus Ward had to be physically restrained from attacking Ben, which probably would have resulted in an even worse situation. Lydia Ward was having hysterical fits and screeching at Ben, in a voice that could be heard in the next county, to get out of her house. Michaela was so furious she could barely speak to Ben except to say tersely, 'We're going. Give me the keys to Simeon's car.'

'I haven't had that much to drink,' Ben protested. 'I can drive us back.'

'No, Ben. We're not going back together.'

He found out what she meant soon afterwards, when she pulled the Lotus up outside Caterham railway station and told him to get out of the car. He couldn't understand why she was so upset. He kept trying to tell her what Eddie had done, but she wouldn't listen. With tears streaming down her face she sobbed, 'I don't know what's wrong with you, Ben. I don't. I can't take this any more. Go!'

Ben took the train back to Oxford, returned to Christ Church and kept a low profile in Old Library 7 for a couple of days. It wasn't until the third day that he spoke to Michaela. After returning the car to Simeon, she had spent some time with him talking things over, opening her heart to him as only the closest of friends can. Simeon was someone you could turn to. By the time she and Ben met again, she had made up her mind.

'It's over between us, Ben,' she told him. 'That was the last straw. You're too wild. It's in your blood. You'll never change.'

'Did your parents put you up to this?' he demanded, bewildered and hurt. But nothing he said could bring her back, and after a lot of tears and pain he said nothing more.

Soon after that, the young Ben Hope would quit his studies and leave Oxford, not to set eyes on the place again for a long, long time.

He knew then, and he still knew many years later, that

Michaela had been right to dump him. The wildness in his blood was something he had not yet learned to control. But she was wrong to believe that he couldn't change. That missing element was what his military trainers would begin to instil in their young recruit when, some time afterwards, he turned up at the Armed Forces Careers Office in Reading and signed up as an infantry soldier.

The army instructors could see the untamed force in him too. But they could use that. They knew how to model it, hone it, channel it, cool his blood, give him purpose. In time, they would turn him into one of the most dangerous and effective fighting men their most elite regiment had ever produced.

And in many ways, in retrospect, the wiser, calmer Ben would have Cousin Eddie to thank for what he had become.

Chapter 19

Ben drove away from Nick's place and headed north out of the city, passing through the suburb of Summertown before he hit the A40 dual carriageway going west. He had no particular destination in mind. Once on the open road he put on the CD that was currently living in the Alpina's audio system, the Miles Davis Quintet live at the 1969 Antibes Jazz Festival. He turned it up loud and put his foot down. Driving hard, overtaking everything in front of him as the Oxfordshire countryside flashed by to the wild sounds of 'Miles Runs the Voodoo Down'. His body was relaxed, but there was a fire burning inside.

Because while he'd been talking to McAllister, something had come to him. Now he needed the time and space to work his thoughts through, step by step, methodically, analytically. Some people did that by taking windy walks, others by sitting in a favourite chair with carpet slippers and pipe. Ben Hope did it by blazing down the road at a hundred miles an hour with frenetic jazz-rock fusion screaming in his ears.

He stayed on the A40 until he was nearing the market town of Witney some thirteen miles west of Oxford, then took a turnoff to the left and raced down a long, straight and narrow country road that took him to the village of Aston. Five miles the other side of Aston was another village called Little Denton. He hadn't intentionally come this way, but as he rolled into the village he wondered what subconscious impulse had chosen the route for him. Who was he to argue with the subconscious mind?

He followed the familiar road through Little Denton and pulled up outside the gated driveway entrance to the old vicarage. The house was unoccupied, which Ben knew for a fact as he employed a private security company to keep an eye on it, and a gardening services firm to keep the lawn mown and the ivy around the windows trim. Despite the maintenance, the place looked sad. Or maybe it just looked that way because that was how it made him feel.

This had been the home of Michaela and Simeon Arundel for many years. Jude had grown up here, and the house technically belonged to him even if he didn't use or look after it. He was currently in America, living with his girlfriend, Rae. Helping her to save the world, Ben supposed. Rae was the ideological type. Ben didn't know how long the relationship would last, but as long as Jude was happy, it was fine with him.

Happy. As if anyone who'd had both their beloved parents brutally snatched from them in a horrific car wreck, only to discover that they'd been brought up believing a lie, could ever truly be happy ever again. Michaela and Simeon had raised Jude as though he were their biological son. The truth was a closely guarded family secret that had only been revealed after their deaths, both to Jude and to his real father. The revelation had come in the form of a letter that Michaela had written to Ben shortly before she died.

It was hard to say which of them, the child or the real father, had had the toughest time accepting it. Jude had flipped off the rails for a while, quitting his university studies, toying with ideas like joining the navy. As for Ben, it had come as no less of a shock to him to discover, right out of the blue, after all those years, that he had a grown-up son. He still sometimes had trouble believing it, even now. And he could only wonder at the saintliness of his dear old friend Simeon, who had been there to step in and support Michaela when Ben hadn't been. Few men would have done what Simeon did, or shown as much selfless devotion. For all the high-risk challenges and crazy odds Ben had happily faced down in his life, he didn't think he'd have had the courage or the integrity to raise another man's child as though he were his own, and never speak of it to anyone.

As Ben had once said to Michaela, the very last time he'd been alone with her before she died, 'You ended up with a much better man.'

Ben got out of the car and stood looking for a while at the empty vicarage, then heaved a sigh and drove on until he came to the Trout pub on the edge of the village. Inside, he took a corner table at the back where he could sit facing the entrance and watch the approach to the pub through the window. Defensive planning was a deeply ingrained habit of his that would never die. He ordered a pint of local real ale and a home-made beef pie, which he ate half-heartedly just to get something inside him. The pie was probably excellent, but he was too deep in thought to even register its taste.

After mulling it over all the way from Oxford, Ben was almost completely certain that the idea that had come to him back at Nick's place was right. To eliminate all doubt, he now went back over it once more, flashing back to the events of yesterday like a movie replaying in slow motion through his mind. He saw himself standing by the display cabinet in Nick's apartment, peering through the glass at the manuscript with J.S. Bach's signature on the top. Then as if from faraway, he heard his friend's echoing voice saying, '*Don't be taken in. It's a fake.'* Followed by his own voice, replying, '*You could have fooled me. It looks real enough. But then, I'm hardly an expert.*'

Nick had sounded so sure. Had he been lying? Ben didn't believe his friend had possessed a single deceitful bone in his body. He could have come on the big authority, but instead he'd been quite candid in his admission that he was far from being an expert himself, not one of the hardcore scholarly types who devoted themselves to collecting valuable, original music scores. Why would he have pretended?

But there was no doubt that someone out there believed it *was* real. Someone who knew about these things, and who knew the value of the manuscript if, indeed, it was what it purported to be.

What was it Nick had said? Ben replayed the words in his mind. *Believe me, if it was the genuine item, it'd probably be worth as much as this apartment and everything in it, plus that daft car outside.*

Which sounded like a lot of money for a piece of paper covered in funny little squiggles, even if those squiggles could be translated into heavenly music. Ben took out his smartphone and did a quick google of original music manuscript values. Within moments, his search took him to the site of the famous London auction house Christie's, where he found that a rare, original copy of a Prelude in E flat major, catalogue number BWV 998, handwritten by J. S. Bach, had sold in July 2016 for over £2.5 million.

Ben whistled to himself and put the phone away, needing no further proof that there was, indeed, a lot of money to be made out of those funny little squiggles. Nick had been right about that. But assuming he'd been wrong about it being a fake, it would take a rare breed of expert to recognise the manuscript for what it was. Obviously someone who knew more about them than a hands-on performer like Nick Hawthorne.

As Ben had said to Tom McAllister, that already thinned out the list of potential suspects quite considerably. The more you narrowed down the profile, the closer you got. Like whittling a stick until its point is so sharp that it can only point to a single person.

That person would be a specialist. A highly distinguished music scholar. An academic, not a criminal. Someone who'd spent their life in museums and music libraries and poring over books, studying these things in extreme detail. Someone educated and refined, mild-mannered, middle-class, what they used to call a *gent*, who shared the same social circles as Nick Hawthorne and knew him well enough to have visited his home and seen the manuscript on display there.

Someone who, if they wanted something like this badly enough to be driven to steal it, would have to employ a rougher, more brutal breed of man to do the job for them. Even if they did so in the knowledge that the kind of rough, hard men whose services they could afford would likely commit violence to obtain it.

Therefore, someone with a pressing motive that overrode the bounds of morality and civilised behaviour by which such an individual would normally be constrained.

Someone desperate.

In Ben's experience, desperately pressing motives usually boiled down, directly or indirectly, in whatever form, to money. Therefore, the mild-mannered scholarly academic of Ben's developing psychological profile might well be someone under severe financial pressure. Debts, bad investments, secret addictions, blackmail, the list of potential factors was a long one. Whatever the cause, that person would be eaten up with stress, and that stress would show itself in all kinds of ways. Sudden displays of temper. Unexpected flare-ups of anger at polite social engagements. Just like the one Ben had witnessed with his own eyes, only the day before, at Nick's lunchtime party. Just steps away from where the Bach manuscript had been sitting, exhibited for all to see.

The profile was complete. Every box was ticked. Ben knew he had to be right.

He decided to pay a visit to Professor Adrian Graves.

Ben took his phone out again. Finding Graves' address was a simple task that took him a matter of seconds online, using the 192.com people finder. Most innocent members of the public didn't realise just how easy they were to track down. Nor did some others who might not be so innocent. Adrian Graves lived in the exclusive, high-priced residential district of Boars Hill, which lay a little south of Oxford city and some eleven miles east of Little Denton.

Ben set off without finishing his lunch. Eleven fast miles later the sat nav was leading him down the wooded lanes of Boars Hill, past fine homes of Cotswold stone, until he found the place. Graves' house was a handsome Victorian pile set a long way back from the road, barely visible through the trees. The gates were open. Ben contemplated a more discreet entry, then thought *fuck it* and drove straight in. He parked the Alpina beside a stately dark grey Bentley Arnage that was the only other vehicle in front of the house. The Bentley's engine was still warm under the bonnet. Wherever Graves had been off to, he hadn't been home long.

To his surprise, Ben found the front door open. For the second time in as many minutes, he thought *fuck it* and went inside without knocking. A grandly sweeping staircase led from the huge entrance hall. There were gleaming hardwood doors on both sides.

Ben was considering which one of them to try first when he heard the muffled gunshot from upstairs.

129

Chapter 20

Earlier

Professor Adrian Graves had been one of the estimated 74,000 listeners across the county to have heard the BBC Radio Oxford news broadcast over breakfast that morning, but he was the only one with such particular reason to be so shaken and upset by the announcement of last night's sudden, violent, and apparently suspicious death of a yet-unnamed male in his forties at an address in north Oxford.

Now Graves was jumping into his car and speeding away from his house, still feeling weak and nauseous with rage and grief as he went to make the prearranged rendezvous with his partners in crime.

He knew, down to his bones, that the victim was Nick Hawthorne. It wasn't meant to have happened this way. What had those idiots done? How could everything have gone so wrong? Tell me *how?* He banged the steering wheel and yelled it out loud, then thumped the wheel even harder, making the Bentley wobble on the road, and screamed it again. 'HOW?'

The events of the last two days had moved at such a whirlwind pace that he'd felt stunned by it all, even before this awful news had hit him like a kick to the stomach. His jumbled thoughts came to him in flashes and bursts of memory as he drove, clutching the wheel with white-knuckled fists. When he thought of Angelique, he wanted to screw his eyes shut and cry.

He had been her client for over a year now, and in love with her for much of that time. It had all been business at first, just a need that had to be satisfied like scratching an itch – but as the months slid by and his visits to the Atreus Club had become more frequent and habitual, he'd come to adore that sweet girl.

Angelique. So beautiful. So mysterious. He knew so little about her – just that that wasn't her real name, and that her wonderfully alluring accent placed her homeland as some-where in Eastern Europe. He wanted to know everything.

Their conversations in the post-session glow had become longer and more personal. She had revealed little about herself, but he'd sensed a sadness in her that he wanted to heal, in return for all the joy she gave him, and so he'd taken to bringing her little gifts. She'd refused at first, because the club had policies about things like that, but in time she'd begun to accept his offerings, and they had grown more generous and expensive. He loved nothing more than to see the smile on her face when she opened a jewellery box to see some new ring or silver chain inside.

Slowly, slowly, he'd pressed to get her to open up to him. He harboured wild, impossible fantasies about leaving Clarissa, his wife of thirty-two years, and running away with Angelique. Love in a cottage. Perhaps up in Scotland, a romantic little croft in some remote glen near a village where he could teach music and support them. They might be poor, but they would manage, and they'd have each other.

He knew it was the craziest idea, but he couldn't get it out of his head. He'd persuaded her to give him her mobile phone number, and so many times he'd been burning with temptation to call it and arrange to meet her outside the club. It was only his fear of stepping into the unknown that made him hold back, and he hated himself for his cowardice.

Now, as he drove, his burning thoughts returned to that day two weeks ago when, after a particularly satisfying session, he'd made her a gift of a pair of diamond earrings and watched as she put them on. 'Imagine,' she'd laughed. 'A poor Bosnian Serb girl like me, with rich men giving her diamonds.'

'I'm not as rich as you think I am,' he'd replied, chuckling. 'Not even close.'

'People like you, they do not realise what they have. Back home where I grew up, you would be like a billionaire.'

'You had a hard childhood?'

'All of life is hard. It does not stop when you get older. Then you die. This is how it is. Unless you are very lucky person.'

He'd paused, shocked by her sincerity and looking seriously at her. 'It doesn't have to be hard, Angelique.' He'd wanted to add, 'Come away from all this. Let's throw caution to the wind, you and I. Happiness is there for the taking – all we have to do is grab it.' But he still didn't have the courage.

She'd snorted at his optimism. 'You have no idea. You have never been hungry. You have never seen what poverty is, how it wrecks lives. I have seen it. Growing up in Banja Luka after the war, we had nothing. There was no work, no money. Sometimes not even any food. Then Dragan and I, we came to Britain, where everybody said it would be easy life for us. But it's not.' She'd shrugged. 'That is why I have to do this work I do, and Dragan has to do the things he does. One day, maybe, we will both be free to do better things, make a better life.'

'Dragan?'

'My brother. He is six years older than me. He look after me when our parents are killed in the war. I was only seven.'

'I had no idea,' Graves had said, full of sympathy and hiding his relief that Dragan wasn't a husband or boyfriend. 'And what does Dragan do?'

'He does what he can to get by. Know what I mean?'

'I can't say that I do. Are you saying that your brother does things that are . . . illegal?'

'If you cannot earn money, you have to take it from people who have too much.'

'That's theft, isn't it?'

'You are like a child. You know nothing about the world.'

She was quite right, of course. Poverty, hardship and struggle were utterly alien to Adrian Graves' comfortable life. He had never known anyone even indirectly connected to the criminal world. 'I'm sorry,' he'd said, in all sincerity.

But he would be sorrier. And his cosseted existence was soon to be blown apart.

The bombshell had landed two days ago, in the form of a large brown envelope delivered to the Graves residence in Boars Hill. Just by luck, his wife hadn't been the one to open it. When Graves had slit open the envelope and found the set of eight-by-six photo prints and the extortion demand that came with them, he'd almost died of shock.

The pictures were very professionally done. There was no possibility whatsoever of anyone seeing them and not instantly recognising him, Adrian Graves, in just about the most compromising positions imaginable: standing in the window of what was very obviously some kind of S&M brothel, naked and tethered with rubber chains, and receiving a whipping from a semi-nude blonde. Some of the images showed him with his eyes closed and mouth open in ecstasy.

When he'd looked at the grisly collection as many times as he could bear to, he tore the lot up into pieces and burned them in his study fireplace. As if that would do him any good. There would be plenty more copies out there, ready to sink him.

It was a blackmailer's dream. The extortion note stipulated a hundred thousand pounds in cash, in exchange for the SD card on which the images were stored. Graves had a week to pay up, or else.

It was too awful to contemplate. Graves spent the first day staggering about his home in a daze, waiting to wake up from the nightmare, racking his brain to think of ways to escape the quicksand. Could he somehow convince Clarissa that the man in the pictures wasn't him? That the images had been digitally altered, as part of some mysterious conspiracy against an innocent man? Some hope.

The second day, the reality of his situation had begun to hit him even harder. The last thing he wanted, when he felt so wretched and strung-out, was to have to plaster on an artificial smile and attend a bloody social occasion with Clarissa, the buffet lunch at Nick Hawthorne's place. But she kept insisting, and short of feigning the sudden onset of some acute illness he'd been unable to worm his way out of the engagement. He'd tried to console himself that maybe a few drinks, and meeting up again with an old acquaintance he hadn't seen in a while, would help ease his mind and distract him from his situation.

That hadn't been the case.

Instead, something incredible had happened.

The instant Graves had laid eyes on the faded sheets of handwritten music notation in their display case, he'd known it was the real thing.

The lost Silbermann manuscript. Here it was, by some

incredible twist of fate, right under his nose. So old Birdlegs had been right after all. None of his peers at the time had ever wanted to believe him, dismissing him as a nutty professor with an overactive imagination – but the mad old coot had been dead right all along. It really did exist, and it was just as he'd described it to the young Adrian Graves, then a research student, all those years ago in Vienna, 1977.

Graves' initial excitement was amplified tenfold soon afterwards when he'd managed to mention it casually in conversation with Nick. 'That's an interesting item you have there, Nicholas.'

'Quite convincing, isn't it?' was the reply. 'Whoever faked it didn't do a bad job.'

Sweet Jesus, he really thinks it's a fake!

'Well, obviously it couldn't be genuine,' Graves said, affecting amusement. 'Still, shame about that mark on it. Does spoil the effect somewhat.'

'I think someone must have spilled coffee on it. Not that it really matters. It's just a novelty item, at the end of the day.'

Coffee! Novelty item! Graves could scarcely believe his ears, much less his incredible good fortune.

'May I ask where you got it?' he'd asked, ever so nonchalantly, while his heart pounded so hard he thought he was going to pass out. Hawthorne had proceeded to tell him about the backstreet shop in Prague and the little man who'd sold it to him for a song.

Graves had studied his former student's face very carefully as he related the story. There was no lie there. Hawthorne really believed that this rare and precious discovery was just another forgery.

'I'll give you fifty quid for it,' Graves had offered, trying

135

desperately to sound offhand. 'A hundred.' Any more, and it would have seemed suspicious.

'I kind of like it,' Hawthorne had replied. 'It's a fun thing to have around, you know?'

In other words, not for sale. It wasn't as though Hawthorne needed the money.

But Graves had to have that manuscript. Suddenly, he could see a way out of the mess he was in. There was no other option, short of robbing a bank to pay off the blackmailers.

Robbing banks. Theft. Criminal acts. As if he could be capable of such a thing. But maybe he knew someone who might be. The more he entertained that terrifying thought in his mind, the more his resolve cemented itself. He'd hardly spoken another word to anyone at the party, becoming so taciturn that Clarissa kept asking him if he was all right. He'd used that opportunity to feign a migraine coming on so they could leave early. The instant he'd got home that afternoon, he'd managed to escape from Clarissa, locked himself in his study, put on some music and dialled the mobile number he'd never dared call until then.

'Angelique? It's – it's me. Can you talk?'

She'd sounded amazed to hear from him. 'Professor?'

'Listen, I – I have a problem. You said your brother was, ah, involved in, ah, *things* of a certain nature.'

'I don't understand. What problem?'

He'd told her all of it, in a tumble of words. 'Someone has pictures of me. Of us. It's not your fault. You're not in any trouble. But I am. A great deal of trouble. Whoever these people are, they want a hundred thousand pounds from me. I mean, well, that's completely absurd. Ludicrous. I don't *have* money like that. My wife's the one with the money. And how can I tell her about this? She'd leave me in an instant. I'd be left with nothing. It's awful.'

'What can I do?' she'd said after a long pause, sounding shocked.

'I need help. I know where I can get money, fast. And your brother is the only person I can think of to help me pay these blackmailing bastards off.'

'I don't understand.'

He'd had to force himself to slow down and speak calmly. 'There is something of great value that, if I could just get hold of it, would be the key to making this whole awful bloody nightmare go away just like *that*. I know exactly where it is. It will be easy to steal. The person who has it has no idea of its worth, so it's not even like real stealing at all. A victimless crime is barely even a crime, if you think about it. I have the connections it can be sold through. But I need someone to do the stealing for me. That's why I thought—'

'Dragan? No. You should not be asking me this. Are you crazy?'

'Please, Angelique, I have no other choice.'

The wild plan had come to Graves' mind in such a feverish rush that he'd forgotten all about having offered money to Hawthorne for the Bach manuscript earlier that day. Remembering it now, he realised that its theft so soon afterwards might potentially point a finger of suspicion at him. But he couldn't be worrying about every little detail at this moment. He'd leave that concern for later. As he'd said to Angelique, he really didn't have a choice.

'I'll pay Dragan five thousand pounds. That's really all I can afford now.'

'Five thousand is not a lot of money when you are asking someone to risk their freedom.'

'Then I'll double it. Five up front, on the understanding that there'll be another five later, when I can sell the item.'

'Dragan will not like it if you make promises and then do not pay.'

'There won't be a problem,' Graves had assured her, his mind speeding as he thought about how he could sell the manuscript under the table to a collector, how much of its value would be scrubbed off in the transaction, how much would be left over. Even allowing for the most punitive margins, he would still come away with more than enough to dig his way out of this situation. He might even make a small profit.

'Ten thousand,' she'd said.

'Yes, ten thousand. Do we have a deal?'

'You will hear from Dragan soon,' she'd told him, then ended the call.

Chapter 21

If only he'd known at the time, Graves kept telling himself
in retrospect. But once the boulder had been set in motion
down the mountainside, no force on earth could stop it
from crashing all the way to the bottom.

Things had happened quickly after his call to Angelique.
Minutes later, Graves' phone had rung and he'd found
himself speaking with the gruff-sounding Serb whom he
would only ever know by his first name, Dragan. Dragan
said little as Graves nervously outlined the situation to him
and described what he needed to be done. 'Nobody is to be
hurt in any way,' he'd repeated several times. 'There must
be no violence involved, whatsoever.'

'Nobody will get hurt,' Dragan had assured him. 'Me and
my crew, we are professionals.'

'Can you give me your absolute guarantee on that? I
cannot impress upon you how important that part of the
deal is. Nobody must be hurt, in any way.'

'Chill out, my friend. We are not animals, hey?'

From there, the horrible events had unfolded out of
Graves' control. The rendezvous spot he was driving to now,
the morning after the awful deed, was the secluded
Piddington Wood, a forty-acre patch of forest in north-east
Oxfordshire, between Thame and Bicester. As Graves drove

139

the Bentley deep into the trees along a bumpy, rutted track dappled by sunlight, he saw the plain white Transit van already waiting there for him, its doors open.

His heart gave a lurch as he saw Angelique standing by the van, looking serious and dressed as he'd never seen her before in jeans and a leather jacket. She was accompanied by three large, muscular, tough-looking men. The biggest of the three bore a slight facial resemblance to her that his coarse features, shaven head and blue spiderweb tattoos on both sides of his thick neck couldn't quite disguise. That would be Dragan, Graves supposed. The big man's arms were folded and he was eyeing the approaching Bentley with something between a smirk and a scowl.

Alone in the woods with a bunch of hardened criminals who had just, to his certain knowledge, murdered someone, Graves should have been intimidated and terrified, but at this moment he was too furious for either. He got out of the car and marched towards them. 'You promised!' he yelled. 'You told me nobody would be hurt! You killed him, didn't you? Why did you do that?'

Dragan uncrossed his arms and leaned back against the side of the van, taking out his cigarettes. 'He saw our faces.'

With that simple statement, all of Graves' worst fears became stark, inescapable reality.

'Why weren't you wearing masks or something? I thought you people were professionals at this! And you didn't have to . . . My God, this is so awful. Don't you realise what you've done?'

'Hey, cool it, professor man,' Dragan said. 'Shit happens.' He puffed smoke, then turned and reached into the open door of the van. He came out with a sports bag, zippered it open and produced from inside a large padded envelope which he held up for Graves to see, but didn't give it to him.

'You got what you wanted, right? So forget about this piece of *govno*.'

Graves was sweating, still palpitating with rage. But he couldn't forget what he was here for. His own survival depended on what was inside that envelope. 'Give it to me. You have no idea how valuable it is.'

Dragan looked pensively at the envelope. 'This weird writing is music, right? Just a bunch of old shit some dead guy wrote hundreds of years ago. How can this garbage be worth money?'

'Believe me, it's worth plenty. Please, be very careful with it.'

'Speaking of money, you forgetting something, professor man?'

Graves stepped back to the car and took out his own Jiffy bag he'd brought. 'Five thousand, as agreed,' he said, tossing it to Dragan. 'The other five, you'll have as soon as I sell the item. It shouldn't take more than a few days.'

'Yeah, right.'

'You have my word,' Graves said. 'Some people keep their promises.'

Dragan frowned, making the flesh on his brow corrugate into rubbery folds. He cracked a predator's smile and waved the manuscript at Graves, still not letting him have it. 'If it's worth so much, then why should I let you have it for ten thousand? Maybe I hold onto it, hmm? See what we can get for it ourselves.'

Graves stared at him, then at Angelique, who was looking back at him with a coldness in her eyes that stabbed his heart. 'You can't do that. We had an agreement.'

'Do not tell me what I can and cannot do, mister pervert. Here is a deal. You give me fifty thousand for this piece of shit paper. On top of the hundred thousand you already owe me.'

'*What?*'

'A hundred and fifty thousand. For that you get the music, the photographs, and we let you walk free. Okay?'

At which point Graves realised, in a moment of utter horror that almost caused his bowels to let go, that he'd been set up from the start. 'You bitch, you planned this whole thing!' he yelled at Angelique, or whatever her real name was. All he got back from her was an icy stare.

'The rich guy doesn't like to spend his money,' said one of Dragan's guys.

'On some things, he has no problem spending it,' Dragan said. 'Like my sister.'

'I never touched her.'

'Oh, we know all about what you did. You are one sick little creep, my pervert friend. Now you pay. And remember, creep, we know where you live. We can come for you any time.'

Graves reeled with shock. He was in free fall now, plummeting headlong into the abyss. As bad as the prospect of exposure and humiliation, divorce, scandal had seemed to him, now he not only faced responsibility for murder but personal harm at the hands of these mindless thugs.

'I'll pay,' he croaked.

'Sure you will, professor pervert. You have three days to get the money.'

Graves knew it was useless to protest. 'I'll do what I can. Give me the manuscript.'

Dragan shook his head. 'You think I am fucking stupid?'

'I can't get the money without it.'

'That is your tough shit. Use your imagination. You say you have no money, then get it from your bitch of a wife that you love so much. What the fuck do I care? Just get it.'

'Are you insane? I can't possibly tell her anything about this.'

'Three days,' Dragan said. 'Or we will come visit you and tell her ourselves. And break your motherfucking legs.'

Graves stood there limp, breathing hard. He looked at Angelique and his eyes filled. 'I loved you.' It was all he had left to say.

Her expression was full of nothing but derision and contempt for him. 'Go fuck yourself. You don't love nobody.'

'Tell me your real name. Do that one thing for me. Please.'

But she just snorted and got back into the van. The negotiations were over. Dragan and his two guys climbed in after her. 'Three days,' Dragan repeated through the window as he started the engine. The van took off, spewing dirt from its tyres.

Graves went wobbling back to his car and drove home as though in a trance. His life, as he'd known it, had just come to a sudden and jerking halt. With nothing to trade, how was he supposed to raise a hundred and fifty thousand in three days?

Home again, he stumbled in through the front door and left it open behind him, not caring. The big house was empty and very quiet. He vaguely recalled Clarissa saying she would be spending the morning with friends.

Graves dragged his feet upstairs to the study. He dumped his car keys on the desk and fell into the leather chair. The finality of the situation had become clearer to him with every mile towards home. No way out. He was done.

He reached for his wallet, took out the Atreus Club business card with Angelique's name and mobile number on the back and sat gazing at it for a long time. Suddenly, he wanted to talk to her again one last time. Tell her once more that he loved her. Let her voice be the last human voice he ever heard before—

He took out his mobile phone and dialled the number

from the back of the business card. As it began to ring, he quickly killed the call.

What was there to say? She hated him. She'd only used him.

What a fool he'd been.

Despair enveloped him like a thick, black blanket. He took a sheet of paper from the desk drawer, a fountain pen from the leather holder on the desktop, and in his scratchy handwriting composed his brief goodbye note. It was the sum total of everything he was feeling at this moment. All he could think of or bring himself to express.

I'm so sorry.

Sorry for his stupidity in falling for a girl who despised him. Sorry for betraying Clarissa. Sorry for causing the death of poor Nicholas Hawthorne. A decent man, a highly talented musician. Snuffed out for money, for no good reason at all.

He didn't even have the energy to sign his name at the bottom of the brief note, so he just scrawled his initials: AG.

Eleven letters. The final statement of Adrian Graves.

From another drawer of the desk he took a ring with two keys. He slowly rose from his chair and stepped over to the grandfather clock by the bookcase. He unlocked the hidden gun cabinet that the clock case concealed, quite numb and detached as he considered his options. As well as his legally-held guns, the safe contained a few items that his father had left him. The pistols were strictly prohibited, but he'd kept them fondly all these years, never imagining there would come a moment when he'd contemplate using one. Least of all for this purpose.

A pistol would be easier for the job he had in mind. Under the chin, or against the temple. But there was less of a guarantee with a pistol. What if something went wrong and he only brain-damaged himself? No. If it must be done, let it be done as thoroughly as possible. One squeeze, and oblivion.

He reached inside the cabinet for the twelve-bore. Took a single cartridge from the safe's ammo compartment, loaded it and returned to the desk to sit in the chair with the gun's butt resting between his feet and the barrels pointing upwards. Then he pressed the cold steel muzzles against the fleshy underside of his jaw, reaching down to make sure the tang safety catch was off. It was awkward doing it this way. But he wouldn't be the first to make it work. He put his thumb through the trigger guard and felt the curve of the slender trigger. Now all he had to do was apply a light downward pressure, and the nightmare would be over for him.

It hadn't been a bad life, really. If it hadn't been for one terrible, terrible error of judgement, it could have gone on a bit longer.

Oh, well.

Graves pushed down with his thumb and his world disintegrated in a white flash.

Chapter 22

Standing in Graves' hallway, Ben froze at the sound. It had come from an upstairs room.

A single report of a gunshot from behind a closed door, followed by deathly hush, was one of the more ominously telling sound combinations in the wide repertoire of human damage. There were just three things it could signify. At the most mundane end of the scale, an accidental discharge while messing with or cleaning a firearm whose user would protest 'I didn't know it was loaded', would generally be met by a stunned and guilty silence, unless other people around began yelling at the idiot who had done it, or unless the idiot had gone and accidentally shot someone – in which case the yelling would quickly turn to screaming. At the most fanciful end of the scale, the solitary gunshot could signify the presence of an armed assassin, now standing quietly surveying his dead victim and ready to flee any second after listening for the sound of running footsteps.

But there was a more common reason for the single, flat report Ben had just heard coming from upstairs. In the majority of cases it meant that someone had just taken a self-inflicted step they would never live to regret. The ultimate solution to all of life's problems, or so it might seem in the desperation of the moment. Tragic in some cases, less tragic in others.

Ben paced up the grandiose staircase, the luxury carpet thick underfoot, and reached the first floor towards where his instincts told him was the source of the shot. Years of sweeping buildings where a closed room might contain either a bound and captive hostage or a terrorist or kidnapper waiting for you with a machine gun had honed his naturally sharp sense of directional orientation to a razor edge. He was certain the shot had come from behind the handsome oak door at the top of the stairs. Reaching the door in absolute silence, he stood immobile for a full two minutes and heard only the utter stillness that told him he was the only living person inside the house. He eased the door open and stepped through it.

He found himself inside a richly-appointed study. Burnished wood, fine antique furnishings, a whole collection of old stringed instruments on stands and hangers – lutes or mandolins, Ben couldn't tell them apart. Matching oak bookcases stood ceiling high at opposite sides of the room and were filled with leather-backed volumes. The tall double window offered a view of meadow and woodland. The study walls were decorated with beautiful silks and oil paintings that must be centuries old. By contrast the section of wall behind the broad Chesterfield desk at the far end of the room had been much more recently decorated with something else, much less pleasant. The ugly spatter of blood and brains was about five feet wide and had reached up as far as the ornate coving, from which it was dripping back down to the floor.

Ben had seen a lot worse sights in his life. That still didn't make it a nice experience. Not wanting to touch anything he pushed the door shut after him with his elbow, and approached the desk. The room was full of the stink of blood and burnt nitroglycerine propellant from the gunshot.

The corpse was seated on the other side of the desk, still upright in his leather chair and facing Ben like a company director greeting a client, though he no longer had a face. The twelve-bore clamped between his knees had done the business. Shotguns might provide an effective means of suicide, but those who picked that route were mighty inconsiderate of the unfortunate folks who would have to clean up afterwards.

The dead man was Graves, all right. Aside from the fact that he was in his own house, Ben could identify him from the same yellow bow tie he'd been wearing yesterday, now yellow and red. The clincher was the initialled signature on the suicide note that lay in front of him on the desktop, beside the fountain pen that had been used to write it. The note was written in the chicken scratch of a person more used to typing on a keyboard, and said simply:

I'm so sorry.
A.G.

Maybe it was a note to the cleaners, Graves apologising for the mess. Or perhaps he'd been tormented with contrition for something else he'd done, like being involved in the murder of an innocent man.

'What are you so sorry for, Graves?'

No reply. If only they could talk.

Ben ran his eyes over the desk. The most incongruous item sitting on its top was the box of 12-gauge shotgun cartridges, freshly opened with one missing. Aside from that were a leather wallet and a set of car keys with a Bentley fob, a mobile phone, a compact laptop whose keyboard was sprinkled with dandruff, a brass banker's lamp, a leather holder with a selection of pens, a pair of reading glasses, a box of Kleenex tissues, a couple of books on ancient music, a business card printed in glossy black and gold, and a small alabaster bust of J.S. Bach similar to the one Nick had possessed. Whoever sold these things was obviously doing a roaring trade among music scholars. Ben was getting to recognise the composer's face quite well by now.

But that wasn't the item on the desk that drew Ben's attention. The glossy business card lay just inches from the suicide note, as though Graves had it to hand in his final moments. The last thing a despairing man looked at before blowing his brains out couldn't but be important somehow.

Ben took out the switchblade and used its point to spear the card and pick it up off the desk. Examining it more closely, he saw that the elegant gold script on the front of the card was the name of something called the Atreus Club. Below that, two short lines of smaller script read:

Exclusive Membership
Discretion Assured

There was no address, no phone number, no website URL. Whoever these people were, they weren't in the business of making themselves easy to contact.

Ben said, 'Hmm.'

The printers had left the reverse of the card plain white. Scrawled on the back in the same scratchy handwriting as the suicide note, the ink a little faded from contact with the wallet in which Graves might have carried it, were the name 'Angelique' and a mobile phone number.

Graves' own mobile lay close by on the desk. On a hunch, Ben plucked a tissue from the box of Kleenex and wrapped it around the phone to pick it up. He used the point of the knife to open the menu of recent calls, and wasn't immensely surprised to find that Graves had called the number for this Angelique, whoever she was, only minutes before shooting himself. People didn't make insignificant phone calls just prior to blowing their brains out.

Ben slipped both Graves' mobile and the card into his pocket.

Next Ben used the knife again to flip open Graves' wallet on the desk and shake out its contents, which were the usual collection of credit and debit cards, driving licence, eighty-five pounds cash and two more business cards, one for a Bentley dealership in Berkshire and the other for a specialist violin restoration firm in Headington. Nothing too interesting there.

The same was the case when he went through the drawers of Graves' desk. Discovering anything obvious there to connect the late professor to Nick Hawthorne's murder was probably too much to hope for, and Ben wasn't surprised when he found nothing beyond the usual paperwork, receipts, tax documents, printouts of music-related articles, and a ream of other useless stuff.

More interesting things were to be found elsewhere in the study. Turning away from the desk, Ben noticed the grandfather clock standing against the wall by one of the twin bookcases. The clock was unusual, because the case where the pendulum should be instead comprised a secret panel that would, if it hadn't been hanging ajar, cleverly conceal a hidden steel-lined gun cabinet. That explained where the twelve-bore had come from.

Prying the heavy panel door a little wider with the knife blade Ben saw a couple of other weapons inside, a little .22 rifle for hunting small game and an expensive Italian

16-gauge pigeon gun. Nothing suspicious about those: like the suicide weapon they would be legally registered to Graves and entered on his shotgun ticket.

By contrast, a separate compartment of the gun safe contained some items that were definitely not legally registered to anyone, because to be caught with such a collection in Britain meant an automatic five-year stretch in prison. They were wrapped up in lightly-oiled cloths, which Ben delicately peeled away with his knife to reveal the collection of pistols: a couple of old Colt revolvers, a C96 'Broomhandle' Mauser and a Yugoslav variant of the Soviet-era Tokarev automatic.

From their age, which ranged from the late nineteenth century through to the mid-twentieth, he guessed they were family hand-me-downs, perhaps with sentimental value, that Adrian Graves must have chosen to keep rather than hand in to the British government for destruction – or in reality to be sold off to dubious dictatorships overseas – under the draconian 1996 handgun ban. His having the illegal weapons didn't necessarily point a finger of suspicion with regard to Nick's death, but it said something about Graves' potentially flexible attitude to the law.

Of one thing, Ben was quite certain. Graves might or might not have had a hand in orchestrating Nick's death, but he hadn't been the one to personally put him through the window. Bad men were out there, and Ben's path was going to take him on a collision course with them.

Turning back to the grandfather clock, he knelt down and checked the contents of the unlocked ammunition compartment at the bottom of the safe. He found two more cartons of shotgun cartridges, a small supply of subsonic hollow-points for the .22 rabbit rifle, plus what he'd hoped to find: fifty boxed rounds apiece for the Colts, the Mauser and the Tokarev.

It might have been his old SAS comrade Boonzie McCulloch who'd once said to him, 'Better tae have it an' no need it, than tae need it an' no have it, laddie.' In Ben's experience, need often arose when you were least prepared. He'd lived by that saying for a long time, and its wisdom had saved him on more occasions than he cared to count. He picked up the Tokarev, checked it over, slipped it in the waistband of his jeans, then dumped the fifty rounds of 7.62x25mm ammo in his jacket pocket, next to the business card for the Atreus Club.

Ben as yet had no idea what that was, any more than he understood the significance of the woman called Angelique whose name Graves had written on the back of the card. His intuition was telling him that, somehow, the secrets of the late Adrian Graves were all intertwined together in one ugly little knot. Ben intended to unravel it.

The last item he removed from Graves' study was the set of keys for the Bentley. Then he left the empty house and its silent occupant. Outside, he glanced about him to check nobody was around, then unlocked the car, got in and turned on the ignition without starting the engine. It was the inbuilt sat nav system he was interested in. After taking a moment to familiarise himself with how it worked, he found the recent destinations folder and scrolled through it, copying addresses, postcodes and GPS coordinates into his notebook. When he'd finished he wiped everything down and closed up the car. He left the key in the ignition. Graves wouldn't complain.

Minutes later, Ben pulled his BMW into a quiet layby near Hinksey Hill and spent a few minutes going back through the Bentley's sat nav destinations list, checking each one on his smartphone. Graves was a frequent visitor to music museums like the Bate Collection in Oxford and the Royal College of Music, Royal Academy, the Victoria and

Albert, and the British Museum in London. Other destinations were tagged with labels, such as one that said 'MOTHER' and led Ben to a private residential care home in the Cotswolds.

But another frequent destination, mysteriously tagged 'AC', showed far more promise. The sat nav's data log indicated that Graves had visited 'AC' several times within the last month alone.

When Ben checked the GPS location, he came up with an address for a manor and country estate called Wychstone House, just outside the Oxfordshire village of Wychstone, not far from Kirtlington to the north of the city. Twenty minutes' drive away, if you were a sedate academic behind the wheel of a stately Bentley. Twelve to fifteen, if you were Ben Hope.

It was a beautiful afternoon. What else was there to do, with the stink of a dead man's blood still clinging to your clothes like smoke and the vision of your friend impaled on the railings still hovering before your eyes, than to take a scenic drive in the countryside?

Ben waited for a chubby young woman to walk by with her cavalier spaniel tugging like a miniature locomotive at its leash, gave her a friendly smile and a wave which she returned cheerfully, then took out the Tokarev. A tough, rugged weapon, the handgun equivalent of the Red Army's virtually indestructible AK-47. It weighed thirty ounces in Ben's hand, with plastic ribbed grips emblazoned with a Soviet star and the Cyrillic letters standing for *Soyuz Sovetskikh Sotsialistichskikh Republics.* It was one of the unaltered models with no safety, except for the half-cock notch on the hammer. Safety catches. Who needed them, anyway? Just one more impediment to letting the tool do its job.

Keeping the weapon below the level of the window he locked open the slide, dropped out the magazine, and laid the pistol in his lap while he pressed loose rounds from his pocket into the mag until it was full. He reinserted the mag, popped the slide release to chamber the top round, lowered the hammer to half cock, and the gun was ready to rock and roll.

So was he.

Ben started the car.

Chapter 23

The drive to the village of Wychstone took him just thirteen minutes, plus another three to find the country estate just beyond its outskirts. The first thing Ben noticed about Wychstone Manor was the interesting level of security about the place. The walls were high, the tall iron gates were shut, and cameras kept watch from both gateposts. His instinct was to hang back a while and observe the place before making any moves.

The country road leading out of Wychstone village past the manor house was narrow and quiet, with verges of unkempt grass and wildflowers and a small patch of oak woods a little way offroad on the opposite side to the manor. Ben scouted the terrain on foot and found a spot among the trees that was about eighty yards from the entrance to the estate, out of view of the security cameras and accessible by car. He parked the Alpina in the long grass where he could see the house through the trees and the gates, then killed the engine and made himself comfortable.

He didn't care how long he might have to wait. A man conditioned to withstand long reconnaissance missions hidden among the rocks of a barren mountainside or the stinking vegetation of the most godawful jungle couldn't complain about spending a little time in a comfortable car on a pleasant spring afternoon. He wasn't hungry, wasn't thirsty. He had everything he needed.

Nor did he feel any undue pressure. Sooner or later someone, most likely Mrs Graves, was going to make the gruesome discovery of the late professor sitting at his desk; Ben was pretty sure that Tom McAllister wouldn't be slow to pick up the trail and put the two dead men together, Graves and Nick Hawthorne. But McAllister's evidence bag would be minus Graves' mobile phone and the connection with the Atreus Club, and that put him a big step behind. Ben liked it that way.

While he waited, he used the pair of binoculars he always kept in the car to scan the front of the manor house. Some expensive vehicles were parked outside, but he could see no movement within.

Just twenty minutes later, a shiny new Jaguar rolled up at the gates. Ben watched through the binoculars as its portly middle-aged driver, the car's sole occupant, stepped out and spoke briefly into the intercom panel on the gatepost. He got back into the Jag, the gates swung open, and he continued up towards the house, unaware he was being observed all the way. The gates closed behind him.

As Ben kept watching, a conspicuously attractive woman in her thirties came out to greet the visitor at the front door of the manor, took his arm with a dazzling white smile that Ben could have seen from that distance without binoculars and led him inside, very tactile, very attentive. She was wearing a tight short skirt, a top that might have been painted on, and extremely high heels that made her tower over the portly little man by at least four inches. He seemed happy to see her, too. He could barely keep his tongue from lolling out.

Ben said, 'Hm.' He was beginning to understand why the

Atreus Club's business card didn't give away very much detail about the services on offer to its members.

He leaned back in the driver's seat and smoked a Gauloise as he pondered what to do next. Then restarted the car, pulled it sharply around in a circle and drove up to the gates. As the previous visitor had done, he stepped out to announce himself to the intercom box that was half-hidden among the ivy on the stone gatepost.

'Professor Adrian Graves.'

And just like before, a moment later the gates swung open to let the visitor through. Ben drove up to the house and parked the Alpina next to the still-ticking Jaguar, on the end of the row of five other luxury cars that presumably belonged to other members. He got out and walked to the entrance, where the same alluring hostess stepped out to greet him, wearing the same megawatt smile.

Ben smiled back. 'Hi. Nice day, isn't it?'

Her smile dropped, and it was as if the sun had disappeared behind a cloud. 'Here, wait a minute. You're not Professor Graves. Who are you?'

Ben pointed at the plaque above the doorway that said THE ATREUS CLUB. 'Exclusive membership, discretion assured,' he said, pushing past her. 'Sounds good. Where do I sign up?'

'I don't know what you're talking about.'

'Really?'

'Hey! You can't just walk in here.'

The entrance foyer was like a five-star luxury hotel, except the collection of erotic paintings on the walls lent the place a particular theme that Ben had never noticed on any of his travels around the world. Maybe if he'd visited Amsterdam, it might have been different. From the reception area a flight of stairs was visible through an arched doorway. Ben caught the tail end of a glimpse of the portly little Jaguar guy climbing the stairs, escorted by someone wearing red stiletto heels. They disappeared out of sight. Here down below, the welcome committee had lost what remained of her charm and was tugging at Ben's arm to prevent him from going anywhere. 'Membership's by invitation only. You can't barge in like this.'

'Who's barging?' Ben said. 'Professor Graves introduced me. You can cross him off the members' list, incidentally. He won't be doing much kissing in future.'

'I'm calling security.' The woman's heels clattered on the polished floor as she hurried over to a desk to snatch up a phone. Eyeing Ben like a tigress she said into the handset, 'Terry, Alan, can you please step into reception? This guy's just forced his way in here and I'd like him removed.'

Terry and Alan appeared seconds later, dressed in dark tuxedos like the pair of club bouncers they, in fact, were. Six hundred pounds of muscle and lard advanced towards Ben across the foyer. He could almost smell the testosterone. These two looked as if they probably injected themselves with it every day.

'Do you have to get those tuxes tailor made?' Ben asked them. 'It'd be a real shame to get them all messed up. I'd stay back, if I were you.'

One of the bouncers, Terry or Alan, Ben would never know and didn't care, tried to make a grab for him. Ben rolled the big fist aside in a deflect parry that unbalanced the guy's top-heavy mass, then gave him a shove to the shoulder that sent him toppling sideways. He hit the floor like a sack of concrete. The other one hesitated, frowning uncertainly at Ben as though considering the wisdom of charging into the attack.

'What are you two arseholes waiting for?' the hostess

snapped at the bouncers, pointing a red claw at Ben. 'Sort him out!' She looked as if she wanted blood. From siren to vampire in ninety seconds flat.

'Relax, guys,' Ben said. 'It's not worth it. I was just leaving anyway.'

The heavy on the floor seemed to be having trouble getting up, clutching his side in pain as though he'd ricked something on his way down. The one still on his feet obviously didn't feel the need to walk Ben back to his car.

At the bottom of the driveway, the entrance gates were already open for the Alpina, as if to say 'Now get lost and don't come back'. He made a big show of revving the engine and driving off in a hurry. He turned right out of the gate and continued for about a hundred yards on the country road away from Wychstone, then pulled into another observation point screened by oak trees. The high stone perimeter wall hid the house itself from view, but that was unimportant as long as he was out of sight of the cameras and could keep an eye on movements in and out of the gates: specifically *out* of the gates.

He resumed his wait. Now his suspicions about the nature of the Atreus Club were confirmed, he figured that the duration of a typical client's visit to the place couldn't be more than an hour or so, possibly a good deal less given the probable age and general physical condition of the average club member. Which suggested to Ben that one of the clients whose cars were parked outside the manor would be due to leave at any moment.

Sure enough, Ben was just five puffs into his next Gauloise before he saw the automatic gates glide open once more and a pearly white Range Rover, which had been on the far end of the row, passed through, turned left and started picking up speed towards the village of Wychstone. Ben could have chosen to wait instead for the portly fellow in the Jag to reappear, but it really didn't matter to him one way or the other. He fired up the Alpina and followed the Range Rover.

When shadowing dangerous criminals or men with military training, as he often had done in the past, caution dictated holding back a good distance and keeping out of sight with other vehicles between himself and the target. But Ben didn't think the kind of middle-class saddo who frequented the Atreus Club would be on the lookout for a tail, not even one as relatively conspicuous as a BMW with French plates and the steering wheel on the left. Ben maintained a steady distance behind as the Rover got onto the M40 at Chieveley and wound its unhurried way northwards towards Banbury. Ten miles further north, leaving Oxfordshire for the southern edge and rolling hills of Warwickshire, the Rover led Ben into the parish of Burton Dassett, a quaint little place full of old stone houses and thatched cottages called Knightcote, where it finally pulled up in the driveway of a large, detached home with a conservatory, separate garage and lily pond, on a large plot edged by a low, neatly clipped leylandii hedge.

Welcome to bourgeois heaven. Ben pulled up on the road a little way from the house, grabbed his binocs and watched. A remote mechanism opened the garage door and the Rover slotted itself inside. The other half of the garage was empty. Unless there was another car parked round the back somewhere, nobody else was at home.

A yellow dog appeared from a kennel and ran across the garden to meet its owner as he got out of the car, and Ben saw him for the first time: late fifties, overweight, balding, glasses, perhaps a senior executive or company director. And harbouring some dirty little secrets that probably accounted for the lingering grin on his face as he opened the front door and disappeared inside the house.

Ben left his car, skirted around the property and found a spot where the hedge was less thick and shielded from view of neighbouring homes by a beech tree. He skipped over the hedge and into the garden, where the friendly yellow dog met him and gladly accepted a treat from the pack of Storm's favourites that Ben carried in the glove box. Now a friend for life, the dog let Ben explore the property unhindered. The German shepherds at Le Val would have eaten him by now. McAllister's dog Radar too, by the look of him.

Ben moved stealthily around the perimeter of the house until he spotted his guy through the French windows of a large living room. He was still wearing the mile-wide grin after his enjoyable start to the afternoon. Ben watched him open up the doors of a tall faux-antique cabinet that housed a large-screen TV, pick up a remote control and start flicking through channels. A football game was playing on one of them. The man took off his jacket, tossed it over the back of a chair and settled contentedly to watch the match.

Even with the sound muted, the man would never have heard Ben slip into the room. The first he knew of the presence stalking up close behind him was the touch of the cold steel muzzle of the Tokarev against his cheek. He let out a startled cry, which Ben quickly stifled with a hand over his mouth. Ben moved round so the guy could see him, and the gun.

'Quiet,' Ben said. He took his hand off the man's mouth, picked up the remote control from the armrest of the chair and turned up the sound until the roaring of the football crowd and the hyped-up chatter of the commentator filled the room.

'Wh-wh-who are you?' the man stammered. But he did it quietly, and didn't try to move from the chair. His eyes bulged as though he might be about to drop dead of a heart attack.

Ben sat in a chair nearby, keeping the gun pointed at him just for show. 'What's your name?'

The man's eyes darted nervously and Ben could see the wheels spinning in his mind. 'L-Lester K-Kimble. I-I don't have any m-money. The only valuables in the house are my wife's jewels. Take them!'

'That's very generous of you. Is Mrs Kimble at home?'

'She's at w-work in B-Banbury.'

'That's fine, Lester. I'm glad I didn't have to scare her. And I'm not interested in taking any of her nice things. I just have a few questions. If you cooperate nicely, Mrs Kimble will never know I was here. If you don't tell me what I want to know, she's going to come home to find her loyal, devoted hubby dead with a bullet in his skull. And none of us wants that, do we?'

Poor Lester must have believed the threat, because he made a gibbering sound of terror that Ben knew from experience was quite genuine. It took him a lot of stammering to blurt out, 'W-W-What questions?'

'Ones you'll be glad you got to answer in private,' Ben said. 'Let's talk about the Atreus Club.'

Chapter 24

Getting people to open up was all about applying pressure, in the right way and the right amount. The old saying that everyone has their breaking point, Ben had largely found to be true. Some of the harder ones you virtually had to torture, though real torture was a dark art that Ben had no taste for, never had, never would. A minor criminal like Paul Midworth the crusty took far less pressure to crack their resistance. But a soft, flabby babe in the woods like Lester Kimble, about as far a cry from the true hardmen of the world as it was possible to imagine, gave way like a rotten twig under a boot heel.

After less than sixty seconds of interrogation, Lester was already weeping with fear and shame. Ben forced him to divulge exactly what he got up to at the Atreus Club, then soon wished he hadn't. In between great gasping sobs and floods of tears, Lester's confessions regarding his sessions with his favourite girl there, Cindy, were as candidly detailed as they were predictably sleazy. He'd been a member for almost three years, couldn't get enough of the place and had dug himself into a credit hole as deep as the Mariana Trench to pay for his secret addiction.

'Just imagine if Mrs Kimble were to hear about these little extramural activities of yours,' Ben said. 'I wonder how she'd take the news?'

Rage flared magenta-coloured on Lester's chubby, tear-streaked face. 'Is that what this is? You're a private investigator, aren't you? Elizabeth paid you to shadow me, didn't she? That rotten bitch!' Then his anger subsided just as fast as it had risen, and he started sobbing again. 'Please. Whatever my wife's offering you, I'll double it. I'll give you everything I own, just *please* don't tell her! It would be the end of me. I'd have to kill myself.'

'You wouldn't be the only one,' Ben said. 'Relax, Lester, I'm not a detective. I might have been, and then you'd be in pretty hot water with Mrs Kimble. Luckily for you, I'm here for another reason.'

'So you're not a robber, and you're not a detective – then who are you?'

'Just someone in need of some answers.'

'How am I supposed to help?' Lester asked. The terrified stammer was gone, but his voice was still hoarse with panic.

'One of your fellow members has got himself mixed up in a lot of trouble. I have reason to believe the Atreus Club is involved in some way. I need your help to find out exactly what the connection is.'

A faint ray of hope lit up Lester's eyes, as he realised he was at least part way off the hook. 'I don't know anyone else there. Not by name, that is. I mean, people come and go, but we don't say much, except the odd hello, or talk about the weather and things.'

'But you'd remember a face. Like this one.' Taking out his phone, Ben pulled up the image of Adrian Graves that he'd lifted from the archives of the Oxford University Faculty of Music website and let Lester see it. 'Know him?'

'I've seen him there a few times,' Lester said, recognising Graves immediately. 'He's a regular.'

'He's been seeing a girl there called Angelique. Do you know her?'

Lester shook his head. 'No. They have a number of girls. Are you trying to hire her or something? Get a number for her? I can't help you with that.'

'I already have her number. But I need a description of what she looks like. A photo would be best.'

'Oh, I get it,' Lester said slyly. 'You want to check her out first. I don't think the Atreus Club let their girls do any moonlighting, though. I mean, if they did, I'd be the first in line to—'

Ben put the gun to his head.

'Don't disappoint me, Lester.'

Lester swallowed. He nodded. 'All right, all right. Please point that thing somewhere else, and I'll help you. Then will you go away? Promise?'

'As if I was never here,' Ben said, lowering the pistol. 'Scout's honour.'

'We'd have to go into the other room. The computer's there.'

Keeping hold of his arm in case he tried to bolt, Ben accompanied Lester through the house to a downstairs room that had been converted into a home office. Above a desk hung framed certificates proudly proclaiming Lester J. Kimble's law degree and subsequent professional achievements, including his letter of appointment from the Queen. Lester was a QC.

The man himself looked much more humble as he seated himself at the computer and went online. Ben stood at his shoulder. The gun was back in his pocket by now. He didn't think Lester was going to pull a concealed weapon on him.

'Each member has his own special passcode to access the club's website,' Lester explained as he keyed in a password

165

on a blank screen. He hit ENTER, and the website home page flashed up in all its colourful glory with a picture of Wychstone Manor that made the place look like a respectable country hotel or conference centre. The introductory spiel began, *'Set in the elegant surroundings of the Oxfordshire countryside, the Atreus Club has been offering highly discreet personal services to our elite membership since 1993 . . .'*

'Looks like quite a business they're running there. How many members?'

'Oh, hundreds,' Lester replied, then added with a note of something like pride, 'But they won't let just any old Tom, Dick or Harry join. It's very exclusive.'

'Only the cream of society need apply. I get that. And how many prostitutes do they have working there?'

'They're not prostitutes,' Lester said, bristling momentarily.

'Call it what you like. I don't judge them, only the sad little losers whose money they take. Now give me the guided tour.'

The way Lester navigated the website, it was obvious he'd been a very frequent visitor. He clicked on a tab that said SERVICES and a new page opened up with a header that promised *'A selection of feminine beauty to suit all tastes and preferences, guaranteed to meet your every need.'* Below was a row of separate tabs each with a name on it. Ben ran his eye across them. The club offered the services of ten different girls: VENUS; ARIA; INDIA; KYMBERLEE; JYNX; BRANDY; KIRA; CINDY; TARRA; ANGELIQUE.

'That's my Cindy,' Lester said, melting at the sight of her name. He moved the mouse as though he was about to click her tab open.

'Never mind Cindy,' Ben said. 'Show me Angelique.'

Lester reluctantly shifted his cursor to click on her tab.

The screen flashed up a high-resolution glamour pic. 'Angelique' had pouting lips and blond hair that seductively covered part of her face. The sharply-drawn features and high cheekbones suggested to Ben that she might be of Eastern European origin. A short bio below the image, carefully worded to be as vague as possible, gave her age as 23, but it could have been anything five years either side. At the bottom of the page, a pink button flashed alluringly, saying CLICK HERE TO SPEND SOME TIME WITH ME.

'You want me to click?' Lester asked, peering tentatively up at Ben.

'You want me to call Elizabeth?' Ben replied.

Lester shrank away as though he'd been punched in the head. 'No.'

'Do yourself a favour, Lester. Get some help. And I don't mean paying some poor girl wearing a thong to tickle your feet with a feather boa, or whatever it is that's been floating your boat. You need therapy.'

'You mean, like a counsellor?'

'There's always electric shock treatment.' Ben stepped towards the door.

'You're leaving? Just like that?'

'I was never here. Not a word to anyone, Lester. Remember that, won't you? Or I might have to pay you another visit.'

Ben needed to say no more. In a world full of strangeness and uncertainty, one thing he could depend on was that Lester Kimble QC would be as good as gold about keeping his mouth shut.

Ben drove straight back to Wychstone that afternoon and took up position in his original OP across the road from the entrance to the manor, where the screen of trees camouflaged the car from the cameras and he could watch the house through his binoculars.

This time, he had to wait longer before he got the result he was hoping for. Several more cars came and went, each time a middle-aged driver on his own. The clients didn't interest him any more. Just after five a blond-haired woman, young, slender, wearing jeans and a leather jacket, appeared from a side entrance of the manor house. She paused momentarily to fish a pack of cigarettes from her handbag and light up, and Ben was able to focus the binocs on her face.

If she wasn't Angelique, she was her twin sister.

Ben tracked her until she disappeared around the corner of the building. He kept watching, scanning from side to side so he wouldn't miss her if she reappeared. Which she did four minutes later, this time behind the wheel of a pale blue Nissan Micra that must have been parked somewhere around the rear. It looked as if she'd finished work for the day and was leaving for home.

By the time the little Nissan reached the gates, Ben had started up the BMW and pulled out of the cover of the trees back to the road. Like Lester Kimble's Range Rover earlier, the Nissan turned left towards Wychstone – and just like earlier, Ben followed. Once she was clear of the village, she accelerated to a steady forty miles an hour and he matched her speed, maintaining a fifty-yard gap between them. The road was a minor one, and quiet this time of day. He couldn't assume she wouldn't notice the lone BMW following her.

But this time, he wasn't planning on following his target all the way home, where for all he knew some big burly husband or boyfriend was expecting her. That would only upset Ben's plans. What he was about to do required a greater degree of privacy.

As the Nissan reached a long straight with trees either side and no other traffic in sight, Ben punched the accelerator and the Alpina responded like a spurred horse. He shot past the Nissan, then swerved abruptly into her path, hitting the brakes and forcing her to a squealing, hissing stop. He got out of the car and walked quickly towards the front of the Nissan with his arms spread wide.

Angelique did what he'd have expected her to do in that situation. She revved the little car hard and sawed at the wheel to try to get past him. But he sidestepped her one way and then the other, blocking her off. He didn't believe she'd have the guts to run him down, and she didn't. In her panic she slammed the horn button as though that might scare him off. Faster than she could react to prevent him, Ben strode up to the car, wrenched open her driver's door, reached inside and turned off her ignition and pulled out the key.

At moments of acute stress, expatriates often revert back to their native tongue. Angelique let out a stream of what Ben immediately recognised as Serbian. With his natural talent for languages he'd picked up some of it back in the day, hunting war criminals with the SAS in the wake of the Bosnian conflict. But even if he hadn't, he'd have been able to get the gist of what she was yelling at him. '*What the fuck? What are you doing, you fucking asshole? Give me back my keys!*'

'A woman driving on her own should always lock her doors,' Ben replied in Serbian.

That stopped her dead. She fell silent and stared at him like a cornered wild animal, breathing hard, slim hands gripping the wheel. She had long, perfect nails that were varnished blue to match her eyes, which were smouldering with hostility. 'Who the fuck are you?' she demanded after a long pause, switching to English. 'You asshole, did you just follow me from work?'

'I'm not going to hurt you,' Ben said, showing her his palms to look less threatening. 'That's a promise. I just want to talk, okay?'

'Fuck you. Give me back my keys!'

He dangled the ignition keys in front of her. She made a lunge for them, but he jerked them back out of her reach. 'You can have them back,' he said. 'But only after.'

'After what? You want to screw me, you have to pay like everyone else, up front. You want to do it in your car? This will cost you a thousand pounds. You can transfer the money online with your phone.' All business. Ben got the feeling this wouldn't have been the first time she'd done these kinds of transactions.

'I told you, I only want to talk. But I am happy to pay for your time. Five minutes, a hundred in cash.' He showed her his wallet with the money inside.

'Talk about what?' she asked slowly, still eyeing him with extreme suspicion.

'About someone you know.'

Her face hardened even more. 'Who?'

'Professor Adrian Graves.'

The words jolted her like a million volts of electricity. Before Ben could stop her, she scrambled across the middle console of the Nissan and out of the passenger door. Her car was at an angle at the side of the road with its left-side wheels up on the grassy verge where she'd skidded to a halt. As fast as a cat, she leapt across the verge and plunged into the trees beyond.

'Shit,' Ben muttered. He couldn't let her get away.

Only one thing for it. He chased after her.

Chapter 25

Ben had expected a reaction from her. Perhaps angry denial that she'd ever heard of this Graves person. Or perhaps a cool upping of the price for information about him. But the suddenness and speed of her flight at the very mention of Graves' name took him by surprise. Now she was crashing through the dense thicket of the roadside woods like a deer running from a huntsman.

Ben sprinted after her, twigs whipping in his face, brambles tearing at his trouser legs. She was fast, but the pursuit of predator and prey over difficult terrain was something he was much more accustomed to than she was, and the little flat shoes she was wearing weren't designed for rough work. He was three strides behind her when her toe snagged on a hidden tree root and she fell hard, sprawling in the damp moss and leaf litter.

Ben knelt astride her body and pinned her down with his hands and knees. She fought him as if he was a rapist, trying to rake him with those blue claws, snapping her teeth, spitting, wriggling like a wild thing. He kept repeating, 'Hey! Hey! Stop that, I'm not going to hurt you!'

Nothing he said could calm her down. In her position, Ben wouldn't have believed him, either.

The gun in her face shut her up quite quickly. She froze

and lay still on her back, her blond hair tangled and fanned out over the dirt, looking up at him with cool defiance in her eyes. But there was also a certain acceptance in her look, which Ben found interesting. When you point a gun at an innocent person, they'll freak out even more and want to know why this awful thing is happening to them. She hadn't even asked him who he was. Stick a pistol in the face of a guilty person, they'll either fight you to the death or lie back and wait for what they know is coming to them. Live by the gun, die by the gun. Ben wondered what that said about Angelique.

'Adrian Graves. Let's have it. Everything you know.'

The repetition of the name got her going again. She spat and hissed, '*Govno jedno, da bog dobio gljivice na jajima!*' Roughly translated, 'You piece of shit, I hope you get fungus on your balls.'

'That's lovely,' Ben said. 'Tell you what, why don't I make this easier for both of us, and tell you what I already know? First off, Graves is dead.'

The look in her eyes told him that she hadn't known. Her gaze flicked to the pistol muzzle that was pointing inches from her face. 'You killed him?'

'Now why would I go and do a thing like that?' Ben said. 'Fact is, I didn't have to. He did it to himself. How does that grab you?'

She humphed. 'What the fuck do I care if the bastard is dead?'

True love. Nothing like it in the world.

'Here's my guess,' Ben said. 'You're such a charming young lady, I can see why a man like Graves couldn't stay away from you. Like a fly around a honey jar, even if it meant the ruination of his safe, cosseted little life. I think he spent all the money he had on you, and more. In fact, he got

172

himself into so much hock, just to enjoy your delightful company, that he ended up doing something very, very stupid to pay his way out of the mess he was in. A friend of mine died because of it. How am I doing so far?'

'You don't know shit!'

'That's okay by me, because now I have you to fill in the blanks, *Angelique*. What's your real name, anyway?'

'Fuck you!' She shouted it so loud that the sound of her cry echoed over the trees.

'You're going to talk to me.'

She spat up at him. 'You would have to kill me first, pig!'

'Have it your way,' Ben said, and fired the gun.

The report made her scream, but the flat boom was so much louder that no sound appeared to come from her open mouth. He'd turned the pistol away just a few inches from her face before pressing the trigger. The bullet slammed into the ground by her right ear. The force of the impact and the jet of hot gases from the gun's muzzle kicked up an explosion of dirt that plastered the side of her face. Bits of moss and dead leaves stuck in her hair. She would have tinnitus in that ear for a few days. That was as much harm as Ben was prepared to do to her. But she didn't know that.

'That was your warning,' he told her. 'You only get one. Now talk.'

The look of defiance was gone now, and real fear clouded her eyes. 'My name is Lena,' she blurted. 'Lena Vuković. I know what happened to your friend, the musician man. But I swear, I did not have anything to do with it. I was not there!'

Ben had to pause a moment to take in what he was hearing. He'd approached this Angelique – now Lena – thinking that, at best, she might help to shine light on the secret life of Adrian Graves. Now she was telling him that

173

she knew about Nick Hawthorne. He couldn't understand the connection.

'Who killed him?'

Lena's face tightened and tears filled her eyes. She hesitated, then glanced at the gun and quavered, 'I don't know who. Dragan is head of the gang. Danilo and Miroslav were there too. I think maybe it was Dragan's idea to kill him. They did it together.'

'Who's Dragan?'

'He cannot know that I told you his name. He would kill me, too.'

Ben pressed the pistol under her chin. He repeated, 'Who's Dragan?'

'Dragan Vuković. My brother.'

'You're telling me that your brother and his pals beat Nick Hawthorne half to death and then threw him out of a window.'

'Yes! You do not understand. Dragan is violent. He is not a normal person. There is something wrong in here, inside his head. He is like this ever since the war in my country. That is why he could kill his own sister if he knew.'

'Sounds like a close family,' Ben said.

'Dragan is all the family I have left.'

'Is this the kind of thing he does for a living?'

'He does what he can to get ahead. It is the same for me, no? For you, for everyone. But with Dragan, it is more than this. He likes to hurt people.'

'How many in his gang?'

'Danilo and Miroslav are the ones I know. There are others. Maybe five or six.' Wide-eyed and streaming tears of fear, she reached up and grasped the folds of Ben's jacket with both hands. 'Promise me that you do not tell them I have told you this. I would do anything. You can screw me

174

as many times as you like. Here, your place, my place. Now, anytime. You would not have to pay me. It is all I have to trade.'

He knocked her hands away with the butt of the pistol. 'Get that out of your head, Lena. Why did they kill Nick?'

'Why do you think?'

'Graves paid them?'

'Not to kill him. To steal. Your friend was some rich guy, no? He had something the professor man said was worth much money. He offer Dragan ten grands to get it from his place. Dragan said afterwards, they find a lot of grass there, and so they take that too. I don't know why they killed him. Maybe he try to stop them. This was a stupid thing to do. He should not have got in Dragan's way.'

Ben shook his head, thinking. None of it made sense. An Oxford music professor was in cahoots with a gang of hard-core Serb criminals, and just happened to be a client of the gang leader's call-girl sister?

'How could someone like Graves even know your brother? He was an academic, not a crook. Why would he get into something like this?'

'He needed money,' she said. 'Because of the scam.'

Chapter 26

Ben looked at her, more confused than ever. 'What scam?'

'You are hurting me. Get off me and take that gun out of my face, and I tell you, if you do not hurt me any more.'

Ben stood up and lowered the pistol, but kept hold of it in case she tried to run. Lena sat up, brushed the dirt from her face and plucked leaves from her hair.

'You have a cigarette? Mine are in the car.'

Ben tossed her the pack of Gauloises and his Zippo.

As she knelt in the leaves and smoked her cigarette like a condemned prisoner with nothing left to hide, soul bared to God, Lena made her confession.

The scam had been Dragan's brainchild, a new addition to the range of profitable criminal enterprises that he and his gang were already running. Lena's line of work had given him the idea that snaring plump, middle-aged Atreus Club members with dirty little secrets and everything to lose could be a highly lucrative operation.

In short, it was an extortion racket. Miroslav was Dragan's cousin, as well as being a skilled photographer and the owner of a camera with a long lens. Miroslav was pretty good at climbing trees, too. He'd used the big oak in the manor house gardens to achieve a bird's-eye view of the window behind which her clients received their regular chastisements at the business end of Lena's well-practised whip. She explained to Ben that was her speciality, the S&M stuff. With the juicy pictures in the bag, all that remained was to deliver the blackmail demand: pay up or face scandal, humiliation, divorce.

'How long has this been going on?'

She shook her head. 'Not long. Graves was the first. Dragan say, if it works we will do others. Like, how you say? An experiment.'

'Why pick on Graves, with dozens of others to choose from?'

Lena shrugged. 'Because he like me. He say he was in love with me. He buy me expensive presents all the time.'

'And that's how you decided to repay his affections.'

'I told you, it was Dragan's idea. Once he makes his mind up about something, you cannot say no to him. So they tell Graves he must pay a hundred thousand or they show the pictures to his wife. He have three days to come up with the cash.'

Now Ben understood why Graves had seemed so stressed-out at Nick's lunch buffet, with a blackmail demand crushing him into the ground. 'But why would he offer money to the crooks who were already extorting him for ten times that much?'

'Are you dumb? He did not know it was Dragan, until this morning.'

'Then how did he come to approach Dragan in the first place?'

'Because I had told him about my brother, the poor Serbian immigrant who cannot find honest work and must make his living stealing things.'

'Nice job, Lena. If he hadn't known that, none of this would have happened. A man like Graves wouldn't have known which way to turn. There would have been no robbery. And Nick would still be alive.'

Her eyes flashed. 'Hey, what do you want? This man, he know nothing about real life. He annoy me with his attitude, like the world is this big happy place where everyone is so fucking civilised and a girl like me only sell herself because she like it. He was an asshole.' Lena's favourite word.

'I don't give a damn about Adrian Graves,' Ben said. 'You want to run your little schemes, entrapping a bunch of perverts and putting them through the grinder, fine by me. They had it coming. But Nick Hawthorne didn't.'

'How was I to know what would happen? It is bad luck for him, that is all.'

'Bad luck for Dragan, too,' Ben said. 'Because I'm in this now.'

She looked up at him. 'I do not even know who you are.'

'Dragan will find out who I am, soon enough. So will Miroslav and Danilo, and whoever else gets in my path.'

Her eyes went to the gun. 'You will kill them?'

'Then at least you wouldn't have to worry about what they might do to you for selling them out.'

'This would not be so easy to handle as you think. They have dogs.'

'That's okay,' Ben said. 'Dogs love me.'

'Not these dogs. And they have guns, too. Some to sell, others for defence. Like I tell you, Dragan is a bad man.'

'Whatever he is, I'm worse.'

Lena looked at him. She nodded. 'I can see you are not afraid. Maybe you are crazy. Or maybe you are dangerous. Dragan is still my brother. I don't want him to die.'

'Help me to catch him,' Ben said, 'and maybe he won't have to. He can spend the next few years in a prison cell instead.'

Lena said, 'You want me to betray my own blood?'

'You already have,' Ben said. 'Now's the time to make good.'

'And if I say no?'

'Worse for him, worse for you. You're not in a position to refuse, Lena. Where does Dragan live?'

'He has a place in Blackbird Leys,' she said after a reluctant pause.

Ben knew where it was. A sprawling estate the other side of Cowley on the eastern side of Oxford, built in the fifties and sixties to relieve the dilapidated inner city and house the workforce of the then-booming Morris Motors car plant. Across the town-and-gown divide that dominated the social identity of the city, Blackbird Leys was the extreme opposite pole to the serenity and beauty of a sanctuary like Christ Church. By the early nineties the estate had earned itself an ugly reputation for knife crime, riots and joyriding. Ben was sure it had become a culture haven for tourists since those days.

'What about the rest of them?'

'They live close together. They are always together. Hang out together. Party late every night, with girls, booze, smoke dope, do meth.'

'Sounds like my kind of social occasion,' Ben said. 'What about you, where do you live?'

'Barton.'

'Alone or with someone?'

'I get enough of men in my work. Men are dirty, smelly, like apes.' She pulled a disgusted face, then looked at Ben. 'Maybe not all,' she conceded, with a sly glimmer in her eye. 'Anyhow, I like to be by myself.'

'Sure about that? I wouldn't like to think there's a seven-foot rugby player waiting in your front hallway. He might get a nasty surprise, you turning up with someone like me.'

'Why would I lie?'

'Of course, I forgot. You're a paragon of truth, *Angelique*. Okay, so here's what we're going to do. We're going back to your place for a few hours. Bide our time, wait until evening.'

Lena looked as if she was still waiting for him to take her up on her earlier offer of a trade. She frowned, then asked, 'And then what?'

Ben said, 'And then you and I are going to crash a party.'

Chapter 27

'Here you go,' Billie said, setting McAllister's coffee cup down on the tiny patch of desk that wasn't heaped high with clutter.

'Thanks, Billie,' he murmured distractedly, not taking his eyes off his screen. He was staring at it so intently that the glass might melt.

The vending machine at Thames Valley Police HQ in Kidlington vomited out something resembling sewage; this was the good stuff from the nearby deli. Tom McAllister was the only superior officer she'd fetch coffee for, just like she didn't tolerate anyone else in the department calling her Billie and not Detective Sergeant Flowers. Likewise, he was the only one of her colleagues who knew that she sang in jazz clubs in the evenings. They enjoyed a cosy working relationship, unlike the one he had with Forbsie. It had been that way ever since McAllister had broken two knuckles of his right fist teaching an arrested drug dealer not to refer to her as a 'jungle bunny'. Things like that brought people closer together, even if it had almost cost him his job at the time.

She looked around her and asked, 'What was it, a seven-point-five magnitude?'

'A what?'

'The earthquake that hit this office. You should tidy up once in a while.'

'I like the mess,' McAllister said, slurping the coffee. 'That way I know where everything is. Hmm, that's good.'

'Full-on day?'

'Shaping up to be, aye.' It was half an hour since McAllister's return from Boars Hill, after the discovery of Professor Adrian Graves, dead from a single close-range gunshot wound to the head, presumed self-inflicted. Not the prettiest suicide Tom had ever been called out to, but not half as messy as the guy who'd thrown himself in front of the 12.18 from London to Stratford-upon-Avon outside Bicester that time. Yugh. The things you had to do for money.

'How's the wife doing?' Billie asked, frowning. Clarissa Graves had been the one who found him and called the police.

'You know. It's not every day you come home and find your husband sitting at his desk with his face dripping from the ceiling.'

'Maybe the gun went off while he was cleaning it.'

'Yeah, and maybe the Devil ice-skates into work every morning.'

He returned to his screen. Billie touched his shoulder and left him to it, giving the earthquake zone a last disapproving look on her way out.

Tom McAllister had spent the first part of the day fretting about this worrisome Ben Hope character who'd burst into the picture the night of Nick Hawthorne's death. Now he had other fish to fry, in the shape of the second dead classical music nerd to turn up on his turf in as many days.

He'd sensed immediately that it couldn't be a coincidence. Now, as he sat looking into the background of this Adrian

182

Graves, the link between the two dead men was growing right in front of his eyes.

First, and most glaringly obvious, the pair had known each other. Graves had been Hawthorne's music professor, years back. McAllister found an old picture in the university archives of the two of them together, along with an article about some grant that had been awarded for the restoration of the cathedral organ.

Second, and even more interesting to McAllister, was the matter of the old music manuscripts. It hadn't taken a lot of research to uncover that Graves was something of an expert in that department. More than that, he was recognised as one of the top authorities in the world on the matter.

To Tom McAllister, classical music was just something you could listen to while cooking, his favourite pastime. He'd had no idea until now that there was a whole academic sub-industry devoted to locating and rescuing forgotten, stolen or otherwise lost works of great composers, which otherwise would never come to light. Nor had he ever given any thought – although it made a lot of sense now as he went on digging – to the potential value of these old bits of paper. He'd been astonished to learn that collectors routinely bid six- and even seven-figure sums of money for them at auction, especially when the composer in question was one of the biggies, a 'name'.

J.S. Bach was definitely a name. Even a big ignorant savage from the Falls Road had heard of that one.

McAllister leaned away from the computer, slurping his cooling coffee and thinking about what Ben Hope had told him about the manuscript allegedly missing from Hawthorne's flat. Hope didn't strike him as the kind of man to get the details wrong, and his description of the missing item had been pretty clear, right down to the brown coffee-or-maybe-something-else stain on the front page and the composer's signature at the top.

According to Hope, Hawthorne had believed the manuscript was a fake. But what if that wasn't the case? What if, hypothetically, there were people in the world far better qualified than Hawthorne, for all his performance expertise, to tell what was genuine and what wasn't? And what were the odds that Hawthorne had just happened to be buddies with one of the top guys in the field – who just happened to show up dead soon afterwards?

'You don't have to be Inspector frigging Morse to see there's a connection here,' McAllister growled under his breath. It was time to take a closer look at Professor Adrian Graves.

McAllister's computer skills were self-taught and he was clumsy on the keys, but he had a sharp instinct for needling out information. He soon found a more detailed biography of the reputed academic on a specialist music institute site. Graves had been born in London in 1953, the son of a museum director, and gone on to study music at New College, Oxford in the seventies. Before returning to Oxford to pursue his postgraduate studies, Graves had spent eighteen months in Vienna cutting his teeth under the tutelage of one Professor Jürgen Vogelbein at the Wiener Institut für Musikwissenschaft. McAllister wasn't even going to try and pronounce it.

From what he could gather, it was there in Austria, and thanks to the influence of his mentor Vogelbein who by all accounts was a legend in that field, that Graves had first formed his interest in old music manuscripts. McAllister followed his nose and ran a more specific search on Vogelbein. Born in Dortmund in 1918, the young Vogelbein had interrupted his music studies to take up military service at the outbreak of the Second World War, which had seen him in the thick of the Battle of Berlin in 1945 as the final push of the Soviet invasion crushed the remnants of the Third Reich.

After the war, Vogelbein had returned to his former studies and eventually become one of the world's most prolific researchers, famously devoted to tracking down lost music manuscripts. He'd received acclaim in 1973 for unearthing a trove of priceless medieval chants thought to have been destroyed centuries earlier. But Vogelbein's true passion was for the works of Johann Sebastian Bach, and the quest to restore his lost works to the treasure trove of musical heritage.

McAllister was surprised to learn that only an estimated fifty per cent or so of Bach's compositions were thought to have survived to the present day. A vast number were said to have been lost in the years following his death in 1750, when the composer's mountain of musical manuscripts were bequeathed to various members of his large family and then subsequently scattered. Others had been destroyed in wars, others still were believed to have drifted into private collections and simply vanished. Before the age of recording, once the physical paper on which it was written came to harm, the music died with it. Preventing that tragic loss was perceived by music historians as a race against the clock, before the ravages of time ate the precious manuscripts away to nothing.

McAllister was definitely learning stuff here, but it wasn't what he wanted to know. 'Ah, bollocks to this,' he muttered to himself.

Just as he was about to abandon his reading about this Vogelbein guy . . . that was when he stumbled on it.

Chapter 28

The small article McAllister found was buried deep in the website of the Viennese music institute at which Vogelbein had worked for most of his life. Judging from the date, the piece had been reproduced from an old edition of an academic journal, presumably part of some initiative to digitise all their archives.

The text was in German, and McAllister had to depend on the Google auto-translation to understand any of it.

PROF. JÜRGEN VOGELBEIN: DIE JAGD NACH DEM SILBERMANN-MANUSKRIPT. Juni, 1980.

The Hunt for the Silbermann Manuscript. June, 1980.
    Professor Jürgen Vogelbein has conceded that his long search for the legendary J.S. Bach composition, said to have been taken from its owner Abel Silbermann by the Nazis during the French Occupation in 1942 and since vanished into obscurity, may never come to fruition. Professor Vogelbein has long maintained his belief in the existence of this obscure composition, claiming to be the only living Bach scholar to have actually laid eyes on it while a soldier in Berlin, 1945. However, its existence has been disputed by Vogelbein's academic peers. Professor Heinz Busch of

Berlin University has dismissed his claims, and further insisted that the mysterious bloodstains rumoured to mark the lost manuscript are nothing more than a figment of the academic imagination . . . READ MORE

McAllister looked at the empty mug on his desk. 'Coffee stain, my arse,' he muttered. Damn right, he wanted to read more. But when he clicked on the link, it took him to an error message that said, 'Sorry, the link you selected can't be used.'

He swore, grabbed his coat and ran to the Plymouth, telling Billie on his way out of the HQ building that he'd be back later. 'Where're you going?' she called after him, but he was in too much of a rush to explain.

McAllister gunned it all the way from Kidlington into the city centre to Broad Street, past the Sheldonian Theatre. He couldn't find a parking space for love or money, so parked illegally on the corner of Broad Street and Catte Street and dared any bloody traffic warden to lay a ticket on him. The reason he was here was the grand Bodleian Library, which had to have a copy of every book, periodical and article published anywhere in the world, going back forever. Which was why the place was so damned big, with vaults and tunnels mining deep under Broad Street, filled with archives so ancient and dusty that most hadn't seen the light of day for decades and centuries, and probably never would.

McAllister charged into the venerable old library with his police warrant card drawn like a pistol, and told the dead-faced woman behind the desk that he needed to see everything they had by a certain Professor Jürgen Vogelbein. He had to spell it twice for her. 'It means a bird's leg,' he added, proud of his new knowledge of German. Not that the dead-faced lady really needed to know.

The library staff kept him waiting for more than an hour,

during which time McAllister hustled across the street to Hertford College and, with a good deal of urging and a little bit of bullying, was able to collar a reedy, bespectacled lecturer named Dr Willard from the Modern Languages department to help him with his 'urgent police business'. Willard might have been reluctant to oblige, but he was too overwhelmed by McAllister's powers of persuasion to say so. By the time McAllister returned to the library with his press-ganged lecturer in tow, the library gofers had come up with the goods: a stack of fusty old academic music periodicals and journals from some recess of the Bodleian's underground bowels.

'What are we looking for?' Willard asked.

'Bloodstains,' McAllister said.

They got to work, or Willard did, while McAllister twiddled his thumbs impatiently. The afternoon was rushing by and Forbsie would be getting his knickers in a twist wondering where the hell he'd gone, but this was important. At any rate, he hoped it was.

It was the better part of two more hours before Willard came up for air. McAllister said, 'Well?'

'I think I found your bloodstain,' Willard said, holding up a yellowed page covered in tiny German print.

'Tell me.'

'It's part of a paper Vogelbein wrote in 1974, about his search for the lost so-called Silbermann manuscript. According to Vogelbein, the music was a *solfeggio* study for clavichord composed by Bach in 1743, seven years before his death. It passed through the hands of various collectors, the last of whom was Abel Silbermann—'

'The guy the Nazis stole it off of,' McAllister said. 'I know.'

Willard frowned at the paper. 'He doesn't give his sources for the information, but he writes that the manuscript is recognisable by the distinctive alleged bloodstain on the lower right-hand corner of its front page. No indication as to where the blood came from, or how old the stain might be. Anyway, it seems that after the manuscript fell into the hands of the Nazis, it went to Berlin but was moved to Silesia in 1945, along with a lot of other Nazi loot, to protect it from the Allied bombings. Silesia was taken over by the Soviets at the end of the war.'

'Okay. And?'

Willard tapped the paper with a chewed fingernail. 'Again, he doesn't give sources, but Vogelbein claimed that the manuscript was among a whole consignment of stolen artifacts that were grabbed and stashed away by the KGB. That's why, having tracked it that far, Vogelbein gave up hope of ever finding it. Is he still alive?'

'I doubt it,' McAllister said. 'He'd be a hundred years old.'

'In which case it appears to be a dead trail, I'm afraid.'

McAllister recalled what Ben Hope had told him about Nick Hawthorne finding the manuscript in an old shop in Prague, only last year. The Soviet Union had collapsed in '91. It was impossible to say how it might have found its way out of KGB hands, maybe sold on the sly and then drifted from place to place until Hawthorne eventually stumbled on it without even realising what it was.

What mattered was two things. First, that it was almost certainly genuine, and highly sought after. Second, that Adrian Graves undoubtedly knew that, even if Hawthorne didn't. The plot had just thickened.

Willard was peering at McAllister over his glasses. 'I don't understand why this is urgent police business, Inspector?'

'Thanks for your time, Dr Willard. Much appreciated, so it is.'

McAllister walked back to his car. It was too late to go back to HQ, so he drove home. He lived alone, just him and

Radar, in a remote riverside cottage on the banks of the Thames, near a minute hamlet called Chimney in west Oxfordshire. When he got home, he took the dog for a ramble along the river and through the woods, then fed him a plate of shredded boiled chicken supremes for dinner. Afterwards, McAllister started preparing his own evening meal in his small but very well-equipped kitchen.

Cooking was his joy. Tonight he was making a classic cheese soufflé tart, a very delicate affair for which he'd carefully prepared the pastry the day before and kept it chilled overnight. He'd selected a fine bottle of Chablis Grand Cru to go with his meal. Tom McAllister often surprised people with his good taste. He could be a bit of a mystery to himself at times, too.

The soft spring evening fell. He slowly began to relax and stop thinking about old music manuscripts with someone's blood on them. Radar curled up in his basket by the fire. The Thames flowed gently by outside. A solitary owl hooted from the trees. All was well with the world and it was possible to imagine that that feckin eedjit Forbsie no longer existed.

The table was set for one, McAllister's soufflé tart was almost perfectly browned in the oven and the Chablis was at the exact right temperature, when the call came in.

It was Billie.

'Boss, you'd better get your skates on. There's a major disturbance in Blackbird Leys and the cavalry are rolling. Reports of automatic gunfire, smoke, all hell breaking loose over there. It's like a war started.'

'Ah, shite. I'm on my way.'

As he hurried to the Plymouth, McAllister was remembering the words he'd heard only that morning.

'Don't get in the way of what happens next.'

And he was thinking,

Hope.

Chapter 29

Earlier

Ben took his bag from the Alpina and left the car at the side of the road. 'I'll drive,' he said, pointing at Lena's little blue Nissan. He still didn't trust her not to bolt at the first chance she got, so was keeping hold of her handbag with her purse and house keys inside.

'You are crazy leaving a car like that out here. Someone is bound to steal it.'

'I'll just have to trust that not everyone's a dirty thief,' Ben said. 'Now please get in the car.'

She climbed in the passenger side without a word, lips tight. The Nissan felt cramped after the BMW. He adjusted the driving seat further from the wheel, fired up the tinny-sounding motor and they took off.

As he drove, he took out his smartphone and handed it to her. 'You know how to use that?'

'You think I am an idiot? Of course I can use it.'

'Wonderful. I want you to go online and tell me the location of the nearest big garden centre. We can stop off there en route to your place.'

She stared at him. 'What for?'

'Because I need some potassium nitrate for my tomato

crop back home. You mix that stuff into the soil, they shoot up like nobody's business.'

'You really are crazy.'

'Tell me something, Lena. Are you a good home-maker? Or are you one of those people who lives on takeaway food and doesn't own a saucepan?'

'I look after myself just fine,' she replied, looking at him strangely.

'I'm sure you do. I thought maybe I could whip something up for us tonight.'

'You? What kind of a man cooks a meal for a woman?'

'I'm a progressive kind of guy,' he replied.

After searching online for a few moments, Lena read him out the location of a big out-of-town garden centre superstore that was open late, off the Oxford bypass at South Hinksey. Ben pushed the Nissan hard around the ring road and they were there within twenty minutes. 'Come with me,' he told her, 'where I can keep an eye on you.'

Ben led her inside the superstore and between racks filled with garden tools, boots and gloves and a thousand kinds of miracle potions and plant food additives. Lena looked around her with a frown and commented, 'This is a very weird place.'

'People like to grow things other than cannabis,' Ben said.

'Only an asshole would come to a place like this.' She was pouting now, like a teenager made to suffer the indignity of shopping with a parent. Ben shook his head and decided to ignore her.

He soon found what he was looking for. The store sold kilo bags of potassium nitrate, otherwise known as saltpetre. One kilo was more than enough for his tomatoes – or would have been, if Ben had had the remotest interest in cultivating fruit and vegetables. The three other items he purchased were a rubber hammer, a pack of strong plastic cable ties and a pair of latex gloves.

'What is all this other stupid shit for?' Lena asked on their way back to the car.

'Why, these things have all kinds of uses around the garden,' he replied. 'It's a healthy lifestyle. You should hang up your whip and try it sometime.'

'Fuck you.'

'Now to your place. Let's go.'

Lena lived in a one-bedroom apartment in a modern development off North Way in Barton, an area to the east of the city that had originally been built mostly as social housing and never quite shaken off its downtrodden aura. 'Welcome to the shit hole where I live,' she said as they got out of the car.

'It's a better neighbourhood than Dragan's.'

'I hate this place,' she said sourly. 'It is full of chavs.'

Which Ben thought was quite a statement, coming from the sibling and accomplice of a racketeer, blackmailer, murdering gangster, thief, drug dealer and gun runner. 'Are you bringing that bag of shit inside my place?' she asked, eyeing him as he grabbed the potassium nitrate from the car's tiny boot.

'Wouldn't want the chavs to steal it, would we?'

Her apartment on the second floor was almost as small as her car, and in need of a clean-up. The carpets were floral, and every wall in the place was painted bright pink. Posters of cute ponies hung on the walls and cuddly toys lay piled on her armchairs and sofa, like a collection belonging to a little girl. Maybe that part of her, the little girl part, was something she needed to hold onto.

'I would like to take a shower,' she said stiffly. 'Is that allowed? Don't worry, I will not try to jump out of the bathroom window.' When Ben looked into the bathroom, he could see why. The window was so narrow that a cat would have trouble squeezing through.

'Okay. Take your time. Don't bolt the bathroom door.'

'You want to watch me?'

'No, Lena, I don't want to watch you.'

When he heard the water splashing a few moments later, he went into her poky bedroom and looked around. At the foot of the bed was a little dressing table with a mirror and shelves either side of it crowded with a collection of lipstick tubes and makeup products. A cheap photo frame held a picture of Lena and a guy who might have been a couple of years older and bore a slight facial resemblance to her, apart from being a foot taller and shaven headed, with muscular arms and a neck like a tree trunk laced with tattoos.

Ben picked a bottle of coloured nail varnish off the dressing table. Blue was obviously her favourite. He glanced at the contents label and slipped the bottle in his pocket, then opened Lena's wardrobe. Some of the garments hanging inside were ordinary dresses, others were mail order items definitely not for everyday wear, like the nurse uniform and various costumes that mostly consisted of see-through lace, straps and buckles whose purpose he could only guess at. But he wasn't interested in her clothing. At the bottom of the wardrobe he found a shoebox containing a pair of red high heels. He dumped those out and took the empty box, which he carried out of the bedroom and up the narrow passage to Lena's kitchenette.

Like the rest of the place, it was built on a miniature scale, but she had all the essentials. Ben searched through the wall cupboards and found a large bag of sugar and a tub of baking soda, which he laid on the worktop. From another unit he took a plain water tumbler, five good-sized bowls and a heavy frying pan. In a drawer by the cooker he came across scissors, a ball of string and a roll of aluminium foil.

Perfect. Everything he needed for a cosy cook-in, SAS style.

His first step was to dump the contents of the nail varnish bottle into the glass. Next he scissored off a two-foot length of string, coiled it up in the bottom of the glass and set it aside to soak for a while. Laying out the five bowls in a row, he measured out three parts of potassium nitrate to two parts sugar, then tipped the whole lot into the frying pan and started heating it gently on the electric hob, stirring it with a wooden spoon and taking care not to let it overcook. The mixture started to turn brown as the sugar caramelised. When it had turned into a gooey paste the right colour and consistency, he added a spoonful of baking soda, which made the goo bubble up and start turning turquoise-blue. He took the pan off the heat and set it aside to cool, removed the acetone-soaked string from the glass and dangled it over the sink to dry. The fumes from it made his eyes sting.

Next he turned his attention to the empty shoebox, which he lined with a big piece of aluminium foil. As he worked, he could hear the water stop pattering in the bathroom, and the sounds of Lena bustling around. He was nearly finished. The mixture in the frying pan had cooled off enough, and he poured it into the foil-lined box. As it cooled further it would harden solid, so while it was still soft he laid the acetone-coated string into the mixture with eighteen inches or so dangling over the side of the box. Then he wrapped the box over with more foil, to hide its strange contents.

He'd put everything away and was washing up the dishes when Lena came into the kitchen, wearing a fluffy white bathrobe and her hair wrapped in a towel. She smelled of shampoo and soap. 'That photo in your bedroom,' Ben said. 'The guy in it with you is Dragan, yes?'

She nodded, frowning. 'So, you been sneaking in my

room? You were probably looking for dirty pictures. I don't do porno.'

'Actually, I was looking for the kitchen.'

She sniffed. 'What is that fucked-up disgusting smell in here?'

'I had a go at making us a pasta sauce,' he said ruefully. 'Didn't quite turn out right. We'll have to order in a pizza instead.'

She humphed. 'So much for the great chef, hmm? You let a man loose in the kitchen, this is the shit you get. This place will stink forever.'

The pizza was from Domino's, and was brought straight to the door by a little guy on a scooter. By then, Lena had finished drying her hair and changed into jeans and a sweater. Ben had found a bottle of inexpensive white wine in her fridge, which would have been better used for cleaning paintbrushes but was still preferable to drinking the tap water. He poured out a glass for each of them and sliced up the pizza.

As they ate, Ben said, 'So you grew up in the Yugoslav wars?'

'I do not talk about it.'

'I know how you feel.'

She looked sharply at him. 'Bullshit, you know how I feel. If you had been a child in Banja Luka, like me, when the NATO forces drop a thousand bombs all around, then maybe I would believe you.'

Ben was familiar with the history of Banja Luka, the second largest city in Bosnia and Herzegovina after Sarajevo. During NATO's Operation Deliberate Force between August and September 1995, devastating air strikes against VRS Bosnian Serb Army enclaves had been launched on over three hundred targets in that area. The true number of civilian casualties had never been openly disclosed.

'That was a tough time.'

She shrugged, and replied with her mouth full, 'Afterwards

our family move to Serbia. But things in Belgrade were not much better. My mother die there. It is like I always say. All of life is tough. You are born, you suffer, then it is finished and you rot in hell.'

'Sounds like you've been reading Schopenhauer.'

'I never heard of this asshole. Who?'

'I only caught the end of the conflict in your country,' Ben said. 'My squadron was supposed to be there for intelligence gathering, to support the UN troops. But there was more than that going on. I saw a lot of the things that were done there to innocent people. I was sorry about it. Later on, we went back there, hunting war criminals. We didn't get enough of them.'

'I have told you, I do not want to talk about those times.'

Lena chewed thoughtfully on a pizza slice for a while, gazing at her plate, then said, 'This music paper, this—' She paused, searching for the word.

'It's called a manuscript.'

'This manuscript, is it really worth much money?'

'Apparently so,' Ben said. 'Wherever it's gone. I didn't see it there among Graves' things.'

'Dragan has it. He is keeping it somewhere safe.'

'I didn't realise Dragan was musical.'

'He is not,' she said, missing Ben's sarcasm. 'He is going to sell it.'

'Right. Through his academic contacts in the world of classical music, art and culture?'

'He has contacts of a different kind,' she said. She hesitated to say more, then added, 'Like Zarko Kožul, back home.'

'Zarko Kožul,' Ben repeated. 'Who's that, a friend of his?'

A dark look washed over her face, like storm clouds passing behind her eyes. The corners of her mouth downturned and she shook her head. 'Nobody gets close to Kožul.

197

He has no friends. He trusts no one. And no enemies, none left living. You cross Kožul, you die. Everyone knows this.'

'Serbian mafia?' The wars and resulting massive economic destabilisation in the former Yugoslavia had been good for organised crime gangs in the Balkans. Their business empire was built on arms and drug trafficking, protection rackets, illegal gambling and prostitution, heists and smuggling. Ben had never run into those guys personally, but he'd known people who had.

'Yes, mafia. Before that, he was in the war. He fight with the Scorpions. You understand what that means, yes?'

'I know who the Scorpions were,' Ben said.

That had been the self-styled name of the Serb so-called paramilitary unit who were involved in some of the worst atrocities of the Bosnian war. They had used the conflict as an excuse to go on a rampage of rape and murder. Eight thousand innocent people slaughtered at Srebrenica. Thousands more women, children and elderly people beaten, abused and tortured in a systematic campaign of sadism and cruelty.

'Then you understand what kind of man Zarko is,' Lena said.

'I also understand what kind of a man would work for him. Like your brother.'

Lena took another bite of pizza, pulled a face as if she'd bitten into a turd, and dropped the limp slice on her plate. 'Dragan never work for Zarko. But he want to, very much. Before we come here, he always try to make an impression, so that Zarko will let him join his gang. One day Zarko say to him, "Go and make a name for yourself in UK, become big man, get experience, make connections. When you have something to offer me, then maybe you come back home and work for me." That is how it works, in their world.'

Welcome to Britain, land of opportunity. 'So that was why

Dragan came to this country, to cut his teeth and learn how to be a real criminal? How come you tagged along with him?'

'What else was there for me to do?'

'So now Dragan plans on taking Nick's manuscript to Zarko in Belgrade?'

'If it is worth a lot of money, Zarko will want it. He will be pleased with Dragan and maybe take him into his gang. That is what Dragan is hoping.'

'I'm so impressed by your dear brother's enterprising talents that I'd like to congratulate him myself.' Ben drained his wine glass and looked at his watch. 'I think it's time to pay a visit to Blackbird Leys. Give him a call.'

Lena's eyes clouded with anxiety. 'What should I tell him?'

'Tell him there's nothing good on TV, you're bored and in the mood for a party, and you're coming over to spend the evening with him and the gang.'

'What about you?'

'What about me?'

'I have to ask if it is okay that I am bringing a friend along. How else can I explain it when I turn up there with a strange man? Dragan will not like this.'

'Say nothing. Do not mention me.'

She didn't look convinced. 'He will know something is up.'

'You act out fantasy roles for a living,' Ben said. 'So act. Sound natural. Use the landline – that way I can listen in on speaker. Stick to what I told you to say. And remember, I understand Serb.'

The phone was in the hallway, perched on its base unit, which had a separate keypad and a speaker covered with a wire mesh that was furred with dust. Lena looked nervous as she stabbed a number on the keypad with a pointed blue fingernail, then pressed a button to put the call through the base unit's speaker. She chewed her lip in agitation as the dial tone pulsed for several seconds. When someone answered, Ben could hear the *boom – boom – boom* throb of loud music thumping in the background, distorted and metallic-sounding over the speaker.

'Yeah?'

'Dragan, it's me,' Lena said in Serbian, shooting an anxious look Ben's way as she spoke.

'Hey, sis, whassup?'

Lena repeated it more or less exactly as Ben had told her to. 'You partying tonight? I'm on my own, nothing to do. How about I zap round there?' Her manner sounded relaxed, she was forcing herself to smile, and Ben didn't pick up on any note of suspicion in Dragan's tone of voice.

'Yeah, sure, we're having a good time, come on over.'

She glanced again at Ben, hesitated and said, 'Is Radomir there with you? I'd like to see him.'

Ben frowned. Radomir?

Dragan paused, then replied, 'Oh yeah, he's coming round later. He'll be glad to see you, too.' Dragan laughed. 'I'll be expecting you, sister.'

There was a brief snatch of unintelligible conversation in the background, then Dragan hung up.

Lena put the phone back on its cradle. 'What?' she said to Ben.

'I thought we agreed to stick to the script. What was that about Radomir?'

'He is one of Dragan's friends. I had to say something, or else Dragan would wonder why I am coming over just like that. If he thinks I have crush on Radomir, it makes it more okay.'

Ben looked at her. He could see no lie in those clear blue eyes.

'All right, then,' he said. 'Let's get it done.'

Chapter 30

Night had fallen by the time they set off towards Blackbird Leys. This time, Lena drove. Ben sat in the passenger seat with his bag containing the foil-wrapped shoebox on his knees. The mixture inside was now fully hardened and ready for use. His bag also contained the other items he'd purchased from the garden centre. If Lena wondered why he was bringing them, she kept it to herself.

Ben had no doubt that the housing estate looked a lot better by night than it did in the daytime, the amber glow of the sodium lamps and the lit windows that spangled the high-rise blocks managing to soften the edge of the brutish architecture. Still, the place gave off an aura of decay that would have suited the set of a post-apocalyptic zombie movie.

Lena pointed out Dragan's squat six-storey block as she pulled up in a parking area surrounded by a wire fence. 'He is on the top floor, on the right. See? Those are his windows.' They were curtained, chinks of orangey light shining through the gaps. Ben could faintly make out the thump of the music even from forty yards away, inside the car. He slipped the Tokarev from his belt and checked it over. Hammer on its half-cock safety notch, a round in the chamber, eight more in the mag. The steel was warm from the heat of his body.

'What is your plan?' Lena asked, looking at him with liquid, anxious eyes.

'You know what my plan is.'

'Do not kill my brother.'

'Whatever happens here tonight is all up to him, Lena. He brought it on himself.'

'You do not have to do this.'

'I'm afraid I do. And so do you.'

They got out of the car. Ben took the key from her, blipped the locks and put the key in his pocket.

'Now what?' she asked.

'What you came here for. Walk over there and go and see your brother. I'll catch up with you in a minute.'

Lena flashed him a last nervous glance, then began walking towards the building with quick, tense steps. The entrance to Dragan's block was a pair of grimy glass doors that led through to a neon-lit stairwell. One of the neons was flickering as though about to die.

Hanging back in the shadows near the car, Ben could see half a dozen figures hanging about the stairwell, young white guys dressed in the usual hoodies and tracksuits with loud sports logos, smoking, laughing among themselves, one slouching on the concrete stairs, another leaning against the door, the rest just loitering about in that shambolic, round-shouldered, can-kicking way of young guys going nowhere.

From the way their conversation seemed to falter when they saw Lena approaching, and the one leaning against the door peeled himself off it and yanked it open to let her through, Ben could tell they knew her. Which signalled to him that these weren't just any old kids hanging tough. They were sentries, posted by Dragan's guys to scout for trouble, or rival gangs, or maybe the police.

202

The one holding the door open nodded a greeting at Lena. Even from this distance Ben could see the kid had watchful, wary eyes too old for his face. They scanned past Lena, peering into the darkness, not spotting Ben.

But Ben knew they already knew he was there. Dragan's people had been alerted to the situation the moment Lena had phoned him. Ben suspected that the giveaway had been that bullshit line about Radomir, which was probably a prearranged code for 'we've got trouble'. There might have been no visible lie in her eyes when he'd quizzed her over it, it didn't mean she was being truthful. He could see the lie in other ways, like her nervy body language on the way over here, and the whole vibe of anticipation she was giving off. She couldn't wait for Ben to walk right into the trap. The moment she reached the sixth floor she was going to spill the whole story about this guy who'd carjacked her after work that day, pointed a gun at her head and tried to coerce her into betraying her dear sibling.

Ben was neither surprised nor disappointed. If it was a choice between handing Dragan over to justice and luring him, Ben, to his death, she was never going to give up her brother. In her place, Ben would have done the same. But if they'd thought he was just going to walk in there like an idiot and let himself end up like Nick Hawthorne, they didn't know who they were dealing with.

They soon would.

Ben slipped on the latex gloves, then shouldered his bag and hopped the wire fence. He began making his way around the side of the building in a wide loop, staying in the shadows. They would be watching from the windows, but see nothing.

It took him six minutes to complete his flanking manoeuvre of the block, by which time he knew that Dragan and his boys upstairs would have had a detailed description of him from Lena, and would have gone into full alert mode expecting trouble to kick off soon.

A concrete path ran up between a row of dismal shrubs and the side of the building. As Ben crept carefully along the dark alley he triggered a movement sensor and a light above him flashed into life. Quickly, he reached into his bag for the rubber mallet and smashed the light, plunging the side of the building back into darkness.

He waited, breathing shallow, listening hard, then moved on. A few yards further, he came to a ground-floor window and peered inside. The room was dark, but by the faint strip of light shining under its door he could see it was a boiler room. He slipped the Tokarev from his belt, pressed its muzzle against the windowpane with one hand and gave the butt of the pistol a sharp rap with the other. It poked a tennis-ball-sized hole in the glass, big enough for him to reach his arm through and undo the window latch.

Thirty seconds later, he was inside the building. The boiler room doubled as a cleaner's storeroom, full of mops and buckets. He crept to the door and stood immobile for a full minute, straining his ears for the slightest sound from the other side, before he slowly opened the door and stepped into the passage beyond. A maze of corridors took him back through the building, until he reached the stairwell by an internal door. The six youths were still on guard at the entrance, all looking much more serious than before as they kept watch through the grimy glass doors.

Ben's sudden appearance from inside the building took them completely by surprise. By the time they sensed him quietly stepping up behind them and turned round, the Tokarev was already in his hand and pointing.

Ben said softly, 'Phones. On the floor. Now.'

The guards gaped at the gun, saw the look in his eyes,

and quickly took out their phones and tossed them in a small heap at their feet.

Ben said, 'Leave. Don't come back.'

This time, there was no hesitation at all. The eldest one batted through the glass doors and the other five followed in his wake as fast as they could. Ben watched them sprint off into the darkness and knew they wouldn't return in a hurry. They might go and find another phone to call Dragan's crew on the sixth floor, but by then Dragan's crew would already be too busy to pick up the call.

Ben picked up the phones and dropped them in his bag. Next, avoiding the main stairs, which were bound to be guarded at every level, he traced his way back through the maze of passages and found a fire escape that nobody had thought to watch. Clever, these gangsters.

He ran up the twisting flights of fire escape steps until he reached the top floor, then peered out of the reinforced glass window of the fire door that separated the stairway from the corridor beyond. It was a long, narrow L-shaped passage lit by bare bulbs on wall holders and had several apartment doors along its length. At its far end the passage branched off to the right, towards the main stairway.

Ben pushed silently through the fire door and stepped into the passage. He could smell the oversweet scent of sandalwood incense wafting from inside the apartment nearest the fire escape. The thumping music he'd been able to hear from down below sounded much louder up here. It was coming from the door at the far end, which tallied with the position of the curtained windows Lena had pointed out to him. Either this was a crafty diversion, or it really was Dragan's apartment and these guys were even stupider than Ben had thought by drawing attention to themselves this way.

Clutching the pistol, Ben paced the length of the corridor, unscrewing each light bulb a quarter turn as he went, leaving only the one nearest the end door still burning. He returned to the darkness of the fire escape exit and waited.

A minute later, the end door swung open, the volume of the music was suddenly amplified, and a large man stepped out into the light of the remaining bulb. He was burly, tattooed and shaven-headed, but he wasn't Dragan Vuković. He was clutching a double-barrelled shotgun that was sawn off at both ends, so it was little more than a chunky pistol. A favourite weapon of thuggish morons everywhere, as destructive as it was indiscriminate, but useless at anything more than across-the-room range. The guy looked around, saw nothing that made him want to start blasting, then stepped back inside the room and closed the door behind him.

Definitely Dragan's apartment, then. And really not so smart. One thing was for sure, though: they were expecting company. Ben smiled to himself as he pictured Dragan inside the apartment, with Lena and the rest of the gang. Get ready, folks.

Ben stepped fast and lightly up the passage. He reached into his bag and took out the foil-lined shoebox and removed its covering. Took his Zippo from his pocket, thumbed the striker wheel and touched its flickering petrol flame to the acetone-soaked string that dangled from the side of the box.

The string began to burn ferociously. Eighteen inches of fuse wouldn't last long, no more than a few seconds before the hardened mixture inside the box ignited, but that was all the time Ben needed.

He thumped loudly on the door, twice, then stepped quickly aside.

What happened next was exactly as he'd anticipated.

Chapter 31

With a muted crash, a ten-inch circle in the middle of the door suddenly exploded outwards in a swarm of splinters. It looked as if a giant fist had punched right through the wood. A sawn-off 12-gauge would do that, at close range; and the blast would have separated Ben's upper half from his lower if he hadn't got out of the way.

The string fuse had about two seconds left to burn before the fizzling flame touched off the volatile mixture. Ben quickly stepped back to the door, shoved the box end-on in the hole and punched it all the way through so it fell inside the room. By then, it was too late for anyone to stop it.

Ben had long ago been taught the art of improvising munitions out of whatever makeshift ingredients an SAS unit might be able to lay its hands on behind enemy lines. It was amazing what you could find lying around in old barns. Certain agricultural chemicals, mixed with things like sugar, could be made to go bang to powerful effect. But the concoction he'd prepared in Lena's kitchen wasn't going to hurt anyone, unless they were already half dead with asthma. It was a smoke bomb, not as effective as the British L83A1 smoke canister grenade but pretty useful nonetheless.

In the final second between the box hitting the floor and going off, Ben heard pandemonium break out inside Dragan's apartment, everyone thinking BOMB. If the guy with the shotgun had had either sense or reflexes he would have blasted the box to pieces where it lay before the fuse ran out. Instead he discharged his second panicked shot through the door, to lay waste to whoever might be standing the other side of it. The payload ripped another ten-inch bite out of the wood-work just above the first, turning an O into an 8.

Next, thick grey smoke started billowing out of the hole in the door. Within seconds, the yells of panic from inside were turning into guttural coughing and spluttering. Nobody would be able to see much as the smoke enveloped them, and it was very unpleasant to breathe. They had a dog in there with them. Ben could hear it barking frenziedly in fear and confusion. He felt sorry for the animal.

The door opened. A wall of impenetrable smoke poured out into the corridor, and from the smoke staggered the big guy with the shotgun. First-line troops, cannon fodder, an expendable footsoldier dispatched to tackle the threat outside. But he was so badly choked by the noxious fumes that he could hardly see. His face was a mess of tears and he was doubled over with coughing. Ben came at him out of the darkness and hit him a single hard blow to the forehead with the rubber mallet. The big guy's eyes crossed, his knees folded and he hit the floor with the shotgun pointing at the ceiling.

One for one. Ben snatched the sawn-off from his hands, ejected the two live rounds, pulled the fore-end and barrels off and threw the bits away into the darkness.

He didn't have to wait long for the next thug to come charging out of the smoke-filled apartment. This one was brandishing a machete and screaming at the top of his lungs. If the first was a big stupid bear, this one was a mean little ghoul. He looked like he knew how to handle the machete, and had probably done damage with it in the past.

But not today. Ben sidestepped the swing of the blade and dropped the guy with a solid rap of his hammer to the crown of the head. Two for two.

By now, the smoke alarms all over the top floor of the building were screeching. The grey fog spilling from the doorway of Dragan's apartment was thickening to a black pall, so much so that Ben could hardly see a thing himself. His eyes were burning. Maybe he'd overdone the baking soda. He retreated into the darkness once more, unshouldered his bag and waited.

Just then, the apartment door nearest the fire escape opened. A tall hippy guy in his twenties, with lank ginger hair and a tie-dyed T-shirt, stood framed in the light of the doorway, thrown into a panic by the whoop of the alarm. One thin hand was still holding the bottle of beer he'd been halfway through when he'd realised something was going on. Noticing neither Ben standing in the shadows nor the unconscious bodies on the floor, he saw the smoke billowing down the corridor, and his bleary eyes opened wide to stare as if it was a living mist creature coming to get him.

'What the fu—?'

But the hippy guy's yell died on his lips, because at almost the same moment Dragan Vuković appeared out of the dark pall swirling from his own apartment doorway. Dragan stepped over the slumped shapes of his men without a downward glance. In one hand he had a towel pressed over his nose and mouth. The other hand was tightly gripping one end of a taut steel chain, at the other end of which was a large brindled male pit bull. The dog had half an ear missing and its muzzle was laced with white scars from dog fighting. Strings of drool flew from its jaws. It was so wild with desperation to slip its leash and rip something apart that it was rearing up on its hind legs, all solid muscle and sinew, its teeth snapping like castanets over the noise of the alarm.

In Dragan's wake came Lena, pale and coughing and retching from the smoke, and two more of her brother's associates, both of them variations on the same muscles-and-ink hardman theme. Danilo and Miroslav, Ben supposed. One of them had his fists locked around the hilt of a long, wicked-looking samurai sword. The other had an Uzi. One long thirty-two-round magazine protruding from its pistol grip, and another sticking out of his jeans pocket.

The sword was one thing. Ben was more worried about the Uzi.

The hippy guy was either too far gone from his evening's beer drinking to recognise the gun for what it was – or else maybe Serb gang heavies toting Israeli-made 9mm machine pistols were such a common sight on the Blackbird Leys estate that residents barely noticed any more. For the moment, he didn't seem that worried about the dog, either. 'What the fuck are you bunch of fascist fuckheaded nutters doing in there? Lighting a fucking barbecue?'

Dragan Vuković had more pressing matters to deal with than complaints from his hippy neighbour. His quick eyes, red from the smoke, were scanning the darkness of the corridor beyond the hippy's doorway, searching for the assailant that his sister must by now have described to him in plenty of detail. He was looking right at Ben but couldn't see him, or the pistol in Ben's hand whose sights were trained right on Dragan's centre of mass.

But Dragan must have sensed the presence in the darkness. He jerked on the dog's chain and yelled in Serbian, 'Go, Demon! KILL!'

He let go. With a savage yowl, the dog instantly flew down the corridor, straight towards where Ben was standing hidden in the shadows.

Chapter 32

Ben didn't want to harm the animal, but he didn't want to get his flesh ripped from bone either. He adjusted his aim towards the charging pit bull and prepared to fire, knowing he'd have to pump half a magazine into the dog to stop its frenzied attack.

He didn't need to pull the trigger. The dog's mad eyes locked onto the hippy guy standing there, and it veered off course like a heat-seeking missile to go for the closer target instead. The hippy guy let out a shriek and went staggering backwards through his doorway, tripped and fell.

The dog launched itself at him with a roar, still trailing its length of chain. Its alligator jaws closed on a trouser leg and began shaking its head viciously from side to side, the way it would to kill a rat, cat or other dog by breaking its neck.

The hippy screamed and wriggled, trying to hit the dog with his beer bottle and kick it in the face as it mauled him. His foot glanced off the dog's head and caught the edge of the open door; the door swung shut and his cries and the dog's crazed barking were muffled behind it.

'Fuck that retard!' Dragan yelled in Serbian from behind the towel over his mouth. He turned to Danilo and Miroslav. 'Find this other bastard for me! I want his fucking head on a plate!'

Whichever of the two he was, the thug clutching the Uzi reached forward to grasp the cocking bolt knob on the top of the receiver. That was the instant Ben realised, as he watched from the darkness, that the gun wasn't yet in battery and ready to fire. That gave him a split-second advantage, and he took it.

He stepped forward into the smoky light and pointed the Tokarev.

'Dragan.'

All eyes snapped onto him. Lena's were pink and puffy, and still streaming tears because of the irritation of the smoke. She let out a cry seeing Ben approaching, but her voice was drowned by the shrill alarm.

Ben advanced another few steps, past the closed door of the hippy guy's apartment. Dragan's friend with the Uzi stood frozen in mid-movement, his hand still on the cocking knob. Ben swivelled his pistol sights onto him and said, 'Drop the weapon. Now. Or die.'

Dragan's guy quickly made his choice. The uncocked Uzi clattered to the floor.

Dragan Vuković stared at Ben with eyes more crazed and brimming with hate than those of the dog he'd beaten and goaded into a becoming a vicious pit fighter. 'Who the fuck are you, man?' Switching to English, his accent was thicker than Lena's.

'I'm the part of your plan you didn't account for,' Ben said. 'The guy you didn't reckon on having to deal with. Now here I am.'

'You think I am fucking scared of you?'

'Yes.'

Ben didn't blink as he watched Dragan through his gunsights. The Tokarev's trigger sear would break at around seven pounds, typical of a clunky military sidearm of its time. Ben's finger was applying six pounds of pressure on it at this moment, and he was thinking about what might make him want to lay on the extra pound.

If he'd encountered Dragan Vuković and his cronies in the remote forests and hills of their own country, he would not have hesitated for one instant to gun down first Dragan, then Danilo and Miroslav, right there on the spot. He would have ended their worthless lives without a second thought, and left them where they fell, for the foxes and wolves to feast on, and for the crows and the worms to finish what the animals didn't eat.

But Ben wasn't stupid enough to openly commit a triple murder in urban Britain, the most heavily-surveilled European police state since East Germany. Not with half his movements throughout that day recorded on CCTV, and a smart cop like Tom McAllister already aware of his involvement in the hunt for Nick Hawthorne's killers.

No, Dragan Vuković was not worth going to jail for – but that was where Dragan was headed himself, and his cronies with him. Three square meals a day, and all the leisure time they could cram in at the UK taxpayer's expense. At least, once locked behind bars, they wouldn't be free to enjoy themselves by throwing more innocent people out of windows.

Dragan spread his hands, trying to look casual. 'What you want with us, man? It's about that guy, right?'

'That guy,' Ben said.

'Look, we did not mean to hurt him.'

'You mean, you didn't realise he couldn't fly?'

Dragan smiled. 'Just one of those things, you know? We can square this up. You want some money to go away?'

'I want you, Dragan. You and your pals here are coming with me.'

'I am thinking you want my sister too, huh?'

Ben shook his head. 'I have no quarrel with her. She can go on whipping perverts' arses the rest of her life, for all I care.'

'Fuck you,' Lena yelled.

'Walk away, Lena. That was the deal I promised you when you sold your brother out to me, remember?'

Dragan's eyes flicked in Lena's direction.

She gave a quick headshake. Nervous. 'He's lying.'

'It's over, Dragan,' Ben said. 'Let's go.'

The alarm was still shrilling. Smoke was still roiling from the doorway of Dragan's apartment. The muffled barking of the dog and the cries of the hippy could be heard from the closed door of the other apartment, to Ben's back. Dragan said nothing. His expression was as hard as the steel in Ben's hand, but Ben could see in his eyes that he knew he was done.

Then everything suddenly changed.

The apartment door behind Ben flew open and the hippy guy came bursting back out into the corridor. His trousers and T-shirt were hanging off him in tatters and his hands and face were bloody. 'Call it off!' he screamed. 'Get the fucking thing off me!' The dog appeared in the doorway, fire in its eyes, pink drool foaming from its gnashing jaws. It stiffened as it saw Ben for the first time. Recognising him as a threat to its master, it instantly forgot all about the hippy guy and charged the new enemy instead.

Ben wheeled around, shifting his point of aim from Dragan's crew to the dog and ready to shoot.

Dragan yelled, 'Demon, attack!'

The dog raced towards Ben. The steel chain attached to its neck snaked along the floor behind it. Ben was about to shoot when the end of the chain snagged under the bottom of the open door of the hippy guy's apartment. The dog's charge was suddenly checked. It roared and strained on the end of the chain, eyes rolling, snapping like a landed piranha fish.

The two seconds that Ben had been distracted by the attacking pit bull was enough time for Dragan's friend to make a grab for his fallen Uzi and rack the cocking knob. Like a slowed-down audio replay, over the noise of the alarm Ben clearly heard the metallic crunch of the action working, the bolt snapping forward, a nine-millimetre cartridge chambering from the long thirty-two-round stick magazine. Not a good sound to hear when the enemy has the drop on you and is about to unleash hellfire on you from just a few steps away.

If Ben had tried to get his pistol back on target and snap off an accurate shot, he'd have been dead. Instead he did the only thing he could, which was to move, and move fast. He dived back, dodged the teeth of the trapped pit bull, hit the floor and rolled towards the dark end of the corridor.

At the same instant, the Uzi in the thug's hand fired with a deafening continuous thunder that drowned out the shriek of the alarm, and a bright strobing muzzle flash that lit up the smoke like a magnesium flare.

Chapter 33

Six hundred rounds a minute. One nine-millimetre copper-jacketed bullet spitting from the Uzi's short barrel every tenth of a second, propelled by burning gas at a velocity greater than the speed of sound, every one of those bullets kicking the recoil of its acceleration straight back into the shooter's hand. Even for an experienced operator, the beast was hard enough to tame. In the hands of a criminal thug who probably posed in the mirror with the gun every day but had never put in any range time, it was almost impossible to control.

And that was what saved Ben's life. The Uzi's wild full-automatic gunfire lifted its muzzle and stitched a ragged line of holes in a climbing zigzag. Dragan's guy grappled to control the bucking weapon, his face twisted up in a crazy grimace as the whole corridor in front of him was peppered with a random shower of bullets. They shattered the over-head lamps and blew electric switches apart. Blasted the cheap acoustic tiling from the ceiling. Smacked through stud walls into neighbouring apartments. Drilled into the flimsy wood of the hippy guy's open door. And slammed through the body of the hippy guy himself as he tried to stagger out of the way, not fast enough. The impact of multiple strikes jolted him back and slammed him into the wall. He bounced off, leaving a big bloody smear, then crumpled twitching to the floor.

Ben made it to the fire escape door by throwing himself down and sliding the last couple of yards, feet first. Bullets thunked into the heavy wood above his head as he battered the fire door open with the soles of his boots and slithered through. More gunfire shattered the reinforced window and showered him with glass. Even in the hands of an idiot, the Uzi was a deadly force. But like any other lethal storm, its fury couldn't last forever. After just three seconds that felt more like thirty, the gun had shot itself empty and fell silent. Through the ringing in his ears Ben could hear the steady shrill of the smoke alarm, and behind that the sound of screaming and panic from other residents of the block.

He struggled upright and slammed back through the fire door at a sprint. Dragan, Lena and their friend with the samurai sword were already escaping the other way, along the L-shape of the passage in the direction of the main stairs.

The one with the machine gun was still standing in full view in the middle of the smoky corridor, now grappling with the weapon's magazine release catch on the grip so he could load his spare. The twisted body of the hippy guy lay near his feet. The dog was still caught by its chain under the bottom edge of the door, and was going wild.

Ben raced along the passage, skipped once more out of reach of the snapping dog, and bodyslammed the guy with the Uzi into the wall. He tore the weapon from his hands and rammed its steel-box receiver hard into his face once, twice, three times. Blood spurted from the guy's split lips and nose. Ben grabbed him by the neck, spun him up onto his feet and sent him sprawling towards the dog. The pit bull was so crazed with frustration and aggression that it no longer differentiated friend from enemy. The guy screamed as the dog's jaws closed on his arm, ripping his flesh.

He wouldn't be getting away in a hurry. Ben left him to his fate and ran after the others.

The smoke was thinning now. Ben reached the head of the stairs. The staircase wound downwards in a rectangular spiral with a minimalistic concrete shaft running up its centre. He glanced down and caught a glimpse of movement two floors below him. He could hear the echo of their footsteps clattering up the shaft. He gave chase.

Ben had reached the landing of the floor below him when the figure emerged from a recess and came at him. Something shiny and long glinted in the lights as it whooshed at his head.

Ben ducked low out of the path of the sword blade. It hissed over him, moving so fast and with so much force behind it that Dragan's crony, clutching the hilt with both hands, couldn't slow its momentum. The blade's sharp point thunked into the wall behind Ben. Before his attacker could yank it out and swing it at him again, Ben knocked him away.

They circled one another. The guy was big and powerful, thick arms laced with spiderweb tattoos like the ones that adorned the sides of Dragan's neck. Ben saw the punch coming before the idea for it had even formed in the thug's brain. He rolled the big fist aside like deflecting a beach ball lobbed to him by a child, then used the guy's speed and weight against him to trap the arm and break it.

The guy let out a howl of agony and staggered back, gaping down in disbelief at the jagged stick of bone that was protruding from the torn flesh of his arm. Ben hit him in the throat, not hard enough to kill. Then pitched him headlong down the stairs.

That might kill him, but only if he was really unlucky.

Ben sprinted down the stairs after him, trampled over the

top of the unconscious body and kept going. Down and down, until he reached the empty stairwell entrance where the youths had been standing guard earlier. Through the grimy glass doors he saw the shapes of Dragan and Lena under the sodium lamps of the estate, running full pelt away from the building, already sixty yards away. An Olympic sprinter couldn't have hoped to catch up with them.

Ben instinctively brought the Tokarev up to aim, then thought better of it and lowered the pistol. To shoot meant to kill, unless he missed. To miss was to risk a stray bullet going through a window across the way, into someone else's apartment, through someone's baby as it lay gurgling in its cot. None of those were good options.

Ben had no choice but to let them run. Moments later he heard the rasp of a diesel engine, then spotted a battered white van tearing away. He had Lena's car keys in his pocket, and thought about giving chase. He had as much hope of catching them in the underpowered Nissan Micra as he would on a bicycle.

Ben said, 'Shit.'

He didn't have much time before the police and fire brigade turned up. He rushed back up the stairs. The thug with the compound arm fracture was awake, and moaning loudly in pain as he tried to stand. Ben pinned him with a knee to his throat and shoved the muzzle of the Tokarev hard against his cheek.

'Which one are you, Danilo or Miroslav?'

'Miroslav.'

Then Danilo was still upstairs, serving as a dog's dinner. Ben said, 'Here are your options, Miroslav. You can either take a bullet in the head now, or spend a very long time in jail for your part in killing my friend. You don't have a lot of time before the police arrive, so choose fast.'

219

Miroslav was breathing hard and in a great deal of pain. Sweat was pumping from the pores of his forehead and cheeks. 'I don't want to die.'

'That's what I thought. Then tell me where Dragan goes from here.'

'He is going home.'

'Home, as in, back to Serbia?'

Miroslav nodded and gasped, 'He tell us tonight he is going back.'

'He's taking the manuscript to Zarko Kožul?'

Miroslav stared at Ben through the mist of his agony, as if wondering how this crazy guy could possibly know that.

Ben asked, 'Where is Zarko?'

Now the look in Miroslav's eyes was the same fear Ben saw in Lena's at the mention of Kožul's name. 'You don't want to tell me? Fine.' Ben pressed the pistol harder into the side of Miroslav's face.

'He have a nightclub in New Belgrade. The Rakia. You can find him there, many nights.' Miroslav seemed to forget his pain for a moment, and gave Ben a little smirk of satisfaction. 'But you should be careful what you wish for, my friend. You go looking for Zarko Kožul, you might find him. And then you will wish that your father had never met your mother.'

'Enjoy prison,' Ben said, and knocked Miroslav out cold with the butt of the Tokarev.

Leaving the limp body there, he ran up the remaining flights of stairs to retrieve his bag from where he'd left it near the fire escape landing. The pit bull had managed to wrench its chain free, and had escaped. That would be something for the police to worry about, when they got here.

Danilo lay in a pool of blood in the passage, a few feet away from the man he'd shot to death. There was nothing

Ben could do for Dragan's hippy neighbour. Danilo was at least still breathing, but the dog had torn him up pretty badly. Ben took the pack of plastic cable ties from his bag and used two of them to secure Danilo's wrists and ankles, in case he made a miracle recovery and decided to leave the scene of the crime. The gunshot residue all over Danilo's hands and his prints on the Uzi would quickly and easily tie him to the killing.

As for Ben, he planned to be out of here very soon. He used more cable ties to truss up the two of Dragan's crew he'd knocked out with the rubber mallet, before returning down the stairs to Miroslav and repeating the same procedure on him. Then he left the building, his exit as unseen as his entrance.

Ben dumped Lena's car keys down a drain outside, along with the latex gloves and the dismantled parts of the Tokarev. He was walking away in the darkness, just another shadow among the trees and buildings, when the first police armed response vehicles came screaming into the estate, flooding the night with swirling blue light. He had a feeling that, if he stuck around a little longer to observe, he might see DI Tom McAllister's Plymouth Barracuda arrive on the scene, too.

But Ben had no intention of remaining any longer than he had to. By the time McAllister had figured out what had happened here tonight, he would already be en route for Serbia.

Chapter 34

Novi Beograd
Serbia

Prior to its conversion into one of the wildest and most notorious nightclubs in the concrete jungle of Novi Beograd, the three-storey warehouse on the left bank of the Sava River had been an abattoir and meat-processing plant. In some ways, it still served a similar purpose – if you were unlucky or stupid enough to cross its owner, Zarko Kožul.

New Belgrade: it wasn't called that for nothing. Up until and during the Second World War the whole area had been swamp and wasteland, home only to the Sajmište extermination camp that was used by the Nazis to execute political prisoners and Jews from Bosnia, some fifty thousand in total. After the war, the area had been completely razed, then in 1948, years of work had begun shipping in vast quantities of sand and construction materials to create the base for the new city.

Like so many buildings in Novi Beograd, the Rakia nightclub was a brutally utilitarian concrete cuboid that looked more like a military installation than a popular entertainment venue. The bikers who patrolled the outside of the building like circling sharks on Harleys from dusk till dawn, and the teams of men hand-picked for their intimidating appearance and violent ways, only served to reinforce the impression of a fortress. Which, of course, was all deliberate on the part of its proprietor. Many more of Zarko Kožul's footsoldiers stood guard inside, heavily armed and working in shifts to protect their boss from trouble and keep an eye out for unwanted visitors. There was often trouble, but only ever of the kind that Kožul's men could settle themselves. It was unheard of for any Belgrade cop to be crazy enough to go poking his nose into what went on at the Rakia.

As a result, it was a place where the most hardcore criminals could let their hair down and feel relatively safe. Local legend held that it had once been a favourite watering hole of Milorad 'Legija' Ulemik, former Legionnaire, one-time member of Arkan's Tigers and the Serbian Red Berets, later to head up the notorious organised crime gang the Zemun Clan, before he'd been sentenced to fifty years in prison for his part in the assassination of Zoran Đinđić, the Serbian Prime Minister.

True or not, stories like that couldn't hurt the reputation of Kožul's business one bit. And they certainly didn't put off the partygoers, who descended on the place in their thousands every night to drink and dance until they dropped.

It was three in the morning and the strobing lights were flashing like the firebursts of a tank battle across the quayside and over the rippling waters of the Sava as Kožul's joint got into full swing. New Belgrade was called 'the Berlin of the Balkans', and it was easy to see why. Bathed in the blood-red of the neon sign that said, simply, RAKIA, a swarm of some three hundred people, many of them already drunk and loud, formed a giant scrum at the entrance of the nightclub, desperate to join the massed crowds already crammed inside. Enormous men stood by the doors with their arms folded, eyeing the throng. Motorcycles slowly patrolled the street.

Among the cars and taxicabs that came and went, a black Mercedes limo pulled up at the entrance. Its driver stepped out and opened the back door.

Dragan and Lena Vuković got out of the limo. They'd come straight from the airport, looked somewhat bedraggled from hours of travel, and were carrying nothing with them except for the small backpack that Dragan had over his shoulder. Lena gazed up at the looming shape of the Rakia, then darted an anxious look at her brother. Unlike him, she had never visited the top floor of the building, but she'd heard the tales and knew enough about the man they'd come to see.

'Are you sure we're doing the right thing, Dragan?' she asked him for maybe the eightieth time since they'd managed to grab the last-minute flight from Heathrow earlier that night.

'Relax, babe, we're golden.'

Dragan led the way, pushing through the crowd towards the main entrance, until the way was blocked by a bouncer so tall and broad that he towered over Dragan and made Lena look like an infant.

'I'm expected!' Dragan had to yell over the percussive thunder of the music blasting from inside. The bouncer unzipped the backpack, opened the plastic folder inside and stared at its contents in bewilderment, as if he'd never seen an original eighteenth-century music manuscript before. He scrutinised Dragan for a long moment, then Lena, then drew a radio handset from his pocket and called upstairs to check. A moment later, the go-ahead came back and he nodded them through the door.

The volume of noise was ten times greater inside the

nightclub. The place was so packed, if you collapsed from exhaustion or too much drink, you were likely to get trampled by the heaving ocean of bodies. Lightning strobes flashed overhead, making the dancers and the forest of upheld waving arms appear to move in jerky stop-frame animation. A second guard led Dragan and Lena through the crowd to a door marked PRIVATNI.

Through the door, they found themselves in a red-lit corridor where the crash of the music was muffled enough to talk. Lena glanced around her, saw more men with guns and shot another anxious look at her brother. But Dragan appeared relaxed and in his element. He nodded greetings to a couple of guys he hadn't seen for four years, and burst into a wide smile as a man in his thirties, dark-haired and much smaller than the bouncers, as well as Dragan himself, came walking over to meet him.

They embraced. 'Welcome back, Dragan. It's good to see you again.' Alek Bosković was one of Zarko Kožul's inner circle. He was lightly built, but twice as dangerous as the hulks guarding the entrance. The closer you got to Kožul, the more deadly the people you would encounter.

'What kind of mood is he in?' Dragan asked.

Alek grinned. 'Never seen him in such good spirits. He hasn't killed anyone for – oh, it must be weeks.'

'Shit. Is he feeling all right?'

Alek clapped Dragan's shoulder. 'Come on up, man. He's waiting for you.'

They walked down winding corridors to the open-shaft paternoster lift that was a throwback to the building's earlier days, once used for transporting carcasses and butchered meat between floors. The double lift was on a continual loop with no doors and no buttons, the left side perpetually going up and the right side going down, like a huge vertical revolving door. The rumble of wheels and pulleys could be felt through the walls and underfoot. The three of them stepped aboard the rattling, shaking platform. As the paternoster hauled them skywards, Alek glanced at Dragan's backpack and said, 'Whatever it is you've brought Zarko, it better be good, my man.'

'Good enough to cost me half my crew.' Dragan told him about the man named Hope who had caused him so much trouble back in England.

'Who the hell is this person?'

'He's a walking dead man, is who he is.'

Zarko Kožul had grown very cautious after all the attempts that had been made on his life over the years. As they stepped from the paternoster onto the top floor, Dragan and Lena were patted down for weapons and concealed wires as a bunch of Kožul's oversized heavies stood around watching every move. The contents of Dragan's backpack were carefully inspected once again for anything suspicious. Finally, after being subjected to a more thorough search than any airport security check, the two of them were led to the holy of holies, the suite of rooms that comprised Kožul's luxurious executive headquarters.

Alek paused with his hand on the doorknob. 'You know the routine,' he warned Dragan. 'Don't speak unless you're spoken to, no direct questions, and don't challenge him in any way. And keep the eye contact to a minimum. He considers it disrespectful.'

'You said he was in a good mood.'

Alek grinned. 'He is.'

They stepped through the door into a large space the colour of blood. Zarko Kožul loved red. Everything was either painted or carpeted or upholstered the same shade of crimson, from the walls to the padded stools that lined the bar at one side of the huge room, even the bar itself. Some said that was so the spatters didn't show up so much after Kožul personally executed enemies and troublemakers with his gold-plated Walther automatic. Others said he made everything red because he couldn't wait to take over from Satan down in hell, so did all he could in the meantime to recreate it on earth.

By the red-curtained windows to one side, a blonde a few years younger than Lena, clad in skimpy red underwear, lay on a red leather couch next to a mountain of cocaine that looked like a kilo of sugar on a low table. She was unconscious and didn't appear to be breathing, but none of Kožul's entourage was paying her any attention. The man himself was seated at the far end of the room, glowering at the visitors from behind a red leather-topped desk the size of an aircraft carrier. Alek gripped Lena's arm to hold her back, and motioned for Dragan to go forward.

Kožul said, 'Sit.'

The wooden chair in front of the desk was painted red and had had its legs sawn short to bring whoever sat in it closer to the floor. The reason for that was obvious to anyone who knew Zarko Kožul.

Kožul got to his feet. He had to be fifty now, but didn't seem to have aged a day since Dragan had last seen him. The only change in his appearance was that he'd filled out a little, if that were possible. After a lifetime of pumping iron, Kožul was literally as broad as he was tall. That was one way for a man who measured just half an inch over five feet in height to get respect in his profession. Another way was to torture, mutilate, and execute anyone who offended him in the slightest way. He'd had many years' practice at that, too.

Zarko Kožul stared at Dragan for a long time. His eyes

were pale, almost colourless. Dragan sat in the low chair, and looked down at his feet, not wanting to show disrespect. One of the guards walked up and laid Dragan's backpack on the desk. Kožul waved him away.

'So the boy comes back a man,' Kožul said to Dragan.

'You said to go make something of myself, Zarko,' Dragan replied, still looking down. 'That's what I did. But all I ever wanted was to work for you. You know that, right? I still do.'

Kožul smiled. He jerked his chin at the bag on the desk. 'What's this you've brought me?'

'It's my gift to you. Out of respect.'

'Respect, huh? That's good, Dragan. That's what I like to hear. Better be true.' Kožul reached out a short, thick arm, fished inside the bag and pulled out the sealed plastic file it contained. He took his time opening it. The smile dropped from his face when he saw what was inside. He eyed the manuscript with disgust, then snapped his glare back towards Dragan.

'What is this?'

'Music.'

'Music? I run a fucking nightclub. I already got all the fucking music I need.'

'It's, like, old. You know, valuable.'

Kožul stared at him. 'My grandmother's old as balls. Doesn't make her worth shit.' He looked back down at the manuscript. 'Jesus Christ, is that toilet paper, or what? Looks like someone wiped their ass on it.'

One or two of the guards chuckled. Kožul liked it when his jokes were appreciated.

As deferentially as he could, Dragan tried to explain. 'The guy we stole it from was totally, like, a real expert. A professor. Seriously, he'd have done anything to get it. There are collectors who pay a heap for these things. There's a market, like you wouldn't believe. See the name on it, this Bach guy? Stuff like this is worth a ton of money.'

'A ton, huh? That sounds like a lot. That sound like a lot to you, Alek?'

'It does, boss.'

'Sure it's a lot. You're talking millions of dinar,' Dragan said. The truth was, he had no idea of a figure and he was going way out on a limb with such a guesstimate.

At the other end of the room, Lena was tensing in anxiety for her brother. Alek's grip on her arm was tight.

Kožul's brows furrowed into a deep frown. 'Even if it was worth something, how the fuck am I supposed to sell it? I don't know anyone who would buy trash like this.'

'Come on, Zarko.'

Kožul's eyes flared. He leaned forward with his knuckles on the desk. 'Are you disrespecting me? First you waste my time with this bullshit, then you talk back like a fucking punk?'

'No, Zarko, you know I'd never—'

Kožul stood there, quivering with silent fury. Then he said in a flat tone, 'Alek, take this piece of toilet paper off my desk and burn it.'

Alek stepped forward. He produced a cigar lighter from his pocket, set to maximum like a miniature flamethrower so that a tongue of fire roared out when he lit it. He picked up the pages of the manuscript and offered the flame up to a corner of the crinkled old paper.

'Wait,' Kožul said, holding up a hand.

Alek extinguished the flame and laid the manuscript back down. Kožul was silent for a few moments, then seemed to relax as though the rage had ebbed back out of him. He sighed. 'Look, you're a good kid, Dragan. I haven't forgotten what you did for me, getting rid of that piece of filth Orlić.'

Radomir Orlić had been one of Dragan's reasons for leaving Serbia four years earlier: an informant who, if he'd lived another week, could have capsized the whole of Kožul's operation by ratting to the police certain information about a certain string of armed robberies. More than a few lower-ranking members of the criminal fraternity had jumped at the chance to ingratiate themselves with Kožul by eliminating Radomir. Dragan had got there first, slit the rat's throat and dumped his body in the Danube.

'I'd do the same again, any time.'

'You would, huh?'

'Any time you say. You're the man, Zarko. I have nothing but love and respect for you, like a son to a father.'

Kožul sat, leaned back in his chair and drummed his fingers on the desk, thinking. Total silence in the room. The blonde on the red couch still hadn't stirred. Her sprawled-out body looked dead.

After a lengthy moment's consideration, Kožul came to a decision. He tapped a finger against the manuscript. 'Okay. I'm not an unreasonable man. Let's give this a try. I know people who know people. I'll make a call or two. See what's what. Maybe you're right. Maybe it's worth something to some collector prick out there. If it is, then you can come and work for me. Always room for one more gun.'

'You'll see I'm right, boss,' Dragan said.

Kožul's expression hardened again. 'Oh, you'd better be. This better be everything you say it is. In the meantime, I got a job you can help me out with. Call it a test.'

'Anything, boss.'

'Alek will fill you in on the details. Now get the fuck out of here. I have business to attend to.'

When Dragan and Lena had left, Kožul dismissed the rest

of his troops and ordered them to take the overdosed girl out of his sight and dispose of her. Alone in his crimson domain, he snorted up a tug-rope of coke and became angry again, wanting to burn that stupid-ass bit of paper after all, then have that time-wasting upstart Dragan Vuković put in the crusher, and his whore sister given a starring role in one of the snuff movies that were a growth area of Kožul's business empire. Then Kožul changed his mind again, and reached for the phone.

The man he spoke to was a criminal fence, a useful associate with fingers in all kinds of pies.

'You think there's money in this old music crap?' Kožul asked, after he'd finished describing the item in front of him.

'I'd have to ask around, but yeah, there might be. Depends.'

'Depends on what?'

'Whether it's genuine, for a start. Believe it or not, that might matter to some people.'

'The guy I got it from says it is. They took it from some egghead who knew about this kind of shit.'

'Does it have any provenance?'

'Any what?'

'Never mind. What you say the composer's name was?'

Kožul had to check the manuscript again to see. He spelled it out. 'B-A-C-H.'

'I heard of him,' the fence said. 'So what's in this for me?'

'What do you want, a finder's fee?'

'I'd settle for fifteen per cent of the sale price.'

'Go fuck yourself.'

'What you worried about, Zarko? If it's bullshit anyway. Nothing to lose, right?'

'Ten.'

'Twelve.'

'Eleven and a half.'

'Give me a break, Zarko.' The fence was one of the very few people who could get away with talking that way to Kožul, though even he was careful not to push his luck.

'Okay, twelve. Then what?'

'Then I'd dig out the contact for this guy I knew, way back.'

'What guy?' Kožul demanded, not liking the idea of getting others involved. The more links to the chain, the weaker it got.

'This guy's solid, trust me. Calls himself Ulysses. Used to be based in Bucharest but he handled stuff all over the world. I haven't spoken to him in years. If anyone can help you find a buyer for merchandise like this, he can. He's gonna want a percentage, but your cut is still gonna be more than you'll get otherwise.'

Kožul thought about it, then said, 'Yeah, fuck it, why not? But I want this wrapped up fast, understand?'

The fence said, 'Leave it with me. I'll talk to Ulysses.'

Chapter 35

Grand Junction, Colorado, USA

The fugitive was a forty-year-old Caucasian male named Ozzy Crumm. He'd never held down a straight job in his life, was considered a primo loser by anyone who'd ever known him, and now he'd skipped bail over a DUI charge, the latest miserable addition to a police file that showed multiple past arrests for auto theft, possession and sexual assault. A psychological evaluation on his prison record indicated a tendency to sudden, irrational outbursts of extreme violence. He was believed to be armed.

Ozzy had now been on the run for three days. There would not be a fourth, but Ozzy was as yet unaware of this fact. Just as he was unaware of the person who was, at this moment, several steps ahead of the police on his trail and very soon about to close in for the kill.

Ozzy was holed up at the Western Hills mobile home park a few miles outside Grand Junction, the rundown single-wide belonging to a friend of his, Garth Boyle, who was currently doing a stretch for dealing amphetamines. Ten in the morning and already hotter than hell inside the cramped trailer. Having just finished off the last of the six-packs of Coors that had been sustaining him in his flight from the law, Ozzy was craving more beer. His bright green '95 Thunderbird, which he'd stolen in Redlands, Mesa County, the previous day, was parked outside in the baking heat. Ozzy happened to know there was a liquor store less than three miles down the road. The temptation was powerful.

Ozzy peered out of the dirty window. The trailer park was enclosed by a mesh fence. He could see the road some way the other side of it, but he could see no sign of the Grand Junction PD black-and-whites that he was certain were cruising the whole county looking for him.

Screw'm anyway. He couldn't stand it any longer, cooped up in Garth's stinking asspit of a trailer, sweating like a pig with nothing to drink. He snatched his Ruger .380 auto from the rumpled bed, stuffed it in the back of his jeans under the hem of his floral shirt, and stepped out into the nuclear heat.

He was a few paces from his Thunderbird when a woman's voice called out, 'Hey there.'

Ozzy turned to look. Her tan was the colour of Tualang honey. Wild dark gypsy hair. Tight jeans, artfully ripped at the knees. A black biker jacket over a light T-shirt emblazoned with the word LOVE. All the right curves in all the right places. Ozzy liked what he was seeing. He liked it a lot.

Ozzy broke out into his trademark big, broad smile, Jack Nicholson meets Dennis Quaid. 'Well, hey there to you too, sweetheart. I'm Larry. You got a name?'

She smiled back, kind of seductively, Ozzy thought. His heart was skipping beats. Zowee.

'Madison,' she replied. Nice teeth. Heck, everything about her was nice. She was well over 21, but he liked 'em a little more mature once in a while. She was eyeing him as if he

234

was the only guy in the world. 'That your trailer?' she asked, pointing back at the asspit.

'That? Hell no, I'm just looking after it for a friend. What about you, Madison? You live around here?'

She cocked her head, still smiling. 'Not really. I'm here for work.'

'Here for a couple days, maybe?'

'Maybe not that long. This job's kind of over already.'

He leaned against the side of the T-Bird, spreading himself out a little to show off his muscles. 'That's a real shame. What is it you do, Madison? Let me guess. You're a dancer, right?'

'You really want to know?'

'Sure.'

'Well then, let me show you.'

She reached into her jacket. Took out a black leather wallet and flipped it open to show him her seven-pointed gold star agent's badge. Before Ozzy had time to react, and long before he even thought of reaching for his concealed .380, she'd whipped out a big custom Kimber 10mm auto and had it stuffed in his face. Next poor Ozzy knew, he was being slammed belly-down on the ground, eating dirt, relieved of his weapon, caught and helpless. The cold steel cuffs bit into his wrists.

'Oswald Hale Crumm?'

'Aghh! Jesus, you're hurting me!'

'I'll take that as a yes. Nice to make your acquaintance, meatsack. I'm Special Agent Madison Cahill of the National Fugitive Recovery Agency. And you were the easiest catch I made this week.'

By midday, Ozzy Crumm had been safely delivered into the hands of the GJPD and Madison Cahill, 37, professional manhunter, was on her way to her next assignment. This time, a personal one.

From Grand Junction regional airport she hopped on a flight to Las Vegas, and from there caught a Hawaii Airlines connection to Honolulu International. There she rented a Jeep Cherokee and set off for the hour's drive to Haleiwa Town on the North Shore of Oahu.

The sky was the most perfect blue, palm trees waved in the gentle ocean breeze and the sweet-scented warm air wafted through the open windows of the Jeep, but Madison was too worried to enjoy the ride. She had left her father six messages in the last two days, with no reply. His health being what it was, and her being his only remaining family, she made a point of keeping in frequent touch with him. It wasn't like him to fail to return her calls.

Madison reached Haleiwa Town and took the winding little coastal road to her father's home. The house was just a stone's throw from the warm sand of the beach, surrounded on three sides by lush tropical vegetation. Her father had lived here alone for eight years. Madison was his only regular visitor, apart from Noelani, the nice local lady employed as a housekeeper.

Madison wasn't someone to flinch from the hard realities of things. She knew that, at the age of 87, Rigby Cahill probably did not have much time remaining on this earth. Yet, it was neither his advanced age nor any kind of physical illness, per se, that were killing him. The affliction that would eventually take him down was one he'd been dying of for many years. Her father had once been a great man, but he was a shadow of his old self and declining so fast she could see distinct changes in him every time she visited, which was often. The possibility of turning up at his house only to find him dead had been on her mind since yesterday.

The terrible thing was knowing what would make him better. It wasn't heartbreak that had made him this way: his wife Kathleen, Madison's mother, had passed away when Madison was just a child. It wasn't financial ruin, either. Enough of the fortune that Rigby Cahill had made during his years at the top of his profession remained to ensure that he'd die a rich man.

No, what had burned her father out, destroyed his mind and ravaged his physical state, was an obsessive quest of discovery that had ended in failure and eaten into him like a cancer. If it hadn't been for that one thing, Rigby would still be his indefatigable old self that she remembered from her childhood, probably still running his operation in New York, travelling the world, living out his dream and making millions.

Madison hated his obsession, detested the part of him that could have become so fixated on it, and the way it had dominated his life for about as long as she could remember. His single-minded drive when it came to achieving his goals had been the reason for his success. That was simply his way. The obsession that had destroyed him was also the only key to saving him. Which meant that, barring a miracle, her father was doomed to live out his little remaining time mired in bitterness and defeat.

She parked the Jeep in the carport at the side of the house and went inside. The front door was never locked.

'Dad? It's me, Maddie.'

Her anxiety rose when there was no reply. As she went through the beach house, she was steeling herself for the sight of him dead. She had seen many corpses in the course of her work. She'd been responsible for two of them herself. But her father – she didn't know if she could handle it. It was hard to imagine her life without him in it.

'Dad? Are you there?'

She found him sitting on the white wood veranda,

237

motionless in his recliner, his pale rheumy fixed towards the ocean. He was alive. If you could call it that. Madison's relief was tempered by her sadness at seeing him looking so shrivelled and sunken. He had been drinking, too. A bottle of Koloa rum stood near-empty by his feet. Koloa was his favourite, judging by the quantity of the stuff he got through in a year. Madison could have instructed Noelani to stop buying it for him, but she didn't have the heart to take away the only comfort that remained to him.

'Dad, don't you even pick up the phone any more? I left you six messages in the last couple of days. Any idea how worried I was? No, of course not.'

Rigby Cahill gave no response, except for a slight flicker of his eyes in her direction and the faintest ghost of a smile when he recognised her.

'You eat anything today? How about yesterday?'

No reply.

'Anyway, I'm here to look after you now. Starting with this. I think you've had quite enough already.' Madison took away the rum, put the bottle back in its cupboard in the kitchen and then went to the answerphone in the living room to delete the messages she'd left him.

To her amazement, in addition to her half-dozen messages from the last couple of days, the display on the answer machine was showing five more that had come in within just the last few hours.

That was very strange. Few people knew his number, and fewer still would have cause to dial it nowadays. Aside from hers, the only calls she could think he might receive would be those routed from his long-abandoned offices in New York, technically still operative but in practice nothing but an empty, sad shell where the phone hadn't rung in years.

And now, all of a sudden, five messages all at once, in the same afternoon?

What was even more astounding was when Madison listened to them and realised not only who they were from, but what they concerned.

Back in the dim and distant past, when as a girl she used to travel the world with her father and partake in his adventures, 'Ulysses' had been one of his most reliable contacts in the sometimes shadowy sphere in which he operated. A secretive man whose real name was an unknown. To her knowledge they had never physically met, though her father trusted him implicitly and they had enriched one another through the years. It had been so long since she'd heard him mentioned that she'd almost forgotten.

Madison replayed the messages over. They were short, clipped and urgent, and all repeated the same information almost verbatim.

'This is Ulysses. You need to call me at once. I have news. The Silbermann manuscript has resurfaced.'

Chapter 36

Ben walked a fast mile through the night from Blackbird Leys, then managed to flag down a taxi. He offered the happy driver a wad of cash to take him out into the countryside near Wychstone village, where he'd left the Alpina earlier that day. The BMW hadn't been touched.

Within minutes he was cutting eastwards towards the M40, then racing southwards down the crowded motorway towards London. He made a lightning pit stop for fuel on the M25, where he spent a moment searching online for a last-minute flight from Heathrow to Belgrade. With luck, he might not even have to step aboard a plane, if he could intercept Dragan and Lena at the airport.

But the delay getting back to the car had cost him, as he realised when he discovered that he was going to arrive at Heathrow too late to catch the last flight. He'd have to wait until morning.

With no longer any reason to rush things, Ben reached the airport at a more sedate pace, drove to Terminal 4 and booked himself into a hotel room for the rest of the night. All the comforts, but none that could compensate for the knowledge that Dragan Vuković and his lovely little sister were most likely already in the air and a big step ahead of him.

In his frustration, Ben raided the mini-bar for some cheap and nasty blended scotch. There were No Smoking signs everywhere and a sensor alarm in the middle of the ceiling, ready to denounce him at the first whiff of burning tobacco. Doing his bit for militant smokers everywhere, he pulled the battery out of the alarm and stood at the window, taking alternate sips of whisky and puffs on a Gauloise while he watched the twinkling lights of an aircraft taking off from the nearby airport, and frowned and fretted and thought about what he needed to do next.

The following phase of his plan would now take him into a very different situation. It wasn't guesswork to figure out that the moment Dragan landed in his home country, he'd be heading straight for Zarko Kožul. From what Lena had told Ben, and Miroslav had confirmed, Dragan's mission wasn't to sell the manuscript but to offer it to Kožul as a tribute, hoping to be taken on as a fully-fledged member of the great man's crew. If Dragan's plan worked, that meant finding him was going to entail penetrating Kožul's operation.

That was where things stood to become serious. Tackling a bunch of wannabe gangsters in the comparatively harmless environment of east Oxford was one thing. Tackling the likes of Zarko Kožul was a different matter altogether. For one man, unsupported, without backup, virtually impossible.

Ben liked working alone. But he also liked staying alive.

When he'd finished his cigarette, he refilled his glass with the paltry remnants of the mini-bar whisky and sat on the bed with his phone. It was almost one-thirty a.m. in Italy, but he dialled the familiar number and waited.

The gravelly voice of ex-sergeant Boonzie McCulloch, 22 SAS, now retired to a life of peace and tranquillity in the hills of Campo Basso with his Neapolitan wife, Mirella, answered on the fourth ring.

'Ben?'

'I'm sorry to disturb you this time of night, old friend. I need your help.'

Boonzie's Glasgow accent was still as strong as it had been the day forty-five years ago when he'd left Clydeside to join the army. He was the only person Ben knew who said things like 'och' and 'jings'. Boonzie's real name was Archibald, but anyone who called him that would get their arm ripped out of its socket and beaten about the head with the wet end.

'I ken ye wouldnae call if it wiznae wurth callin'. Hud on a minute.'

Ben heard the rustling sounds of Boonzie slipping out of bed and carrying the phone out of the room so as not to wake Mirella. A few moments later, Boonzie's voice came back on the line. 'What's aun your mind, laddie?'

Ben replied, 'Bosnia.'

The truth was, the SAS had been much more involved in the Bosnian conflict of the mid-1990s than had ever been officially revealed. Elements of 22 SAS A Squadron had been dropped into the country early on in the war, masquerading as regular troops. Once deployed, they had quickly become involved in key intelligence roles, as well as combat initiatives against Bosnian Serb fighters, who were to prove a tough and determined enemy. As the war grew ever more intense, one classified operation had seen a five-man SAS team dropped deep behind enemy lines to snatch a prominent Serb leader and war criminal from his mountaintop hideaway and smuggle him away for interrogation. The mission had helped to turn the tide of the war.

Boonzie McCulloch had been one of that five-man team.

As usual, much of the work of Special Forces units in that war would have been impossible without local help. The

SAS were expert in the 'hearts and minds' approach to warfare, cultivating contacts on the ground to facilitate infiltration and intelligence gathering. Boonzie had been in the thick of the operation, more so than his younger comrade who had only seen the end of the conflict and the later pursuit of known war criminals.

'Do you think Husein Osmanović would talk to me?' Ben asked.

Osmanović was a Muslim Bosniak. On the morning of July 16th, 1995, Serbian troops comprising soldiers of the Vojska Republike Srpske and elements of the Serb paramilitary force known as the 'Scorpions' had stormed his village near the town of Srebrenica and perpetrated one of the worst atrocities seen on European soil since the Second World War. Together with other acts of butchery that claimed the lives of some eight thousand innocents over the course of just a few days that month, it came to be known as the Srebrenica Massacre. Soldiers forced the villagers from their homes and lined them up in the street. They began by executing anyone who tried to resist, then started on the women. When Husein Osmanović tried to stop the soldiers from dragging his wife and teenage daughter away, they shot him in both legs and then made him watch as they gang-raped and beat and strangled Dalila and Safija to death in front of him. Afterwards, they shot Husein four more times in the chest and laughed over what they thought was his corpse.

Husein survived, built himself back to strength and devoted the rest of his life to revenge. The name of the fringe political organisation he founded and led, Srbe na Vrbe!, meaning 'Hang Serbs from Willow Trees', said everything about his attitude to his bitter enemies. He and his followers had played key roles in the SAS intelligence operations that eventually helped to win the war. But Husein, like Yugoslavia, would never be the same again.

'I dinnae ken, laddie,' Boonzie said. 'It's bin a long time. What do ye need tae ask him aboot?'

'Everything he can tell me about a Serb gentleman named Zarko Kožul. A little bird told me he was a member of the Scorpions, back in the day.'

'Diznae surprise me. We never did catch all the fuckers.'

'Nowadays, Kožul is an organised-crime boss in New Belgrade. A pretty powerful one, by all accounts.'

'Aye, an' I can guess the rest,' Boonzie said with a sigh. 'Ye're in trouble again. Am I reet?'

'You know me.'

'I do, laddie.' Boonzie paused, sounding thoughtful. 'Where are ye noo?'

'Now I'm in London. Tomorrow I'll be in Serbia. The clock's ticking on this one, Boonzie.'

'Leave it wi' me. I'll see what I can do, but no promises.'

'I appreciate it.'

'Jesus Christ, you're a mad basturt, ye really are.' With that line of flattery, Boonzie ended the call.

An hour and a few cigarettes later, when the mini-bar was somewhat emptier, Ben's phone rang. He picked up. 'Husein Osmanović?'

There was a few moments' silence on the other end. Then a raspy voice with a heavy accent replied, 'I believe you are mistaken. I have no knowledge of anyone by this name.'

It was all part of the age-old ritual of spy games. Ben said, 'My apologies for the misunderstanding. May I ask to whom I'm speaking?'

'My name is Adnan Tatarević. We would not be having this conversation, if it were not for my regard for our mutual friend in Italy.'

'I understand,' Ben said. The man's voice sounded like a blunt band saw cutting ironwood. You get shot four times in the chest and survive, you end up with a voice like that. Ben knew he was talking to Husein Osmanović, but he didn't contradict him.

'And I understand that you are in need of information.'

'Zarko Kožul,' Ben said.

'Why?'

'Let's just say I have a particular need to get close with him.'

The man calling himself 'Tatarević' was silent for a moment. When he spoke again, the raspy voice was dripping with hatred like molten lava. 'That Chetnik motherfucker is one of the worst of them. He is the most feared organised-crime leader in Serbia, responsible for more murders than anybody knows. As a younger man he was a member of the Scorpion paramilitary unit who butchered many of my people in the so-called "ethnic cleansing". Srebrenica, Podujevo, and many other terrible massacres. But I am thinking you already know this.'

Ben said nothing.

The voice rasped, 'May I ask what your intentions are, assuming you can, as you say, "get close"?'

'I have what you might call a bone to pick with one of his associates,' Ben replied. 'My quarrel isn't with him personally. But that could change, if he gets in my way.'

'As I understand it from our mutual friend, you generally settle your quarrels in a most decisive fashion.'

'I do what I have to do.'

'Yet, I fear this undertaking will be more difficult than even a man of your talents can deal with. Do you not think that many before you have tried, and failed, to penetrate the ring of armour that surrounds Kožul? He is protected by an army. Informants are everywhere, watching, spying. If Kožul sees you as a threat, to come within a mile of his stronghold would be suicide.'

'Just the kind of odds I like.'

'Nobody is that good, my friend. Not even you, not even if half of what I have been told about you is true.'

Ben smiled. Boonzie, putting in a good word for him. Osmanović almost certainly wouldn't have called otherwise. Ben sensed his interest, and knew what was coming next.

'You walk in there alone, without question Kožul's men will take you down,' Osmanović said. 'You kill five of his, he will only send ten more to take their places. Frankly, I cannot see you coming out of this alive. Not unless you had some assistance.'

Ben flipped another Gauloise from the pack and lit up. 'Assistance of what kind?'

'I know some people who would love to get back at Kožul for the things he has done. It seems to me that your plan could serve a mutual purpose. You help them, perhaps they will agree to help you.'

'How many?'

'Three.'

Ben had no doubt that Osmanović was talking about himself, along with two associates. 'You vouch for these people personally?'

'You have my word, and my word is my bond.'

'In that case, I would be interested in meeting with them,' Ben said.

'When you get to Belgrade, call this number.'

Chapter 37

The next day just after midday, Ben's flight touched down at Nikola Tesla Airport. Belgrade felt chilly after southern England. The sky was a shifting mosaic of grey slates, and a diagonal rain was slanting down out of it, the kind of rain that finds its way into every crevice and soaks a man to the deepest core of his soul.

He was tired. Tired of chasing, weary of fighting. He'd left his near-empty bag in the boot of the Alpina at Heathrow, and felt oddly naked without it hanging over his shoulder. As he stood under the rain outside the airport and dialled the number he'd been told to call, he had to struggle against a strange feeling of dread that rose up inside him. It was like no sensation he'd felt before, going into a hundred battles. If he'd been a superstitious man, he'd have thought his peculiar apprehension was a premonition of something bad about to happen.

A different voice from the one he'd spoken to last night, but with the same heavy accent, answered the phone on the third ring and told him to take a taxicab to the Despot Stefan Tower. 'It is a well-known landmark of the city. Climb the steps to the top of the tower and wait there for a man in a green hat.'

Ben found a taxicab for hire a minute later, and the car

took off on its eighteen-kilometre journey towards the city. The driver wanted to chatter, but Ben wasn't in the mood. He tossed the guy a bunch of the dinar notes he'd got from the airport bureau de change, closed his eyes and didn't open them again until they'd reached their destination.

Back in the mists of antiquity, the then-tiny population of Belgrade had dwelt within the thick walls and ramparts of a stone fortress. The Romans had conquered it, various besieging armies had hammered it over the course of many centuries, and all that had survived to the present day were the scattered gates at its four corners. The Despot Stefan Tower was attached to the north-eastern fortress gate, named after a fifteenth-century Serbian ruler. It was the last piece of Belgrade's older history still standing, and now a tourist attraction giving sweeping views from its ramparts over the breadth of the city skyline. Four astronomical telescopes stood mounted on posts, presumably to encourage visitors to observe the heavens. Ben didn't suppose that the man in the green hat had chosen this rendezvous point out of an interest in astronomy.

Unsurprisingly on a gloomy day like today, the tower was deserted. The rain had thinned to a drizzle, which Ben didn't mind so much except that the dampness made his cigarette fizzle out. Standing at the ramparts gazing across the city, he hadn't been waiting long before his phone buzzed in his pocket. More instructions, he thought. Or else maybe the man in the green hat had got cold feet.

But it was a different voice, and a more familiar one, that spoke when he answered.

'It was you, wasn't it? Don't tell me it wasn't you, because I know it was. I warned you.'

'Detective Inspector McAllister, I have no idea what you're talking about, but it sounds like you're accusing me of some heinous act.'

'You sound like you're on Mars. Where the hell are you?'

'A long way away from your turf, so relax. I'm not even in the country.'

'Germany? Russia?'

Ben frowned. 'That's an odd question. Why would you ask me if I was in Germany or Russia?'

'Because of the Silverman or Silbermann manuscript, or whatever the frig it's called,' McAllister said impatiently. 'That's what this is all about. Nazis, KGB, and some guy called Bird Leg. That's why I've got an impaled organ player in the morgue, a music professor with his face blown off, and half my city looking like frigging Beirut on a bad day. And it's all down to you, Hope.'

'Bird Leg?'

'Don't change the subject.'

'You have nothing on me, Inspector. As you know very well, or you wouldn't be calling me like this. Besides, I thought we were friends.'

'Oh, sure. Bosom buddies. Two peaches in a blender.'

'Always with the cooking metaphors, McAllister. You're in the wrong job. Should get back into the kitchen, where you can do something worthwhile for a change.'

'Wherever the hell it is you've run off to, Hope, you'd better stay there. Show your face in my city again, I'll be down on you like . . . like . . .'

'A sack of potatoes?'

'Watch it.'

'I don't think I'll be attending more college reunions any time soon. Everyone I knew is dead.'

'Aye, and the rest of us will soon be joining them, if you get half a chance. So do us a favour and don't ever come back to Ox—'

Ben ended the call and cut him off. He was still trying to

figure out what the hell McAllister had meant about Nazis, the KGB and someone called Bird Leg when a figure appeared at the top of the stone tower steps. A man in a long black coat and green baseball cap walked towards Ben, hands in his coat pockets, shoulders hunched. He looked in his mid-fifties, heavyset, greying beard, cautious eyes. As he came within a few steps of where Ben was standing at the rampart, the man stopped and pulled a small automatic from his pocket.

The pistol pointed at Ben's stomach.

'Major Hope?' said the raspy voice.

'I might have expected a more friendly welcome, Mr Osmanović.'

Osmanović glanced down at the pistol, hesitated for an instant and then slipped the gun back into his pocket. 'Forgive my lack of trust, Major. It is in short supply these days. I am taking quite a chance meeting you like this.'

'You know who I am, I know who you are. If I'd thought you intended to use that pistol, you'd already be learning to fly.' Ben jerked his thumb behind him over the top of the rampart. 'And you can call me Ben.'

'Husein.' They shook hands.

Osmanović beckoned Ben over to one of the telescopes. He angled it downwards on its pivot, so it aimed across the city skyline like a miniature cannon. He pointed through the drizzle. 'Do you see that square concrete building in the distance, there by the river?' Ben looked through the scope at the faraway building magnified several times in the eyepiece. The most unexpected feature was the rooftop helipad on top of the warehouse, marked with a big H.

'That is the objective,' Osmanović said. 'The Rakia nightspot, on the site of an old slaughterhouse, owned and operated by our friend Zarko Kožul. He uses it chiefly as a money-laundering operation and legitimate business front, while the vast bulk of his profits come from peddling misery and death. The upper floor is where he has his offices, if you can call a dive of degeneracy an office. To reach it, one must pass through several layers of security. A gauntlet of Kožul's men surrounds the building and guards their master's lair day and night.'

'If you have doubts about this target, why not hit his home instead?'

'I have already lost two good men trying to discover its location. This is a secret known only to Kožul's very closest associates. You see the helipad on the roof? Kožul never crosses the city by car. He flies into work each day from a private airstrip outside the city. He uses multiple vehicles to transport him between home and a hangar at the airstrip, always changing routes, and fitted with dark glass so that it is impossible to know which one he is in. Believe me, he is as devious as he is cruel. And so, we have no choice but to hit him here, at the Rakia. Though it will not be easy. His fortress is virtually impregnable.'

'Look around you,' Ben said, pointing at the ruins where mighty walls and turrets had once stood. 'If history teaches us anything, it's that nothing is impregnable.'

Osmanović smiled. 'Your reputation is clearly no lie. I have a plan for getting inside, which requires the skills and bravery of a man like you. I will tell you all about it. But first, let me introduce you to my associates. They are waiting.'

Osmanović led the way back down the tower steps, to where a shabby, grime-streaked old-model Mercedes sedan was parked on the street below. Its interior hadn't been cleaned out in at least ten years. Ben sat in the front passenger seat and lit a fresh Gauloise without asking permission. Osmanović didn't object. Not car-proud, seemingly.

251

They drove through the glistening wet streets in silence, heading westwards from where the Danube and Sava rivers split and carved the city into segments. On the western fringes they arrived at what might once have been a thriving industrial park but now looked like a ghost town of old abandoned warehouses and cracked concrete, with weeds that sprouted tall in the car's headlights.

Osmanović stopped the Mercedes outside the dilapidated entrance to one of the warehouses. It looked like the kind of place you might take someone to execute them. Belgrade, city of culture and beauty.

Osmanović got out of the car. He said, 'Follow me.'

Chapter 38

Ben did as he was asked, and walked into the warehouse after Husein Osmanović. Rusty old lifting equipment and bits of chain lay around the bare floor. The walls were daubed with graffiti and scorched in places where kids or vagrants had lit small fires.

Osmanović muttered 'This way' and led Ben deeper into the building and down a flight of crumbly concrete steps that led to a steel door. Their footsteps echoed off the bare walls of the large, empty space. If this was Osmanović's HQ, it was a little more spartan than Ben imagined Kožul's to be.

The other side of the door was a smaller room, just a bare concrete cube lit by dirty skylights. In the middle of the room stood a long, rough wooden table covered in an array of miscellaneous weaponry. At a glance Ben saw there was a mixture of modern hardware and stuff dating back to the Second World War. Old guns never died; they just fell deeper into the dodgy black market underworld. The other item on the table was a Samsonite cabin-size suitcase, its lid closed. Ben could only wonder what was inside.

Two men stood by the table, one scraggy and gaunt and bald, the other wide and swarthy. They watched Ben keenly as he walked into the room. The scraggy one badly needed a wash. Ben could smell the sour body odour from several metres away.

'These are my associates, Duša and Nidal,' Osmanović said. 'They have my complete trust. Aside from that, all you need to know about them is that they have reason to hate and despise Zarko Kožul almost as much as I do, which is saying a great deal.'

'All these years he's been operating,' Ben said, 'and nobody's put a stop to him?'

'I told you, many have tried. It would be a mistake to underestimate his power. However, we are not completely without the means to rid our country of scum like Kožul.' Osmanović waved a hand over the rows of weaponry.

Ben stepped closer to the table. It looked as though someone had raided a firearms museum and loaded a small truck with everything from American M16s to Russian Kalashnikovs; a massive Nazi-era heavy machine gun on its field bipod; an assortment of submachine guns that ranged from slick Steyr machine pistols to agricultural-looking British Stens from the 1940s. At the smaller end of the scale, Ben's hosts had laid out a mixed collection of pistols and revolvers, some modern, others that wouldn't have looked out of place in Adrian Graves' secret collection of historic arms.

'This selection is all we could assemble at short notice,' Osmanović said, noticing Ben's expression. 'You have a preference for a specific make and model?'

'Whatever works,' Ben said. 'If I need to bang in a nail, I don't worry about who manufactured the hammer.' He picked up a Glock .45 auto, checked it over, inspected the fully-loaded magazine, and worked the action a few times to make sure it functioned properly. Duša and Nidal were watching his every move like a pair of hungry dogs.

Osmanović smiled. 'A good choice. The Glock is a reliable tool and the forty-five slug will put a man out of action every time, with just one hit.'

Ben tossed the gun back onto the table. 'As long you can get the hit on the man when it counts. Are Tweedledee and Tweedledum here up to the job?'

The scraggy one, Duša, seemed to understand. He flushed red, snatched a big chunky Colt Anaconda .44 Magnum off the table and twirled the revolver around his index finger like a cowboy. Proving what a fearsome gunslinger he was. Maybe Ben was supposed to be impressed. Instead he turned to Osmanović and said, 'Being able to do tricks with a sixgun doesn't make you a shooter, any more than owning a Fender makes you Eric Clapton.'

Osmanović signalled to Duša to put the gun down, then shrugged his shoulders. 'Who would understand your wariness of us better than I? But you must believe that I would not expect you to walk into the lion's den without expert backup. Be assured, these men are among the best you will find in Serbia. Nidal was with the Military Police Battalion. Duša has spent three years with the Falcons, 72 Special Brigade, fighting terrorism.'

'And avoiding soap, by the smell of him,' Ben said.

If Serbia was anything like Britain, it was full to the brim with wannabe warriors going around bragging to anyone who'd listen that they'd been part of this or that elite unit. Ben had encountered more SAS fakers in his time than had ever actually served with the regiment. But he was just going to have to take Osmanović's word for it.

'You said you had a plan.'

'Here it is.' Osmanović went up to the table and opened the Samsonite case. It was filled with polythene-wrapped bricks of white powder, stacked in three tiers.

'Is that what I think it is?'

Osmanović chuckled. 'The bottom layers are nothing more than white sugar. But the top layer is pure uncut heroin, taken from a dealer who, shall we say, will no longer be needing it. Street value, thirty euros a gram. Not what it used to be worth, but you can be sure Zarko Kožul will be interested in purchasing it from us for the right price. To be more precise, from you.' He pointed at Ben.

'Not exactly my cup of tea, Husein.'

'If you can think of a better way to get inside his fortress, Mr Hope, I would welcome any ideas. This will get his attention better than anything.'

'Until he discovers the sugar.'

'By which time, you will have made your move against him.'

Ben paused, weighing up the options, visualising the scenarios as movie images unrolling on a screen in his head. 'And you?'

'On your signal, we will launch the attack from below. This will create a diversion and keep Kožul's men busy. If the man you seek—'

'Dragan Vuković.'

'—if Vuković is in the building, he is yours to deal with however you like. All we want is Kožul.'

'Want, as in, taken captive?'

'I would just as soon put a bullet in his head myself. But if you were to beat me to it, I would not shed tears.'

'In other words, you want me to kill him for you.'

Osmanović spread his hands. 'We would consider it a great favour. For a long time we have waited for someone like you to come along.'

'I'm not an assassin,' Ben said.

'But you want your man. This is the price for getting inside. Are you with us, or not?'

Ben didn't like the arrangement one bit, and he was liking it even less the more he thought about it.

'We haven't talked about the police. Things start kicking off, it won't be quiet. We'll have five minutes, ten maximum, before they roll in.'

Osmanović shook his head. 'Forget about the police, my friend. This is New Belgrade, not Little England. Kožul owns most of the cops, and those he does not own have more sense than to step inside his territory. Nobody will come.'

Ben was silent for a minute longer. Still thinking, still not liking.

'Okay, I'm in,' he said finally. Osmanović looked pleased, until Ben pointed at the open case and added, 'But we're not going with this crap. No drugs. If we do this, we do it my way.'

'As you wish. I have a reliable source that informs me Kožul will be in his office every evening this week. I propose we hit him tonight.'

'You seem to want this very badly,' Ben said.

'I would gladly risk a bullet to see another of those Scorpion motherfuckers dead. Never forget, never forgive. That is my credo.'

'What about money?'

'All I have in the world, I would give up without a second thought if it helped to nail Zarko Kožul's worthless hide to a wall.'

Ben smiled. 'Seeing as you're prepared to be so generous, how much cash can you get together in the next few hours?'

Chapter 39

Hearts and minds. When an experienced and perceptive operator got deep inside the enemy's way of thinking, it was possible to anticipate their moves. Not to gift-of-prophecy levels of prediction, but accurately enough to provide an edge. Ben was at war, and in warfare, having an edge was everything.

Thanks to Lena, he knew that Dragan was as anxious to prove himself to Zarko Kožul as he was to offload the stolen Bach manuscript. Therefore, Ben could safely anticipate that Kožul would have been Dragan's very first port of call the instant he stepped on Serbian soil, offering the precious item to his would-be boss in the hopes of winning his favour.

Which led Ben to consider how Kožul might respond to Dragan's unusual pitch. If he was any kind of businessman, he would have protested and blustered and made a lot of noise about how this wasn't his marketplace, how am I supposed to flog this piece of crap, yadda yadda, then gone and started making enquiries anyway to find out whether the thing might be worth even just a few bucks. Any gangster worth his salt would have a well-developed network of fences and other criminal handlers through whom all manner of tainted goods could be filtered and converted into nice clean cash. The moment Kožul had possession of the manuscript, he'd be on the phone. Soon afterwards, the word would be spreading to any number of black market connections. It would all have happened fast. A man like Kožul would expect rapid results.

So Ben had decided on the play. He could describe the manuscript accurately enough and – thanks to Nick Hawthorne – had picked up enough scraps of knowledge about its background to be able to pass himself off as expert, at least to the likes of Kožul. If he could talk his way into a meeting masquerading as an interested cash buyer, and if Kožul took the bait, that gave Ben the means to penetrate his defences. Even the thickest armour always had a soft underbelly, if you knew where to look.

Once he was inside, the plan would dissolve into total improvisation. A lot could go wrong. The most obvious of which was that Dragan might be present when Ben turned up at Kožul's headquarters, or Lena, or both, which would send things instantly south as Ben was recognised. Worst-case scenario, the fight would break out within moments of his arrival. Best case, it was still a hairy and reckless proposition, with many unknown factors of which the quality of his backup was one of the most concerning. He would be walking in there unarmed, which was even less comfort.

But Ben had gone into less favourable situations in his time, and he was still breathing. He'd still be breathing when the dust settled after this one. So he kept telling himself – but the strange feeling of dread that he'd felt at the airport was still there, like a sour taste at the back of his mouth that wouldn't fade away.

While Ben worked on his game plan, Husein Osmanović was busy assembling enough stacks of cash to pack tightly inside the Samsonite case in place of the heroin and sugar. Nidal went off in search of food and returned with a sack of hamburgers and fries, which the four men consumed in the silence of the warehouse and washed down with Coke. Ben smoked and said nothing to anyone.

Finally, as midnight approached, it was time. Osmanović and his men gathered up their chosen weapons and the four of them walked out into the cold night and piled into the Mercedes, Ben in the front passenger seat with the case at his feet, Nidal and Duša in the back. Osmanović drove across the lit nightscape of Belgrade to a quiet, dirty street a block away from the Rakia nightclub.

Osmanović killed the lights and the engine. The pulsing thump of the dance music could be heard even from here. Ben turned to address the two surly, shadowy faces in the back. 'Everyone knows the drill. I go first, the rest of you split up and slip inside one at a time. Be ready to act on my signal the moment things kick off. I'll be relying on you, okay? Let me down, and I swear I'll shoot you myself.'

The surly faces nodded. Osmanović clapped a hand on Ben's shoulder. 'We will not let you down.'

Ben lit a Gauloise. There was a big, empty space behind his right hip where there should have been a fully-loaded Glock nestling in his belt. Feeling naked and unsettled, he grabbed the case, kicked open the car door and began walking towards the nightclub.

As Ben got closer to the Rakia, he craned his neck upwards to see if Kožul's helicopter was visible on the roof, but the angle was too steep. If they'd had an extra man available, Ben would have posted him on top of the Despot Stefan Tower with a two-way radio to report on any comings and goings. But they were short of manpower as it was.

A street lamp across from the nightclub was flickering. The shadows seemed to contain all kinds of hidden menace. Ben watched the red light spilling out of the Rakia's main entrance doorway like a fiery glow from the gates of hell. The ear-numbing nightmare primal cacophony coming from inside sounded like hell, too. He didn't think Johann Sebastian Bach would have approved. Miles Davis would probably have just pulled out a revolver and shot the degenerate responsible. Miles was Ben's kind of musician that way.

A hundred young males and females thronged around the building, eager to press their way inside past the heavy security. Ben wondered whether all these people really didn't have anything better to do with themselves. He pushed through the crowd. As he'd expected, a bouncer intercepted him before he reached the door. The guy was seven feet tall and all in black, with a beard like a forest and arms like the steel girders on a battleship. Maybe the demons of hell looked like he did, too. He held up a hand the size of a catcher's mitt in Ben's face.

'Ticket.' The big man's voice was about three octaves lower than normal. Genetic freak.

'This is my ticket,' Ben said, and showed him the case. 'I'm here to do business with Zarko Kožul. I'd let me in.'

The big man regarded him with hostility, then ushered him inside with a nod to a pair of other bouncers, just as large, who stepped up and closely flanked Ben as he was led through the wall-shaking noise and flashing lights to a door with a sign that said PRIVATNI. He could have broken their necks without too much effort, but that might spoil the timing of his plan.

Forest-beard opened a door and guided Ben into a small office. 'Who the fuck wants to see Zarko?' Even with the closed door muffling the din from outside, the guy still had to shout. His beard quivered when he spoke, as if there were things living inside the tangled mass.

'The name's Richter,' Ben shouted back. 'Lutz Richter.'

Speaking Serbian with an Austrian accent was hard, but the muted pounding of the music covered up his bad intonation. 'The word on the street is, your man upstairs has something to sell. I'm buying.' He pointed at the case.

The word on the street. Why did shady crooks always get the worst lines?

They made Ben open the case and lift out its contents, then frisked him carefully. When they were satisfied that he wasn't carrying any guns or bombs, they allowed him to cram the money back inside the case and close the lid. 'Happy?' he yelled to Forest-beard. 'Now lead the way, big boy.'

The big guy said something to the others that Ben didn't hear, then left the room. He was gone five minutes, during which time seven hundred pounds of flesh, very little of which consisted of cerebral matter, stood guard over their charge. Ben contemplated the pros and cons of bashing their heads together to see what was inside. Same bad timing.

Then the beard was back. He nodded to the others and motioned to Ben as if to say, 'Let's go.' Evidently the green light had been given from upstairs.

Point of no return. Whatever was to happen up there, Ben was committed now.

Zarko Kožul's men led him deeper inside the building. Rounding a corner, Ben realised that the strange vibration he could feel thrumming through the walls and underfoot was coming from a paternoster lift. 'If I'd known we were going on a fairground ride, I'd have bought candyfloss.'

They got on, which was like boarding a moving tram, only vertically, and a harder task for Ben's oversized and less-than-nimble escorts than it was for him. Mistime it and you might lose a leg or an arm, or get crushed between the rising platform and the access doorway, but what was that to hard guys like Kožul's hand-picked gorillas? The wooden platform creaked and groaned on its perpetual loop. There was another platform about ten feet above, and Ben supposed there would be another ten feet below, all daisy-chained together. Round and round, all day long. Serving fresh victims up to Zarko Kožul and bringing down the remains for the gorillas to cart away and bury in a lime pit somewhere.

As they juddered their way up through the floors, Ben was mentally rehearsing what he would say when he found himself face to face with the crime boss. He'd be winging it all the way and everything depended on how he was received. If it turned nasty, he planned on killing Kožul first and then going looking for Dragan Vuković. If it went well, he planned on killing Kožul first and then going looking for Dragan Vuković.

They stepped off the paternoster at the top of the building, into a dingy narrow passage with badly whitewashed walls and old floorboards that were slick and shiny from decades of dirt and grease. Ahead, the passage led past a set of doors, behind one of which Ben presumed was Kožul's office suite Osmanović had described. The passage was barred by two more very large guards, both armed with tiny Czech-made Skorpion submachine guns that looked like toys in their hands. They halted him and insisted on frisking him a second time.

'They don't breed them for smarts where you come from, do they?' Ben said as they patted him down. 'You think I magicked up a ballistic missile on the way up here?'

'He's clean.'

By now, Osmanović and his guys Nidal and Duša would be inside the nightclub downstairs. Ben pictured them working their way around the sides of the dance crowd, nervously fingering their concealed weapons, psyching themselves up for the action that might start exploding at any time. Perhaps wondering if any of them would leave this place alive tonight. In Osmanović's case, perhaps not caring that much whether he went down fighting, as long as he could take a hated enemy with him.

The beard juddered. 'This way.' At a door, one of the armed guards said, 'I'll take that,' and grabbed the case from Ben's hand, letting his submachine gun dangle from his shoulder as he clutched the case under his thick arm.

'Be careful,' Ben said. 'There's more cash inside that case than you'll ever make.'

The guard wasn't impressed. He motioned at the door. 'In there.'

Ben expected the door to lead into Zarko Kožul's office. Instead, behind it was a tiny, bare room with nothing in it but a wooden chair.

It wasn't a place for business transactions. It was a makeshift holding cell.

And that was when Ben realised he'd walked into a trap.

Chapter 40

A big hand shoved Ben into the tiny room. The door slammed, shutting out all light. He heard the clunk of a strong lock closing him in, and knew that there would be little point in trying to force his way out. The guards whose presence he could sense on the other side of the door would just shoot him through the wood.

The holding cell was little more than cupboard-sized, small enough to touch all four walls without moving his feet. No light switch. He sat in the chair and closed his eyes, letting his body relax, his mind drift and his breathing slow. Conserving energy. He would need it soon enough.

Ben could wait like that for hours, days, barely stirring, shutting out his thoughts, only vaguely aware of the passage of time. But fewer than ten minutes went by before he heard movement outside the door, voices, the scrape of the key. The door opened. He didn't blink at the sudden bright light.

The same massive guards stood outside the doorway, now boosted to half a dozen in number and armed with automatic weapons that were dwarfed in their bear-size paws. All identical Skorpions. Ben wondered whether Zarko Kožul favoured the weapon for its light weight, extreme portability and high cyclic rate of fire, or whether the name just gave him fond memories of his days with the paramilitary Serb Scorpions.

Along with the guards were two smaller men. One was a slender, dark and medium-tall man in his thirties, casually but smartly dressed in jeans and a white shirt, whom Ben had never seen before. One of the better-looking gangsters Ben had come across in his time. Nicely groomed and smelling of some kind of expensive, refined aftershave.

The other man was Osmanović's guy, Duša, the scraggy gaunt bald one. Duša just smelled of rank body odour, as always. He was standing with them as though he was totally at ease and belonged to their group. Which, as Ben now realised, he did.

It seemed that Husein had contacts a little deeper inside Zarko Kožul's organisation than Husein had thought, too.

Duša pointed. 'That's him. This bastard arrived in town just today. His name's Hope. He's working with Osmanović.'

'Thanks, Duša,' Ben said. 'You know, these guys hate a snitch even more than they hate their enemies. You should bear that in mind.'

The dark-haired man in the white shirt nodded, not taking his eyes off Ben. 'Zarko will be pleased with you, Duša. I'll let him know the tip-off was good and give him the all-clear to come back. Just as soon as we dispose of Osmanović and the other one. Where are they?'

Duša replied, 'Somewhere on the bottom floor. The plan was to split up and wait for the signal. We were meant to be backup. This one was gonna rub out Zarko and then go looking for Dragan Vuković. Got some beef with him, apparently, but don't ask me what. All I know is, he came over from England or someplace to find the guy.'

The dark one gazed dispassionately at Ben. The others all had the dead eyes of dull-witted footsoldiers who just did what they were told. This one had the spark in his eyes that indicated something substantially more was going on upstairs, to compensate for his lack of bulk. Ben made him for a higher-echelon member of Kožul's forces, a second- or third-in-command. It was a principle he'd noticed in the past. When it came to hardcore gang crime, rank tended to run in inverse proportion to physical size, on a scale with the big stupid ones at the bottom and the small vicious ones at the top. By that reckoning, Zarko Kožul himself was probably a midget.

'How interesting,' said the man in the white shirt. 'It seems Dragan must have made a greater impression in England than we thought. So you are this Ben Hope I've been hearing about.' He considered for a moment, then motioned to the big men behind him without looking round. 'Get everybody together. Find the other two and bring them to me, dead or alive, doesn't matter. Duša, you go with them.'

Forest-beard and two of the other large men instantly obeyed, clutching their weapons like toys in their beefy fists as they hurried off. Duša, the snitch, hustled away after them. Ben was left alone with the man in the white shirt and the remaining three hulks. A six-foot-six monster with a faded blue swastika tattoo in the centre of his forehead motioned towards Ben with his gun barrel and asked the one in the shirt, 'Hey, Alek, what do we do about this guy here?'

'Same thing we always do, you dimwit. Take him to the junkyard, shoot him and put him in the crusher.'

'So you're Alek,' Ben said. 'I'll make a note of that.'

Alek paused and looked at Ben with a faint smile. 'On second thoughts, let's not shoot him. Let me call Dragan, see if he's finished the little job Zarko gave him to do last night. I'm sure he'd love to help feed our cocky British friend here into the crusher alive and video him dying in indescribable agony as his guts pop out of his mouth and his eyeballs burst from their sockets like champagne corks. Zarko will be amused to watch that afterwards.'

Ben said, 'You people must be really stuck for entertainment around here.'

Alek's mouth downturned at the corners. 'Take this piece of trash out of my sight.'

Large hands grabbed Ben by the arms and he was hauled out of the tiny room. Fighting back wasn't much of an option, with three guns pointed at him and surprise not exactly on his side.

'Nice meeting you, Mr Hope,' Alek said. 'At our next encounter, you'll be as flat as a piece of roadkill.'

'I'll be seeing you again,' Ben said.

Alek chuckled and walked away, shaking his head in disbelief at this guy's attitude and taking out his phone to dial a number. Ben heard him say, 'Hey, Dragan. You still over at the yard? Don't go anywhere. I have a surprise for you.' Then he disappeared around a corner and was gone.

Now it was just Ben and the three hulks. The one with the swastika motioned back in the direction of the paternoster and grunted, 'That way. Keep your hands where I can see 'em. You so much as fart at me, I'll splatter your brains all over the wall.' He shoved Ben round to face the way he was pointing, and jabbed his gun into Ben's back. Ben put up his hands like a model prisoner and started walking slowly.

'I say we should just waste him now,' said one.

'You heard what Alek said.'

'I know what he said, I just don't like it, is all. This guy is bad news. I can smell it on'm like shit.'

'That's your own ass crack you can smell, Vladislav,' the other replied, and laughed like a hyena.

'Shut your holes,' said the one with the swastika. He

pressed his gun muzzle harder into Ben's back, steering him towards the right-hand paternoster shaft entrance, the side for down.

Ben could never understand why these thug types always seemed to like jamming their barrels into you. Maybe it was some Freudian thing. Or maybe they were just such terrible shots that they couldn't hit the target unless the weapon was physically in contact with it. Either way, it wasn't a good idea to get that close to your opponent.

That was a lesson of wisdom Ben had never needed to be taught. And it was one that someone was about to learn, the hard way.

Chapter 41

'Move it, English,' growled the big guy with the swastika.

Ben asked him, 'Would it help my case if I told you I was only half English?'

'I'm so gonna enjoy watching you get squished.'

They were almost at the head of the paternoster shaft. With each step Ben could feel the vibrations thrumming through the old floorboards more strongly. The hidden mechanism that kept the rising and falling lift platforms on a perpetual loop was juddering and thrashing away in the background, drive belts slapping, pulleys turning, cables creaking. Like a giant industrial meat grinder or some kind of fiendish mangle that could chew you up and spit out the bones.

Ben let his step falter as they got close, and the big guy bumped into him from behind. That much mass took more effort to stop. Momentum that could be used in all kinds of ways.

Ben put an elbow in his left upper abdomen, hard enough to rupture the spleen and too fast for anyone to react. Then the big man was sprawling towards the shaft mouth and tumbling over onto his face, crying out in pain and surprise and fear all at once as he went sliding on his belly over the greasy floorboards, scrabbling desperately to halt himself.

His head and shoulders went into the open shaft, poking in between the platform that had just come rumbling past and the next one rumbling down ten feet behind it. A lightweight, nimble man might have been able to get out of the way in time, but this guy stood no chance. He saw it coming and knew what was about to happen. A shriek burst out of his mouth and was cut short.

Ben turned away, not because he was squeamish at the sight of a man getting his head squashed like a ripe pumpkin, but because the Skorpion submachine gun that had been poking in his back a second ago was now in his hands and he was swinging around to open fire on the swastika guy's two astonished comrades before they hit their triggers first. He mowed them down left to right with a sweep of full-auto fire that filled the narrow passage with deafening thunder. They crumpled without a sound or a shot fired, and their bodies collapsed in a mountain of flesh with their weapons under them.

Smoke oozed from the muzzle of the Skorpion in Ben's hands. He turned back towards the paternoster. It was making all kinds of different sounds now as the mechanism had suddenly jammed up solid. The part of the swastika guy's body that wasn't snarled up between the underside of the descending platform and the lower edge of the shaft entrance was convulsing in its death throes on the greasy boards. The old machinery didn't have the power to shear through that much flesh and bone. Hidden driveshafts and pulleys were clattering and banging and rattling as if the whole contraption might explode at any second.

'More than one way to get squished,' Ben said.

A sound behind him made him wheel around. Alek had heard the shots and was racing to the scene with a gun of his own. The AKM assault rifle was much, much louder in the confined space. It was also much more powerful. Ben threw himself down and rolled behind the heap of the two dead guards to use them as cover, like sandbags.

Alek opened fire. Ben felt the impacts slamming into the heavy flesh of the dead men, and the little wet splashes on his face as their blood spattered him. Their bulk might absorb most of the rounds, but an unlucky bullet could easily carve its way out the other side and find a path to Ben. Not a good place to be. He pointed the Skorpion up over the top of the mound and rattled off another burst without looking to see where he was shooting. That was enough to drive Alek back down the passage. It was also enough to empty the Skorpion's magazine. The perennial problem with these greedy little machine pistols was keeping the damn things fed.

Alek was back an instant later and hosing bullets down the corridor. Ben had the unpleasant realisation that he was no longer fighting Dragan Vuković's morons. He couldn't get to the dead guards' weapons because they were buried under a ton of bullet-riddled meat. It was time to get out of here.

There was a sudden pause in the gunfire as Alek ejected the empty mag from his smoking assault rifle and slammed in another one. Ben used the brief lull to roll out of cover. The paternoster would have been the perfect escape route, but now it was blocked solid and making terminal noises. He saw a door and crashed through it, with no idea what was on the other side and no time to worry about it.

He found himself running blind into a storeroom stacked full of drinks crates. The only light in the room was filtering through the grime-filmed windows from the Rakia's blood-red neon sign outside. By the same light, Ben could see the silhouette of the iron fire escape the other side of the glass, bolted to the outside of the building.

Behind him, Alek was bursting into the room waving the AKM. Ben shoulder-slammed the window and his leather jacket saved him from being badly cut as the glass burst out in an explosion of shards. Bullets punched through the window frame an inch from his head. He dived through the shattered hole and latched onto the rough, rusted steel of the fire escape and he began to race downwards. The fire escape zigzagged down the side of the building with a plate-steel landing every twenty feet. Ben was two steps from the first landing down when Alek appeared at the window above and let off a rattle of shots that cracked out into the cold night air. The bullets kicked sparks off the fire escape. As Ben darted out of sight and hit the iron landing with a clang, he saw Alek take out a radio handset and start yelling orders into it.

The fire escape landing had a service door leading back inside the building. Ben booted it hard and it burst inwards. He ran through it, vaulted some garbage sacks near the entrance, sprinted for an internal door and wrenched that one open. The heat and noise of the nightclub hit him like a slap, even though he was still only one floor closer to the riot happening on the ground.

Over the beat of the music, he could hear screams and gunfire. He was pretty sure that was an unusual sound, even on a typical night at the Rakia. Now he knew the answer to the question he'd been asking himself, whether the shooting on the top floor would have been audible down below. It was. What he was hearing was Osmanović reacting to what he must have taken to be Ben's signal. The plan was coming apart even faster than Ben had feared.

Ben muttered, 'Shit.' He ran on, tried a door that opened into a stinking toilet, tried another and found that it led to a bare-brick stairwell going down. He raced down the stairs three at a time, heading towards the chaos below. The gunfire down there seemed to have stopped, but he could still hear plenty of screaming. Maybe Osmanović and Nidal had realised the plan had gone south and fled the building. Or maybe they were already dead.

As he rounded a corner between floors a stairwell door flew open and Ben found himself staring face to face at the big man he'd first encountered outside in the street. The one with the forest beard and steel girder arms. At the sight of Ben a look of puzzlement flashed over his hairy face, then quickly turned to fury. He was carrying a Skorpion subgun identical to the one Ben had used upstairs, except this one was still loaded. He wrestled it off his shoulder and pointed it Ben's way, an operation that took half a second longer than it took Ben to spin a roundhouse kick that caught his right forearm and sent the weapon clattering down the stairwell.

The kick should have broken his arm, too, but the giant just scowled.

Ben backed away a step, like stepping away from a tall building to be able to see all of it. This wasn't someone he would have chosen to get into unarmed combat with.

But you seldom got a choice in these matters.

Chapter 42

The big man charged. A fist as large and hard as a frozen turkey launched towards Ben with about three hundred and fifty pounds of muscle behind it. Enough thrust to knock a man's head off his shoulders. But slow. Ben could have sauntered over to the bar and waited in line to get himself a whisky in the time the punch took to get within three inches of his face; then he twisted easily out of its path and rolled the blow right past him. The fist connected with the bare brick of the stairwell wall with a crack like a rifle shot. Brick and masonry dust sprinkled the steps.

The big man gave a howl. Encouraging to know the creature could feel pain. Ben drove a kick into the barrel of his ribcage and felt a couple of ribs give under the impact. The big man staggered, but didn't go down. He came at Ben again with pincer hands grasping for his throat, to throttle the air out of him and maybe tear his head off as well. Ben bent his knees and ducked low, then drove up again and forwards with all the force in his legs and rammed the crown of his skull into the big man's stomach. The big man tottered further back this time, right to the edge of the flight of steps going downwards. He windmilled his arms for balance, but it was like trying to stop a falling tree. He went swaying backwards over the edge. As he fell, a massive claw hand flailed out in desperation for something to grab onto, and found Ben's sleeve.

The two of them tumbled down the concrete steps. The guard landed heavily on his back with a wheezing grunt and Ben landed on top of him and rode him like a toboggan to the landing below. His opponent was badly winded now, all the air driven out of his lungs by the sledgehammer blow to his back. Marquess of Queensberry rules would probably have dictated that Ben shouldn't take unfair advantage of the situation, and instead let him have a moment to catch his breath before they resumed.

Except Ben wasn't playing by those rules. He got to his feet and kicked the guy hard under the chin to push his head back and expose the curve of his larynx. Then stamped his heel down hard to collapse his throat. The biggest, meanest creature on earth was nothing if it couldn't draw air any more. Hit a man hard enough in the throat, and even a single blow can kill him instantly. Ben didn't settle for once. He stamped four times, until he was certain the job was done.

The big man's weapon was lying on the dusty concrete a few steps below. Ben snatched it up and raced onwards to the ground floor. He was halfway down the final stairway when he heard the gunfire resume, and realised that at least one of his backup team was still in the game.

Ben crashed through the doorway at the bottom of the backstairs and found himself on the edge of the nightclub dance floor. It was deserted, apart from the dead bodies littered over the floor and the men shooting at one another and the last of the punters running in terror from the scene. The strobing of the lights made everything look like stop-frame animation. The noise of the music was ear rending. The staccato rattle of full-auto gunfire was louder. In a matter of minutes, the Rakia had reverted back to its original purpose as a slaughterhouse.

A long, glitzy bar covered in mirrors stretched the whole length of the far wall. Husein Osmanović was backed up against it. White muzzle flash was erupting from the barrel of his weapon as he sent a burst left, a burst right, and took down another of Zarko Kožul's men who were entrenched behind some overturned tables across the room. From his angle, Ben could get a better shot at them. He opened fire with the Skorpion. The stream of spent brass arcing out of the ejector port looked like a shower of gold in the light. The overturned tables became colanders as Ben's bullets punched through them. Two more of Kožul's men went down.

Ben couldn't see Nidal, until he recognised one of the bodies lying a few steps from Osmanović near the bar. Osmanović fired another burst towards the tables, but the survivors there had had enough and were scurrying back in retreat. Ben caught Osmanović's eye across the room. The Bosniak signalled to Ben. He was grinning wildly from ear to ear, manic with the adrenalin of battle. Maybe he was thinking their mission had been successful, that his money had been well spent, and Zarko Kožul was lying dead somewhere upstairs.

Ben knew he was going to disappoint him on all counts.

Suddenly, more gunfire was erupting from another direction, and Ben whirled round to see a whole contingent of the enemy appear from a doorway to the left. Someone yelled in Serbian, 'Kill them!'

Ben whipped behind a corner as bullets smacked off the wall next to him. Osmanović went to scramble over the top of the bar for cover. He was halfway there when Ben saw him twist and fall back to the floor. Ben pointed his Skorpion around the corner, returned fire at the man who'd shot

Osmanović, and the shooter crumpled and fell. Ben's gun was already half empty and he thought *fuck it* and rattled the rest of the mag off at the incoming enemy, taking down a couple more and driving the rest back through the doorway they'd emerged through.

He looked over at where Osmanović lay under the strobing light. Not moving. Always a bad sign.

Ben broke from cover and ran across the dance floor. He jumped over one large body, and Nidal's smaller one, and reached Osmanović. He crouched beside him and rolled him over. Blood was bubbling at both corners of the Bosniak's mouth, staining his grey beard purple-black under the lights. He was struggling to breathe. Ben tried to help him sit up, but nothing could help that he'd been shot through the lungs. He'd been lucky once; now his luck was out. He rolled his bulging eyes up at Ben and rasped, 'Tell me . . . tell me we got that bastard.'

'Yeah, we got him,' Ben said. 'Everything went according to plan. You can rest easy now.'

A big part of Husein Osmanović had already died years ago, after the things that had happened in that damned war. Now the rest of him slipped away in Ben's arms with a smile on his bloody lips. Sometimes a lie is the kindest thing you can say to a person. Ben felt the life go out of him, and lowered Osmanović's body to the floor.

He and the dead were no longer alone. Ben looked up at the semicircle of Kožul's big men who had gathered round, peering down at him through their gunsights. He rose slowly to his feet, and the gun barrels rose with him. Too many to fight. More were coming.

Ben put up his hands.

The dark man Ben knew as Alek came storming over, glancing around at the bodies and the wreckage of the nightclub. Duša followed in Alek's wake. He barely looked at the bodies of his former associates Nidal and Osmanović, and instead gave Ben a lopsided 'ha ha, you lose' kind of leer.

Alek wasn't sharing in the snitch's amusement. 'Three men!' he was yelling, gesticulating in anger. 'Three men did this! And that's with a tip-off. What if we hadn't known it was coming?'

'Zarko is going to love you,' Ben said to Alek. 'He'll be so pleased, he'll probably give you a promotion. New house, new car, maybe an enhanced dental plan.'

'You're done, English.' Alek snapped his fingers at his men, as if they were dogs. 'Let's go. Move, move.'

They grabbed Ben by the arms and he was marched roughly outside with guns stabbing at his back. The night sky above New Belgrade was starless and cold, a ghostly mist rising up from the river and shrouding itself over the city. The street lamp opposite the Rakia that had been flickering earlier had now expired and was standing surrounded by a pool of dark shadow. By now the street was almost completely deserted, only a few stragglers from the Rakia still making their hasty exit from the scene. A distraught woman with ruffled-up hair, smeared makeup and a torn dress hanging off her shoulder was staggering about alone in the street, half hysterical and crying out 'Miloje! Miloje!' over and over; but Miloje was either already long gone or he was among the collateral damage still inside, part of the mess that Alek was going to have to clear up before Zarko returned.

First, though, Alek had other business on his mind. He led the way from the building and down the street towards a waiting black minivan. Ben's guards followed, hustling their captive along at gunpoint. Ben supposed the minivan was his ride to the junkyard, where his promised fate awaited him.

Alek was still wearing the white shirt, with no jacket, and he was rubbing his hands and slapping his sides as the chill of the night air quickly got to him. As he walked closer to the black minivan he paused and danced from foot to foot as though undecided about something, then seemed to make his mind up and turned to face his men.

'To hell with this,' he complained bitterly. 'I'm damned if I'm driving all the way to the junkyard and freezing my ass off waiting for Dragan to turn up.' He turned and pointed at Duša, then turned the pointing finger Ben's way. 'Change of plan. Duša, cap this motherfucker right here and put his miserable carcass in the river.'

Duša appeared only too happy to perform the service. After all the good work he'd have done for Zarko Kožul tonight, he was sure to be handsomely repaid. He stepped up to Ben and pointed his gun. The men holding Ben quickly stepped out of harm's way.

Ben said to Duša, 'Remember what I said happens to snitches.'

'Not before it happens to you, moron.'

Duša raised his weapon and was about to fire, then hesitated and came another step closer. This was his big moment and he didn't want to foul it up by missing the mark.

If the snitch came one step closer, Ben intended on grabbing the weapon from him and braining him with it. He'd still get shot anyway, but at least he could go out knowing he'd lobotomised this little bastard.

Duša halted. His eyes were gleaming under the street lamps. He was grinning from ear to ear. He took careful aim, as though he were a sniper preparing to engage a target a thousand metres distant and not a cheap thug about to execute an unarmed prisoner five steps away.

What happened next all took place within the space of a

280

second. Duša's eyes suddenly darted downwards as a strange glowing green dot of light, the size of a beetle, appeared on his chest. The gun faltered in his grip as he stared at the hovering dot for a moment and the grin quickly evaporated from his face. Then he dropped the gun and started frantically brushing and swatting at the green dot, as though it were a bee attacking him.

The dot abruptly fell to the level of his knees.

The sharp crack of a pistol shot sounded from across the street.

Chapter 43

Duša let out a screech and instantly hit the ground. In the same instant, more pistol shots were popping out of the darkness. Alek darted towards the black minivan while the rest of the men scattered. Duša was screaming and writhing on the ground, clutching his shattered right kneecap. A second later, one of the big guys gave a loud yell as his left shin exploded in a spray of blood and he, too, went down.

Ben alone had realised that the green laser sight was pointing from the pool of darkness beneath the dead street lamp opposite. Now the dark-clad shooter stepped from the shadows, holding the pistol in both hands and firing in a steady, rapid stream. The side window of the minivan burst apart, the shot narrowly missing Alek as he ducked down for cover. Without a split-second's hesitation the shooter swivelled the pistol back round towards the heavies, chased them with the green laser dot and kept firing. A third one had his leg shot out from under him as he tried to escape.

Ben stared at the shooter. He couldn't understand why the guy wasn't shooting to kill. Maybe he was a cop; whatever the case, the speed and precision of his surprise attack was the mark of a trained professional.

Then the shooter moved further out of the shadows and Ben saw that he was wrong.

The shooter was a woman. She was wearing a black leather biker jacket and had her dark hair scraped back in an unruly ponytail under a black baseball cap. Ben had no idea who she was, only that at this moment she was his best friend in the world.

Not all of Kožul's men were scattering for cover. A porker with a screaming skull tattooed on one cheekbone raised his Skorpion and was about to return fire at the woman, when Ben dived for Duša's fallen weapon, kicked Duša out of the way, and double-tapped the skull guy in the chest and head before he had time to pull the trigger. Duša's face was contorted in agony and he was trying to get up. Ben saw his hand go to his belt and start drawing out the heavy Colt Magnum that was stuck through it. Ben shot him once through the heart and once more between the eyes, so fast the two shots sounded almost like one. He would have preferred to make the moment linger, but you couldn't have everything.

The black minivan started up and took off with a screech of tyres. Ben popped off four shots at its rear, but he was worried about bullets going through the windows of background buildings. He wheeled round to engage any more threats, and saw there were none left. Kožul's injured were lying about the pavement, groaning and clutching their wounded limbs. The rest had fled.

Ben turned to the woman. 'Who the hell are you?' he asked in Serbian.

The woman seemed not to understand what he was saying. Now it was his turn to have the little green laser dot hovering over his body as she pointed the pistol at him. Her eyes were hard. They flicked to the Skorpion in his hand.

'DROP IT!' Speaking English.

And Ben's second surprise that evening was that she

283

wasn't Serbian, which also meant she couldn't be a local cop. She was American. New York, by her accent, but the regional phonology of her speech was a detail Ben could think about later. Right now, she was burning with energy from the gunfight and ready to take him down next.

'I SAID DROP IT, MISTER!' She wagged the pistol towards the ground. The universal sign language for 'put down your weapon right now or I will shoot you'.

Ben's choice was either to shoot first, which he didn't want to do, or get shot himself, which didn't appeal to him either, or drop his gun. He dropped his gun.

'Who are you?' he repeated, in English this time.

She frowned at him over the gunsights, picking up his accent the same way he had hers, and just as surprised as he was.

'I thought you were police,' Ben said.

She gave a snort. 'Funny, I thought the same about those guys until I saw they were about to plug you. I couldn't let that happen.'

'Appreciated. If you don't mind I'll express my gratitude later. First, we need to get out of here. Have you got a car?'

'Forget it, buddy. This is not a rescue mission for your Limey ass. You're on your own, whoever you are.'

He was about to reply when they both heard the urgent revving of a vehicle approaching at high speed. Its lights appeared around the corner of the street. The black minivan was back, and it seemed that Alek had picked up some reinforcements. Two men were hanging out of the side windows with submachine guns, and they'd be within effective range in about three seconds.

'No time to argue,' Ben said.

'Yeah, I think you're right.'

They broke into a sprint just as the gunfire erupted from

the oncoming minivan. The woman ran around a corner, Ben right behind her. Their racing footsteps and the roar of the chasing vehicle echoed off the walls of the narrow street. The smell of the nearby river was strong.

A beige Skoda Octavia sedan was parked up ahead. The woman blipped the locks as they ran towards it. She piled into the driver's seat and Ben clambered into the passenger side. The engine burst into life and she took off with a wail of spinning tyres, the rear end of the car sliding all over the road. Bullets punched out the back windows and the side mirror.

Now the chase was on. The Octavia skidded around another corner and onto a long illuminated stretch that ran alongside the river. The black minivan was right behind them. Ben twisted around and glimpsed Alek at the wheel, his face obscured by the riverside lights flashing over the windscreen. His two men hanging out the open windows left and right were rattling off bursts from their Skorpions. Most were going wide, but some weren't. The Octavia was getting badly riddled from the rear.

'Damn it, I don't know these streets!' the woman yelled. She had the pistol cradled in her lap as she drove. Ben said, 'May I?' and snatched it. She was too distracted to stop him.

He pressed through the gap between the front seats, keeping low. The pistol was a Beretta 98 with a nineteen-round capacity. He checked the magazine and found only two cartridges left. 'You have a spare mag?'

'Sorry, I forgot to ask the moron I took it off back there if he had any,' she shouted back at him.

'Touchy,' Ben muttered.

Fine. Then he'd have to make do with two rounds.

Chapter 44

Ben fired out of the shattered rear screen. The guy hanging out of the minivan's left side dropped his weapon and went limp, dangling from the window like an empty sack. The van began to swerve all over the road. Ben took careful aim at his moving target and snapped off another shot. The guy on the right threw up his arms and sprayed blood from his mouth and slithered back inside the minivan. Two for two.

The minivan faltered and began to slow. Alek couldn't know that Ben was all out of ammunition. The power of the bluff.

Now the Octavia was quickly lengthening its lead over their pursuers as the woman sped along the banks of the Sava River. Ben clambered back into the front seat and replaced the empty Beretta on her lap. 'Thanks.'

She glanced at him but said nothing and concentrated on her driving. Which she could do with as much skill as the way she handled a pistol. At the end of the riverside drag she swerved up a side street without losing an ounce of speed, and hammered up onto a main avenue that led into slow-moving traffic through the city. She carved through the traffic as though it were standing still.

'We might want to slow down a little,' Ben suggested. The woman went faster.

Finally, she swerved into the car park of an all-night Maxi supermarket and killed the engine. She slipped the empty pistol into the side pocket of her leather jacket and zipped it shut, then flung the driver's door open and stepped out to frown at what was left of the Octavia's rear end. Ben joined her.

Aside from the shattered back windscreen and side mirror, maybe sixty or seventy bullets had perforated the bodywork. Not the kind of damage that could easily be hidden, or patched with a little filler putty and a lick of touch-up paint.

'Crap,' she breathed. 'This was a rental. Hertz are gonna kill me.'

'Story of my life,' Ben said. 'Believe me, I've been there. But speaking of life stories, maybe it's time we went on with the "who the hell are you?" thing.'

She looked at him. 'Fine by me. But seeing as you owe me for stepping in back there, you can go first. Quid pro quo.'

'Fair enough. What do you want me to tell you?'

'Whatever there is, mister. I'm not in the habit of picking up strangers.'

He shrugged. 'I'm Ben Hope. I'm five feet and eleven inches tall and I'm a Sagittarius. I know that's important to you Americans.'

'Kiss my ass. Keep going.'

'I was born a few years before you, and raised in England, but my mother was Irish. I spent a while in the British Army, now I live in France. I'm here to attend to an unresolved personal matter between myself and a man named Dragan Vuković, an associate of one Zarko Kožul, who as you possibly know is the proprietor of the nightclub back there. Is that enough detail for you?'

'Army, huh? Is that where you learned to shoot like that?'

'It appears you're no slouch yourself.'

The corner of her mouth gave a twitch that could have grown into a smile, but didn't. She cocked an eyebrow, looking at him with a steady, penetrating gaze. 'And by "unresolved personal matter" I take it we're talking about the kind that means these folks don't like you very much?'

'I'd feel the same way, in their shoes. If I wore that kind of shoe.'

'And they'd really rather you weren't around any more.'

'I'd say their intentions were fairly clear.'

She narrowed her eyes at him and pursed her lips, thinking. 'So what are you, a collector for the mob? Zarko and his guy welch on a deal and someone sent you here to take names and break bones? I've known a few guys with your background who wound up doing that kind of work.'

Ben hated talking about his personal affairs, but under the circumstances he could understand why she needed to know more. He replied, 'That's not who I am. Dragan Vuković stole something from a friend of mine, in England. While he was at it, he threw my friend out of a top-floor window that happened to have iron spikes below.'

'That doesn't sound so nice.'

'Vuković isn't such a nice person. Now he's here in Belgrade, and he's passed what he stole to Zarko Kožul.'

'And you're here to get it back?'

'It's more a matter of principle,' Ben said. 'The stolen item itself is of no real interest to me.'

'So we can't be talking about money.'

'This isn't a business thing. I told you, I'm not in that line of work.'

'I see. So what line of work are you in?'

'I help people,' Ben said. 'Or try to. This time round, I didn't do such a great job. I need to make that right.'

'Help people?'

'When innocent people are in trouble, when they have a fight that they can't fight on their own, when things get bad.'

'You're there for them. How noble. Like the Equalizer. Chasing down the bad guys, and chewing up a bunch of rental cars in the process?'

'You make it sound more glamorous than it really is.'

She paused, still eyeing him, still weighing up her thoughts. 'That big douche back there with the skull tattoo would've shot me if you hadn't got him first. And you had the chance to use that Beretta on me in the car if you'd wanted. All things considered, I might be prepared to take a wild risk and venture to assume you're one of the good guys.'

'Assume nothing,' Ben said. 'You have my word.'

'Your word.'

'Yes. And now it's your turn to tell me who you are and what this is all about.'

The woman looked at him a little longer, then reached up and took off her baseball cap and yanked the elastic from her ponytail. Glossy black gypsy ringlets tumbled down over her shoulders. She brushed a few curls from her face, and glanced over at the lit-up frontage and windows of the supermarket. 'I see a cafeteria in there. I haven't eaten a bite since I landed. I'm lagged as hell and my body clock doesn't know if it's coming or going. What do you say to a late-night snack and a cup of coffee with me, Mister Ben Hope?'

Ben said, 'Lead the way.'

They walked inside the brightly-lit supermarket cafeteria, where the smells of stewed coffee and cheap food hung in the air and a few customers sat about with that hangdog late-night look about them. Nobody glanced up as the two of them came in and sat face to face at a generic Formica table by the window.

The woman scanned the greasy plastic menu card on the table, pulled a face and said, 'Now it comes to it, suddenly I'm not that hungry.'

'Your countrymen invented this kind of food,' Ben said.

'Doesn't mean we have to eat it.'

A droopy, limp-looking waitress came and took the order. Two coffees, black, and a cheeseburger for Ben. When it arrived, it looked as droopy and limp as the waitress did. Ben bit into it. Six thousand years of Serbian history and culture and here he was eating the same plastic food you'd find anywhere else on earth. The coffee was as stale as it smelled, but it was hot and strong. Just what you needed when your evening could have ended inside a crusher.

'Don't look now,' the woman said. 'I think your burger has a severed human ear in it.'

Ben kept munching. 'First rule of soldiering, eat when you can, sleep when you can.'

'So you're going to go to sleep on me now?'

'No, I'm going to listen to your story now. Start talking.'

She sat with her elbows planted on the table and the steaming coffee cup in both hands. She had draped her black leather biker jacket over the back of her plastic chair. It was hanging heavily with the weight of the Beretta in the zippered pocket, but the cafeteria staff and clientele were too faded to get jumpy about it, even if anyone had noticed. Underneath the jacket the woman was wearing a black T-shirt. Her arms were toned, and her hands were slim and small, but strong. No rings or bracelets. She had an easy way about her, like a relaxed athlete. If the evening's excitement had left her in any way stressed or shaken, she wasn't showing it.

'Okay. My name is Cahill, Madison Cahill. I am, as you

have noticed, from the United States. And as you may also have gathered, I'm not here as a tourist. I'm here for the same kind of reason you are. Personal business.'

'With Zarko Kožul's people?'

'Small world, ain't it?' Her mouth gave that nearly-smile twitch again. 'Kožul is a bad guy, what I hear. And chasing bad guys is what I do for a living. Like you.'

Ben swallowed down the last of his burger and wondered whether his first impression of her being a cop might have been correct after all. 'FBI agents don't go moonlighting on personal business. Not halfway across the world, all alone, no backup.'

'Who said I was a Fibbie? I wouldn't go near that. Not a team player. I work alone.' Madison reached behind her, took a black leather wallet from the pocket of her jacket, and skimmed it onto the tabletop between them.

He picked it up and looked at the seven-pointed gold star badge. At its heart was an American bald eagle, and around the eagle was a blue circle with gold lettering that sparkled under the neon light and said SPECIAL AGENT – BAIL ENFORCEMENT – FUGITIVE RECOVERY.

'An American bounty hunter in Belgrade,' he said. 'What happened, did one of your chickens get out of the pen on your watch and you have to catch it before anybody notices?'

Two little frown lines appeared above her nose and her eyes hardened. They'd been fairly hard to begin with. Now she looked dangerous. 'I don't like being called a bounty hunter.'

Ben put up his hands. 'I take it back.'

'And like I said, I'm here for personal reasons. I didn't exactly plan on things happening the way they did tonight. I don't know what I was expecting, if I'm honest. All I had was the name of the nightclub. I drove there straight from the airport, heard the shooting going on inside, figured something was wrong.' She shrugged. 'You know the rest.'

'If you're not here on agency business, where did the weapon come from?'

This time, the twitch did grow into a smile, but it was a nasty one. 'One of Kožul's boys was kind enough to let me have it. Another sucker for my feminine charms. He'll be okay in a couple of days. Might need to see a dentist, though.'

'But he still has both knees intact.'

'I guess he was just lucky.'

'They were all lucky,' Ben said. 'A one-legged man can still shoot back. It pays to put them down properly.'

'Call me sentimental, but I didn't want to kill anyone. Not off my own turf, not unless I had to. You, on the other hand, seem to have no such scruples.'

'Whatever gets the job done.'

'Like the chest-head double tap. They don't teach that in the regular army. Special Forces, right?'

Ben gave a grim smile. 'Aren't we the observant one?'

'I get paid to be smart. And I'm seldom wrong.'

'Maybe so. But I still don't get what kind of personal business brings a sweet young lady to a place like this.'

She paused, sipped coffee, then set her cup down and leaned back in her chair with her arms folded. 'Sweet. I like that. Sweet is good. Now, you said this guy Vuković took something from your friend and he needs to pay for what he did?'

Ben nodded.

'Same for me. From what I hear, this Zarko Kožul character is a crook like any other. He steals things he has no right to possess, and right now he has his hands on something that means a very great deal to me, and to someone I care for more than anyone in the world. At least, that's what I was told by Ulysses.'

'Who the hell is Ulysses? What are you talking about?'

Madison leaned forward again, and this time when she replied the coolness was gone from her voice and Ben saw anger flashing like summer lightning in her eyes.

'I'm talking about my father, the once-great Rigby Cahill, a broken-hearted, sad and lonely and wonderful old man who spent the best years of his life hunting for that goddamned music manuscript. How a piece of trash like this Kožul has got his hands on it, I don't know and I don't give a damn. What I do know is that I won't tolerate it. I aim to take it back from that sonofabitch, and I'll roll right over the top of anyone who tries to stop me.'

Chapter 45

Madison Cahill fell silent and looked away, her face flushing as though she thought she'd said too much.

Ben stared. 'What did you just say?'

She waved a hand, flustered. 'Forget it. It doesn't concern you. I don't think you'd be interested, anyway.'

Ben said, 'Try this on for size. Four pages, bound together with wax. Handwritten music stave, the ink slightly faded after more than two and a half centuries of changing hands from one place to another, and maybe not always as well cared for as it should have been. The signature of Johann Sebastian Bach at the top of the front page. On the bottom corner of the front page, a funny-shaped stain that some people seem to think is coffee. Personally, I have my doubts, and I'm not the only one who feels that way. Some people seem to think the manuscript is a fake, although I have my doubts about that as well, and I'm definitely not the only one who feels that way about that either. It was discovered in an old music shop in Prague last year. Bought cheap and taken to England as a novelty, from where it was recently stolen to order by a bunch of killers who reneged on their arrangement with the guy who hired them, and brought it here to Serbia.' Watching the change in her expression, he smiled. 'Does that sound like the kind of thing you're looking for?'

The colour had drained from Madison's face and now she was staring back at him with eyes so intense that they could have nailed him to the back wall. She opened and closed her mouth a couple of times and shook her head in disbelief. 'I . . . I don't—'

'I thought it might,' Ben said.

'Your friend—?'

'His name was Nick. He's the guy who found it in Prague and didn't think it was real. But someone else knew better.'

'Dragan Vuković—?'

'The guy who stole it. Who now works for Zarko Kožul, who now has the manuscript. Which you already knew, because someone called Ulysses tipped you off. Which is how you came to be here, and now I'm waiting to hear more. It seems you and I have a lot more in common than either of us realised.'

Madison's mouth was still hanging open in amazement and she had to struggle to regain her composure. 'Ulysses isn't his real name.'

'That's a big surprise.'

'He's a specialist in lost and stolen artifacts. A dealer, fence, call it what you like. He used to work with my father sometimes.'

'Your father, Rigby Cahill?'

Madison nodded. 'You haven't heard of him. But if you were in the antiquities world, you would have. My father was, is, one of the most legendary treasure hunters of the last fifty years.'

'Tell me about him.'

'It's a long story.'

'I don't have anything else to do tonight.'

They ordered more coffee. Ben lit a Gauloise. 'I don't think you can light up in here,' Madison said, pointing at the sign that said ZABRANJENO PUŠENJE.

Ben glanced over at the hunched shapes scattered about the rows of empty tables. 'I don't think anyone really cares what I do in here.'

'In that case, screw it. I'll join you.'

He offered her the pack of Gauloises and lit up for her with his Zippo. She took a couple of drags, then plucked the cigarette from her lips and stared at it. 'Jesus, these French smokes sure pack a wallop. What's in them, nitroglycerine?'

'If a thing's worth doing,' he said, 'it's worth overdoing.'

Madison smoked, and began to tell the rest of her story. Talking about her father made her face soften. She would pause now and again, and gaze sadly into space for a quiet moment before continuing. Ben listened, kept the Gauloises coming, and nobody came over to complain.

Rigby Ignatius Boddington Cahill had founded his company in New York in 1970, at the age of 40, following a successful but not sufficiently rewarding career as a scholar, dealer and valuer of all things antiquarian. Thanks in part to his vast knowledge of his subject, his new agency quickly gained a strong international reputation searching for – and in most cases locating – lost or stolen art treasures. He named the firm Cahill Associates even though from the get-go it had essentially been a one-man outfit.

'Dad was as famous for his energy as he was for his talent,' Madison said. 'He'd only have burned out anyone who tried to work alongside him, or driven them nuts.' She explained that then, like now, the police avoided getting too involved in stolen art and antiquities recovery cases, lacking the expertise and connections to pursue them effectively and preferring to leave such work to specialists, who functioned like private detectives and could make a lot of money by charging commission on the value of recovered goods.

And make money Cahill Associates did, in spades. Rigby's searches all over the world for lost art treasures seemed to draw him like a magnet, time and again and with uncanny precision, to the exact spot that others in his profession had consistently missed. He raked in generous commission for locating paintings stolen from museums and private collections. He tracked the often tortuous path of war plunder, a great deal of which had been looted by the Nazis before and during the Second World War and stashed away in all kinds of ingenious locations to keep it safe from Allied hands as the Third Reich crumbled in the latter years of the conflict. The sheer volume of what the Nazis had stolen during their twelve-year heyday between Hitler's rise in 1933 and his downfall in 1945 was mind-boggling. Rigby soon became known as a specialist Nazi-plunder hunter. Even accounting for the vast quantity recovered by the Allied forces' Monuments, Fine Arts and Archives Program after the peace, stashes of plundered gold bars, silver coins and ornaments, paintings, jewels, furniture, rare books, ceramics and sculptures, tapestries, and religious treasures taken by the Nazis were still turning up all over Europe.

Rigby didn't find all of it. One of his misses was the legendary Amber Room, the eighteenth-century wonder dismantled and removed from the Catherine Palace near St Petersburg during Germany's invasion of the Soviet Union. He smarted over that one, but not for long. In September 1974 he succeeded in locating one of several Nazi treasure trains reputed to exist, this particular one hidden underground in a collapsed tunnel deep in the heart of Poland and all eight of its carriages loaded to the roof with bullion, artwork and 1940s paper currency. The cargo's value was in excess of $50 million, of which Rigby walked away with an eye-watering thirty per cent.

'He could have retired young and lived like a king,' Madison said. 'Instead, he just ploughed the money straight back into expanding his operation into bigger and more ambitious ventures. He lost a packet trying to resurrect a sixteenth-century Portuguese treasure ship from the ocean bed off the coast of Sumatra, and squandered more millions hunting for Paititi, the Incan City of Gold. He never cared about wealth. Forget fast cars and palatial homes. Half the time he'd be going about with odd socks, holes in his clothes and just a few cents in his pockets, because he didn't give a damn about anything much except his work.'

She gave a wistful smile. 'I guess that explains why I came along so late. When I got older, my mom told me she hardly ever saw him during those years. He was like a force of nature, totally fixated on whatever was his goal at that time. Even after my mom died in 1991, when I was eleven, he just kept on working through his grief. I don't even know if he realised how sick she was, until it was too late.'

'A little one-track minded, perhaps,' Ben said.

'Raging obsessive would be more like it,' Madison said. 'Even to the point of total self-absorption. He could drive you crazy at times.'

'But you still love him.'

'Yes, I do. I bleed for him. When I see him now, I just want to cry. I'm ready to cry now, just talking about it.' As if to prove her point, a tear rolled from the corner of her left eye. She brushed it quickly away.

'What happened to him?' Ben asked.

'The Silbermann manuscript happened,' Madison said.

Chapter 46

Madison said, 'You know, I've been hearing this goddamn tale all my life. Never thought I'd find myself retelling it to a total stranger in an all-night café in the armpit of Belgrade.'

'We saved each other's lives tonight,' Ben said. 'That's about as closely connected as two strangers can get.'

In the spring of 1975, Rigby Cahill's New York offices received an unexpected call from a prospective new client by the name of Miriam Silbermann. She was fifty years old, currently resident in Zermatt, Switzerland, and a retired classical violinist of international repute, who in her prime had been favourably compared to contemporaries like Michèle Auclair and Patricia Travers. At the peak of her career she had toured with the New York Philharmonic and performed the Brahms Violin Concerto at Carnegie Hall, three times.

Rigby Cahill had just so happened to be in town on a rare trip home that week. As a lover of Brahms and patron of the NY Phil, he was excited at the prospect of meeting the famous violin virtuoso.

'But he could never have predicted what she was about to tell him,' Madison said. 'Even less the effect their meeting would have on his life forever afterwards.'

Miriam Silbermann travelled to New York City and first met with Rigby Cahill for lunch at the Russian Tea Room on West 57th Street, 23rd April 1975, the same day that President Gerald Ford declared an end to US military involvement in Vietnam. For Cahill, the day was no less momentous. At 50, five years his senior, Miriam Silbermann was still bewitchingly beautiful; many years later he would confess to his daughter that he hadn't been able to stop staring at her throughout lunch.

'I'll never forget what he told me,' Madison said, 'about the amazing quality she had in her eyes, a light so bright it would blind you to look into them for too long, and a pool of sadness so deep and dark you would be lost forever if you let it swallow you up. But what she had to tell him was even more amazing.'

Madison related that the Silbermanns had been living in France when, in July 1942, the Germans came knocking on their door to deport them.

'Silbermann is a Jewish name,' Ben said. 'The Nazis had been detaining French Jews since 1940, but April '42 was the start of the major round-ups and deportations. Something like thirteen thousand of them were scooped up within a couple of days and taken to the Drancy internment camp outside Paris.'

'That's the story she told Dad. She would have been about seventeen at the time, if I remember. Now, the Silbermanns were a musical kind of family, as you might guess from Miriam's later career. She spent a long time telling Dad all about her little brother Gabriel, who she said was this tremendously gifted pianist. Her father, Abel Silbermann, taught at the Paris Conservatoire for quite a few years, but then being Jewish got in the way of his career, thanks to the Nazi puppets who were running France by then. He was also a collector of all kinds of musical artifacts, I guess mostly a bunch of valuable old instruments. And also—'

'A certain Bach manuscript?' Ben already knew the answer.

Madison nodded. 'You got it. After all those years, she still remembered the name of the German commander of the soldiers who raided their home that day. I've heard Dad repeat it so often, it's branded on my memory too. He was SS Obersturmbannführer Horst Krebs. As it turns out, he was something of a musician himself. When he spotted the manuscript sitting on the Silbermanns' piano, he snatched it for himself.'

'And then?'

'Dad said Miriam Silbermann wouldn't talk much about what happened next. All I know is that the family never saw their home again after that day. They were taken and loaded into a truck with a bunch of other Jewish families, and imprisoned. The house was commandeered by the Wehrmacht for quartering officers, and later on was wrecked by Allied bombing. And that was that.'

'And so, thirty years after the end of the war, Miriam Silbermann came to your father asking him to recover the stolen manuscript. Why wait so long?'

'I think she simply assumed it was lost forever, until she heard about Dad's reputation for finding plundered Nazi loot and realised that maybe there was hope after all. Or maybe that's how long it took for her to put the pain of the war behind her. Who really knows?'

'What happened to her and her family after they were taken away?'

Madison shrugged. 'She never talked about that, either. But whatever it was, it wasn't good. Dad said she would go quiet whenever the subject came up, and the pain in her eyes would become so intense that it was terrible to look at. I think she channelled those emotions into her violin playing, you know?'

'If we don't know what happened to the family, what about the manuscript?'

'That became Dad's mission, from that moment on. He was so deeply touched by Miriam Silbermann that he lost interest in any of the other projects on his books, even though they could have been worth millions to the business. Like I told you, money wasn't what drove him. He went at it full steam, literally not sleeping for weeks at a time. When I was born five years later, he was still at it.'

'Did he ever get close?'

'You're talking about the journey of a skinny little document, in the middle of a giant war that was ripping the whole world apart. It was almost an impossible quest, but Dad tracked the path of the manuscript to Berlin. He thought Krebs might have taken it there as an offering to Hitler. Old Adolf loved music, apparently, and not just Wagner. In fact the Nazis thought Bach was the most "German" of all the great composers, whatever that means exactly, and they revered his music more than anyone's. Might have been a real feather in Krebs's cap to hand a trophy like that to his supreme leader.'

If the theory was right, Ben was thinking, then it was a pretty rich parallel. The SS commander Krebs taking the manuscript to Berlin to ingratiate himself with his Führer; three-quarters of a century later, Dragan Vuković stealing the very same artifact away to Belgrade as an offering to his prospective employer, Zarko Kožul. History sometimes repeated itself in the most bizarre ways.

'Whatever the case,' Madison went on, 'Dad was pretty sure the manuscript was still in Berlin in 1945.'

'Why?'

'Because he wasn't the only one searching for it,' Madison replied.

Chapter 47

Ben's cigarette was burned down to its stub. He crushed it on his saucer and lit another. 'Who else was in the hunt?'

Madison replied, 'A man called Jürgen Vogelbein, a professor at a Vienna music institute. Vogelbein was much older than Dad. He'd been a soldier in the Battle of Berlin, when the Russians were closing in on the city right at the end of the war. He was part of a special detachment in charge of evacuating art treasures out of Berlin ahead of the Soviet push, and claimed that he actually saw the manuscript being loaded on a truck. He spent years, decades, searching for it after the war, despite being mocked by other academics for believing it even existed. I guess that's academics for you.'

Ben suddenly remembered Tom McAllister's mysterious reference to Nazis, the KGB and a man called 'Bird Leg'. 'Vogel' was German for bird, 'Bein' for leg. No fool, that McAllister. He'd been figuring a lot of things out from his end.

Ben asked Madison, 'Did the manuscript by any chance end up in Soviet Russia, in the hands of the KGB?'

She looked at him. 'Is that just a wild guess, or do you know more about this than you're letting on?'

'A little birdie told me. Did it?'

'The convoy that evacuated the treasures out of Berlin

went to Silesia,' Madison said. 'That's a region spread between Poland, Germany and the Czech Republic.'

'I know where Silesia is. Go on.'

'Well, the Nazis' idea was to keep their precious stolen merchandise safely out of enemy hands, but it didn't quite work out that way for them because pretty soon afterwards the Soviets came swarming in and took over Silesia. Vogelbein believed that the manuscript, along with the rest of the goods, was grabbed by Stalin's secret police, the NKVD.'

'Which after the war eventually morphed into the Soviet Committee for State Security, the KGB,' Ben said. So McAllister had been right. It was a rare thing for Ben to take his hat off to a police detective.

'Which was as far as Vogelbein was able to track it before he gave up the chase,' Madison said. 'As for Dad, he refused to let it go that easily. He kept on kicking at doors for as long as he could, spent fortunes on bribes and offered all kinds of rewards to anyone who could come up with a lead. He had a whole network of contacts, not all of them legal. The most shadowy of all of them was this specialised art and antiquities fence who was rumoured to be Romanian, but nobody had ever met him or knew his real name; guy called himself "Ulysses".'

'We've heard that name before.'

'He and Dad did a lot of work together in the past, made a lot of money together. But this time round, nothing doing. The trail was looking deader with every passing year. Meanwhile, Dad met up with Miriam Silbermann several more times in New York, and at her home in Switzerland, reporting his progress to her, probably trying his best to sound optimistic. But even he knew, in his heart, that nobody could ever hope to penetrate the KGB. Once those guys had it, the game was over.'

'I'm guessing your father didn't accept that too happily.'

'No, it broke his spirit. He started drinking around that time, and his relationship with my mom suffered a lot. It's a wonder I was even conceived.' Madison managed a small smile. She paused, scratching at the Formica tabletop. 'On top of everything else, I think he was already in love with Miriam Silbermann, even if he'd never have admitted it to himself at the time.'

'They had a relationship?'

'Never. Dad wouldn't have done that to Mom. But Mom could be a difficult woman, and he wasn't exactly the most attentive husband, and things were strained between them through most of the marriage. He was captivated by Miriam, talked about her endlessly, even years later. It's not a big stretch to imagine he had stronger feelings for her. I know he did.'

Madison paused again, and gave a sigh. 'And so it went on, for sixteen years. Somewhere in the middle of it all, I was born and started growing up. Dad was still travelling about the world, dabbling in other projects, but without much enthusiasm. I sometimes went along with him, and even though I was just a kid I got the taste for it, the travel, the detective work, the hunt.'

'Except in the end you gravitated towards a slightly different profession, hunting people rather than treasure.'

'And I'm damn good at my job. Anyway, then 1991 came around. A big year. First, Mom died, within just weeks of her diagnosis. It was a terrible shock. Next major event in our lives, same year, the Soviet Union collapsed. Suddenly, right when he should have been deep in mourning, Dad starts getting as jumpy as a bloodhound on a scent. He'd come back to life. Quit the booze, packed his case, and off he went to pick up the trail. Why? Because he'd had a tip-off from Ulysses that with the USSR falling apart, former KGB agents had been selling off valuables from the state coffers on the sly. Armed with a contact number or two, Dad set sail for Moscow.'

'And?'

'And came back almost a month later empty-handed and even more twisted up about it than before.' Madison shook her head and heaved another deep sigh. 'And that was pretty much the last we heard about the manuscript. There was no telling what might have happened to it. Even knowing it was locked up in the hands of the KGB was better for Dad than imagining it being sold off to a private collector, or drifting around Christ knew where, or being lost again.

'But the worst thing of all was having to tell Miriam Silbermann that it was over. He flew to Switzerland to break the bad news to her in person. When he returned, he headed straight for the nearest bar and woke up three days later in Central Park. Never said a word to me about it, but he was never the same again after that. A sixty-one-year-old multi-millionaire, and he looked like a hobo twenty years older. He abandoned his career and embarked on his next great project, drinking himself slowly to death. Eventually, the phone stopped ringing. The office sat empty, just the way it is now. I haven't had the heart to terminate the lease.'

'Where is your father now?' Ben asked.

'He moved to a little beach house on Oahu, Hawaii, eight years ago. My idea. I figured he'd be better off someplace warm. Maybe a mistake, I don't know. I go to see him when I can – in fact I visited just a couple days ago – but I don't think he even registers my presence. All he does is sit on his veranda, staring out to sea. I don't know what he sees, or what goes on inside his mind. I think he's just waiting for the end. And I guess the end will come, soon enough.'

Ben was silent for a moment as he digested Madison's

sad account and tried to fit all the pieces of the puzzle together in his head.

'But it's not the end of the story, is it? While your father was wasting away on his beach and you were off hunting fugitives, the manuscript resurfaced. We'll never know what journey it made from Moscow, who had it, how many hands it passed through before it popped up in a little backstreet shop in Prague a year ago, and my friend Nick brought it home without even realising what it was. But someone else did.'

Ben told her about Adrian Graves, his scheme to acquire it, the sticky end to which he'd come and the manner by which the manuscript had landed in the possession of the Serbians, first Dragan Vuković and now his lord and master, Zarko Kožul.

'I think I understand how the rest goes,' Ben went on. 'Kožul probably had no interest in the manuscript to begin with, but then he had second thoughts and made a call or two, put the feelers out and realised that maybe it was worth something to him after all, even if he just flogged it off on the cheap. He's probably got a network of criminal fences ten times bigger than your father ever did, back in the day. And that's a pretty small world. I think word of the manuscript's reappearance on the market reached the ears of this man who calls himself Ulysses. Ulysses then contacted your father's old office in New York and left an urgent message, maybe more than one, to alert him. Which then got relayed to his home in the Hawaiian Islands. Your father might no longer be in touch with reality enough to answer the phone or pick up messages. But it so happened that his devoted daughter was there for a visit, the only other person who knew the story of Rigby Cahill's quest to find the Bach manuscript.'

Madison arched an eyebrow. 'Nice work, detective. You're a real smart guy. A regular Mike Hammer.'

'You called Ulysses back and convinced him to deal with

307

you personally, on your father's behalf. Ulysses handed you the connection to Kožul, along with the nightclub address here in Belgrade. You didn't waste time jumping at the opportunity to finally get back the one thing you believe could make the old man happy again. And here you are.'

'Here *we* are, Mr Hammer,' she corrected him. 'Question is, what happens now?'

'What happens now is that you get on the next flight home and forget this,' Ben said. 'It's not worth the risk you're taking.'

She gave him the fierce frown again. 'Because I'm a woman? You don't think I can handle myself in a tough spot?'

'Tell me something. What exactly were your intentions when you came to Belgrade? To set up a meeting with the charming Mr Kožul and make him a tempting cash offer for the goods?'

'Negotiate with these scumbags? You must be kidding, right? Even if I had the money, no chance. That's not how I do business, baby.'

'That's what I thought. Which leaves the one and only option of doing it the hard way.'

'Which I have no problem with at all.'

'Zarko Kožul isn't your regular class of murderous lunatic. This is someone who's most in his element when he's torturing and butchering large numbers of innocent victims. Ever heard of the Srebrenica massacre?'

Madison said nothing.

'If you don't know what his unit did to those people, then keep it that way. You don't want to know. This is a man who gets his kicks from putting his enemies inside a car crusher and filming them getting squished to death. We're not talking about serving bail bonds or enforcement of speeding tickets here.'

Madison stiffened like a cobra about to strike. 'Oh, because I'm not used to dealing with hardcore crooks. Like the jerk last year in Tucson who beat his wife and three kids to death with a hammer and burned their bodies in a pit because she told him he looked like Baxter Burnett. Wasn't a movie fan, I guess. Or the other psycho dickhead in Nashville who chopped off both a guy's arms with a chainsaw because he looked at his sister, then blew away three Sheriff's deputies who came to arrest him. There's only one reason neither of those slimeballs is gonna taste freedom again, if they live to be a hundred. And you're looking at her.' She jabbed her thumb to her chest.

'Fine,' Ben said. 'I have no doubt you can look after yourself. You proved that tonight. So let's say you did manage to get past an army of Kožul's men and snatch the manuscript back. Assuming he hasn't already sold it on by now. Let's also say you were able to get out of this in one piece and deliver the damn thing to your father on Oahu. What do you think that's going to change?'

'I have to believe it will,' she said. 'It's my only chance to bring him back from wherever he is right now.'

'Even though he's virtually catatonic? You said yourself, his brain's gone. He's hardly more than a vegetable.'

She flinched as though he'd slapped her. 'Don't mince words, Ben. Tell me how you really see it.'

'If my choice of words is brutal,' Ben said, 'that's because I'm trying to make you understand the reality of this situation. As much as I admire your dedication to your poor old father—'

'Cut the crap,' she interrupted. 'Will you help me with what I came here to do, or not?'

'The answer is no, Madison. I'm not going to help you get yourself killed for nothing. For your father's sake, as well as your own, go home.'

She shook her head. 'No way. You'd have to drag me on

board that plane inside an iron box with chains around it. Even then, I'd break out and whoop you like a red-headed stepchild.'

'This is my hunt. I work alone.'

'We've already seen how that went for you.'

'I'd have got out of it.'

'Bullshit.' She fixed him with the steely manhunter stare that he could imagine her giving to some fugitive desperado she'd just nailed, .45-calibre eyes pointing at him. Her face was hard as slate. Then the twitch came to the corner of her mouth, and flickered into a crooked, one-sided smile. The hardness in her eyes gave way to a twinkle of mischief.

'Besides, I know something else,' she said. 'Something I'll bet my butt you don't.' She paused, waiting for a response.

Ben said nothing.

'Like you said, small world. Ulysses has all the same shady contacts Kožul does.' She paused again, waiting and watching for his reaction.

'So?'

'So Ulysses knows people who have done business with Kožul in the past,' she said. 'He might even have done business with him personally, though he might not say so.' She paused again. Teasing.

'And?'

'And it so happens that Ulysses is in on the big, big secret. Closely-guarded information he wouldn't divulge to a living soul, except maybe to sweet little ol' Maddie, the daughter of the legendary Rigby Cahill, for old times' sake.'

Ben was tiring of this game. 'What secret?'

Madison's smile twitched wider. She leaned across the table towards him.

'I know where Kožul lives.'

Chapter 48

The nav coordinates Ulysses had given Madison to locate Zarko Kožul's remote hideaway were over ninety kilometres from Belgrade, a short helicopter ride but too far to drive in a car whose bullet-chewed rear end was all too likely to attract police attention. Ben had her call the rental agency's 24-hour customer hotline from the supermarket cafeteria to report the Octavia stolen.

'Whoops. Not happy,' she said when she'd finished making the call.

'They'll get over it.'

'What are we going to do for transport?'

'That won't be a problem.' He pointed at the table menu. 'You want to eat something now, or would you rather wait until breakfast? We're in no rush.'

'I thought you wanted to go to Kožul's place.'

'It can wait. Kožul probably isn't even at home right now. My guess is he'd have flown into town to check out the damage to his operation, and won't be back there till morning. Some heads will have to roll for what happened tonight. One or two of his people will probably end up in the crusher.'

'You really got that crusher on the brain, haven't you?'

'We'll wait for the dust to settle, let him get home and

311

let off steam. Then we'll hit him in the afternoon, when he's not expecting it.'

'So what do we do until then?'

'What normal people do, get some rest. It's been a long day and tomorrow will be longer.'

They walked outside into the night. The mist had blanketed itself more thickly over the city, and the temperature had dropped another degree. They left the supermarket car park without a glance at the Octavia, and set off up the road at a brisk pace.

'A damn sight colder than Colorado this time of year, that's for sure,' she said, rubbing her hands together.

'Is that where your home is now?'

She laughed. 'When you hunt fugitives for a living, you can forget having anything much of a home life. Grand Junction was my last job. The next one, I don't know yet. Could be someplace down in New Mexico, could be way up in Alaska.'

He nodded. 'I used to live that way, moving around all the time. Sometimes I used to forget where to go back to afterwards.'

'Settled now?'

'In theory.'

'Married?'

He shook his head. 'You?'

She gave a shrug. 'They say Maddie Cahill always gets her man. But that's one guy who's escaped me, so far.'

'I'm sure the White Knight will come along eventually. As long as you don't shoot his kneecaps out on the first date, it could be the start of something beautiful.'

'Geez, now I realise where I've been going wrong all this time.'

They walked on in silence. After a few kilometres, they

were in a low-grade suburban residential area inland from the river. The streets and houses were dark, with the darker silhouettes of cars in driveways and dotted along the kerb-sides. Ben stopped outside a driveway, walked a few steps towards the house, glanced at the darkened windows, and whispered, 'This one will do.'

'This what?' she whispered back, but he was already too busy examining the vehicle he'd picked out to reply. An old-model Range Rover. Four-wheel drive. Minimal security. Not in the best condition. Easy to break into, cheap to replace. Within two minutes, he was inside and working on the ignition wiring. The house was still in darkness.

Madison poked her head in the open door and hissed, 'Car theft? You can't be serious.'

Ben removed the fat wad of Serbian banknotes that was overstuffing his wallet. He plucked out a sheaf that felt about the right thickness and gave it to her. 'Go and post this through the letterbox.'

'You're crazy.'

'But I'm not a car thief.'

Madison stared at him, then scampered up to the house, shoved the cash through the front door and came running back to jump inside the Range Rover as Ben got the engine fired up and the rasp of the engine broke the silence of the night. An upstairs light came on. A man's silhouette appeared at the window, looking out in alarm at his car skidding backwards out of his driveway. There was a shout. Then the Range Rover was screeching away down the street in a cloud of diesel smoke, and was gone.

Five kilometres away, Ben switched the plates for ones he removed from a rusted-out Lada, and dropped the originals down a drain. 'You've done this once or twice before, I see,' Madison dryly observed.

'Practice makes perfect. Now let's go and find a place to hole up for the night.'

'Like normal people,' she replied.

On the far edge of town, they spotted a motel with a vacancy sign and pulled in. The old fat guy in reception was fairly drunk, but still mostly coherent, and spoke better English than Ben spoke Serbian. He looked surprised when Ben told him he wanted to book two rooms, but before he could answer Madison nudged Ben's arm and cut in, 'Why splash out for two rooms when one will do fine? We just spent most of our cash on a car, remember?'

Ben looked at her. '*Our* cash?'

'In any case, we only have one room available,' said the old fat guy.

'We'll take it,' Madison said, then turned to Ben. 'Pay the man.'

'Whatever you say,' Ben said, and paid the man.

The room was small, with a ramshackle double bed covering most of the worn carpet and just enough space to walk around it. The en-suite bathroom was as functional as most military latrines Ben had encountered. 'I'll sleep on the floor,' he said.

Madison clucked her tongue. 'There you go again.'

'There I go again what?'

'Pandering to the little woman. You think this chivalry thing is cool, or something? I'm as happy sleeping on the floor as the next guy. You take the bed.'

'Do what you like, but I told you I'm having the floor and that's that,' Ben said, grabbing a pillow from the left side of the bed and tossing it down on the carpet.

'Dumb as a rock and twice as stubborn,' she muttered. She grabbed the other pillow and dropped down out of his sight to stretch out on the floor on the other side. A hand came up and yanked a blanket down off the bed to cover herself with.

'Look who's talking. I thought Roberta Ryder was the most obstinate female I'd ever meet.'

She craned her head upward to peer at him over the bed. 'Who's Roberta Ryder?'

'Good night, Madison.'

Ben clicked off the sidelight, then lay down, closed his eyes and was dreaming within a minute. In the middle of the night, he awoke, heard Madison Cahill's soft, regular breathing as she slept nearby, and realised she'd climbed up into the bed after all.

He smiled and went back to sleep.

Chapter 49

The next morning, Madison demonstrated that she'd regained her appetite by attacking the biggest breakfast Ben had ever seen in a truck stop down the road from the motel. Even the largest truckers were gawking at her in awe. 'Eat when you can, right?' she said between mouthfuls of egg, sausage and bacon. It might not have been traditional Serbian fare but at least there was little danger of finding a human ear in there.

Ben had only a cup of coffee in front of him. He generally didn't eat much before a battle. And a battle was coming that day. That was for sure.

'Finished?' he said, draining the last of the bitter dregs. 'Then let's go shopping.'

'Boy, you're so much fun to be with.'

It took an hour of scouring the city before they found what Ben was looking for. The backstreet army surplus, camping equipment and sporting goods store was run by a little old man with a Fu Manchu beard and a shopkeeper's apron, who never stopped smiling the entire time. Ben was wondering if a stroke had frozen his face in a permanent grin.

The store had everything Ben needed. He built a pile of goods on the counter as the old man went on grinning, now maybe for another reason. Two pairs of zoomable field binoculars; a pair of walkie-talkie radios with a kilometre range; a coil of strong, thin rope; a sheet of plastic waterproof tarp; two identical heavy-duty survival knives with blackened carbon steel blades, pretty faithful copies of the US military M9 bayonet right down to the lug on the scabbard to enable the weapon to double as a scissor-action wire cutter.

Madison was watching Ben as though wondering what they needed so much kit for. He held up one of the knives and asked her, 'Do you know how to use one of these?'

Madison frowned at the weapon. 'Uh, is the pointy end the part you stick into the other guy?'

'Good enough.'

Ben was about to settle up with the old man when he noticed the item hanging on the wall at the far side of the store, and asked to see it. The old man happily took it down to show him. The crossbow's stock was made of glass fibre painted in gaudy camo colours, and up close the weapon looked cheap and flimsy. 'Let me show you something else,' the old man said. Still grinning, he vanished into the back shop to return a moment later holding another crossbow. This one was a very different proposition. Black and businesslike, with a carbon fibre stock, scope, onboard quiver and a carrying sling like a rifle's.

'An Excalibur hunting crossbow, made in Canada,' the old man said proudly. 'Expensive. But for the buyer who appreciates real quality, what is expense?'

Ben would sooner have been able to purchase a firearm, but this was Europe, not America. Firearms required permits; bows didn't. 'I'd need the right kind of bolts,' he said. 'Hunting tips.'

'May I ask what kind of game you have in mind?'

'Wolves. Big nasty ones. Lots of them.'

The old man reached under the counter and came up with a box full of aluminium crossbow bolts. Their bladed tips were so razor sharp that you could shave with them. He explained to Ben that from this bow, these bolts would launch at four hundred feet per second. Half the speed of a pistol bullet. Nothing on earth could outrun them. Not even the biggest, baddest wolf.

'How much for everything?' Ben asked.

'I like wolves,' Madison said as they were leaving the store. 'I hate the idea of skewering one with an arrow.'

'I feel the same way,' Ben said.

By mid-morning they were setting off in the stolen Range Rover, using Ben's smartphone as a sat nav to guide them the ninety-plus kilometres to Zarko Kožul's private residence. Madison's thick black mane of gypsy ringlets was tied back under the black baseball cap. Her combat hairstyle. Her eyes were hidden behind mirrored aviator shades. She had gone very quiet, sitting motionless by Ben's side, emanating a brooding energy that told him she was mentally preparing for whatever they might find when they got there. He left her to it, and drove in silence with just his dwindling supply of Gauloises and his own thoughts to occupy him.

As far as he could, he'd worked out his strategy. The more he thought about it, the less likely it seemed that they would find Dragan Vuković at Kožul's private residence. If his suspicions proved right, Ben intended to capture Kožul and force him into luring Dragan out to meet him with the offer of a cushy full-time position in his gang. No wannabe gangster would refuse such an opportunity. Dragan would be dead before he'd even realised he'd walked into a trap.

That was, if things went to plan. Assuming they could get past the guards. Assuming a lot of things.

As midday approached, the city was a distant memory

and the terrain had grown forested and mountainous. Kožul's use of a chopper to commute back and forth to his Belgrade base meant that he could choose to live in the middle of nowhere, and that was exactly what he had done. The satellite led Ben onto a succession of ever-smaller, rougher roads, not a farm or homestead in sight for kilometre after kilometre. When the metalled road ran out altogether and became a steep, rock-strewn track, he shifted the Range Rover's four-wheel drive into low range and locked the axle differential to help the transmission scramble over the rough ground. If you were going to steal a car, make it one appropriate to the conditions. The Range Rover bounced and lurched on, kilometre after kilometre, higher and deeper into the craggy mountains where majestic white-tailed eagles soared and circled far overhead.

Eventually, the 4x4 could go no further. If the terrain didn't kill it, the hot, complaining engine would. Ben pulled up and shut it down. 'We walk from here.'

Madison nodded. Her mental preparation was over. She was ready.

Ben jumped out of the cab, opened up the tailgate and hefted out the big holdall he'd bought from the old man in Belgrade to carry his gear. Silence hung over the mountains, just the whistle of the cold wind through the pines and the distant shrill cry of a bird of prey. By his reckoning they were still about six kilometres from Kožul's place.

He shouldered the bag and nodded to himself.

He was ready, too.

They hiked onwards, speaking little. Madison had removed her jacket and carried it slung over her shoulder. She moved with agility and ease over the heavy terrain. Ben felt confident that he could trust her capabilities, if things got nasty. Which he was confident they would. He sensed she was thinking the same thoughts, about him, about what was coming, about potential outcomes. The banter between them was gone, just as Ben had experienced a thousand times before between military comrades when a fight is imminent and the mind clears itself for more serious considerations.

Sometimes the rocky track took them through wide open terrain, where Ben kept glancing up and around in paranoia that Kožul might have spotters posted on the higher ground to watch for approaching danger. There were none. Other times, the path of the track was swallowed up by a thicket of gnarly trees and overhanging branches, and Ben could feel the presence and cautious eyes of the creatures that lived there, watching unseen from the deep cover of the forest. Serbia was home to brown bears as well as wolves.

Ben felt a sense of kinship with the wild things. His quarrel was with a far more dangerous species. Predator against predator. And he was the most dangerous of all.

The track left the forest behind and followed the curve of a sweeping rocky ridge that teetered high above the wooded valley below. Ben no longer had to check the GPS coordinates. He was one with this place. As he made his way towards the vertiginous edge of the ridge, he looked down and saw that he'd calculated their bearings perfectly.

There, two hundred feet below them, nestling at the end of a private road that cut through the trees, lay the remote private residence of Zarko Kožul.

Chapter 50

Ben had seen criminal kingpin mansions as grandiose and magnificent as regal palaces, but one glance at the distant group of buildings told him Kožul's home wouldn't be joining that list. He took a pair of binoculars from the kit bag and settled himself behind a large rock to observe the place more closely. It was more like a paramilitary compound than a country estate, roughly three acres in size and oval in shape. Judging by the halo of thick green woodland that densely surrounded it, the whole area had been levelled out of what had once been forest. The approach road carved through the trees and led up to a set of tall iron mesh gates inset into the high-security fence that encircled the compound. Once inside the gates, the road snaked towards a collection of buildings that occupied a rough semicircle across the rearmost half of the fenced area.

The largest of the buildings was the house itself. It was a rambling single-storey hacienda-style affair with a lot of big windows. Aside from the expanses of glass and the terracotta-tiled roof, every inch of the house was painted bright red. Red walls, red doors and window frames. A fancy red mosaic-pattern patio area stretched out to the rear, with a covered pool. The terrace at the front of the house was enclosed behind a low wall, also painted red.

Madison had grabbed the second pair of binocs and positioned herself a few metres away from Ben among the rocks. 'Looks like hell,' she said. 'The man has taste, make no mistake.'

Ben scanned back across the compound. Moving clockwise from the house he traced the semicircle of other buildings, lingering for a moment on each one to study it. Nearest to the red house was a whitewashed block building with a flat roof and square windows facing in the direction of the gates. It could have been anything from a storage facility to an accommodation block for Kožul's men. He guessed Kožul must keep a number of personnel on full-time duty here at the compound, maybe alternating them in shifts with the men who guarded the Rakia.

A little distance from the whitewashed building stood a large sheet-metal hangar that was very likely to be for Kožul's helicopter. The hangar's steel roller doors were closed, making it impossible to tell whether the chopper was inside or not. A smaller building adjoined the hangar, block-built like the other but windowless, unpainted and rough-hewn with a rusty corrugated roof. Maybe a workshop or generator room, Ben thought, judging by the aluminium electrical mast sticking upwards from its side wall with wires stretching to each of the buildings and the house.

Nearest to their side of the fence was an elongated carport, open front and back, under which sheltered a variety of utility vehicles and big-wheeled offroaders. Those might belong to the men, Ben thought, or else maybe were Kožul's own little fleet.

Madison was still watching the house. She said from behind her binocs, 'I can't see a living soul down there.'

'Nor me.'

She lowered the glasses and glanced anxiously across at Ben. 'What do we do if the sonofabitch isn't home?'

'Then we hang around until he is.'

'Could be days.'

'I'm sure you've been on stakeout plenty of times before now,' he said. 'There are worse places.'

'Sure are. This is like a picnic next to the bayous of Louisiana. Or the wilderness of northern Minnesota. Shot my first man there, after stalking him for four days straight, no food, no sleep. He was holed up in a cabin with a thirty-ought-six hunting rifle and all I had was my Kimber.'

'Who fired first, him or you?'

'I've been shot at plenty of times. If you're thinking I'm liable to go all hysterical when the shit starts hitting the fan, think again.'

'That's good to know.'

She paused a beat, then asked, 'What was your first time?'

'First time doing what?'

'Killing a man.'

He thought about it. 'I don't remember.'

Madison humphed, put the binocs back up to her eyes and resumed watching, now scanning away from the house and sweeping her field of vision carefully back and forth. Ben looked up at the sky. A bank of dark rainclouds was moving in from the east, pushed by the cold mountain wind that was whistling around their ears. He crouched lower behind his rock and used the sheltered space to light a cigarette. He offered the pack to Madison. She waved it away and went on watching.

A moment later she stiffened and said, 'Wait, I see something. Six o'clock from the western edge of the fence, in the woods.'

Ben shifted position and snatched up his binoculars. The view in his lenses blurred as he swivelled across to pinpoint what she'd seen. Then he spotted them. 'Got it. Good call.'

323

The figures of two guards were slowly ambling among the dense thicket of spruce and beech trees that enclosed the compound. Ben zoomed in as close as he could without losing focus. They were big guys in keeping with Kožul's evident recruitment policy, both in their thirties. One had a beard and the other had long hair, which made them look like irregular militia troops in their surplus-store combat fatigues and black woollen beanie hats. Both were armed with what looked to Ben like full-size M16 battle rifles. Out here in the wilderness there was no need for compact urban-style weaponry, just as keeping up with the latest Belgrade dress fashions didn't matter quite so much. The bearded guy was holding his gun diagonally across his chest and the longhaired one had his slung pointing downwards behind his left shoulder. Casual carry positions, the body language of for-hire soldiers with not much to do and little interest in their duties but following orders nonetheless. They were talking. Longhair turned towards his comrade, who rocked backwards on his feet as if he was laughing at a joke.

'That's something, at least,' Madison said in a hopeful tone. 'If the guards are on patrol, must be they've got something to guard, right? Means Kožul might be home.'

'Or they might be guarding something else. For all we know, they've got forty tons of heroin or Saddam's missing WMDs stashed in that big building down there.'

'My gut tells me he's home,' Madison said firmly. Her eyes had narrowed to fierce slits and her jaw was set. 'He's home, all right. Probably had a late night and is tucked up all nice and warm in his little bed. Which would make this the ideal time to hit the sonofabitch.'

Ben didn't want to approach the compound until the time was right. The time wouldn't be right until he knew for sure Kožul was at home, because to spring an attack on an empty house would be disastrous. They had to wait for visual confirmation. Ideally for Madison, Kožul would magically signal his presence by appearing at the window waving the Bach manuscript in his hand and yelling, 'Yoo-hoo, come and get it.' Ideally for Ben, when Kožul showed his face Dragan Vuković would be standing there next to him, with a big target stuck to his chest. For both to happen at once seemed unlikely, but stranger things had happened.

'No,' Ben said. 'We keep waiting and watching for now.'

They kept waiting and watching. Time ticked slowly by. The two guards continued their endless meandering circuit of the perimeter. Ninety minutes later, they were joined by another pair who emerged from the block building. Ben watched as the four men stood around for a few moments, visible in a clearing among the trees, talking and sharing cigarettes. Then they split back up into twos and resumed their patrol of the woods outside the fence. The doubling the guard had to mean something, but Ben didn't know what.

Still no movement from the red house.

Ben unzipped the crossbow from the bag and used his waiting time to familiarise himself with how it worked. The prod was so powerful that the bow couldn't be drawn back into the firing position without a special rope cocking aid. The weapon might be super-effective and quieter than any silenced firearm, but the trade-off was that it would be as slow to reload as an antique musket. Ben cocked it, fitted one of the hunting-tipped bolts into position and six more into the onboard quiver, ready for action. Being shot with a bullet wasn't a nice prospect at the best of times, but the idea of an aluminium shaft driving a razor-sharp arrowhead through your body at four hundred feet per second was ghoulish enough to make even Ben shudder.

They waited. The sky darkened steadily as the rainclouds closed ominously in, ready to dump a million gallons of rain over the landscape at any moment. The guards kept circling. Madison's body was tense and her face was tight and pale as she constantly scanned the compound through her binoculars.

'This is taking too damn long,' she muttered.

'Look on the bright side,' Ben said. 'No guard dogs, at least none I've seen or heard yet.'

'Maybe Kožul's allergic.'

'Bad for him, good for us.'

Two hours and sixteen minutes into their stakeout, the first heavy splat of a raindrop hit the rock next to Ben. Within the next minute, the sky opened up and delivered its promised downpour. Ben unrolled the waterproof tarp from the bag, crawled over to Madison's position and the two of them huddled together under their makeshift bivouac shelter as the rain drummed hard on the plastic sheet and ran down in rivulets to pool in the hollows around them. Up close like this, Ben could feel the tension coming off Madison like heat ripples.

Two hours and forty-two minutes in, the rain stopped and the sun crept out from the clouds, painting the landscape in vivid colour as though the deluge had washed off a layer of dust. Three minutes after that, something else happened.

'You see them?' Madison said in a voice husky with anticipation.

'I see them.'

Chapter 51

The procession of vehicles was visible to the naked eye from a long way off. The sunlight peeking freshly out from the dissipating rainclouds glinted off glass and paintwork as they coiled their way closer along the approach road to the compound. Through his binoculars Ben counted eight of them, black, boxy, top-of-the-line SUVs with tinted glass. Moving single-file like a military convoy. Fat all-terrain tyres throwing up dirty spray from the puddles left by the rain. Headlights blazing like a twenty-one-gun salute, even in the renewed brightness of the afternoon.

'Hello,' Madison said. 'We most definitely have company.'

'Quite a bit of it.'

'Bring it on,' she replied. 'I'm dying of boredom here.'

Ben lost sight of the convoy as it reached the ring of trees. He anticipated the moment the lead vehicle would reappear close to the compound perimeter, and regained visual contact. The convoy slowed to a halt at the closed gates. Either they were dead on time for a prearranged rendezvous or someone had radioed ahead to say they were incoming, because the guards seemed to be alerted to the imminent arrival. The woods patrols converged towards the gates while four more armed men emerged from the block building and came running to greet the new arrivals.

The gates were unlocked and hauled open. When the last of the line had passed through, the guards closed and relocked the gates. The new four trotted after the vehicles as they drove up towards the red house. The original four split back up into pairs and returned to their patrol duties.

'What do you think's up?' Madison asked.

To Ben's eye, going by the body language and behaviour of the guards, the developments down below looked exactly like the arrival of some kind of top brass or VIP dignitary at a military base. It wasn't Kožul. Something else was happening. 'Looks like a meeting,' he said. 'Ulysses told you Kožul does business at the house?'

'That's what he said.'

'Maybe that's what this is. We'll soon find out.'

Ben and Madison crept along the rocky ridge to find the best elevated observation point overlooking the house. At this range, the high-powered field binoculars on maximum zoom offered a crystal-clear view of the front.

The SUVs pulled up in an orderly line along the red terrace wall. Black bodywork flashed in the sunlight as doors opened. Men stepped out. Ben scanned left and right, trying to count heads before they all started disappearing inside the house. He'd counted nine when he recognised the man in the white shirt. Kožul's guy, Alek. Except now he was clad in a black polo and a grey suit that hung well off his slender frame. He'd been in charge of the men last night and he was clearly in charge today, issuing orders to the gorillas stepping out of the SUVs. There were enough weapons on display to fill the armoury at Le Val.

As Ben watched, Alek walked over to the third vehicle in the line and opened the back door. A tall and slightly stooped man in a linen suit got out, clutching an attaché case that had been laid flat across his knees during the drive. He appeared disorientated and unsteady on his feet, probably because of the black cloth hood he was wearing over his head. Once again, Kožul was being extra-cautious about protecting the location of his home base.

'Not one of the crew, that's for damn sure,' Madison muttered. 'It's definitely some kind of meet going down.'

Alek took the visitor's arm to steady him, turned him towards the house and then reached up and removed the cloth hood. Ben focused his binoculars carefully on the visitor's face. He was older, completely bald, gaunt and grim. The Boris Karloff look.

Alek ushered the visitor from the vehicle towards the house, making apologetic gestures and being as courteous and attentive as a manservant. Maybe the guy was some big cheese they didn't want to upset too much. Or maybe Alek was just lulling him into a false sense of security before whipping out a box cutter and slashing his throat. You could never tell with these people.

Madison touched Ben's arm and said, 'Ben, look.'

The front door of the house had opened and out of it, stepping into the sunlight to meet the arrivals, came one of the shortest adult men Ben had ever seen. He couldn't have been much over five-feet-nothing in height, but he made up for it in width and muscle mass, both of which were considerable. He might have given the impression of a grotesque child bodybuilder, if it hadn't been for the swarthy complexion and weathered features of a man around 50. He was wearing mirror shades that glinted in the light and was clad from head to toe, all five feet of him, in crimson red that matched the house. A human pillar box.

'Zarko Kožul,' Ben said. His guess about the crime boss

being a little guy had been nearer to the mark than he could have imagined.

'It's the small ones you need to watch out for,' Madison said. 'Goes for snakes and scorpions, too.'

Kožul's body language wasn't that of a happy man. He was doing a good deal of pointing and yelling as his heavies milled protectively around him. He didn't appear to extend the same degree of courtesy towards the bald-headed visitor with the attaché case as Alek. Privileges of rank, perhaps.

The last in the line of black SUVs was also the last to open its doors. As its occupants stepped out, Ben swivelled the binocs to take a look at their faces. 'Well well,' he murmured.

Dragan Vuković and his sister, Lena, walked towards the house. Lena was looking nervy and uncomfortable in a short, sleeveless red dress and must have been freezing in the cold breeze. Her brother had the swagger of confidence in his step as though he was completely in his element. He was wearing a dark cotton jacket over jeans, a smart-casual look that was a big departure from his usual pick of the Thugs R Us catalogue. Alek must have taken him out shopping somewhere fashionable.

'Who's the chick?' Madison asked.

'Her name's Lena Vuković. She's on the edge of the gang. The big fellow with her, that's her brother. Looks like he brought little sister along as window dressing.'

'The brother's the guy you have the beef with, right?'

Ben nodded. 'He certainly is.'

Kožul gave Dragan a cursory wave of acknowledgement, and Ben saw Dragan smile the way a dog wags its tail at a pat from its master. Then Kožul turned towards the house and motioned impatiently for everyone to follow. The small crowd began filtering inside. The four guards remained outside the house, manning the front like sentries.

'There they go,' Madison said. 'All the eggs are in the basket. You ready to do this now?'

'I was born ready,' Ben said. He put away the binoculars and snatched up the crossbow.

Madison flashed him a piratical grin. 'So what're we waiting for, bud. Let's rock the house.'

Chapter 52

They stalked their way down the rocky slope, moving cautiously from boulder to boulder, tree to tree, so as not to be spotted from the compound. No yells or alarm sirens sounded from below. No rifle shots cracked out. Reaching level ground they trotted fast towards the cover of the woods.

The ring of forest was about a hundred metres deep, after that they would reach the fence. They walked a few paces apart, treading softly through the trees. The carpet of leaf litter was spongy underfoot and made silent movement easy for people who had been trained to slip unnoticed through hostile territory. Madison Cahill might never have been a soldier, but she worked like one. *I'm damn good at my job*, she'd told him. And he believed it.

Ben's nose picked up the faint, acrid tang of cigarette smoke. A second later, he heard the crack of a breaking twig from about thirty metres away through the trees. He froze and made a fist sign for Madison to do the same. They stood very still, listening hard.

Voices. More crackling and shuffling as the pair of guards circled the perimeter with all the stealth and noiselessness of a rhinoceros herd.

In total silence Ben unslung the Excalibur from his shoulder. Cocked, loaded and ready to go. His right thumb found the push-off safety button and pressed it to the fire position.

He could see them now. The original two they'd observed from the ridge earlier, the bearded one and the longhaired one. They were walking side by side through the trees, just a pace or two apart. Following the contour of the perimeter counter-clockwise, with the fence a couple of dozen metres further away to their left. Their rifles were cradled loosely in their arms. Both were smoking cigarettes.

Ben waited, barely breathing. The two men kept walking. The bearded one on the right was about half a head taller than his companion closer to the fence. Neither of them remotely suspected the presence of intruders. Maybe if they didn't smoke so much on duty, they might have smelled them. Ben would have.

Ben slowly raised the bow stock to his shoulder. Madison was standing to the side, hiding behind a tree with her knife out. She flashed him a look, and he knew what she was thinking. With one shot he could only take down a single guard. Even if he made the cleanest kill in the world, the other would still have all the time he needed to fire off a hundred rounds while Ben struggled to recock the bow, and make enough noise to alert everyone inside the compound. Element of surprise, somewhat compromised.

Ben took careful aim through the scope. The centre of the crosshairs was an illuminated dot. You could choose between red and green. Green was brighter for visibility. At exactly the right moment, Ben let the shot fly.

The release of the bowstring made a dull *thwack*, as soft as a kid's airgun. But there was nothing soft about the impact downrange. The bolt whooshed through the air and hit the taller bearded guard in the neck and passed straight through into the shorter one's head.

The taller guard's knees folded under him and he went down like a demolished chimney tower crumpling into its own footprint. The shorter one remained standing, his body posture sagging slightly, long hair drooping limply forwards from under his beanie hat, hands still clutching his rifle.

For an instant Ben half-expected the guy to turn and start shooting – then realised that he was pinned to the tree trunk next to him by the crossbow bolt that had skewered him through the right temple and protruded from the left.

'Holy fucking shit,' Madison breathed.

Ben walked up to the dead men. Stepped over the body of the first and tugged at the end of the bolt holding the second one up. The aluminium shaft was bloody and dripping. With a couple of sharp twists and yanks, Ben plucked the tip out of the tree bark. He caught the body as it began to fall, and lowered it to the ground. He left the bolt embedded in the guy's skull and wiped the blood off his hand on the guy's trouser leg.

'Talk about killing two birds with one stone,' Madison whispered, still shaking her head in amazement.

'I won't get that lucky again,' Ben whispered back. 'Might have to use our knives next time.'

'Lucky my ass, William Tell.'

He bent down to pick up one of the fallen M16s. It was the proper military deal, with a three-way selector switch to choose between single shots, three-round bursts and fully automatic fire. Thirty-round magazines loaded up with mil-surp 5.56mm NATO ammunition. Thousands of these assault weapons had been circulating in all kinds of the wrong hands since the end of the Bosnian wars. Now two of them, at least, were back in good hands. Ben tossed one to Madison, took the other for himself and slung it over his shoulder. 'For after. You know how to use one of these things?'

Madison arched an eyebrow at him. 'Probably not. I only came second in my urban combat rifle course at Thunder Ranch in Oregon last year.'

'Only second?'

'The guy who beat me was ex-Delta Force. Now *he* got lucky.'

Ben recocked the crossbow and fitted a fresh bolt from the quiver. They gathered up all the spare magazines the dead men had been carrying, then kicked leaves over the bodies and moved on towards the fence. They were stalking their way through the trees some twenty metres short of the wire when Ben gripped Madison's arm.

The second pair of guards were coming straight towards them. Ben and Madison each ducked behind their nearest tree and pressed themselves tight against it. Ben nodded to her. She nodded back, tense and urgent.

The path of the guards took them between the two trees. They were just ambling along, looking sullen as though they were pissed off with patrol duty. Ben and Madison waited until they had passed by, then stepped out from behind the trees.

Ben went, 'Psst!'

The guards glanced quizzically at one another, then both turned round to look behind them. Ben let loose with the crossbow and the one on the left fell straight back with the end of the bolt sticking upwards out of his chest. The other one clawed for his rifle. Ben dumped the spent bow and unslung his M16. Now the shooting would begin and their stealth approach would be over.

Or not. Something flashed through the dappled sunlight between the trees. The remaining guard made a wheezing sound like 'Dooff' and dropped his rifle, both hands going to his belly just below the ribcage. He fell heavily to his knees and then toppled sideways, sprawled out in the leaves. Madison's knife was buried in him up to the hilt.

Ben looked at her. She shrugged. 'As a little girl I could bullseye watermelons at twenty paces. Now I nail 'em at thirty.'

'What an enchanting child you must have been.'

'Admit it, you're impressed.'

'Let's get through the rest of today first,' Ben said.

He left the crossbow where he'd dropped it. The attack would soon be entering its next phase, where the sneak approach would blossom into open combat and noise wouldn't matter. Reaching the fence, he unclipped his own knife from his belt and fastened it together with its scabbard to turn it into a wire cutter.

Three minutes later, he and Madison had both wriggled through the hole he'd made. He used some cut branches to mask the hole.

Now they were inside the open ground of the compound.

'So far, so good,' Madison said. 'Four bad guys down, only about another zillion to go. Walk in the park.'

Ben checked his weapon. Said nothing.

They moved on.

Chapter 53

The bald man inside the house was a sixty-year-old Bavarian called Conrad Heilbronner. In his time he'd been a museum director and senior insurance underwriter specialising in art and antiquities, before turning to more lucrative pursuits as a professional thief responsible for several major art heists and the deaths of five security personnel. Never caught, he'd quit that game while he was ahead. Nowadays he made his money as a middleman, consultant and broker, part of a network of similarly qualified experts across the world whose skills were constantly in demand.

It was a safer existence for him than his former career in violent crime, while still highly profitable. The illegal multi-billion-dollar trade in stolen art and antiquities ranked third in the world's big-money rackets after arms and drugs. Pillaged artifacts from Syria and Iraq had provided a wonderful source of income for many years, all the more so now that dimbo terrorists had finally cottoned onto the fact that they could sell off the treasures they looted from UNESCO heritage sites instead of simply smashing them to bits.

Heilbronner had fingers in other pies too, and his own extensive network of buyers – businessmen, investors, private collectors, they came from all walks of life – constantly hungry to acquire more loot. With Heilbronner's expert guidance they could purchase an item illegally for a relatively reduced price, sit on it for a period of time and then re-introduce it onto the legitimate market for a substantial profit, minus Heilbronner's fat commission of course. Technically, sellers were required to prove that the item was kosher, in accordance with those pesky regulations of the International Institute for the Unification of Private Law, or UNIDROIT. In practice, as usual, the law could easily be circumnavigated: Heilbronner's use of free-port warehouses in tax-free economic zones like Bermuda and the Cayman Islands allowed his clients to discreetly store their illegal purchases for years, if they chose. Most were in no hurry to resell. As long as the stuff wasn't too high profile, by the time the goods reappeared on the market at a massive price hike they were clean enough to eat your dinner off.

Alternatively, as some of Heilbronner's clients preferred to do, they simply added the artifact to their personal collection and enjoyed possessing it, with no intention of ever selling. It takes all sorts.

Whenever the word went out that a special new item was on the market, Heilbronner was well placed to be one of the first to hear about it. On this occasion, as often in the past, it was one of his chief contacts, the Romanian known only as Ulysses, who had put him onto the job, by way of trading favours. Heilbronner already had two interested potential buyers for the Bach manuscript, with the bidding opened at half a mill subject to authentication of the goods for sale: a Saudi prince who was a classical music nut, and a billionaire real-estate tycoon in Miami who would snap up anything he could just for the hell of it.

But first, Heilbronner had to verify the item was what the seller claimed it was, even though it was patently obvious that the seller had not the first clue what they were holding, nor any accurate idea of its value. For that purpose, Heilbronner had flown to Belgrade that morning from his country estate in Schleswig-Holstein. He wasn't too happy about being made to wear a hood on the long, uncomfortable car journey to the house, but business was business and Heilbronner was the consummate professional. His mission was to carry out the initial evaluation, pending the outcome of whatever further tests he deemed necessary to validate the manuscript's authenticity. He had brought with him a custom-made handheld XRF spectrometer, a highly sensitive scanner that used near-infrared light to measure the chemical composition of the paper, such as its gelatin concentration, which would quickly give an accurate reading of its age. It was a more efficient method than many of the older chemical analysis tests, which were often destructive to the sample.

Heilbronner's case also contained a small electron microscope, with which he could examine the ink on the manuscript and gain a pretty fair idea of how old it was, as well as to compare the markings against digitised images of other original Bach handwriting and musical notation stored in his mini-laptop. The world was full of fakes, but Heilbronner considered himself an infallible judge.

Heilbronner was thinking that the only real sticking point here was this idiot Zarko Kožul. Kožul resented having to wait for test results to determine whether the sale could even go ahead or not. He appeared to consider it a personal insult against his good name – what a joke that was – that any testing should be carried out at all. Kožul wanted the cash, and he wanted it right away. What an ape.

They were all gathered together in the long split-level living room, which, of course, was decked out in crimson leather with a scarlet carpet and ruby wall coverings. Heilbronner was the only one seated as he expertly examined the manuscript on a table in front of him. He could tell it had not been well looked after in its recent history. Its life prior to that appeared to have been pretty rough, too.

'What is this stain?' he asked, pointing. He spoke perfect Serbian, plus eight other European languages.

'Dragan wiped his ass on it, what do you think?' Kožul said loudly, and all his men laughed. Heilbronner didn't smile. He carried on with his analysis, working meticulously and with full focus, as though he were alone in an empty laboratory and not surrounded by a gawking crowd of armed crooks.

Lena Vuković didn't share their interest in what was happening. She was standing to one side feeling stupid in this dress and wishing she hadn't allowed Dragan to bring her here. Ever since they'd arrived back in Serbia he insisted on taking her everywhere with him, as though he didn't trust her not to run off.

Lena watched Dragan with his new comrades, and thought about the change in him. For as long as she could remember, her brother had been a violent and hard man – but the long-wished-for opportunity to finally go to work for Zarko Kožul seemed to have brought out his worst tendencies even more. He would do anything to prove his loyalty to his new boss. Like what he'd done last night, with his own sister watching.

Before they'd received the late-evening call from Alek, Dragan had been carrying out a 'little task' for Kožul. Namely, the disposal of a fellow gang member whose wife's second cousin's brother-in-law had been seen drinking in a Belgrade bar with a member of the police Žandarmerija and therefore could no longer be trusted. Given what a fine job Dragan had done with Radomir Orlić that time, Kožul had ordered him to take care of it personally.

Lena had never known what the man's name was. She

only knew what they'd done to him, and she didn't think she could ever forget.

Dragan and two others had taken him out to the junkyard Kožul owned on the edge of the city. Lena, of course, had been made to come along and spectate as the bound and bloodied victim had been given the choice between being burned slowly to death or put in the crusher.

He'd chosen the crusher.

Lena could still hear the screams ringing inside her mind, and taste the nausea that had kept her on her knees in the bathroom most of the night. This was how Zarko Kožul brought his men closer to him, by making them do such sick and awful things. How could Dragan obey such a person? What kind of man did that make him?

When they'd got the call about the capture of Ben Hope, Lena had feared that they would do something as horrible as that to him, or even worse. She had been thinking a lot about this man Hope. She felt bad that she'd betrayed him before, in Oxford. He had been fair with her, and not hurt her the way most other men did. She wanted to burst out laughing when the next call had come to say Hope had escaped. But she didn't dare show her relief to anyone, least of all to Dragan. Lena was more like his prisoner than his sister. Suddenly, she had never felt more trapped in her life.

Heilbronner finally looked up from the manuscript and folded his laptop. Zarko Kožul had been pacing furiously about the room, his face as red as the walls. 'Well?'

'I am ninety-nine per cent certain that the item is genuine,' Heilbronner said coolly. 'However, without further testing I can't guarantee my assessment.'

'Then get the fuck on with it,' Kožul said.

Heilbronner shook his head. 'Not here. I would have to take it away.'

Kožul stared at him the way a mad bull stares at a tore-ador. 'No. You want it, you buy it now. You don't want it, get lost. That's how it is when you do business with me.'

Heilbronner replied, 'But it's not how things work, my friend. I didn't come here to buy it, only to broker the sale. I thought we were clear on that point.' He looked at Alek. Alek suddenly seemed to develop an overwhelming interest in the view from the window.

'Do you know what happens to motherfuckers who waste my time?' Kožul said. The room went deathly quiet. All eyes were on Heilbronner.

Heilbronner was no fool, and knew he had to think fast before this psycho maniac dwarf pulled a pistol and started blasting. Maybe there was an angle here. If the manuscript was his, he could get a lot more selling it on than he'd make on commission. 'Perhaps I might be prepared to reconsider, and make you an offer here and now,' he said slowly. 'I value the manuscript at one hundred thousand dollars. I could have the funds transferred to you immediately.'

Kožul spat. 'That all? I didn't set this whole fuckin' thing up for a few nickels and dimes. You know what my operation pulls in every week?'

'Given its dubious origins and condition, that's all you'd ever get for it, believe me,' Heilbronner lied. 'This is the black market, not an auction house.'

Kožul stepped closer. The two of them squared off. 'Hundred fifty,' Kožul snarled.

At a hundred and fifty, Heilbronner knew he could still make three-fifty plus back on the deal, especially if he sold to the real-estate tycoon in Miami who couldn't tell shit from sugar anyway. He put on a big show of looking cagey. 'You're hurting me. At that price, you've got to offer me something to sweeten the deal.'

Kožul's face darkened to a shade of puce and twisted as though he was chewing on a live hornet. Then he pointed at Lena and said, 'What about her?'

Heilbronner had contacts in Saudi where he could make a buck trafficking human flesh, too. He gave her a once-over. Blond hair, not bad-looking, still young enough to fetch a reasonable price to the right buyer. He acted indignant. 'What good is that to me?'

'You wanted a sweetener,' Kožul said. 'That's a sweet piece of ass, for a stinking filthy whore. Take her away, do whatever you want with her.'

Lena yelled, 'I am not a whore!'

Kožul's men all laughed, Dragan included. Lena backed away, suddenly very frightened and shocked by this sudden turn of events. She looked at her brother. How could he let them treat her this way?

Heilbronner shrugged. 'Okay, one fifty and you throw in the whore. On condition that I get to examine the goods first. For all I know, she's full of disease.'

'Like I said,' Kožul replied with a dismissive gesture. 'Do what you want with her.'

Lena had no possible hope of escaping what was coming. She turned empty eyes on Dragan. 'You'd let them do this to me. Your own sister.'

Dragan snapped back, 'Shut your mouth, you stupid bitch.'

Kožul had two of his men show Heilbronner to a room where he could check out the merchandise. It was a bedroom Kožul sometimes used to entertain prostitutes, who were generally the only women who entered the house. The bed was red satin and the ceiling was tiled with mirrors. A real tigerskin rug adorned the floor, with bared fangs and glass eyes that seemed to watch them as they came into the room.

343

Heilbronner shoved Lena towards the bed. 'Get your clothes off. I need to inspect you.'

She retorted, 'Fuck you. I'm not anybody's slave.'

'You soon will be, so better get used to it.' Heilbronner reached inside his jacket and slipped out the stiletto blade he kept concealed there. He waggled the knife at Lena. 'Now do as I told you, or it will go badly for you. Understood? Quick, quick.'

'Why don't you just kill me? I would rather die than be sold like a horse.'

'You want to do this the hard way, that's fine by me,' Heilbronner said. He slipped the knife back in its sheath. Stepped towards her and shoved her down so hard on the bed that she bounced. Next thing he was clambering on top of her, his foul breath in her face, pinning her down with his weight and batting away her arms as he reached down and started tearing at her dress. Lena screamed, but then his hand clamped over her mouth, twisting her neck painfully and stifling her cries. She felt the dress rip off her, heard him laugh. 'More fun this way, no? Stay still, whore, or I'll cut you. You need to learn some respect.'

She bit his hand and his laugh turned into a sharp yell. She bit harder, tasted blood on her lips. Then the knife was back out again and at her throat. Lena drove her knee upwards and caught him hard in the groin, and he cried out again. She wriggled and struggled and bit and gouged like a wildcat fighting for its life in the jaws of a wolf, no longer thinking about the knife in his hand. They rolled off the bed together and hit the floor, him on top of her, knocking the wind out of her. She wrestled him off her and realised he wasn't fighting back any longer. He was groaning and clutching at his chest.

That was when Lena saw the spreading crimson flower on

his shirt and realised that he'd accidentally stabbed himself in the struggle. She staggered to her feet, gaping down at him. The blood was pouring out of his wound, his shirt now black with it. She held up her hands in front of her and saw they were wet and red and dripping. Heilbronner was trying to prop himself up on one elbow, reaching out with his other shaking hand for something solid to pull himself upright. But the knife had gone terribly deep and his strength was already failing him. He fell back with a gasping groan.

Seized by a surge of hatred that went far beyond what she felt about this repulsive man, she dropped to her knees and yanked the bloody blade out of his chest and stabbed him again, and again, and again. The needle-sharp stiletto made a kind of *shtick* sound at every thrust. Throat, stomach, face, she didn't care. Heilbronner spouted blood from his open mouth. He screamed and squealed, but she wouldn't stop with the knife. Just kept on stabbing him, more and more. *Shtickshtickshtick.*

They heard the commotion in the living room. 'Jesus Christ, what the fuck's happening in there?' Alek said.

Dragan Vuković had turned fishbelly white, frozen immobile with his champagne glass in his hand. One instant they'd been toasting the morning's modestly successful financial score and his acceptance into the gang, the next it sounded as if piglets were being butchered in the house.

Kožul turned to Dragan. 'Go check. That bitch sister of yours better not be fucking this deal up, or I'll roast her eyeballs on a skewer.'

Dragan set off at a run towards the bedroom. But he never got that far, because in the next instant the house was shaken to its foundations by a massive explosion outside, followed by the crackle of gunfire.

Chapter 54

Pressed tight against the western wall of the carport, Ben edged to the corner for a glance towards the red house, a hundred or so metres across the compound on the far end of the row of other buildings. He drew quickly back to rejoin Madison and held up four fingers, signalling to her that four guards were posted in front of the house.

Ben and Madison had managed to come this far from the trees without being spotted, but slipping across the relatively short distance from the fence, using the cover of the carport as a shield between them and the house, was the easy part. Things would get trickier from here. It wasn't so much the four men he could see that troubled Ben, but the rest of Kožul's guards scattered about unseen inside the other three buildings. The larger block was a concern. The more he studied it, the more it looked to him like a barracks or hangout for the men. For all he knew, there were thirty guys in there shooting pool and drinking beer, heavy weaponry at the ready for any sign of trouble. Or maybe he was just being paranoid.

Ben crept along the row of parked vehicles to the eastern end of the carport, from where he could get a clear view across to the hangar and smaller building beside it. During the time they'd been making their way through the woods to the fence, some activity had taken place at the hangar. The large steel doors were rolled open, and the helicopter housed inside had been wheeled half out into the sunlight.

The chopper was a Bell 206L LongRanger, sleek and bright red, the seven-seater version with enough room in the back to allow luxury-loving crime bosses to commute back and forth to work in that extra bit of comfort. Ben could see one of Kožul's men standing beside the helicopter, attending to a flap on the fuselage where the fuel tank was. He had a big electric pump set up beside him and a thick rubber pipe lay like a limp, dead snake across the hangar floor from the aircraft. From the adjoining workshop or generator room another man emerged pushing a handcart on which was loaded a large blue steel drum. It looked heavy. The man wheeled his load to the hangar, and the two of them got busily to work connecting the drum to the pipe and pump. Their boss's daily travels between here and New Belgrade must take a toll on fuel, and keeping it topped up must be their job, on top of regular sentry duties. The handcart guy had a Glock in a belt holster. The other was armed with an M16 that was lying on a metal table near the mouth of the hangar, where he could get to it quickly.

Now Ben knew what the smaller building was used to store. He waved for Madison to join him, and she trotted over with her head low. He pointed forked fingers at his eyes, then pointed in the direction of the building. Saying, *I want to check that out.* She nodded.

To make the dash to the fuel store was to cross more than twenty-five metres of open ground, risking being spotted. But the same risk applied no matter which way they tried to go from here, and the only safe alternative was to stay hidden behind the carport all day and let Kožul go about his business undisturbed. Ben counted to three, and they took a deep breath and broke cover and sprinted across the gap as fast as they could, clutching their rifles tight against their bodies and keeping their heads down.

Nobody saw them from the house. The two men working on the helicopter were too occupied with their activities to notice. Ben slipped inside the open doorway of the fuel store with his knife ready in case anyone else was in there, and Madison followed closely behind.

Ben didn't have to knife anybody. He looked around him. The storeroom was lit by a single dusty bulb on a wire. The craggy walls were cobwebbed and thick with old dirt. On a concrete plinth was an ancient diesel-powered generator connected to a spaghetti of wiring that ran through a hole in the wall to the overhead mast outside. The generator was running loudly, making all kinds of clattering noises and giving off a pungent stink of exhaust fumes. Next to it stood a grime-streaked mechanic's workbench with a metal tool rack on one side and a bay of industrial shelving units on the other, full of motor spares and maintenance parts for the cars and trucks.

The other end of the storeroom was an arsonist's dream. Against one wall stood a cluster of at least a dozen tall propane gas bottles that might be for heating or welding purposes, or perhaps to supply the blowtorches Kožul used to torture his enemies. A large collection of black and green jerrycans for diesel and gasoline took up space nearby. Then there was the mother lode: four large wooden pallets stacked with red metal two-hundred-litre drums with JET B lettered across their sides in white. Fuel for the chopper.

The wall above the drums displayed a big ZABRANJENO PUŠENJE No Smoking sign. Even murderers and gangsters cared about health and safety. Or maybe not, judging by the cigarette butts lying about the concrete floor. Nobody had managed to blow the place up yet, clearly. All the job required was a little care and expertise.

They didn't have much time. Ben said to Madison, 'Time to start warming things up around here. Get ready to run like hell.'

She moved closer to the doorway and peered cautiously out towards the hangar to check on the two men. 'Whatever insane thing you're about to do, do it fast.'

Ben started twisting open the wheel valves on each propane bottle in turn, working his way along the row until they were all hissing in unison and he could smell the rotten-egg smell of gas filling the storeroom. He moved quickly over to the pallets of Jet-B drums. Pressed the tip of his knife against the side of one of them, struck the butt of the handle a sharp blow with his other hand and the tempered carbon steel blade punched through the softer metal. Straw-coloured fuel came sluicing out and pattered on the floor.

He did the same with five more of the drums, until the fuel was beginning to pool rapidly on the concrete and he had to take care not to let his boots get soaked in the stuff. Jet fuel was less highly flammable than gasoline, so Ben stabbed holes in all of the green jerrycans as well. If a job was worth doing, it had to be done right. The air inside the storeroom was getting hard to breathe with all the mixed toxic fumes.

'Hurry,' Madison rasped from the door.

Ben grabbed an oily rag from the workbench, wrapped it around a short length of scrap battening timber, and wet it in the fast-spreading pool of gasoline. 'I'm done. Let's go.'

He stepped outside and breathed oxygen. The two men at the hangar were still refuelling the chopper, and had their backs to them. One was standing by the pump, the other supervising the hose that fed up the side of the fuselage to the tank. It was pulsing and quivering like a living thing as fuel gushed through it under pressure. If either of the two men turned around, they would see Ben and Madison standing there and instantly raise the alarm. But about two seconds from now, that would no longer be an issue.

Ben played the flame of his Zippo under the petrol-soaked rag on the stick and it burst alight.

'Party time,' Madison said. Ben tossed the blazing torch back through the storeroom doorway.

They ran.

There was an angry yell from the hangar.

Chapter 55

The guy by the pump had spotted them. He started to give chase, pulling the Glock from his belt holster and shouting in Serbian. He pointed the pistol as he ran and was about to squeeze off a wild shot at the two fleeing intruders heading for the carport. Nobody would ever hear the shot.

The man was a few paces from the entrance of the storeroom building when it blew, engulfing him in a massive explosion that tore the building apart and hurled its corrugated roof high into the sky. A gigantic fireball rolled upwards. Shrapnel from the ruptured propane bottles flew in all directions, hammering like deadly hailstones off the wall of the carport where Ben and Madison had taken cover an instant before the blast. Windows and headlights of the parked vehicles shattered. Alarms began shrieking. Roiling flames gushed from the windows of the shattered storeroom. A monumental tower of black smoke that could probably be seen from Belgrade was filling the sky and blocking out the sunlight. Small secondary explosions sent stabs of flame through the heart of the smoke.

'There goes our element of surprise,' Madison yelled in Ben's ear.

'Hold on tight.'

The remaining man inside the hangar had leapt away from the helicopter in a panic and snatched his rifle from the metal table when the shockwave of the explosion knocked him off his feet. Now he was scrambling back upright and going for his fallen rifle when Ben stepped out from behind the carport wall and shot him twice in the chest and he went back down.

Ben flipped his M16 to burst fire and sent a couple of bursts into the fuel pipe and drum of Jet-B. The punctured pipe ripped apart and the end still connected to the pump began writhing and leaping like an injured cobra, spraying fuel all over the hangar floor, the dead man and the helicopter. Arcs of Jet-B spouted from the holes in the drums. The flames from the burning storeroom were already licking at the inner wall of the hangar. It took only moments for the spreading rivulets of leaking fuel to reach the blaze.

In those same moments, through the smoke, Ben saw the figures of men emerging from the block building beyond the hangar, and more running from the direction of the house. He heard shouts and snapping gunfire. Then the approaching figures disappeared behind a huge curtain of flame that leaped twenty metres into the air as the jet fuel ignited and the whole hangar and everything around it burst alight. The helicopter was swallowed in the raging fire. Then it exploded, bringing half of the burning hangar down around it.

Out of the wall of flames came a human torch, one of the guards who had been too close when the fuel went up. His face and most of his body were invisible behind the flames that were eating him alive. He was staggering like a drunkard, pawing the air in desperation. Ben could feel sorry for a man's suffering, even when that man would have seen him tortured to death and laughed at the sight. A single round from Ben's rifle ended the pain for the man and he fell back and quietly burned.

More shapes were flitting and darting behind the smoke as Kožul's men spread out to counterattack. Sporadic bursts of gunfire crackled out over the roar of the blaze. Ben and Madison fell back to the cover of the carport and returned fire.

With all hell breaking loose, Madison Cahill was ice-cool. She was hunkered down behind the tailgate of a crew-cab Ford Ranger, using the heavy pickup truck for cover as she picked out her targets left, right and centre and engaged them efficiently, methodically, calmly. The old combat shooting instructors had a saying: *slow is smooth, and smooth is fast.* Madison was all three.

But the enemy were plentiful and they were determined. The muzzle flashes behind the dense black smoke drifting from the burning hangar looked like galaxies of twinkling stars on a dark night. Ben remembered what Husein Osmanović had told him. 'You kill five of his, he will only send ten more to take their places.'

So be it. Then they'd just have to keep killing them until nobody was left.

The carport was drawing such heavy fire that the vehicles inside were beginning to come apart. Shattered glass covered the concrete floor like snow. Ricochets were pinging all over the place like angry bees. Bullets splatted the bodywork of the Ford Ranger and forced Madison to slither away from the tailgate and crawl to a safer position behind the wheels of a truck trailer.

Ben kept shooting until his rifle ran dry. Lightning fast, he switched magazines and kept up his steady fire. BAPBAPBAP; BAPBAPBAP. This way, that way. Another shadowy figure went down behind the smoke. Then another.

With typically black military humour Ben's SAS comrades had used to joke that if they ever found Major Hope dead on the field of battle, he would be sitting in a great big pile of spent cartridge cases. It was getting to be that way now, as fired shells spewed from his weapon's sooty ejector port and heaped up all around where he was crouching. He could feel the hot brass rolling around underneath his legs and burning him painfully through his trousers. Better than a bullet burning through your flesh. Or a petrol bomb going off in your face. With so many bullets incoming, it was only a question of time before one of them holed the fuel tank of one of the vehicles in the carport. One unlucky spark, and Ben and Madison might suddenly become the main course at the barbecue.

But then the enemy fire was slackening. Ben could see the flitting figures, far fewer of them now, retreating behind the smoke. He reached out and touched Madison's shoulder, and she tore her gaze away from her rifle sights to look at him with huge intense battle eyes. Her cheeks were blacked with gunsmoke.

He said, 'Let's go,' and pointed ahead, and they advanced from their position to press forward the attack, firing as they went. A couple of Kožul's men turned to direct retreating fire their way and were cut down. The rest had had enough and were fleeing for the gates. Ben and Madison moved on across the compound, jumping over bodies. His rifle was empty. He dumped it and snatched up a pistol from one of the dead men. Madison did the same. The fight would be close-quarters from here on in.

The smoke from the still-burning hangar and shattered fuel store had thinned and dissipated to become a drifting grey mist over the entire compound, through which they could see the bright red house looming towards them like a surreal apparition as they approached. No more guards emerged from the house to open fire on them. The compound was now silent and empty, just the crackle of the flames and the moan of the wind. The first phase of the attack was over. But unless they'd managed to make their escape during the confusion, Zarko Kožul and Dragan Vuković were still somewhere inside the house. Hiding, or waiting.

This wasn't over yet.

Chapter 56

'The manuscript,' Madison hissed at Ben. 'It's what I came here for and I'm not leaving without it. If that sonofabitch Kožul's still in there, he might try to slip out the back way with it.'

Ben could see the determination in her eyes. 'Split up. You take the back, I'll take the front.'

Madison nodded and broke away from him at a fast trot with her pistol pointed out in front of her, keeping her head down just in case anyone fired on them from the windows. She darted through the row of SUVs parked in front of the house and skirted the low wall running alongside it and then disappeared around the corner and was gone.

Ben felt her sudden absence like a strange hollow sensation inside his chest, and it struck him that he was worried about her. He pushed that feeling to the back of his mind and moved cautiously to the front entrance. Stray bullets had knocked away bits of rendering from the masonry and drilled holes in the red-painted woodwork. He pressed his shoulder to the door and leaned against it. Not locked. It swung inwards, smooth and silent. Solid hardwood, three inches thick, on heavy brass hinges. The carpet inside the entrance hall was deep and soft underfoot. Bright red, like the inside walls, the skirting, even the ceilings. It was as if every square inch of Zarko Kožul's inner sanctum was saturated with so much blood it couldn't absorb another drop. Except there would always be more blood. Ben knew that. And more would surely be coming soon.

His battlefield capture was a heavy Colt 1911. The workhorse sidearm of every major war the US Army had fought throughout the twentieth century. Fully loaded it carried only eight rounds, but those .45-calibre bullets were decisive fight stoppers.

The entrance passage was long and wide, with glossy red doors set a few metres apart on both sides. Ben eased open the first door, ready to blast anyone hiding the other side of it. An empty cupboard, containing a few mops and cleaning products. Ben wondered who did the domestic chores around here. The gang lord as homemaker. He shut that door and opened the next. It was a lavatory, all in red – red bowl, red cistern, red sink; even the toilet paper was red. Thorough.

Ben kept moving. The sights and smells around him seemed strangely enhanced, like the effect of some drug on his system. That was because, with his ears still ringing badly from the battle, his other senses were kicking into overdrive to compensate until his hearing recovered. And it was his sense of smell that saved his life, exactly two seconds later as he reached the third door up the passage and started reaching for the handle.

The whiff of perfume reached Ben's nose and triggered an instant memory. It wasn't perfume, like a woman's scent. It was aftershave. The expensive stuff. He'd smelled the same smell only last night and now it was jangling critical danger warnings.

The glossy red paintwork of the door exploded into splinters as a storm of bullets ripped through from inside. But Ben had already seen it coming and ducked sideways out of their path. The door burst open and through it came Alek, the Skorpion submachine gun in his hands spitting fire. The door led up from a basement, a flight of stone steps leading downwards. Ben kicked the door hard back into Alek's face. The impact knocked the gun sideways in Alek's grip and he staggered backwards through the half-open doorway, still firing, bullets raking the opposite wall. Ben kicked the door again, harder, and caught Alek's gun arm in it as Alek tried to press through the gap. Ben put his weight against the door, trapping the arm hard against the edge of the doorway. Alek let out a roar of pain and rage, but he wouldn't drop the gun and was trying to twist it round towards Ben. Ben whipped out his knife and stabbed it deep through Alek's writhing arm and pinned it to the doorframe, and Alek's roar became a scream. Ben jammed the muzzle of the Colt against his side of the door and fired twice. The screaming stopped. The arm went limp. The Skorpion clattered to the floor.

Ben opened the door. Alek had slumped into a crouch, hanging from his pinned arm. The two .45-calibre holes in his chest had blown out his heart and lungs and he was wheezing his last few breaths, eyes trying to roll up at Ben and rapidly losing their focus. Ben might have been tempted to finish him off with a mercy shot to the head – then again, why waste the ammunition. He plucked out the knife to release the arm, then gave Alek a nudge with his foot and the dying man went bumping and rolling down the basement steps like a bin-liner full of dirty washing.

Ben closed the basement door. His ears were ringing worse now. Up ahead, the entrance passage ended at a wide archway with double doors. He stood still and listened hard, but all he could hear was the whining in his ears. There might be empty space behind the door. Alternatively, Zarko Kožul might be lying in wait there with a bazooka. Only one way to find out. Ben took a deep breath, then booted the double doors open.

The other side of them was a reception room, wider than the hallway. Ben glimpsed the figure standing there pointing a pistol at him and instinctively dropped into a combat aim-fire stance. His trigger was maybe half an ounce away from breaking when he realised it was Madison. She lowered her own weapon at the same instant and puffed her cheeks at him. 'Hey, don't be sneaking up on me like that.'

He asked her, 'Come up against any trouble, your end?'

She shook her head. 'All clear, from the back. I checked the rear grounds, pool house, nobody. You okay? I heard shots.'

'I'm okay. The other guy isn't.'

'Kožul?' She looked hopeful.

'One of his lieutenants.'

'Let's search the rest of the house. The others can't be far away.'

The reception area had more doors radiating off it. One led to an enormous kitchen that looked as though it had never been used. The next one they tried opened up into an even bigger living room, opulently decked out from top to bottom in Kožul's trademark red with enough large heavy leather furniture to stock a small warehouse. The room was deserted. Ben and Madison stepped inside.

'Jesus Christ, what is it with this red colour scheme? It's like freakin' vampires live here,' Madison muttered, gazing around her with a frown.

'Worse,' Ben said.

He was getting a sinking feeling as the conviction dawned on him that the house was now empty and both Zarko Kožul and Dragan Vuković had made their escape, along with Lena and the mysterious bald man in the linen suit. If Alek had taken refuge in the basement, it was easy to see how the rest of them could have fled without him. They could have taken off in one or more of the SUVs parked outside the house, their exit screened from view by the smoke of the burning helicopter hangar. Even if they'd escaped on foot, they could be far away by now. They'd be impossible to find in the wilderness.

Either way, not good.

Either way, mission failed.

'Come on,' Ben said. He motioned towards the door.

'Wait,' Madison said, holding up a hand to halt him. She seemed to have seen something. Ben watched as she hurried over to a table at the far side of the huge room. A black leather attaché case sat open on the tabletop. Even as Ben noticed it, he recognised the case as the one the bald man had carried inside the house earlier. Its contents had been laid out on the table next to it, some peculiar-looking instruments whose function Ben could only have guessed at.

But something else had drawn Madison's attention as she stood frozen at the edge of the table, gaping down in utter amazement at whatever she'd spotted there. She let out a little cry that sounded more like a little girl's voice than her own. Slipped her pistol into the back pocket of her jeans and reached down with shaking hands to pick up the yellowed, curly-edged, tattered, stained document that rested on the polished surface.

Madison turned to look at Ben with tears in her eyes, and held it out for him to see.

No mistake about it. In her hands was the same age-worn music manuscript Ben had seen inside the glass display cabinet in Nick Hawthorne's apartment that day.

'We found it. This is it. It's unbelievable. It's incredible. It's—' Madison shook her head, as though words had failed her.

'It's yours,' Ben said. 'You came a long way to find it. Now take it.'

Handling it as though it were one of the lost Dead Sea Scrolls, Madison edged the manuscript into an internal pocket of the attaché case. She closed the lid and snapped the catches. She stood staring for a moment at the shut case. Caressed the smooth leather, then reached up and wiped the back of her hand over her face. She sniffed. In the short time Ben had known her, he'd never seen her look so emotional. She murmured, 'I'm sorry.'

'Don't be. Now let's get out of here,' Ben said.

She looked at him. Her eyes were wet. 'What about Kožul? What about Vuković?'

'Long gone by now,' Ben said. 'If they've got any sense. That's what we're going to do too.' He stuck the heavy Colt into his belt.

'You wanted to get that guy so bad.'

'And I will,' Ben said. 'Some other time.'

'You helped me. I want to help you.'

'No chance. This time, you're going to do what I say and go straight home with that damn thing before more harm comes to it. Or to you.'

They left the living room and crossed the big reception room, Ben retracing his steps towards the exit the way he'd come. The double doors were right in front of them, leading to the entrance hall and the front door. A half-hour trek back to their vehicle, and they could be in Belgrade before dark. He would see her safely to the airport, get her booked on the first available flight out of Serbia and wait for her to be safely in the air before he resumed his hunt for Dragan Vuković. It was a small world. Ben would find him.

At any rate, that was the plan taking shape in Ben's mind.

But it was all about to change.

They were three-quarters across the reception area when one of the other doors radiating off it suddenly swung open and a harsh voice behind them said, 'You fucking mother-fuckers think you can get away so fucking easy?'

360

Chapter 57

Ben turned sharply round to see Zarko Kožul stepping out of the doorway towards them. All five feet nothing of him, built like a miniature bull and almost as broadly muscular as he was tall, still clad from head to toe in bright crimson that made him blend into his surroundings. His face was flushed dark with pulsating fury and his eyes were bloodshot. The only thing about him that wasn't red was the little gold-plated .380 Walther PPK automatic clenched in his muscular right hand. Gaudy but deadly, and pointed right at Ben's heart.

Ben's reflex was to reach for his own weapon, but he checked himself. Pure survival instinct, because the Colt was tucked in his belt with the safety on. The fastest quick-draw pistoleros in the world could clear the leather and hit two balloons eight feet apart in a tenth of a second. Ben wasn't too much slower than that. But balloons don't shoot back, and a .380 slug would travel the ten feet between Kožul's gun and himself and Madison in a hundredth of a second.

The maths weren't in Ben's favour. He stilled his gun hand. Madison's own weapon was still in her jeans pocket. She had probably come to the same conclusions Ben had.

Kožul was not alone. Dragan Vuković emerged from the doorway after him and stood at his mentor's shoulder, which was barely higher than Dragan's midriff. They looked like a comedy duo together, but Ben didn't suppose that was the reason Dragan looked so amused.

'You got them, boss,' Dragan said in Serbian. He had a big black nine-millimetre in his own hand, loose at his side. 'Blow them both away. Do it, boss, before the bastards cause you any more trouble.'

'Dragan is impatient,' Kožul said in English. 'Young and dumb and impulsive, like I used to be.'

'Maturity can bring such wisdom to the enlightened few,' Ben said.

Kožul wagged the gold Walther. 'Enough bull. Pistols on the floor. Finger and thumb, nice and slow. Any tricks and I'll put one in your eye. I'm a real good shot with this.'

Ben hesitated, then slowly reached down to the butt of the Colt. Inched the weapon out of his belt between thumb and forefinger, dangled it in front of him and let it drop to the carpet with a soft thud. Madison did the same with hers.

'Blades too,' Kožul said. Next the matching pair of survival knives joined the pistols on the red carpet.

'Now the case,' Kožul said. 'What's inside it belongs to me.'

Madison paused, as though she might actually be considering bolting with the attaché case and its precious contents. Then she let out a sigh and set the case down at her feet and slid it towards Kožul.

Dragan Vuković stepped forward and gathered up all the hardware. He thrust the two pistols in his pockets and the knives through his belt, then grabbed up the case and went back to stand close to his boss.

'That's better,' Kožul said. 'Now how about we all go make ourselves comfortable in the other room. I got some calls to make.'

Now Dragan was pointing his nine-mil at them as well. Ben and Madison led the way at gunpoint as they all filed into the living room. Kožul directed them to a pair of red leather-upholstered chairs near the window, ordered them to sit, then took a seat himself in the centre of a broad red sofa opposite, making the leather creak under his squat bulk. His legs were so short that his feet didn't touch the floor, making him look like an evil, steroid-filled, prematurely-aged child of twelve. Meanwhile Dragan walked to a glass-topped coffee table well out of the prisoners' reach, and laid their guns and knives down on its surface. He set the case down next to the table, then pulled a small walkie-talkie radio handset from his pocket and thumbed the call button. There was a garbled crackling of static, nothing else. 'I can't raise anyone, boss,' he said. 'They're all gone.'

'What about Alek?' Kožul asked. Dragan shook his head.

'Alek's taking a nap in the basement,' Ben said. 'A long one.'

Kožul studied Ben for a long moment as he played with the shiny gold pistol, then said, 'So you're Hope. The piece of shit who broke up my place of business and took out half my guys. And now you think you're just gonna come strolling into my home and cost me more fuckin' grief, hmm? For what? You think I owe you money or something?'

'You're not important to me, Kožul. I came here for him,' Ben said. He pointed at Dragan. 'It's a personal thing between the two of us, nobody else. Hand him over to me, and I'll let you live.'

Kožul laughed loudly and twisted round in the sofa to cast a grin back at Dragan, but not long enough for Ben to rush him and put his nose bone through his brain. 'Check out the balls of steel on this motherfucker,' he snorted, and Dragan shook his head in disbelief. Kožul turned back to

363

face Ben, and the amused look turned serious again. 'So tell me, what's my man Dragan done to you that you came all the way out here to fix his business?'

'He killed a friend of mine. I get kind of unreasonable when people do things like that.'

Kožul shrugged. 'So get in line. You killed a bunch of my guys too.'

'That's what comes from mixing in bad company,' Ben said.

'We gotta finish this prick, Zarko,' Dragan interjected in Serbian. 'Just say the word. I'm itching to whack'm.'

'Hear that? Dragan wants you dead nearly as much as I do. And you will be, pretty soon. But why rush things? Like I said, I'm going to make a call or two. Get some other guys over here. I got plenty more. Then we're gonna take ourselves a drive back into town, to this junkyard I happen to own. Lot of problems get solved there.' Kožul waved the gold pistol at Ben. 'And we're going to have ourselves a party getting rid of this one, right, Dragan?'

'Flatten him good,' Dragan said in English, eyes fixed on Ben.

'You won't be alone,' Kožul said with a twinkle in his eye. 'That bitch of a sister of Dragan's is gonna be joining you. We'll have her go first, so you can watch her pretty little body go into the crusher and split open like a fuckin' tomato. People pay good cash for that kind of shit on video. Then it'll be your turn. Won't be such a wise-ass then.'

Dragan was smiling. Ben looked at him. This guy's employer was talking about inflicting a slow and horrific death on his own sister and filming the event for entertainment, and he was smiling.

Ben looked back at Kožul. 'What did Lena do to piss you off so badly, Zarko?'

'None of your fuckin' affair what she did,' Kožul said. 'She fucked up my business. People who fuck up my business pay the price. As you'll find out.'

'I thought maybe she laughed at you when you tried to make a pass at her, because you're just a runt.'

Kožul's eyes flashed dangerously. 'Keep talking, smart guy. The more you wag that tongue of yours, the worse it gets for you. I just added another hour to your death. Believe me, we've had plenty of practice at making it last.'

'The cops are on their way here, right now,' Madison said. 'They could be arriving here any minute, all ready to lock you up for a very long time.'

'Is that a fact, lady?'

Madison said, 'Yup. And if I were you, I'd be running away as fast as my fat, stumpy little runt legs could carry me. Pint-sized prisoners have a much worse time in jail.'

Kožul digested her words, then the corners of his mouth downturned in an inverted U and he replied, 'That's interesting. You want to see what a pint-sized stumpy little runt like me can do? Watch this.'

Before Ben could launch himself in the way to protect her, Kožul turned the muzzle of the .380 automatic towards Madison and fired once. The sharp crack stabbed the air. Madison went over backwards, toppling the chair with her. Her head hit the wall behind her and she slid to the floor with her eyes closed and lay in an immobile heap.

Ben rose to his feet. But the .380 was already pointing his way and the pistol in Dragan Vuković's hand was aiming in the same direction.

Kožul said, 'I would advise you to sit yourself the fuck down, Mr Hope.'

Chapter 58

Ben stood looking at Kožul for what felt like a long, long time. He felt very cold, and he was breathing too fast. His heart was pounding in his throat.

He slowly sat down.

Madison Cahill was not moving.

Kožul glanced over at her as if she was a dead fly he'd just swatted, and gave a chuckle. 'Told you I was handy with this thing, didn't I? One shot, right in the heart.'

'That was a good one, boss,' Dragan said.

'That's why I'm always telling you, practice. Right? Practice is the only way you get to be a good shot like me. A few hours from now, Hope, you're gonna be begging me to do the same to you.'

Ben made no reply. He kept glancing at Madison. The sight of her lying there was more than he could bear.

Kožul smiled. 'Speaking of that, I can't be hanging around here all day. Let's get this show on the road. Dragan, go find that murdering bitch sister of yours, and drag her in here. She's gotta be hiding in one of the other bedrooms. Break her fuckin' arms if you have to, but I want her alive. Understand?'

'I can do that,' Dragan said, and headed for the door with a big grin on his face. Your lord and master tells you to go and fetch your sister for execution, you obey without hesitation. Dragan left the room, still grinning to himself.

Alone with Zarko Kožul, Ben stared at the mean little killer on the sofa opposite him. Looked into his eyes and saw nothing. Then he looked at Madison, and at the smear of blood on the wall, glistening red on red above her fallen chair and slumped body. He couldn't have saved her, but even so he knew the guilt would weigh on him for however long he had left in this world. He looked at the gun in the hand of the man who had shot her. The icy coldness that had taken a grip at the core of his being was slowly spreading through him, numbing him all over. He felt his breathing slow and his heart rate settle. His muscles began to relax.

In a normal person, those were the physiological signs of the body getting ready for rest. For Ben Hope, it meant he was gearing up for action.

Ben stood up from his chair. He took a step towards Kožul.

'I still got seven rounds in this thing,' Kožul warned. 'The first two are for your balls, you come another step.'

Ben said, 'I've known a hundred men like you, Zarko. You like to leave the dirty work to others to take care of. You think you're above attending to the small stuff. Like cleaning the house, looking after the helicopter. Basic maintenance.'

Kožul was glowering, but Ben could see he was already a little unnerved. 'What is this lunatic bullshit you're feeding me? Sit the fuck down and shut up.'

Ben didn't sit. 'Like that gun in your hand. I'll bet you spend hours polishing your pretty little gold rocket, but you don't like to get your hands all black and oily from the parts that matter, like scrubbing out the chamber, or cleaning all

367

the crud off the feed ramp, or making sure the springs are all good and tight.'

'What the fuck are you talking about, you stupid fuck?'

'Just the fact that your gun's jammed, Zarko. Don't take my word for it. Try pressing the trigger and see what happens.'

Kožul stared blankly at Ben, and then pulled the trigger of the Walther.

Nothing happened. Not even a click. The mechanism was locked up solid.

Ben came on another step. 'In the business, we call it FTE. Failure to eject. It's the firearms equivalent of a motorway pile-up. Only happens with automatics, which makes some folks still prefer revolvers even in this day and age. Your slide isn't fully closed, because there's a live round jammed up hard behind the spent case that the ejector failed to pull out after that last shot. Now the slide is stuck partly open, the magazine won't come out, and it's going to take a couple of minutes of basic gunsmithing work to clear the jam. And you don't have two minutes. See what I'm saying?'

Kožul stared at the gun in his hand as though Ben had just worked some conjuror's trick and turned it into a live cobra. Ben took another step towards him.

'So now you're in an awful lot of trouble, Zarko. That's what they call "the tables turning". And you'd better pray that your flunky Dragan comes back soon, because I'm about to snap your filthy neck.'

Kožul threw himself forwards off the sofa and stood braced with his lips peeled away from his teeth in a snarl, showing jagged teeth. It was like being faced with a dangerous little predator, like a wolverine. He hurled the useless pistol at Ben.

Ben ducked the missile and came in fast and low. Fast,

because even unarmed Kožul was a tough little nut to crack. Low, because even with his opponent standing Ben had to direct his strike at a downward angle. He drove an elbow into Kožul's throat. Kožul rocked on his feet and let out a gurgling croak, but didn't go down. He might have charged then, all muscle and gristle and hard little fists and snapping teeth, but Ben wasn't going to allow him time to counter-attack. He followed the elbow strike with a straight kick that drove Kožul's right knee joint inwards and broke his leg with a crunch.

This time, Kožul did go down, and hard. Ben landed on top of him. Kožul was incredibly strong for his size, as powerful and feral and as uninhibited in his violence as a chimpanzee crazed on angel dust. He bucked and twisted and tried to hurl Ben's weight off him, but Ben hung on tight and kept him pinned to the red carpet. Four more elbow strikes to the face, and Ben felt the teeth cave in. Then he grabbed Kožul by both ears and battered his head off the floor at least ten times, until Kožul was beginning to flag and his eyes were rolling back in their sockets.

Then Ben cupped a hand under Kožul's chin and the other one at the back of his skull, and gave his head a sudden, sharp wrench, up and sideways to rend the vertebrae in his neck. Muscles like a bull from years of pumping iron didn't save you from having the same weak spots as any other mortal man. Ben felt the neck break, gave it a couple more violent twists, then let Kožul's dead body sink down limp.

He jumped to his feet and began running over to Madison. He was halfway to her when he heard the door open and Dragan Vuković's voice saying, 'Boss? I couldn't find her, boss. I—'

Dragan halted mid-stride and mid-word, and froze in the doorway.

369

Chapter 59

Dragan's gaze went to Kožul's twisted shape on the floor and lingered there for a moment, before he turned his look on Ben with murder burning brighter than blazing jet fuel in his eyes. He clawed the pistol from his belt and ran into the room, blasting like a crazy man. His first shot hit a television screen. His second shattered the glass top of the little coffee table where Ben and Madison's weapons were piled. The third would have hit Ben, if Ben hadn't already been diving for cover behind one of the red leather sofas. As large and sturdy as they were, they offered little protection. Dragan's bullets ripped through the wood and leather and ploughed into the red carpet inches from Ben's body.

Dragan was screaming, 'You killed Zarko. You fucked up everything. Now you die!'

Kožul's pistol was lying nearby on the floor. Ben snatched it up and hurled it at Dragan's head. He was better at throwing than Kožul. The gun bounced hard off the middle of Dragan's brow and made him cry out in pain. The skin of his forehead was ripped open. He faltered for a second, trying to wipe away the blood that poured into his eyes.

Which bought Ben enough time to belly-crawl over to the shattered coffee table. He could see his Colt lying among the broken glass on the floor beneath it. Dragan had cleared the blood from his eyes and was coming after him again. Ben reached out for the Colt. His middle finger touched the end of its chequered butt, but it was just beyond his grasp to pick up. A couple more inches, and he'd have it. But Dragan had realised he was going for the gun, and fired again. The bullet passed between Ben's fingers and smacked into the floor. He felt the searing pain and the sudden wetness of the blood and drew his hand sharply away.

Now Dragan strode up to him, aiming downwards with the nine-millimetre for the kill shot. Blood was still pouring freely from the flap of skin torn loose from his brow. His face was twisted in hatred, veins standing out on his neck like ropes. Ben rolled on his back and lashed a kick out at him and caught Dragan's shin with his heel as the shot went off. Dragan's aim wavered and the shot burned into the floor beside Ben's left ear.

The back-force of the kick was enough to slide Ben a couple of inches along the floor. Close enough to the table to reach out behind him with his uninjured left hand and grab the Colt from the pile of broken glass. His fingers locked around its butt and he found the trigger and brought the weapon up over his head in an arc and flashed the sights on Dragan's chest and—

The percussive blast of the gunshot that filled the room was twice as loud as a pistol going off. Like a Claymore mine exploding at close quarters. Dragan was thrown violently forwards as though a horse had kicked him from behind. He hit the floor next to Ben, landing on his face with his arms outflung. There was a bloody raw mess of pulped flesh the size of a dinner plate in the middle of his back.

Ben hadn't fired. For an instant he was confused and didn't understand what had just happened. Then he looked up and saw Lena Vuković standing there.

Her hair was wild and her face was covered in tears. The red dress she was wearing was ripped at the shoulder. There were speckles of dried blood on her throat, on her arms, and on the small slim hands that were clutching the black short-barrelled shotgun. A trickle of blue smoke was oozing from its barrel, which was still pointing towards where Dragan lay inert on the red carpet. She slowly lowered the weapon, came a faltering step closer and gazed down at her brother's body.

'Is he . . . is he dead?' she whispered, barely audible.

Ben made no reply. He rolled to his feet, dropped his pistol and scrambled past Dragan and over to where Madison was lying. She still hadn't moved. Kneeling by her side, he looked for the gunshot wound where Kožul had shot her in the chest. When he saw the blood on her his stomach clenched tight. Then he realised it was his own blood dripping and flecking everywhere from his injured hand.

Madison opened her eyes. 'Ben?' she croaked.

She was alive, but how? 'He shot you.'

She groaned and lifted her head off the floor, then propped herself up on one elbow. 'Hurts.'

She tugged open her biker jacket. Something solid and rectangular slipped out of her inside pocket and hit the floor between her and Ben. He picked it up with his good hand. It was the slim black wallet containing the Fugitive Recovery Special Agent's badge she'd showed him in the cafeteria back in Belgrade. The wallet had been punched through on one side. When he flipped it open, a nine-millimetre jacketed bullet fell out, squashed as flat as a coin. The seven-pointed gold star badge attached to the inside of the wallet had a deep circular impression dented into the steel where the bullet had struck. If Ben had a badge that lucky, he would have hung it on the wall back home as a memento.

Madison felt the back of her head and winced. Her fingers came away red. 'Must've knocked myself out when I hit the deck.' Then she saw the blood on Ben's hand, and the sight seemed to shock her back to the reality of the moment. She gasped and looked around her.

'Kožul's dead,' Ben said. 'Dragan too. Lena shot him.'

Madison said, 'Lena?'

Lena Vuković was still standing there over her brother's still form, gazing down at him with a vague expression on her face as if she didn't yet fully grasp what had happened. She turned her unfocused gaze slowly Ben's way. 'Did I kill him?' she asked.

Ben stood up, helping Madison get to her feet. 'It's over for him, Lena. The world's a better place now.'

She nodded, slowly. She was still holding the ugly black shotgun, its weight sagging down to point at the floor by her feet. She looked at it and blinked. 'They were going to sell me to that man. I try to get away. He . . . he stabbed himself. I don't know how it happened. Then I am hiding, because I know they will come for me. Suddenly there is so much noise, gunshots and explosions and shouting, and I get scared. I found this gun in the room where I hid. I—'

She hung her head and screwed her eyes shut, then reopened them and tears leaked down her cheeks. 'Dragan, he was searching for me. Then I hear more shooting inside the house, and I run, and that was when I find you. He was going to kill you. I had to shoot him. I would have killed him anyway.'

'You did the right thing,' Ben said. 'He wasn't much of a brother to you.'

'He would have stood by and seen me sold like a slave.'

Ben didn't add that Dragan would also have been content to stand by and watch as Zarko Kožul fed her into a hydraulic car crusher. He might even have done the honours himself. Some things, maybe Lena didn't need to know.

'Dragan was a bad man. You told me that yourself, remember?'

She nodded again, more tears rolling down her face. 'Yes, I knew this. I always knew.'

'And now he's gone, you're free to get on with your life,' Ben said.

She looked at him. 'You will let me go? After everything that happened here?'

'I never saw you, Lena. Because I was never here either. Nor my friend Madison.'

Lena turned away from Dragan's body and walked a step towards Ben. 'You are a good man, Ben Hope,' she whispered.

'I'll second that,' Madison said, and squeezed his arm.

'Are you sure you're okay?' he said to her.

Madison looked over at the attaché case with the manuscript inside. She smiled. 'Never better. But look at your hand.'

'Just a scratch.' Ben smiled back at her, despite the throbbing pain in his damaged fingers.

'You're going to need surgery.'

Ben flexed his fingers and the blood pattered to the floor like rain. The agony was enough to take his breath away, but he smiled. 'See? Perfectly functional.'

He would tell himself afterwards that it was the distraction of the moment, and the pain, that prevented him from reacting fast enough to stop what happened next.

Behind Lena, Dragan Vuković's bloodied and tattered body suddenly raised itself off the floor as if some demonic force had filled it with a final burst of energy. His eyes snapped open, white in the red mask of his face, and turned towards his sister. The nine-millimetre clenched in his fist came up and pointed at her back.

Madison screamed. Ben yelled, 'Look out!' and Lena began to spin around, and then a tongue of yellow-white fire boomed from the muzzle of the gun. Ben was leaping for his pistol.

Lena's body went as rigid as if she'd been hooked up to a main power line. She tottered back a step and almost fell, but somehow she managed to stay on her feet and bring up the shotgun.

Dragan shot her again.

The shotgun went off in Lena's hands. Its deadly payload of buckshot and the big .45-calibre slug from Ben's pistol both slammed at once into Dragan's chest and the simultaneous impact kicked him flat. This time, Dragan Vuković truly wasn't getting up again.

But he hadn't gone down alone. Lena dropped the shotgun and fell backwards as Ben caught her in his arms. Her eyes rolled up to look at him and she burped a red mist, and then she was gone.

Ben did what he could to revive her. Madison helped, the two of them taking turns until they were both slicked with Lena's blood and there was no longer any chance of bringing her back. Wherever Lena Vuković had slipped away to, Ben could only hope it was a better place than her brother.

The red house, now a deathly tomb, fell into silence. There seemed to be nothing more to say. Ben took Madison's hand, and she hugged him tight for a long moment. Then he broke away from her and knelt by Dragan's body to frisk him for the keys to the SUV that had brought him and Lena to the house. Madison picked up the case with the manuscript inside. It would not be out of her sight again until she reached the USA.

Outside, Ben blipped the key fob at the line of parked SUVs in front of the house. The last one in the line flashed its indicators and unlocked itself with a *clunk*.

'I'll drive,' Madison said. Ben let her. She stowed her case in the back, and he climbed into the passenger seat and lit his last Gauloise with his good hand, and Madison fired up the car and took off. They left the burning ruins of Zarko Kožul's compound without looking back, and didn't talk about it all the way to Belgrade.

A new journey was about to begin, for both of them. The final voyage of the Bach manuscript.

Chapter 60

Oahu, Hawaiian Islands
Two days later

The surf whispered on the white sands, driven by the warm ocean breeze that made the palms gently sway and rustle above the beach house veranda. Rigby Cahill sat in his recliner under the shade, gazing out to sea. He had been sitting there for a long time, too lethargic to even go and get himself a drink. Only he could know what was going on in his mind during the endless hours he spent just watching the blue horizon and the waves roll in. He was barefoot in shorts, wearing a battered straw hat with a torn rim and a fresh, crisp hibiscus-pattern shirt that he hadn't bothered to button up, so that his sunburned belly protruded like a shrivelled balloon. The shirt had been laundered and ironed for him that morning by his housekeeper Noelani, or else he most likely would be wearing the same one he'd worn all week. It didn't matter very much to him what he wore. Month in, month out, nothing much mattered at all. Just serving out his time, was all it was.

Rigby heard the crunch of tyres on the gravel out front, and car doors opening and closing, followed by the sound of two, maybe more, sets of footsteps creaking up the steps to the front door. He could tell it wasn't Noelani returning to attend to some task or other, because the car sounded different from the little Honda she drove, and she always came alone. Rigby was aware of all these things, but he didn't shift in his recliner or pull his tired old eyes away from the ocean. Next, he heard the front door open, and voices. The unexpected sound of his daughter's voice brought a warm tingle. He never told Madison how much he loved her visits. But who was that with her?

He still didn't move, but he was listening more intently now. There was a man's voice, not saying much, one that Rigby didn't recognise. Then, a different woman's voice. Rigby's eyes flickered and something moved deep inside him, as if someone had put a spoon inside a pot of old memories crusted over with time and given it a gentle stir. He knew that voice, but damned if he could remember from where. Rigby let out a long sigh. What the hell?

Behind him, the veranda door creaked open and Madison's familiar footsteps sounded on the boards. 'Dad?' said her soft voice close to his ear as she bent down. 'I came to see you. How are you doing?'

Rigby shrugged. 'Okay, I guess.' He could barely even remember the last time he'd heard his own voice. Sounded croaky and weak.

'Dad?'

He slowly shifted himself around in his recliner to look at her. His beautiful daughter, looking more like her mother all the time. But the expression in her eyes was different from usual. She always looked worried around him. Now it was worry mixed with excitement. He couldn't figure out why. She was holding a case. What was that about?

'Dad, I've got something for you. It's, well, get ready for a surprise, Dad.'

He watched, bemused, as Madison laid the case on the veranda deck next to his chair and opened the lid. From inside she took a slim card folder. She laid the folder softly on his lap. 'Open it, Dad.'

'Is it my birthday?' Not that he celebrated them any longer. Not for decades.

'Better than a birthday, Dad. Take a look inside.'

Rigby uncurled his hands from the arms of the recliner. They seemed to weigh a ton each as he slowly picked up the folder. He glanced nervously up at Madison.

'Go on, don't be afraid,' she said, smiling. Her eyes were shining.

Rigby Cahill opened the folder and looked inside. He didn't comprehend what he was seeing at first. Understanding dawned on him like the golden rays of sunrise over an ocean that had been too dark for too long, filling him with light and warmth for the first time in an age. His heart began to pump. It could not be real. But it was.

'It's . . . it's . . .'

Madison brushed a tear from her eye. 'Yes, Dad. It is. This is it. We found it, after all these years. We got it back.'

Ben had stepped out onto the veranda, moving very quietly, unnoticed by the old man. He'd seen so many people die. Watching Rigby Cahill at this moment was like seeing someone who was already dead come to life, a small but vital flicker of flame rekindled from the cold ashes. It was a strange thing to witness.

The pages of the old music manuscript fluttered in the old man's hands. 'I don't understand. Where did you find it? Who found it?'

Madison flashed a look over towards where Ben was standing behind her father's chair. She looked as though she was about to announce his presence and introduce them. Ben shook his head. He pointed his left thumb over his shoulder, back through the doorway. His right thumb was lost in the bandages that covered the two damaged fingers. The doctor in Belgrade who'd done the patching up had been told the injury was a dog bite. He hadn't looked convinced, but cash is king.

Madison nodded, understanding what Ben was telling her with his signal. She wiped her eyes and bent down closer to her father and put a hand on his arm. 'Dad? I have another surprise for you.'

Her father blinked up at her. From sitting doing nothing for years on end, to not one but two major life-altering incidents in the space of a single afternoon. Madison had talked at length on the journey here about her concern that their plan might all be too much for Rigby Cahill to handle. Ben reckoned the old guy was tougher than that. They would soon find out who was right.

'What surprise?' Rigby said, frowning.

'You have a visitor. Someone who's come a very long way, especially to see you.'

Ben turned to open the veranda door, then stepped aside to let the visitor walk out.

Miriam Silbermann wasn't at all what Ben had expected when he and Madison had met her flight at Honolulu International earlier that afternoon. At the age of 92, she stood as erect as a dancer and was considerably fitter than most sixty-year-olds. Whether it was the clean air of the mountains around Zermatt, or decades of yoga or t'ai chi or simply force of spirit, she carried herself with effortless pride and exuded fierce independence. Anyone who dared to take her arm to assist her up steps or in and out of a car would probably withdraw a stump. Ben was in enough pain as it was.

Miriam was slim and elegant in a Givenchy outfit that was made for a Swiss summer rather than the burning Hawaiian sun, but managed to appear perfectly cool and airy. Nothing whatsoever in her demeanour could have given away the fact that she'd just travelled over 7,500 miles at a moment's notice to be here. The sea breeze rippled her white hair. She removed her sunglasses to reveal blue-green eyes that were as vivid and bottomless as the Pacific Ocean stretching across the horizon.

Ben could fully understand why Rigby Cahill had fallen in love with her, all those years ago. Even now, Miriam probably still had a horde of far younger suitors back home, tripping over one another to win her favour.

'Rigby,' she said.

Rigby Cahill seemed to go rigid for a moment, then slowly turned to look at her. As agile as a ballerina, Miriam crouched down beside his chair to be at eye level with him.

Rigby Ignatius Boddington Cahill, This is Your Life.

The manuscript, still trembling in his hands, now fell into his lap. His mouth hung open. His expression was one of utter bewilderment, but the recognition in his eyes could have been spotted from San Diego.

'*Miriam?*'

Her English was as perfect as her ageless beauty. 'Yes, Rigby, it's Miriam. How are you, my dear old friend? It has been such a very long time.' She clasped his hands tightly in hers.

It was hard to tell what was going on inside the old man's mind as a thousand different emotions played out on his face. He was silent for what seemed like minutes as he stared at her. Finally, apparently accepting that this wasn't some kind of waking dream, or that he hadn't died in his chair and woken up in heaven, he said, 'I feel much better now.'

'Our manuscript,' Miriam said, lowering her gaze to look at it resting on his lap. *Our* manuscript.

'No, it's yours,' Rigby said. As though he'd suddenly received an injection of the Elixir of Life, his voice sounded ten times stronger. He slipped his hands out of hers and picked up the manuscript to offer to her. 'Madison found it for you. Take it.'

Madison flashed another look over at Ben and he could tell she wanted to cut in and say, 'Actually, folks, I can't take all the credit for finding it; meet Ben Hope.' But he preferred to stay out of the limelight and gave her another shake of his head.

'May I?' Miriam took the manuscript gently in her slim, immaculate hands, rose to her feet and turned towards the veranda balcony to gaze at her rediscovered family treasure for a long, long moment. The sadness in her expression would have filled the ocean as she ran her fingers over the yellowed, faded paper. They lingered over the odd brownish-russety stain on the cover sheet. She closed her eyes, and for a strange couple of moments Ben thought she looked like a spirit medium trying to connect with something unseen and otherworldly.

That was when he finally understood.

'Let's leave them alone for a while,' Madison mouthed to him. She nodded towards the doorway. She and Ben drew away from the scene and went inside the house.

Chapter 61

They stood watching through the ocean-facing windows as the two old folks sat together and talked. Madison inched closer to Ben, reached across and took his hand, squeezed it.

'Thank you,' she whispered. 'This is happening because of you.'

'Ouch.'

She realised what she'd done. 'Oh – I'm sorry! I didn't mean—'

'Shh. Look,' Ben said, pointing with his good hand.

Madison looked back out onto the veranda and put her fingers to her mouth. 'Oh my God.'

Rigby was getting out of his recliner. Arm in arm, he and Miriam stepped down the three wooden steps that led to the white sand. Five years his senior, she was the one who had to steady him; but he was on his feet and walking, by his own volition, somewhere other than the short journey to the bathroom or his bed.

Madison couldn't help herself. She gave a sob, and then the tears came flooding. Ben put his arm around her shoulders and she squeezed close to him, crying and beaming and sniffing and laughing all at once. 'Look at them. Aren't they beautiful together?'

'Yes,' Ben said. 'Yes, they are.'

'If only this could have happened years ago.' Madison shook her head, following the two white-haired figures as they moved slowly along the empty sands with the blue ocean and surf beyond. 'This is a moment I'll never forget,' she said. 'Again, thank you.'

'I didn't do anything,' he replied.

'You only think that, because that's who you are,' she said. 'I'm thanking you. Like a gift. You have to accept it.'

'Or else?'

She smiled. 'Or I'll kick your limey-half-Mick ass so hard, you'll be wearing it as a ten gallon hat.'

'Then you leave me no choice. I accept your thanks. But I had a pretty good backup.'

'Neat team, you and me, huh?'

'We ought to do it again sometime.'

Madison pressed closer, reached up with her lips and kissed him.

'Another thank you?' he said.

'Or something.'

Later, Rigby was exhausted from his stroll on the beach and retired to his room for a lie down. As the sun began to descend over the ocean, Miriam Silbermann sat in the beach house with Ben and Madison, and they talked. 'I can't express my gratitude to you for agreeing to come visit Dad,' Madison said, for the hundredth time. 'I could say you don't know what it means to him, but I guess you do.'

Miriam was sitting perfectly upright in an armchair with the manuscript on her knees. Ben noticed the way she kept touching it.

'It has been quite a day for him,' Miriam said with a warm smile. 'And for me.' She looked down at the manuscript. 'It certainly has come a long way, hasn't it?'

'Nobody will ever know for sure where it's been,' Ben said. 'But now it's back where it belongs.'

Miriam nodded. 'It belongs with your father,' she said to Madison.

'That's too much,' Madison replied, shaking her head. 'I couldn't possibly expect you to give it up. Neither would Dad.'

'Please. I insist. I ask only that you let me hold it a while.'

Even as sundown came, the warmth of the day permeated the beach house and Miriam had finally surrendered to the heat by rolling up the sleeves of her Givenchy outfit. Her arms were thin and pale, but still toned and strong-looking. She wore a gold Cartier on one wrist and a platinum chain bracelet on the other, but it was something else that Ben had noticed. Miriam caught him looking, and Ben felt embarrassed; but instead of trying to hide it, she raised her left forearm to let him see the faded blue tattoo on its underside, midway between wrist and elbow. The tattoo was a six-digit serial number. Beneath the number, a small triangle had been indelibly inked into her flesh.

'Memories,' she said. 'Better never to forget them, Mr Hope. Reflecting on our past, no matter how painful, reminds us of who we are. That is the reason I chose not to have it removed.'

The tattoo could only mean one thing. Ben had seen pictures, but he'd never seen one, literally, in the flesh before. During the Nazi Holocaust only one concentration camp had adopted the policy of marking its prisoners that way on arrival. Miriam Silbermann had been prisoner 135287. The triangle was a way of telling the Jewish inmates apart from other groups, such as Gypsies or political detainees.

'You were sent to Auschwitz,' Ben said. 'You and your family.'

Miriam Silbermann closed her eyes again, and held them

385

shut for so long that Ben began to think she must have drifted off to sleep. Then she opened them again, and the blue-green light seemed to penetrate through him. She said, 'Yes. After the internment camp at Drancy, we were put on a train along with thousands of others. I will never forget that train. The noise, the darkness, the smell of fear. There were so many of us crammed into the carriages, like cattle. We all knew where we were going. To the death camp. To Auschwitz.'

'I'm so sorry,' Madison said.

'So much has been said about that place, and yet nobody can understand who was not made to suffer it. Neither of my dear parents survived, of course. My mother died in the first month, my father a month later. Me, I had to make myself strong. To will myself to survive, God willing, no matter what horrors took place there. And so, I did. I was the only one who returned, after the Red Army liberated the camp on January 27th, 1945.'

'Weren't there four of you?' Madison said. 'Dad told me you had a brother. Gabriel.'

The old woman was silent for a beat, then another, then she slowly shook her head. 'Gabriel was never in the camp. I have to thank the Lord that he did not have to endure that torture. His suffering was brief and merciful by comparison.' Again, she passed her long, slender fingers over the stain on the manuscript.

'This is my brother's blood,' she said quietly. 'The day the Germans came, he wouldn't let them take our family treasure. And so, they shot him. Murdered him with a bullet, in his own home. I was not even allowed to touch his body before they took us away. It was the single most terrible moment of my life, and I have had many. Too many.'

'That's why you wanted the manuscript so badly,' Ben

386

said. 'Not because of what it was. It was all you had left of Gabriel.'

Miriam nodded. 'I wanted nothing more than simply to touch him, one last time. Now I feel him again with me. There is no need for me to keep this.'

She gently placed the manuscript on a sideboard next to where she sat. 'When your father awakes, please express to him my undying thanks and give him this token of my gratitude, and my love.'

'He loved you,' Madison said. 'Right from the moment he met you.'

Miriam's lips curled up at the corners. 'I know. Of course, I always knew. He is a wonderful man, your father. He would not give up, even after the search for the manuscript had broken him in body and spirit. I hope he will be happier now, bless him.'

'I think so.'

Then Miriam Silbermann heaved a long, long sigh, as if the pain of the ages had been stored inside her body and now at last she was able to exhale and release it all. She gave Madison and Ben each a beaming smile. Her teeth were white and even, like shiny little pearls. She reached forward with both hands outstretched, patted the arms of the armchair with a decisive flourish, then stood up, from primly seated to rod-straight in one sprightly, flowing movement. There were times when Ben couldn't stand up that fast. After the death struggle with Zarko Kožul on the floor, this was one of them.

'And now,' Miriam Silbermann said, 'may I desire one of you dear young souls to please call me a taxicab back to the airport?'

Ben had never in his life before been called a dear young soul. He stood with her. 'Let me accompany you, Fräulein

Silbermann. I think Madison wants to be alone a while with her father.'

Late that night, after Ben had seen Miriam's flight off, he left the airport and walked slowly under the sultry Hawaiian sky and wondered about what he would do next. Choices.

He'd been away from Le Val so long that a day or two longer wouldn't change anything. A day or two spent by the ocean, taking in the sunshine and relaxing to the pace of island life while his hand healed up. Walking on the beach. Drinking rum and talking history with old man Cahill. And perhaps spending some of that time with his daughter. Ben liked Madison. He liked her a good deal.

But a lot of things that could have been, could not be. Sometimes things were better that way, for everyone. And some choices were really not choices, after all.

Ben walked until he found himself faced with the great black expanse of the ocean. A vast canopy of nebulae and star clusters and galaxies and things he could only begin to imagine filled the infinite sky above him. He stood there, alone in the darkness, and smiled to himself as he thought about Special Agent Maddie Cahill and her father, and a story that had been so long in the telling but finally come out well. Happy endings were a rare and precious thing in this life. Why spoil it?

He could hear the neverending rush and whisper of the surf rolling in. He could hear its voice calling him. Somewhere across that ocean was home. Friendship, a bottle of French wine and a glass or two of single malt whisky. The love of a dog. And a woman whose name was Sandrine Lacombe.

Ben smiled to himself once more, and then slipped into the night.

Read on for an exclusive extract
of the new Ben Hope thriller
by Scott Mariani

The Moscow Cipher
Coming May 2018

PROLOGUE

The city was Moscow and the date was February tenth, 1957.
It was to be the last night in Leo Ingram's life, although he
didn't yet know it.

The bitter cold day was turning to a frigid evening as the
deserted streets darkened, urging Ingram to turn up the
collar of his heavy greatcoat and walk faster along the slippery pavement. His shoes were sodden from trudging
through the dirty slush. The whistling wind carried flurries
of snow that threatened to re-cover everything in white.

Ingram detested the unrelenting cold, as he detested the
palpable fear and oppression that gripped this city. He could
see it in the eyes of the people everywhere he went; could
almost feel it oozing from the grey, dirty, ice-rimed streets
themselves; and the same fear was pulsing deep inside his
own heart that night as he carried out his mission.

Leo Ingram was his real name, as opposed to the identity
shown on the forged papers he was carrying. His spoken
and written Russian were easily good enough to pass for a
native, as long as he didn't get into protracted conversation
with any of the locals, something he had studiously avoided
since being smuggled into the USSR five weeks earlier. His
cover had been carefully set up. For the last five weeks, as
far as anyone was concerned, he had been Pyotr Kozlov,

self-employed piano tuner. Had he been required to actually tune a piano as proof of his false identity, he could have done so, as that had been his profession before the war. How a mild-mannered, cultivated and peace-loving gentleman like Leonard Ingram could be transformed into a highly-decorated British Army captain and then, post-1945, into a special agent of the Secret Intelligence Service: that was a testament to the deep, dark impact that terrible war had had on the lives of everyone it had touched.

Ingram's mission in Moscow was nearly complete. He had been planted to play a relatively brief role, but one that was key to the success of the operation. If all went well tonight, the five weeks of perpetual nail-biting tension, of constantly looking over his shoulder, half-expecting to see the KGB thugs coming for him at any moment, would be over and he would begin the journey home – not that getting out of the Soviet Union would be an easy matter.

If all didn't go well . . . Ingram closed his mind to that dreadful possibility.

The package thrust deep inside one pocket of his greatcoat was the first thing his plan required him to offload that night, before moving to the second phase. The package was innocuous enough at first glance, just an ordinary tobacco tin imprinted with Cyrillic lettering, identical to millions of others carried by millions of men across the USSR. But what that little round tin contained could not have been more explosive if it had been packed full of super-concentrated TNT. If they caught him with it, all was lost. Not just his own life, but all the efforts and risks taken by others in order to obtain the extremely precious and hard-won information inside.

As he rounded an icy corner of the dark, empty street and a fresh blast of bone-chilling wind slapped him in the face and made his eyes water, the warehouses came into view. A mile's walk from his rented digs, this industrialised zone of the city was even more dismal and rundown than the rest of Moscow. Most of the ancient pre-revolutionary buildings were semi-derelict and abandoned behind rickety fences nobody guarded. All the same, he was cautious. The failing bulb of a street light flickered on, off, on, off, throwing long shadows that he watched carefully in case they might conceal enemies with guns.

Satisfied he was alone, Ingram approached the fence and made his way along the snow-rimed wire mesh to the hole, large enough for a man of his slender build to slip through easily, he'd cut three nights earlier.

The warehouse was an old meat packing plant that hadn't been used for many years, its doors rotted off their hinges. Ingram stepped over the half-eaten body of a frozen rat and moved into the darkness of the building. The hiding place was very specific. The package would remain there only a day or so before, if all went according to plan, his contact would collect it. It had been decided back at the start of the mission that a dead drop of this sort was a safer, more prudent way for the package to change hands. Ingram would have preferred to deliver it straight to his contact, but these were not his decisions to make.

The package carefully hidden, Ingram slipped unseen from the warehouse and continued on his way through the cold darkness. Phase two of the plan was the rendezvous with his colleague, a man he had never met and would never meet again after tonight. A small waterproof envelope in Ingram's pocket contained a slip of paper on which were written four lines of code: an enciphered message that, among other information, gave precise directions to the location of the hidden package. Once the envelope was passed on, Ingram would walk away relieved of a tremendous burden. His part in the mission would effectively be complete as his contact decoded the directions using a special key known only to a select few, then retrieved the package and whisked it away to East Berlin, where others in their organisation would be anxiously waiting to take possession.

When the package finally reached the safety of London and its contents analysed, it would cause a sensation. Careers would be made out of this, though the men and women who'd risked their lives to obtain the information would likely get little credit.

Ingram walked on through the half-deserted streets, checking his wristwatch and his bearings and glancing behind him now and then to ensure he wasn't being followed. A police car hissed by, tyres churning brown slush on the road, and made his heart race for a moment before it passed on into the night without so much as slowing down to check him out.

His anxiety was peaking as he walked on. His meeting with his contact, however brief, would be the moment of maximum danger for both of them; when they would be at their most vulnerable if either of them had fallen under suspicion. To be caught together was their worst nightmare. 'It's almost over,' he kept telling himself. 'You'll soon be home free.'

As Ingram crossed a sidestreet, a large figure of a man in a long coat and a brimmed hat appeared from nowhere and stepped towards him. 'Good evening,' the man said in accented English. He was smiling. His right hand was in his pocket, clutching a hidden weapon. And he was most certainly not the man Ingram was supposed to meet.

KGB. The acronym stood for *Komitet Gosudarstvennoy Bezopasnosti*, the Committee for State Security. A name that struck terror into the hearts of those who opposed the Soviet regime, as well as the Russian citizens it oppressed as virtual captives in their own homeland. The KGB had been created only three years earlier and already forged a fearsome reputation as a direct descendant of the dreaded *Cheka* secret police of the olden days. Its agents were as ruthless as they were efficient.

Ingram's stomach twisted as he realised they were onto him. He bolted diagonally away across the icy street, then skidded and almost fell as a second figure appeared around the corner up ahead, cutting off his escape. The second agent wasn't smiling and he had already drawn his service automatic.

Had someone betrayed him? Had the KGB already caught his contact and made him talk? Had a mole inside his own agency given him away? Ingram didn't have time to ask those questions as he sprinted off in the opposite direction with the two agents in pursuit.

A shot cracked out. Splinters of brickwork stung his leg as he darted around a corner. Ingram knew that the KGB would shoot to wound, not to kill. He also knew what kind of horrific tortures they would use to force information from him. He would give them nothing. He and his fellow agents had all been sternly lectured on the risks associated with getting caught. Like his colleagues, Ingram carried hidden in the heel of one shoe a small glass vial containing a cyanide pill, to be swallowed in the event of imminent capture. The death it offered was by no means a pleasant one – but it was, he had been assured, far quicker and kinder than the treatment a spy would receive at the hands of his or her captors.

He sprinted along a cobbled alleyway, vaulted a railing and almost broke his neck hurtling down a long flight of icy steps. A sharp right turn, then a left, then another right; and now Ingram was quite lost in the maze of dark narrow streets, but all that mattered was getting away from his pursuers. Escape was his only hope. Ingram had killed nine enemy soldiers in the war and was quite proficient at armed combat, but the Secret Intelligence Service didn't issue weapons to undercover agents posing as innocent piano tuners. The couple of tuning forks he carried about with him wouldn't be much use.

He paused, heart pounding in his throat, breath rasping. Listened, could hear nothing. Had he lost them? Maybe, but he could assume nothing.

The cipher in his pocket. It must not be found. He snatched out the envelope and looked desperately around him for a hiding place to which, if he made it out of this, he could always return later. The buildings either side of the narrow street were old grey stone, slowly crumbling with decay and neglect. He ran his fingers along the rough, cold masonry, found a crack big enough, and stuffed the envelope inside it and poked it in deep with his fingers. Then he ran on, careering over the slippery pavement.

For a few elated moments longer he thought he'd given them the slip. That was when he heard the rapid thud of footsteps closing in behind him and in front, and realised they had him cornered.

He was done. Ingram felt the strange calmness that can sometimes come over a man when he knows, and accepts, that the end has come. He reached down and slid the false heel off his left shoe, trying to get to the cyanide pill inside before the enemy grabbed him; but his hands were numb with cold and he fumbled with the vial and accidentally let it slip from his fingers. He dropped to his knees, groping about in the shadows for it, but it was too late. Powerful hands seized his arms and yanked him roughly to his feet.

A pistol pressed against his head. If he could have struggled fiercely enough to make them blow his brains out, he would have, but then a cosh struck him hard over the head and knocked him half senseless. The KGB men dragged Ingram down the street to a waiting car where a third agent sat impassively at the wheel, smoking a cigarette. Ingram was bundled roughly inside. The two who had caught him sat either side, boxing him into the middle of the back seat. The car sped off.

Its destination was the infamous Lubyanka prison and KGB headquarters in the heart of Moscow, where men highly expert in extracting the truth from their victims awaited their new arrival.

The last night of Leo Ingram's life would be a very long and agonising one.

Chapter 1

Inside the confessional, filled with the serenity of the magnificent cathedral that was one of only two Catholic churches in his home city of Moscow, Yuri Petrov knelt humbly on the step and prepared to bare his soul to God.

On the other side of the grid, the priest's face was half veiled in shadow. Yuri made the sign of the cross and, speaking low, began the sacrament as he'd been doing all his life.

'Forgive me, Father, for I have sinned. My last confession was over two weeks ago and these are my sins.'

Yuri ran through the list of various lesser, venial sins, such as drinking and occasionally skipping his nightly prayers. But it was something else that was weighing so heavily on him and was the real reason he'd come seeking guidance. 'I'm struggling with a great burden, Father,' he explained nervously. 'A terrible secret has been revealed to me and I don't know what to do. I'm frightened.'

The priest listened sagely. 'Would the right course of action be to share your secret, my son?'

'Yes, Father. But in so doing, I could be in serious danger.'

'The only danger is in doing wrong, my son.'

'I know it's wrong to lie, or hide the truth. I've done that too many times, Father. I've been used to keeping secrets, in my past career. But nothing like this. If I tell, I'm a dead man. I need God's guidance on what to do.'

The priest reflected on this in silence for some time. 'Pray to Him, my son. Open your heart to His wisdom, and the guidance you seek will be heard.' Having given his counsel, the priest gave Yuri the penance of two Hail Marys, invited him to make an act of contrition, and ended the sacrament with the usual 'Through the ministry of the Church, may God give you pardon and peace. I absolve you of your sins, in the name of the Father, and of the Son, and of the Holy Spirit.'

'Amen.'

'Go in peace. Do the right thing, my son.'

Yuri left the Cathedral of the Immaculate Conception and trudged down the steps to Malaya Gruzinskaya Street feeling scarcely any more reassured than before. Moscow was enjoying a warm June; the sky was blue and the sunshine was pleasant, but Yuri was too taken up with confusion and dread to notice. How had it come to this, he kept asking himself. As he walked away from the grand gothic church, he cast his troubled mind back over the events of the last few days and the path his life had taken to lead him to this awful situation.

Yuri Petrov was thirty-nine years old, divorced, single, currently unemployed and going nowhere fast. The reason he'd been so used to keeping secrets in the past was that, for over fifteen years, he had been a spy for Russian Intelligence, albeit a minor and lowly one. Not that any of his former neighbours or acquaintances in Amsterdam, where he had lived for ten of those years, would have known it. As far as anyone was concerned, even (especially) Yuri's ex-wife Eloise and their daughter Valentina, he led the steady, plodding and unexciting existence of a senior technical support analyst working for an international software company based in the Netherlands. The ability to speak Russian being a key part of his phony job, the story fitted well and he'd carried it off for years without drawing suspicion. Each morning at eight he'd kissed his wife and cycled off to a fake office with a fake secretary, and got on with the real job of being an intelligence spook. Whatever that was, exactly.

While the Russian secret service had been stepping up its spying activities across Europe for some time and deploying their spooks on all kinds of cool missions such as nabbing state secrets, orchestrating cyber-attacks, infiltrating protest groups and generally helping to subvert the stability of nations, to Yuri's chagrin he felt his own talents to have been woefully underused. He was not, never had been, Russia's answer to James Bond. He had never carried a gun or been asked to do anything remotely risky. His role in Amsterdam was ostensibly to keep tabs on the intelligence agents of rival nations, but it seemed that his counterparts there had as little to do as he did – which all amounted to a life not much less drab and uninspiring than his fictitious cover, in which he had little to do except trawl the internet, drink too much coffee, eat too much stroopwafel, and become increasingly dissatisfied and frustrated with his career.

It hadn't always been this way. Once upon a time, in the bygone days before he'd been sent into exile in Amsterdam, his Intelligence bosses had seemed to appreciate Yuri's abilities. For Yuri might not have been endowed with many talents in his life, but for some reason and with very little effort on his part he just so happened to be a highly gifted code cracker. Back in the day, Yuri's capacity for deciphering signals intelligence – or 'SIGINT' – encryptions intercepted from rival agencies such as the Brits, the Yanks or those pesky Israelis, had been second to none and earned him quite a reputation in Moscow. On several occasions, when Russian Intel operatives way above his pay grade had been unable to penetrate the firewalls protecting the secret files of MI6, CIA, Mossad and others, Yuri had been called in to assist. He'd cracked security passcodes that had been thought uncrackable, even complex fifteen-digit monsters that didn't appear in a hash look-up table and presented over 700 million billion billion permutations.

But that was long ago, before the relentless march of technology had taken all the intellectual challenge out of codebreaking and pretty much rendered talents like his obsolete. Nowadays it was all just a war between computers: one to weave the incredibly complex code, another to attack its defences, and the winner was simply whoever had the most powerful machine. The human factor was almost completely removed from the equation. After just a few years in the job, Yuri's special skills had become increasingly redundant. Then came the Amsterdam posting, and the long, slow decline. Frustration grew to bitterness; bitterness to hatred: against his employers back home, and the whole damn government.

During this unhappy period he hooked back up with an old friend from school and began regular contact with him on social media. Yuri Petrov and Grisha Solokov had known each other since the age of seven, and had the usual on-off friendship until their teens, when they'd become best buddies for a while until Yuri drifted off to university in St Petersburg to study IT and Grisha went to work for his father, who owned a radio repair shop.

During the years the two friends had been out of touch,

Grisha had discovered the wonderful world of conspiracy theories and become deeply immersed. The repair shop long gone, he now operated his own internet radio station from a hidden bunker at a remote farm many miles from Moscow. He lived alone with only an assortment of feral cats and a few goats and chickens for company, and spent most of every night in the bunker streaming his rants about everything from illegal government surveillance operations to chemtrails to the Illuminati plot to enslave the human race to the covert deportation camps that really existed, according to him, on Mars.

Needless to say, in their Facebook chats Yuri had never divulged to his friend what he did for a living. Grisha had his own secrets, too. Because his show frequently attacked what he considered to be the corrupt dark underbelly of the Russian state and its president in particular, he kept his location extremely hush-hush so as to elude the government assassins whom he believed were intent on silencing him.

In short, Grisha was slightly nuts.

Looking back, Yuri couldn't pinpoint the moment he'd started getting drawn into Grisha's ideology. To begin with, he'd been dismissively sceptical of the whole thing, and almost stopped with the social media contact. The stuff his friend came out with was often more than Yuri could stomach, like his conviction that lizard-like alien beings capable of taking on human form really do run the planet, and that various celebrities as well as members of the British royal family were among these evil creatures hellbent on the total domination of humanity. But the more he'd listened to Grisha's show, the more compelling Yuri started finding its less wacky theories of conspiracy and corruption at the heart of the global establishment. Gradually, tiny doubts about his own government, and the state of the world generally, percolated through his head and wouldn't go away, feeding his increasing sense of restlessness that he was a pawn working for dark powers.

Maybe it was just an expression of his dissatisfaction with his own job, he told himself. Yet, the same creeping paranoia that fuelled Grisha's radio show started haunting Yuri as he cycled the streets of Amsterdam. He became certain he was being watched and followed, his phone tapped, perhaps even his thoughts somehow monitored. A reasonably devout Catholic since his teens, he turned to God for moral support. When an answer to his fervent prayers failed to materialise, Yuri found solace in the sins of drink and marijuana, having developed a taste for both.

What made it so much worse was that he could never tell Eloise a word about his secret life, let alone the anxieties that plagued him. As a result he ended up barely speaking to her at all, with the inevitable consequence that she felt very neglected by him. When the marriage eventually fell apart, Yuri blamed the Russian intelligence services even more bitterly for his woes and took it as proof of their pernicious influence over society. Shortly after Eloise left him and took Valentina away to live in France, Yuri returned to Moscow, handed in his resignation and found alternative employment fixing computer bugs for private cash-paying customers. He managed to persuade Eloise to let Valentina, now ten, travel to Russia for visits. Eloise was difficult about it and barely spoke to him on the phone.

Yuri's preoccupation with all things conspiracy-related had by then grown even more pervasive. Even if he wasn't yet prepared to believed that shape-shifting alien lizards govern the planet, as a parent he was angry that his child would grow up as a drone of the globalist Deep State. He felt he needed to *do* something to make people wake up to the realisation that everything they thought they knew about the world was a lie. The media they trusted was simply an instrument for propaganda; the leaders they voted for in fact controlled nothing; the real rulers were hidden in the shadows and democracy was a myth.

He and Grisha now communicated daily on prepaid phones bought for cash and theoretically untraceable to them. On Grisha's advice, as an extra precaution Yuri followed his friend's practice of replacing his 'burner' every couple of weeks. As a means of living as much off the grid as possible in an urban environment, he also moved to a dingy hole of an apartment that he paid for in cash, utility bills all in the name of a former tenant.

He and Grisha started meeting in person. The first reunion took place at a bar in a small town eighty kilometres from Moscow. Later, as a sign of his growing trust, Grisha let Yuri in on the secret of his farm's location, way out in the country. Never had Yuri mentioned his past as a spook for Russian intelligence. That was history now, anyway.

Over the next couple of years, Yuri visited the farm often. The two friends would spend days and nights in Grisha's chaotic home drinking vodka and talking conspiracies. It was more than a hobby or belief system for Grisha, it was a total lifestyle. Yuri felt the infectious lure of that world. He was becoming seriously addicted.

'It's all building to a head, don't you see?' Grisha had kept insisting during their most recent late-night session. 'It's coming. Just you wait. Something's going to happen that'll prove everything we've been saying. Something that'll show the world what these bastards have really been up to all along. Nobody will be laughing at us then.'

'"Something"?'

'Something huge, my man.'

Yuri believed it too, even if neither of them knew what that 'something' could be.

Then, one sunny day in June two years after he'd left Amsterdam, Grisha's prediction came terrifyingly true, in a way neither of them could have imagined.

The Moscow Cipher
Coming May 2018

THE HUNT IS ON . . .

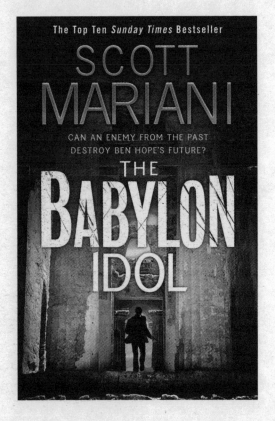

Don't miss the action-packed bestseller

WHERE BEN HOPE GOES,
TROUBLE ALWAYS FOLLOWS . . .

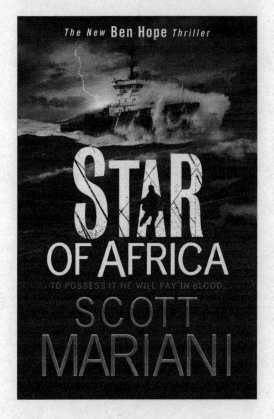

The first in an explosive two-book sequence

HAS BEN HOPE FINALLY
MET HIS MATCH?

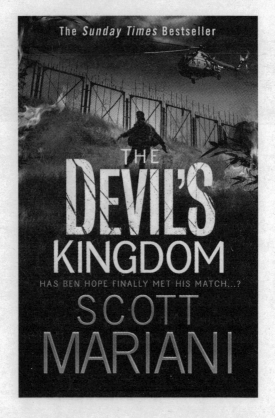

The *Sunday Times* Bestseller

THE
DEVIL'S
KINGDOM

HAS BEN HOPE FINALLY MET HIS MATCH...?

SCOTT
MARIANI

The thrilling sequel to *Star of Africa*